The
DICKENS BOY

ALSO BY THOMAS KENEALLY

FICTION

NONFICTION

Outback

The Place Where Souls Are Born

Now and in Time to Be: Ireland and
the Irish

Memoirs from a Young Republic

Homebush Boy: A Memoir

The Great Shame

American Scoundrel

Abraham Lincoln

The Commonwealth of Thieves

Searching for Schindler

Three Famines

Australians (vols. I, II, and III)

A Country Too Far (ed. with Rosie
Scott)

Australians: A Short History

FOR CHILDREN

Ned Kelly and the City of Bees

Roos in Shoes

The
DICKENS BOY

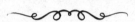

A Novel

THOMAS KENEALLY

ATRIA BOOKS

New York   London   Toronto   Sydney   New Delhi

ATRIA
BOOKS

An Imprint of Simon & Schuster, Inc.
1230 Avenue of the Americas
New York, NY 10020

Copyright © 2020 by The Serpentine Publishing Company
Originally published in Australia in 2020 by Vintage, an imprint of Penguin Random House

First Atria Books hardcover edition March 2022

ATRIA BOOKS and colophon are trademarks of Simon & Schuster, Inc.

For information about special discounts for bulk purchases, please contact Simon & Schuster Special Sales at 1-866-506-1949 or business@simonandschuster.com.

The Simon & Schuster Speakers Bureau can bring authors to your live event. For more information or to book an event, contact the Simon & Schuster Speakers Bureau at 1-866-248-3049 or visit our website at www.simonspeakers.com.

Interior design by Alexis Minieri

Manufactured in the United States of America

1 3 5 7 9 10 8 6 4 2

Library of Congress Cataloging-in-Publication Data has been applied for.

ISBN 978-1-9821-6914-5
ISBN 978-1-9821-6916-9 (ebook)

To the four young pilgrims,
Gus, Clementine, Alexandra, Rory.
Travel well.

"I can honestly report that he went away, poor dear fellow, as well as could be expected. He was pale and had been crying and (Henry said) had broken down in the railway carriage after leaving Higham Station, but only for a short time . . ."

Charles Dickens to his daughter Mary (Mamie), September 1868

I

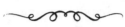

A long ocean voyage seems plentiful in small incidents at the time but is remembered as a blur when it ends. On my journey to Australia on the *Sussex*, a gentleman in the saloon said one day off Africa that only being wrecked would save us from the tedium. But after Cape Town it was all wind and fury as we tore across the Indian Ocean and the base of the Australian continent to our destination.

Even at sixteen, after I arrived in Melbourne, I knew it was a remarkable place and that I would have no trouble writing about it to Mama, Aunt Georgina, and the guvnor. A great city built on the riches provided by the gold of Victoria's hinterland—unlike Manchester or Liverpool or Nottingham or such—it had not grown from some dreary medieval village or fearsome coalpit. It was a lively British city fifteen thousand miles from its parent.

In such a place one finds a particular kind of Briton. My Australian mentor, George Rusden, was a scholarly, British sort of Melbournian. He had come to Australia as a boy with his clergyman father and had later explored the country and driven livestock through it. As clerk of the Parliament of Victoria, he had the final say on parliamentary procedure in a booming and self-governing colony.

Rusden had somehow met up with my father in London some years past. He struck me as a Tory and was certainly not therefore the sort of fellow who would have consorted with my father—and he wasn't pliable in the way I sensed the guvnor was, nor likely to wear a flash waistcoat nor be a critic of slums or an honest roisterer down towpaths. He was, though, a scholar and a billiard-player. The guvnor was indifferent to the sport of billiards.

Mr. Rusden had done a lot for the colony—including building a statue of Shakespeare at Melbourne University. He saw the Empire as a sort of Federated States of Britain, and Melbourne sang from the south to London and Edinburgh in the north, and they—as it were—sang back. Rusden was the sort of fellow determined to ensure the chorus would continue.

But having been charged with helping me, he took his duty by me very seriously from the moment he and my brother Alfred met my ship and took me to the Rusden house in the Brighton area of Melbourne.

It was good to have Alfred there, sitting by Mr. Rusden's desk and winking at me now and then as Rusden spoke to me. For Alfred had become something of a sport, with none of the adolescent sullenness he used to show me when I was twelve. He had been managing a sheep station named Conoble, deep in the hinterland, for some time, and had a slightly weathered face to show for it. Corona, his new post, was a place of some thousands of acres with a hundred thousand sheep that needed to be shorn each year. And that was what I noticed: here tens of thousands of acres was the normal astounding fact, and everyone forced themselves to be calm about it. Alfred had written to my father saying he was happy as a king at Conoble, and now he was going to manage, and be happy as a king, at another station of similar named Corona. "Are you working through the alphabet?" I asked him, but there seemed a quaver in my voice perhaps only I could hear. Like him, I wanted to be happy as a king at the sheep station I was slated for, Eli Elwah, which was five hundred square miles and had a twenty-mile frontage on a river named the Murrum-bidgee.

Alfred winked at me again as Mr. Rusden said, "Do not be seduced by the egalitarian principle here. Do not allow the men working on the station to treat you as a familiar. If they show any tendency to do so, quash it at once with firmness. Under these different stars, you must remain an English gentleman and maintain the reserve associated with that high office."

"I'll remember, sir," I said earnestly, half still a schoolboy.

"Make no mistake, it can be lonely on a station out in the bush," Rusden continued, "and many good men are seduced into rough company. There is an answer to this in matrimony with one of the many sturdy and handsome daughters of neighboring squatters. But you are too young yet, and if you wish to be a pastoralist on your own terms you must maintain your distance from your inferiors. Some of the men are roguish and would not be beyond corrupting you with native women while you're in your cups, do you understand?"

I nodded. As the youngest of ten children I could see that even jovial men might think it somehow funny, as older men considered all bullying funny.

"I hope that advice is not repellent to you," said Mr. Rusden. "But you are as good as a man now."

"As good as a man," Alfred confirmed, smoking his cheroot and calm as Socrates.

"And of course, beware of the wretched habit of drinking nobblers."

Seeing my confusion, Alfred said, "Mr. Rusden means glasses of spirit. Rum or battle-axe brandy. They'll nobble anyone."

"Especially in the early hours of the working day," Mr. Rusden told me. "Hutkeepers, blacksmiths, and other pastoralists will always offer you nobblers because it is part of the courtesy of the bush. But if you yield to the importunity of one you will not be able to refuse others without causing offense because colonial fellows have a great deal of sensitivity in these matters. If you become known for polite refusal from the start, you'll offend no one person."

"Very good advice," said Alfred, winking at me again.

In a way I was pleased he did, but also confused. Alfred seemed to be implying I should have a nobbler when appropriate. But how would I know when was appropriate? I was trying to feel out the rules of the country and hold on to them in the immensities ahead.

I think my father believed that with me on one station and Alfred on another, we would be near neighbors. Now I had seen Alfred, the way his face carried my mother's high brow but my father's refined lower features, I wished it were true.

At last Rusden stopped telling me the facts of the bush and invited me and Alfred for tea on the veranda. Not being married, he vanished awhile to organize things, giving me the liberty to at last ask Alfred what he thought of Rusden's pastoral advice.

"Look, he's right, but you can't get away without being a fellow too," said Alfred, his full dandyish moustache quivering with conviction. "I would have said, join the jockey club, field some of your horses, and join the cricket club. They'll all support you. Go to church sometimes and drink with the squatters at their pub in town. People will stick by you if you make the social effort."

I was delighted to hear my brother's simpler exhortations.

"*Plornishmaroontigoonter!*" he said suddenly in a secretive voice, using my father's nickname for me, generally shortened to Plorn. "Above all, it's important in Australia to be seen as a sportsman and a likeable chap."

In the shadow of that nickname invented by Father, an old shame revived. My father had his empire of readers, not only in the British Empire but in America and France and Russia. But I had never read any of his novels. I had not read anyone's novel, not even Wilkie Collins's *The Moonstone*, which I'd been told that once begun you could not help finishing. I had told no one this but felt I must confess it to the guvnor himself before I left England. I'd intended to tell him that I hoped after I made my way to Australia I would gain in time the power to read his work and behold his great imagination.

Mind you, I was a cunning child and had put together a sense of my father's tales. I knew *Our Mutual Friend* had a boatman's daughter named Lizzie Hexam, a world-beater of a lass in the last book the guvnor had written before I left. (He told me he was too busy with readings to write a new one.) I knew that the book before had a lot to do with the guillotine, and people were crazy for it. I was able, if I needed, to pretend in front of strangers I had read at least some of his books.

I felt it was dishonorable and an insult to the guvnor to pretend to him, however. And though I meant to confess that shame to him, I was at school in Rochester and then at the agriculture college at Cirencester a great deal of the time, and he was often away from Gad's Hill when I was home, reading in theaters or going to France for his health. There was never the right time to tell him. I had wondered whether to tell Aunt Georgie and get her to intercede for me, but I could not bring myself to tell her either.

Before I caught the train at Higham, I decided I'd confess and beg the guvnor's pardon.

The day I left the dear, bright house at Gad's Hill, I said farewell to Aunt Georgie, and to my big sister Mamie who also lived there. Mamie was a quiet and gracious and affectionate woman and was being courted by a brigade major from Chatham named Lynch, who would soon find there was more steel in Mamie than he might have expected. Brimming with tears, Mamie told me she had said goodbye to too many brothers. More than ten years back she had seen Walter off to India, and while she wept she had told him she could not support his loss. Walter was never to return, she said. She told me all this unnecessarily, but with grievous affection. She had seen Frank off to the Bengal Mounted Police four years back, his loss from home insupportable, she said. Then Sydney went to the navy and next came the departure of Alfred for Australia. And here I was, the youngest, the last child, the last of the insupportable losses that Mamie would have to endure.

I was accompanied by the guvnor and my brother Henry to Higham Station, and after booking most of my luggage through to Plymouth the three of us took the train to Paddington. It was a journey we made all the time, but it was elevated this time by the fact it could be my last run to Paddington. That finality demanded I notice every smallest thing along the track. Henry was nineteen and, in so far as any of us were handsome, he was handsome. He was also very bright and, after finishing school in Boulogne, had gone to Brackenbury's military school at Wimbledon, which was considered a good school to prepare a boy for the army or the Indian Civil Service. But Henry hadn't wanted anything to do with either of those destinies. He was going to be a lawyer and, unlike me and the rest of my brothers, Henry could afford to take his future success for granted.

The guvnor was proud that "H," as we called Henry, was going to Cambridge in the new year, an institution which, along with Oxford, had gone unadorned by the shadow of any Dickens progeny before.

I cried on the way to Paddington because I feared I might not manage to tell my father the truth about my failure to read his books. H and Father did not reprimand me for my tears but pressed my shoulder at various points, with Henry telling me, "After you make your quick fortune, Plorn, you should just come back to us. You'll be playing for the Higham cricket team at Gad's Hill again before you know it."

This was good brotherly comfort. And Henry was coming all the way to Plymouth to keep me company onto the ship. Yet it was not entirely cricketing comfort I needed. I felt that without having read my father's work I was going naked and barely formed into the wilderness. I could not believe that at this late hour of departure I had been so negligent as not to speak to him about it before.

At Paddington we went towards the boat train and there by the gate Father stopped. Though he was wearing a sportive hat and a good satin vest of colorful design, he looked tired and thin, as if he hadn't eaten enough lately. His face was seamed, and his dark curls and beard were lank and streaked with an unhealthy gray. But his gift for *being there*, his advanced power to occupy a place, was still intact. He had been going away to France, where he was not as well known, to have quiet times, but he seemed to come back more restless. He still held his weekend court at Gad's Hill, and all his faithful friends turned up, the barrister Le Neve Foster and the painter Augustus Egg. The great tragedian Macready and his young missus also often came.

But since the guvnor had returned from his readings in the United States in the spring, lame, he'd excused himself from the long walks he used to go on. Yes, his life, I see now, was restless and he remained absent a lot and when there were no visitors at Gad's Hill, talked a lot about the charges on him. I hated it when he mentioned how much it cost to keep Mama. He'd even talked about coming to Australia to do readings, to which John Forster had said, "Don't be ridiculous, Dickens. It will kill thee." (Forster was a Northerner and said "thee" all the time.) But I hoped the guvnor would come, and Alfred and I could protect and guide him.

And I must now tell him of the sad state of my reading. The confession would man me for the new world. "The traveler!" the guvnor said when we paused closer to the barrier for the boat train. "The colonist! The King of the Bush!" He had tears in his eyes as he extended his arms, but I shook his hand instead. Henry hung back and seemed to study the contents of a porter's trolley to allow the guvnor and me to talk. I wanted to say, "I'm sorry. I haven't read any of your books. But I will when I learn to penetrate those armies of paragraphs you put in them."

I knew he was famous for not being conceited, not in that way anyhow. But I felt I would expire with shame if I said it. I simply sweated.

"You have everything you need?" he asked.

"Yes, sir."

"Adequate clothes to cut a dash in the cities and on the sheep stations?"

"That's right," I said, still unable to tell him. "Papa, I'm sorry you have the cost of the cabin on the *Sussex*."

He reached out and took my hand and kissed it. "Don't be ridiculous, Plornish. I would not have it otherwise."

"I was not a good student."

"Yes, but you can be a good man."

Tell him, tell him! went the terrible imperative in my mind. I began to cry, not caring who saw me on the platform. I was going away, and as an undeclared entity.

"Dearest boy," the guvnor said, extracting, as if just remembering it, a letter from his pocket. "For you, my dearest Plornishgenter! You must *apply* yourself, Plorn. That is all. You have all the gifts but that one."

If I read one of your books, if I penetrate all that text . . . would that count as application? I wondered.

I got on the train to Plymouth with Henry, who said, "Cheer up, old fellow. I don't doubt Australia's the go. You'll come back able to buy and sell us. Have you read *David Copperfield*?"

"Of course," I claimed through my tears.

"Then there you are! And what about *Great Expectations*?"

"Yes," I lied.

"Well, there you have the convict Magwitch, disqualified from life in England, giving our hero Pip his colonial fortune. Have you ever noticed how close to Plorn is Pip? It's my theory the old man wrote it specially for you."

This idea served to dry up my tears.

"If Magwitch could make a fortune in Australia," said H, "how much more could a robust and free and well-founded boy like you make?"

We went through to the boat train, with a final wave to the guvnor. There were tears in his eyes, but I knew the busy city day at the premises of his magazine in Wellington Street would seize and console him.

~

"My dearest Plorn," his letter read,

> I write this note to-day because your going away is much upon my mind . . . I need not tell you that I love you dearly, and am very, very sorry in my heart to part with you . . . It is my comfort and my sincere conviction that you are going to try the life for which you are best fitted. I think its freedom and wildness more suited to you than any experiment in a study or office would ever have been; and without training, you could have followed no other suitable occupation.
>
> What you have always wanted until now has been a set, steady, constant purpose. I therefore exhort you to persevere in a thorough determination to do whatever you have to do as well as you can do it. I was not so old as you are now when I first had to win my food . . . and I have never slackened in it since.

The guvnor's letter then urged me never to take mean advantage of another, and never to be hard upon people in my power.

As your brothers have gone away, one by one, I have written to each such words as I am now writing to you, and have entreated them all to guide themselves by this book [the New Testament] . . . as questionable as the barbaric Old Testament might be, and putting aside the interpretations and inventions of men.

You will remember that you have never at home been wearied about religious observance or mere formalities.

He concluded by asking me to say night prayers, as he did, writing, "I hope you will always be able to say in after life, that you had a kind father. You cannot show your affection for him so well, or make him so happy, as by doing your duty."

꩜

As it turned out, my stay at Eli Elwah would last only twelve hours in all, and even now my memories of the place are painful. After traveling north by train, then west on the long Murray River, I arrived at a little town named Moama where I made arrangements for the bulk of my firearms and books and bush saddles, my clothes and tools and other impedimenta, to be taken to Eli Elwah by dray. After that I traveled north by coach until it stopped, then continued on my mare, Coutts, a bay with a white blaze. I had bought her in Melbourne on Alfred's advice and named her in honor of the guvnor's friend Miss Coutts.

Coutts appeared to have great stamina, which the man who sold her to me said was because she had some Waler in her, explaining "Waler" was the name of the New South Wales breed of horse that had emerged from a melting pot of thoroughbreds, Arabs, Cape of Good Hope Dutch breeds, Timor ponies, with a little Percheron or Clydesdale thrown in for ruggedness.

My thoughts on horseflesh were interrupted when I came upon a lantern-faced boy drover who was very amiable and forded some creeks and lagoons with me, which he told me the colonials called "billabongs." According to the drover they were astonishingly full for this time of year.

And so I rode into Eli Elwah Station one morning to see a fine old homestead house, with drovers' huts, a blacksmith forge, cook and carriage houses, with a camp for blacks off by a fringe of trees along a creek. It seemed to me that everyone had visible, understandable functions, and I liked that. An ageless-looking manager with a mahogany face welcomed me in a looping accent that showed he was born here or had been here a long time. He told me his name was McGaw and that I had better stay in the homestead with someone called Britton. He informed me, I thought unnecessarily, that if he let this man Britton loose in the drovers' huts half of them would bugger him and he wouldn't even notice.

He told me the time for dinner, and that his wife was away so I needn't dress in either a formal or semiformal way. A drover's wife who was McGaw's housekeeper then showed me to my bedroom— a pleasant room with a bed, a desk, and a long window giving onto a veranda.

I changed my boots in the long melancholy twilight and wore a tie and jacket to dinner. There was another young man with gingery hair, moustache, and complexion standing behind a chair at the set table in the dining room. This was clearly the earlier-mentioned Britton, who was probably two years or so older than me.

Soon after, McGaw entered in shirtsleeves, as was his managerial right, and riding boots. He looked distracted and was holding a cut page of newspaper thick with text, which he put on the table by his plate and continued to read for a while from above, before looking up at me and asking, "You met Archie Britton?"

After Britton and I made affirmative noises McGaw nodded and sat down in his place, where he continued to read the newspaper.

"How are things at the new dam site?" he asked Britton without looking up.

"The men are working with a will," said Britton with an accent that had a bit of Yorkshire in it. "The Chinese men working on the scoop are thorough tigers."

"I was told they were good before I hired them," McGaw murmured, his gaze still on the newspaper. "I wanted a depth of seven feet at the wall. Are they delivering that, do you think?"

"According to my measurements, Mr. McGaw," said Britton, who seemed at home here, which I felt a bit cheered by.

McGaw now looked at me from dark creases within his leathery face. "I think Britton's a bit overawed, Dickens. You are very clear proof that the great man exists."

"I'm afraid I'm a very ordinary fellow," I said, long practiced at people making a nod towards my father's literary fame as a prelude to addressing me.

"I'd say I *was* overawed!" declared Britton. "Who wouldn't be?"

"Well," I assured the two men again, "I don't have my father's gifts."

"But what sort of a *pater* was he?" asked Britton, wanting, good fellow that he was, only to hear the best of my immortal sire.

"We used to have plays and cricket matches in the garden. When boys from school visited us they would be in awe and trembling, but after an hour or so of fun and games they'd say, 'By Jove, Dickens, your guvnor is a stunner and no mistake!'"

This was exactly what Britton wanted to hear, and he laughed as if reassured that God in his heaven and Charles Dickens's power to charm boys in the garden were two signs that all was right with the earth. Even McGaw looked amused.

"And you play cricket?" Britton asked.

"Yes. I'm told by kind people I'm an all-rounder. Middle-order batsman and medium-paced bowler."

"We have a station team," Britton told me. "We're playing Burrabogie a week from Saturday."

It felt as though things were falling my way. The cricket team at Higham had asked me to bat for them whenever I was home during the past two years. My batting figures were better than I had implied.

"I read this surprising press report," McGaw said, looking at me and tapping the newspaper clipping by his plate.

McGaw's reflections on what he had read had to wait awhile due to the arrival of the drover's wife and a little black girl carrying dishes.

After serving the three of us soup, the woman called, "All set, Mr. McGaw?" to which he replied, "Set as houses, thanks, Molly." She and the black girl disappeared.

"Yes," said McGaw, patting the newsprint again, "there were some troubles in your house, I believe. With your ma, was it? I wouldn't mention it except—well, here it is. In your pa's words."

"My parents separated years ago," I said, blushing. "And the press make too much of it," I added. Generally when I blamed the newspapers people nodded sagely and said, "Well, we all know about the press, don't we?" And the conversation then moved blessedly to other matters, but McGaw wasn't finished.

"This is a piece in the *Argus*," he said, "but reproduced from something called the *New-York Tribune*. It quotes your pa as saying, 'Mrs. Dickens and I have lived unhappily together for many years. Hardly anyone who has known us intimately can fail to have known that we are, in all respects of character and temperament, wonderfully unsuited to each other.'"

McGaw turned his dark, lizardy gaze up at me again, saying, "Did he really write that, d'you think? 'Wonderfully unsuited?' Or is that made up?"

"He would put it differently now, I think," I replied. "But, you see, at the time there were so many rumors around." I despised my-self for defending the guvnor as if he were the accused. "I was only six, but even I knew people made too much of it all."

McGaw slowly returned his gaze to the text, and again read. "'I suppose that no two people, not vicious in themselves, ever were joined together who had a greater difficulty in understanding one another.'"

"All this is exaggerated," I said, as if it might save me, or as if McGaw would pity me and leave off.

He did not.

"But they say that these are your pa's own words. Are they wrong?"

"No, but you have to understand . . . when he wrote that he was in a desperate state . . . And people were being mean towards my aunt Georgie. I don't know . . . I was a child, as I told you, Mr. McGaw."

"I mean, we all know about troubles in marriage," he contin-ued, sniggering. "You don't get to know a person by marriage but only by staying married. But if it was as bad as your pa says, why did he marry your mama in the first place?"

Before I could answer, he read on. "'For some years past, Mrs. Dickens has been in the habit of representing to me that it would be better for her to go away and live apart; that her always in-creasing estrangement made a mental disorder under which she sometimes labors—more, that she felt herself unfit for the life she had to lead as my wife and that she would be better far away. I have uniformly replied that we must bear our misfortune and fight the fight out to the end, that the children were the first con-sideration, and that I feared we must bind ourselves together "in appearance."'"

Britton looked away and concentrated on the prints of stallions on the wall, embarrassed for me.

"Mr. McGaw," I began sternly, before being interrupted by the housekeeper and the girl coming back to set up our plates with roasted lamb and vegetables.

Britton took the time to discuss my ship with me, and I tried to give a polite account of my voyage on the sailing ship *Sussex*, mentioning my good cabin and my friend, William Dempster, who'd been on board with me. I lamented I wouldn't see much of him because he was bound for Western Australia.

The woman and child served our meal, and we discussed my journey out under sail, and the fear many had of steamships being set alight by a spark from the engines.

After the women left we set to on our dinner, and even McGaw spent time purely relishing it. But after a while he looked down at the newspaper report again.

"Edward," he said, "I trust you're willing to discuss these matters. You are not so tender in feeling as to avoid these issues, are you?"

"No," I declared. I didn't feel I had had the chance to say otherwise. "But—"

"What about this then?" he interrupted. "'Nothing has, on many occasions, stood between us and a separation but Mrs. Dickens's sister, Georgina Hogarth . . .'"

"My auntie Georgie," I said wearily, hoping it might remind him he was addressing living and breathing entities. It didn't.

"Why would she stay on after your father had sent her own sister away?"

"For us," I cried. "Purely for us."

But the beggar went on reading. "'From the age of fifteen she has devoted herself to our house and our children. She has been their playmate, instructress, friend, protectress, adviser, companion. In the manly consideration towards Mrs. Dickens which I owe my wife, I will only remark of her that the peculiarity of her character has thrown all the children on someone else, indeed on her sister. I do not know—cannot by any stretch of fancy imagine—what would have become of them but for this aunt, who has grown up with them, to whom they are devoted, and who has sacrificed the best part of her youth and life to them.'"

I knew the guvnor had written a letter for the papers, but I hadn't heard it read so coldly and so cruelly.

Again, he raised his eyes to mine. "*Manly consideration towards Mrs. Dickens . . . ?*" he asked with a frown.

"You need to understand, Mr. McGaw," I warned, "he was provoked by malicious people. You see, he was answering the most malicious rumors at the time." But had the guvnor not realized that papers would republish his letter whenever they were short of copy?

"'I hope that no one who may become acquainted with what I write here can possibly be so cruel and unjust, as to put any misconstruction on our separation, so far. My elder children all understand it perfectly, and all accept it as inevitable.'"

McGaw breathed in emphatically. "But let me see here, Edward. It gets very confusing. First he defends your aunt, and then he goes on to mention another 'spotless young creature,' someone as innocent and pure as your sisters, and malicious persons who spread rumors about her. Very confusing to a colonial reader, I would say."

I was not about to tell him the "spotless young creature" was Miss Ternan, who the guvnor had tried to help in her career as an actress. Now and then she visited Gad's Hill, but she was bad at cricket.

My dinner lay cooling before me, but molten steel had begun to flow through my veins. Two of the malicious persons referred to were Thackeray's daughters, Minnie and Annie, who we'd been friends with when we were little. During his life Mr. Thackeray would come to Gad's Hill and play cricket. He and my father would also devise plays and give all us brats a part in them. Then, one day when I was six, the guvnor called us all together and told us that our former friends the Thackerays had betrayed us with vicious rumors. That was the year everything changed, with Mama going back to her other family's house, taking my eldest brother, Charles. It was also the year the guvnor grew old.

"Do you know who this 'spotless young woman' is?" McGaw asked, bully that he was.

"You are *not* a gentleman, Mr. McGaw," I declared, choking with something broader than rage, more demanding than panic. I wanted in truth to kill him.

"I *am* a bloody gentleman, you know," McGaw insisted. "I was quoting your own deathless pa, after all. Come on, Dickens, don't be like that. You need a thick hide to be successful in the bush."

"Damn you, Mr. McGaw. I won't stay under your roof and I will not stoop to work for you."

"You'll feel different in the morning. Look, let's have a nobbler and make peace."

"You are lucky I don't demand honor," I said furiously.

"Demand what?"

"A duel, a trial of honor."

McGaw turned to a flushed Britton, who was sitting, looking at us wide-eyed. "A trial of honor? Can you believe this bloke?"

"My father is a gentleman, Mr. McGaw, whereas you are a lout."

I got up and walked away from the table and was in the corridor before he called out after me, with some anger in his voice, "I'll let all that guff go till tomorrow. We're all bloody human, you know. Me, you, your immortal pa."

It felt like shame was devouring me from inside—shame for my guvnor, for my mama, for Aunt Georgie, for myself, for the entire breathing world. I had to leave McGaw or kill him.

2

Back in my room I packed into my saddle bags and valise the few items I had already unpacked, retrieved my shaving gear, then left the room and sought the front door of the homestead.

I heard McGaw call, "Are you going to join us, Dickens?" as I walked away, up the hall and out into the night. I made my way to the drovers' quarters and asked a man to saddle my mare. He did it, only asking once where I meant to go. I told him it was not his business, to which he reacted as if democracy demanded a person was required to tell any inquirer all their intentions.

"I am leaving," I told him then.

"Tonight?"

"*Instanter*," I said. "As fast as I can."

"Nice saddle you've got," he said as he put my best Australian saddle on Coutts. "But watch for rabbit holes."

"Open the homestead gate for me, will you?" I asked him. "I would appreciate it."

He did that and I cantered out, my shame and outrage still larger than the immensity of stars. Utter darkness soon consumed me, and I put poor Coutts into a gallop for relief. If we killed ourselves it would be a sweet release, at least for me. What I had been through, and the just rage I carried, crowded out everything normal.

It was a long ride. I rested in a few raw slab-timber public houses on the way to a little town named Deniliquin. Southwards then, I reached the great trench of embankments and maze of billabongs where the River Murray ran and so the stage road. I was by then in a more equable frame of soul, and still glad I had made a protest against the abominable McGaw. I reached Melbourne after three days' travel, and took a room at the Savage Club, for which the Dickens name and the patronage of Mr. Rusden qualified me. Then, after putting on a good suit, I made my way to the grand freestone Parliament at the top of Bourke Street, and presented myself at Mr. Rusden's office. But on being admitted, I found myself treated like a miscreant.

"I cannot disguise that I am severely disappointed with you for passing up such an excellent position," he told me. "One not at all easy to procure. What caused you to move away without reference to me or your brother?"

"Please don't tell my father, Mr. Rusden."

"He'd expect that I would," he replied, and I felt that Rusden's letter would join all the unsatisfactory reports on me from a range of schools that had distressed the guvnor and convinced him I could not apply myself. But my defense in this case was the unutterable McGaw.

"Whatever possessed you?" demanded Rusden.

I said I knew Mr. Rusden had gone to a lot of trouble to find me a place at Eli Elwah. All I could tell him was that McGaw was not a gentleman as I felt unable to reprise McGaw's performance because it contained things—Aunt Georgie and Mama and the Irish girl—I could not mention to the austere Mr. Rusden. It was not so much that I wouldn't. I *couldn't* repeat those foul insinuations. I would go too deeply, it seemed to me, into my own depths of shame.

Shame over what? I could not tell Rusden in what sense McGaw was "no gentleman" and later I could not define it for Alfred either. When I wrote to him that night I could only use the formula "not a gentleman."

I now had to report to Rusden daily but could see he'd already concluded I was ill-suited to Australian life. I had hoped he would spread the news that McGaw was a cad. Instead if he spread any news it would be that I was green. And I was not. I had shown the bush what I was made of by racing poor Coutts in darkness down the red soil road amongst great stands of bush. So though I might have been green in colonial terms, I was not in a way that disqualified me for colonial life.

⁓

To my club in Melbourne, the Savage, where I stayed with all the irrelevant comfort appropriate to a London club, with some of the guvnor's friends peering at me from framed photographs or portraits on the walls—Macready as Shylock, mad old Walter Savage Landor. Papa and Mr. Forster used to visit him in Bath to drink a toast to the beheading of Charles I, and to recite the doggerel Mr. Landor had written and Papa taught us as a joke.

> George the First was always reckoned
> Vile, but viler George the Second;
> And what mortal ever heard
> Any good of George the Third?
> But when from earth the Fourth descended
> (God be praised!), the Georges ended.

And, here in this club, even the full-bosomed Lady Blessington, the free spirit who rushed around town with her comrade (at least that's one way to put it) Count d'Orsay, one of Alfred's godfathers.

And most sinister of all, my own godfather, Edward Bulwer-Lytton, who had married for love and then endured his wife writing a novel satirizing him and calling him a hypocrite. However, he was a statesman and a grand writer, and I was honored to bear his name.

None of them helped me here. None of them knew or could silence McGaw. None of them was advised to give up chemistry and Latin and spend a half year at an agriculture school for farmers' sons in Cirencester. The faces of our godparents, seen in full flesh at Devonshire Terrace and Tavistock House or Gad's Hill, were, in their bleared pictures in Melbourne, a reproach.

3

I felt liberated when, one evening a few days after I'd last seen him, Rusden came to the Savage Club and told me I was to be given one last tilt at settling in the bush. He sounded weary, as if he had little faith in me, and I knew I must depart into the interior and stay there. He said he'd found me a place at a station named Momba, a good way north of Eli Elwah. He told me I would need to catch a steamboat up a river named the Darling, which fortunately still had enough water in it after last winter's rain, until I reached a town named Wilcannia. I would then have to report to a certain stock and station agency which sent a monthly wagon of provisions to Momba. "The best thing is," said Rusden, "you'll have a good man, Mr. Bonney, there as a mentor. And the storekeeper, young Suttor, is an educated colonial—do pass on my respects to him."

Though he had also said McGaw was a good man, I had a new ambition. The guvnor had said application was all I lacked, so I would show application now such as would astonish him. I would apply myself like McCready and Landor and Lytton and Lady Blessington. I would relieve my father's anxieties with a heroic scale of application. And one day I would return to him, Daniel from the furnace, as an *applied* man, and one familiar with *Hard Times*, *Martin Chuzzlewit*, and all the rest.

I went north again by rail and stage to a town named Yarra-wonga, then caught a ferry which would take me all the way along the Murray and up the Darling. I had a small cabin in the *Eliza Jane*, which was narrow in the beam to make it less likely to hit sub-merged snags that might damage its red gum hull. The captain of the ferry, Burgess, was a proud man with a wizened face and a basso voice. He boasted of what the *Eliza Jane* carried inland, reciting its inventory like a parson who never gets tired of reciting the Credo or the Paternoster. "We have on the stern and in our shallow hold every requirement for civilization," he claimed. "Woolpacks, soap, kerosene, galvanized iron, drapery, some on order, some on spec-ulation, curtains ditto, sherry, stationery, sawn timber, wire, sugar, candles, potatoes, earthenware, books, glassware, and claret."

I half expected him to say at the end, "For these and other gifts may the Lord be praised!"

There were three men who traveled on the foredeck, sleeping under the stars in comfortable-looking bush swags they called bed-rolls. I was walking up and down the foredeck after breakfast on the long, casual haul down the Murray—we had not yet reached the Darling—when one of these men approached me and said in a native-born Australian accent, "Excuse me, Mr. Dickens." He had a half-amused face and a black beard which would soon reach the dimensions of the blade of a shovel.

Wary of all Rusden's warnings about the trap of over-familiarity, I frowned and said, "Yes?"

"Just," said the man, "I'm on my way to Momba too."

I was surprised, but pleased. He looked like a reliable escort. However, I was still trying to be as severe as Mr. Rusden wanted me to be. "Is that so?" I replied.

The look of amusement did not leave his eyes. He did not take a step back as an English working man would have by now.

"I'm Tom Larkin," he said. "I'm to be blacksmith for Mr. Bonney. He wrote to me and told me to look out for a Mr. Dickens, to say hello and that I was riding to Momba Station from Wilcannia too. So, there you go."

"I am pleased for your company, Mr. Larkin," I said, as much like a threat as I could manage.

"The Bonneys seem decent fellows," he said cheerily. "You see, I grew up on Moolbong with Mr. Brodribb. My father and mother worked for him donkey's years, ever since they left Ireland. I went up to Wagga then to get married myself last month. And said to the wife, 'Time to see the world beyond the Darling, my dear.' She's game for it. A Welsh girl, sea-captain's daughter. She's to come up to Momba in the autumn."

"My felicitations," I risked saying. But I could not let him know I liked him at first sight. I felt I liked far too many people at first sight.

The ferry stopped frequently along the way. Sometimes we would put into timber camps, where tree fellers with smoky complexions had stacked their timber by the riverbank. Sometimes Captain Burgess needed wood for the boilers, but other times he would buy roughly milled timber. Sometimes there was an ageless woman in sackcloth with her bush brats in these camps. You could see these flimsily clad offspring running like rabbits to avoid being seen by passengers as we put in. I noticed Larkin was amused by them, as if they reminded him of his own childhood.

When we stopped at bigger towns, Captain Burgess would often spend time with merchants, while the three fellows from the fore-deck went ashore and started a fire, drank tea and rum, and yarned with each other. The cook and the steward fished for river cod. If it were daytime, one of the first-class passengers, a Mrs. Desailly who lived at some place west of Wilcannia, whom Burgess treated as a sort of bush duchess, disembarked with her face totally veiled in netting to defeat the sun and insects, and sometimes to make social calls. Mrs. Desailly had reacted kindly enough when Captain

Burgess pronounced me the youngest son of the great narrator, but I think she wanted to see if I would last in her country before she took the trouble of warming to me. She asked me a few questions with a fluting voice, and my answers were so plain that she lost interest and said, "I think Captain Burgess must be playing jokes on me."

The narrow dimensions of the *Eliza Jane* made more sense once we reached the town of Wentworth and entered the Darling. The banks were high and red soiled, hosting great thickets of river gums, and when we stopped and ascended the banks while goods were off-loaded I went walking in the rich grassy plains beyond and saw great outcrops of red rocky tor.

When we stopped at a station named Mount Murchison, the overseer came aboard to visit Mrs. Desailly. After he was introduced to me, he declared, "My God, the country's thick all at once with Dickenses. There's one at Corona! Met him at the races at Poolamacca Station three weeks back. He brought along a few likely horses, I must say."

He took me for a stroll beyond the screen of river gums and, just like a reader, said, "Your dear old dad hasn't written a book for some time. Is that so? Last one was *Our Mutual Friend*, I believe. Must be three years back."

"Four," I corrected him. "He does reading tours, you see, and the performances . . . they tire him out."

"I liked the character Lizzie Hexam of course, the daughter of the river, but I couldn't help admiring the fortune-hunting girl. What's her name?"

"Ah yes," I foolishly said, pretending to hunt through the vast cast of my father's creations, with which I was no more familiar than the rivers of Russia. But suddenly I was about to pluck the accurate name. Little Em'ly Peggotty, I thought gratefully, and then said it.

"I think you are mistaken, young Dickens," he told me. "That's the ruined woman who comes to Australia in *Copperfield*. Hang on there—I think I might have it. Wilfer. Bella Wilfer."

"I do believe you're correct," I said tentatively.

I'd had to play this game before with even more exacting Britons; endure such questioning as if every line of my father's works were grafted onto my veins as an inheritance from the grand storyteller.

We were out in the open well beyond the riverbank now, the sun high and every feature of the land sharp. A great plain stretched in front of us, its plenteous grass metallic sounding in the breeze and running away to the west without any limit I could see. Distant hills looked blue, but many quartz outcrops also rose in the midst of the plain.

"How d'you like the look of that, young Mr. Dickens?"

"I do like it," I told him.

"It's the Mount Murchison run, where we do our grazing."

"Where are your sheep, though?"

"They are there, believe me, and their fleeces growing, and their lambs ditto. The country is so vast and the capacity to carry sheep per acre so small here that the sheep are lost somewhere in this place and we will find them in time for mustering. But you, Dickens, with your patrimony, you could be the first great poet of this Darling country. You might make Wilcannia shine with luster in the world's eye," he said with a grin. "I suggested the very same to your brother at the races at Poolamacca. But he thought I was joking."

I thought, No, Alfred didn't think you were joking. Alfred was rebuffing the idea, just as I now did. "I'm a very unmusical fellow," I told him. "I'm a better cricketer than a poet."

"Oh well now," he said, thankfully pleased with the topic of cricket. The colonials seemed to love it with a passion equal only to horse racing.

I simply looked west under a high sun. A country with big pockets. Big enough to hide flocks and people in.

⁓

When our boat reached Wilcannia it seemed a busy town, reputedly one with around three or four hundred people. This busyness might have been because of the flutter our arrival caused. A number of people were drawn down to the high pier on the riverbank, and there was a flurry at the gangplank as the grave, veiled figure of Mrs. Desailly landed. Two troopers in white helmets, blue jacket, white pants, and high boots waiting by the gangway saluted as she passed, and a Catholic priest and an Anglican pastor took their hats off.

"Do you know where Mrs. Desailly's going?" I asked Larkin. "I mean, where her home is?"

"Netallie Station. The Desaillys are legends along the Darling. She has her husband and, a rare thing, daughters. Squatters' daughters are pretty scarce on the ground in this part of New South Wales. If they exist, Mr. Dickens, they often prefer to stay in the cities, and spend their old man's wool check."

" 'Old man' meaning 'father'?"

"Dead right," said Larkin.

As I watched Mrs. Desailly board the surrey I reflected with my new worldliness that women were a mystery. If you put two chaps in the same saloon, unless one of them was blighted with shyness or strangeness, they would be firm friends by the end of such a journey as we had been through. Whereas Mrs. Desailly and I had remained utter strangers, and her only advantage as a fellow traveler was, as far as I could see, that she was not a devout reader of my father's work and so set me no literary tasks.

Several tall young natives waited to one side of the pier to help with unloading the *Eliza Jane*. Two of them wore vests with their loincloths, but most of them were bare chested and looked muscular. Over in the shade of trees were two turbaned Afghans with a string of camels which would be carrying much of Burgess's cargo into the remoter country.

Tom Larkin suggested, "If you wanted, Mr. Dickens, we could set out this morning and travel forty miles before we camp tonight. What do you say to that?"

They surprised you, these people. This man was in a sense a servant, and what servant asks his master, "What do you say to that?" But I had heard it was the custom of the country and I was sensible enough not to try to eradicate it single-handed.

"I am supposed to report to the stock and station agent first. Fremmel's. They have a wagon going out to Momba."

"Good-oh, we can string along with it," he said with a smile betraying full, shovel-bearded amusement.

"What are you laughing at, Larkin?" I asked.

"Well, I'm amused people go to such lengths to meet you because of your old man. Not that you lack merit on your own. They would have got the wagon ready specially to ensure you'd call in and see them. By tonight they'll be bragging about their good mate young Dickens and predicting great things for you. Not without reason either. I too think you'll do well."

"Thank you," I said, feeling oddly grateful.

"Just as a bit of a warning, they'll want you to wait in town a day or two so they can show you off," said Larkin. "Whereas . . . you might prefer us to be on our way."

When I reiterated my intention to go to Fremmel's, Larkin nodded and said, "While you're at the stock and station agents, I might get my sins heard, since the priest is here. After that I can be found at the pub right there, the Commercial."

I had never heard a Papist so frankly and casually mention the requirements of his barbarous religion. "*Get my sins heard.*" And then, a drink at the Commercial. I felt a shadow fall between Larkin and me. The guvnor was a great abominator of Papism, believing it to be an enemy of all progress.

The town's buildings looked to have thick sandstone walls, these being a sovereign repellent of the heat. There were two sandstone churches representing the two abiding faiths, mine and Larkin's. The Commercial, also made of sandstone, offered accommodation. Three warehouses were aligned amongst the shade provided by high white-flowering eucalyptus. And not far away was what I was told were the beginnings of a post office.

As I saw my modest pile of goods assembled on the pier of heavy timbers, I walked ashore myself and said goodbye to Captain Burgess, who was accepting plaudits from a number of people for getting his ship here yet again. The men talking to him turned the slits of their eyes to me as I passed by. Their clothes were fashionable enough, and they had the well-heeled look which I would learn squatters always brought with them, no matter how much they might be in debt, when visiting town from the "real Australia," out there somewhere beyond. They were assessing me in my brand-new wide-awake hat and riding jacket and moleskin trousers. They did not say anything, and it may even have been from a form of shyness, and also a Mrs. Desailly reticence to get to know me until I had "applied myself" to their country and become a permanent figure in it.

Walking on, I found a police trooper at my side, saluting. "Mr. Dickens," he said in one of the softer and less combative Irish brogues. "Then could I assist ye now?"

I told him I wished to visit the stock and station agent and he pointed down past the warehouses into a shimmer of heat. "Fremmel's," he assured me. "You have some business there? I'll escort ye, Mr. Dickens, and my friend will watch your goods against pilferage."

It was not long before we came to Fremmel's Stock and Station Agency, whose door was festooned with crepe decorations. In the window a sign said, "Fremmel's Welcomes Mr. Edward Bulwer Lytton Dickens, son of the Immortal Charles Dickens, to Wilcannia, Future Metropolis of the Darling River."

My Irish constable saluted and left me, saying he would be needed once the transfer of goods from ship to warehouse began, because "the darks," the Aboriginals I'd seen at the wharf, needed eagle's eyes on them since they were pilferers by nature.

I walked into the store, by way of the normal deep-shaded veranda, past a notice board on which horses and tack and properties of sundry sizes were advertised along with information about coming auctions of ewes and lambs. One in particular caught my eye: "290 Merino and Border Leicester Rams Available Through Early Sale of Station and Worth a Further Run!" Even then I thought the notice meant someone had "gone bust." I stood by the agency's long counter, alarmed by the festive crepe hung around the office.

A man in a good suit and a paisley cravat, wearing spectacles, came up to me then. He had about him the feel of someone at the height of his powers and aware he had them. A block of a fellow with slicked brown hair. Apart from his watchful eyes, the chief feature of his face was his out-of-proportion lips. There was too much of them. A person was simply sure that at whatever school he'd gone to, colonial or British, he would have been called "Froggy." An astonishing-looking woman I assumed was his wife appeared beside him, her appearance appealing to the burgeoning man in me. She was a bit taller than her husband and her white dress was just a little disarrayed, as was her black hair, yet you could not tell whether it was artifice or lack of interest that created the effect.

"My wife, Mr. Dickens," said the man.

I accepted the woman's lace-gloved hand when she offered it to me, as a man would.

"My wife is French, sir, and I like to call her Madame Fremmel," he said, his long amphibian lips curved into a huge smile.

"It is an honor, madame," I told her. "My father loves your country. He knew your president Lamartine very well."

"And France loves your papa," she said. "Even the emperor. And for those who do not love the emperor, as I do not, your papa was also a friend to Victor Hugo in his exile!"

I was impressed by Mrs. Fremmel's mention of Hugo, whom my guvnor had once said he liked more than any other Frenchman, though Hugo's wife looked as if she was ready to poison the poor man's breakfast. Looking again at Fremmel he just didn't appear a man who had a wife familiar with Hugo, and who liked to hold opinions on the French emperor in a place like Wilcannia.

Her bit said, however, she drew back again, allowing her husband control over the moment.

"I know you must be tired from your journey," said Mr. Fremmel, "and I would be honored to be your host while you recover. I promise you I can gather a fine company of gentlemen from Wilcannia and beyond who would be pleased to entertain and acclaim you for choosing our settlement as your destination. I believe your birthday is about to take place . . ."

Oh dear. I imagined trying to speak and appear wise to the civic fathers of Wilcannia.

"Sir," I said hurriedly, surprising myself with my desperate firmness, "that is very kind of you, and there may be later occasions where we can all be joined in jovial company. But I must get to my station as soon as I can and apply myself to the business of sheep."

Fremmel's smile immediately went crooked and looked unreliable.

"Oh," he emphasized, "I would be particularly grateful to be your host for a few days at least. After all, I could tell you much about the business."

His wife laughed pleasantly. "Fremmel is not like other men," she said as a genial warning. "He is not uselessly tender, as his wife might be sometimes. He has a clear head."

The urgency to apply myself was acrid in my throat. "No, I have to be on my way to Momba as soon as it can be done. Mr. Rusden expects me to. He mentioned a wagon . . ."

"That is so, but the wagon does not have to go till you're ready," said Mr. Fremmel before calling towards the interior of the store-room. "Maurice! Where in God's name is the boy? *Maur-ice!*"

A young man came hurrying into the office; I thought he must be the Fremmels' son, since there was more than a hint of Mr. Fremmel's lips on this man's face, though not enough to mar his features.

"This is my nephew," Fremmel told me.

The young man gave an unalloyed smile and held out his hand, saying, "Maurice McArden." He must have been about twenty and the only similarity to his uncle besides his lips was that he too had conscientiously pomaded hair.

"I am driving the supply wagon to Momba, Mr. Dickens," he told me, "whenever you're ready to go."

I appealed to this kindlier presence. "Your uncle has generously offered me his hospitality. But Mr. Rusden, our patron, has insisted I go there at once and apply myself. There is also a new blacksmith going there with me. A man named Larkin."

"Well," said Mr. Fremmel, "this Larkin may be ready to go, but it will be rather a rush for Maurice."

"Oh no," said Maurice almost willfully, as if he would be delighted to upset his uncle's plans. "The wagon is as good as ready. My bags and swag are packed too. I need only change into bush kit."

Fremmel was frankly irritated by now, which brought out irritation in me.

"The only way, Mr. Fremmel, to prove I am fit for this life is to begin living it as soon as I can," I said as reasonably as I could. "That is certainly my father's wish."

"Very well then," said Fremmel, grimacing as he relinquished any ambition he'd harbored to be my mentor in town.

"Well," said Maurice, stepping forward and not disappointed at all. "Where should I meet you and this Larkin, Mr. Dickens?"

"Larkin and I will be at the Commercial," I replied.

As Mr. Fremmel turned his attention to a catalogue, Mrs. Fremmel smiled charmingly at me and then at her nephew, saying, "You must both be careful with heat sickness and snakes. Kick your swag before you settle down on it."

"My aunt is half-demented by snakes," said Maurice fondly.

I was myself half-infatuated with the divine Mrs. Fremmel, and given her Gallic accent, her advice on serpents was hard to forget or ignore. To us nearly serpentless Britons, the word "snake" had great power in any case.

"Death adder," she said, shivering. "Taipan. And you are both my darling boys."

"I am nineteen," Maurice McArden told his aunt.

"Yes," she said with insistence. "Boys."

"I need but twenty minutes, Mr. Dickens," said Maurice, glancing at his uncle, who still looked aloof.

4

When I arrived at the Commercial, Larkin was speaking companionably to other men, a pint of dark brown fluid only quarter-drunk before him. I signaled to him and told him we were going.

I itched to ask him about his encounter with the priest while we were waiting for Maurice, for to know a practice is barbarous is not to renounce all curiosity in it. I managed not to. I also managed to tell him the agent had offered me his hospitality, but I had managed to renounce the town of Wilcannia in favor of Momba.

So we drew up our cavalcade, me on Coutts, Tom Larkin on a stocky, shaggy gelding I called a Waler after the distant uplands of New South Wales where they had been bred. I would learn the army in India sent their agents to Australia to buy up as many Walers as they could for cavalry mounts.

I wondered if my brother Walter had ridden a Waler while serving in the 42nd Highlanders in India, where he'd been involved in the campaign that led to the defeat of the rebels at Cawnpore and the relief of Lucknow. The poor fellow had fallen down one day with sunstroke and "smart fever," a sort of brain infestation, and had to be carried to a hill station to recuperate. The guvnor had been very proud that Walter had earned "a mutiny medal with clasp" and gained promotion from ensign to lieutenant and some prize money before he'd even turned eighteen years!

I had barely known Walter when I was young. To him I was the "cursed Plorncaster" or "Plorncabanaster." But he had come to my room at Tavistock House two nights before he left and said, "Plorncaster, I have been dismissive of you." He burst into tears, and his face creased so childishly I had no idea what to do. "I don't want to go. Just because I passed the East India Company exam, why must I go?" And he shook his head. "Little Brother, Little Brother, if I could stay, you and I could be chums."

"Ask Katie to talk to the guvnor!" I'd suggested, knowing our eldest sister could make demands and had the power to make Father stop and take notice. But if Walter had done so, Katie hadn't been able to prevail.

Poor, pitiable Walter, in view of what was to happen!

Maurice McArden, in checked shirt, moleskin trousers, and Prussian boots, sat at the reins of the wagon and a team of four draught horses. We set off without any uttered sentiment and in two street lengths were on black soil fringes where a few Chinese were growing pumpkins, and beyond that we moved onto red soil and into the yellowing grass of this antique and western land. The sun was strong—not so strong as to dement a man but strong in an honest way. There was no vapor in it. The chance of fog in this country was remote. Clarity was all. I guessed one would call it "prairie" had it been America, with glinting outcrops suggestive of gold but generally yielding only quartz. Distant mountains somehow promised infinity, however, rather than any limit.

We drove in silence for a long way, perhaps fifteen miles, before Larkin called, "Reckon it's a little after two."

He dismounted by the rocky rim of a strangely beautiful yellow earth lake with only a smear of mud at its bottom. Every stone that had delineated the lake and its various stages of fullness and decline shone blue and yellow, brown and white.

I dismounted, too, and Maurice hauled his draught horses to a stop and tethered them to a fragile-looking bush.

"Will your horses bolt?" I asked him.

"You don't know how a grevillea can tangle the reins," he told me, possessed of superior knowledge.

That was when we began to talk like fellow travelers, and I learned much of Maurice and Tom Larkin on the way and, inevitably, as we lay on swags beneath huge skies which intoxicated one with their immensity, they learned something of me. For we were like travelers on a raft in immense seas. At every fork on the track so far, Maurice and Tom Larkin seemed to agree where we needed to go, this way, not that way. I might have been one of those hapless British travelers who perished (of thirst, for I would learn that in Australia they used only the verb) and I might have become a cautionary tale.

That first lunchtime was functional. The bread called damper, mutton, black tea. In the afternoon, Larkin and I let Maurice's dray go ahead of us along a route made, in this country of sun-brittle grass, by the stagecoach that brought the shearers to Momba Station in season. As we rode along behind, Tom Larkin gave me further education in the nature of the country, pointing out the mulga trees widely spaced on the plain and telling me you never cut one of them down because the branches were good stock feed in drought.

He also pointed out light-green-blue shrubs called saltbush, which he said the sheep loved. How providential, he solemnly told me, that this shrub that had been here since Adam's day proved just the ticket for sheep to live off!

He showed me pearl bluebush, which was like saltbush but not as palatable. Similarly applebush and rosebush, which looked nothing like their namesakes.

Above all he showed me the tall, orange-brown kangaroo grass, saying, "Prime, Mr. Dickens. Prime!" And then, as if he had committed a breach of etiquette, "Prime, Plorn. Caviar for sheep and cattle. It dies with drought though." Then yellow tussocks, of which he said, "Mitchell grass. Hard to kill."

By the end of the day he had introduced me to clumps of mulga grass with green-gray bulbs, emu grass, feathery and lime-green neverfail, which Larkin assured me was even more durable than mulga and Mitchell grass. And he had no doubt that this was all providence for the wool business, that all this fodder, until now cropped only by kangaroos, had been placed here from time primordial until Britons should need it to grow the world's best wool.

He put names to other items in the nearby landscape until I grew thoroughly confused. It was astounding how much he knew, as if he had sampled them all as provender himself.

In the late afternoon we encountered the front fence of Momba Station, which stretched away, northwest and southeast.

"It's forty-five miles long," said Maurice, a little breathlessly. It was in its way a world wonder—built of tons of wire, and hardwood stumps by the ton, along with mountains of human sweat.

After a dinner of mutton stew prepared by Larkin, my two friends told me of their origins while taking mine for granted.

First, Tom Larkin: "My parents were convicts from Ireland, but loving and worthy of honor. My old man was transported for breaking his oppressive landlord's door down, though if he were here he would argue fully he was no criminal. My dear mother was sent here for stealing a length of cloth in Limerick. She was a good woman, but sadly died in childbirth, and my father passed a few years later of melancholy. I cannot swear, Mr. Dickens, that liquor might not have been involved, for men's souls were marked by their long imprisonment and the passage to Australia."

I listened to this as if it were normal to have such parents.

Maurice had, if anything, an even sadder tale. His parents had both been artists, and their marriage a meeting of souls. They traveled widely together on painting expeditions. Maurice's father had been elected an associate of the Royal Academy and would, in time, have been made a full member. Maurice's parents had exhibited together at the Royal Society of Artists under, said Maurice, "A friend of your family, Dickens—a very generous man named Clarkson Stanfield. Your father dedicated a novel to him, I believe."

I remembered the name Clarkson Stanfield. Though he was an old man—I would say maybe twenty years older than my father— he had the demeanor of a young one and proved he liked children when he came to Tavistock House for fun and games when I was little. (He had lost a lot of his own children, it turned out.) He painted back cloths for the plays Papa put on, and the guvnor said of him that though he was a Papist he lived modestly and without hypocrisy. For fun he imitated someone stumbling over his names, and would make jokes, calling himself Clarkfield Stanson and Fieldstan Transom. Then he went on to tell us how in Napoleon's day he had been *pressed* into the navy by a press-gang. He knew that story would enchant us, and he was right.

So this same man had been a benefactor to Maurice's parents, and we were discussing all this beyond Wilcannia, on the rim of the known earth.

Sadly, three years past, Maurice's parents had died in a huge avalanche in the St. Gotthard Pass. The rest was a familiar enough story: Maurice's father had left his business affairs in the hands of a London lawyer he would have entrusted with his life. The man was unworthy not only of that trust but even incapable of normal honesty.

"Like a child in a novel, I had nothing," said Maurice, "and my father's friends rallied and wrote to my mother's brother in Wilcannia. Not long after I got a wonderful, welcoming letter from my aunt, saying that she and my uncle both believed I should join them in New South Wales, and my parents' friends raised the money for a saloon passage, though I traveled second-class so I had resources left over. And . . . here we are. Tom and I are orphans, but you, Dickens, thankfully in full possession of parents."

Though possession of Charles and Catherine Dickens was not easy to claim at such a distance, and could not even be simultaneously managed in England, with Mother living at her parents' and Father prowling the earth.

At last, without even checking my swag bed for vipers, I unfolded it and, in the cooling desert night, fell asleep on it.

Away at dawn, we crossed claypans where, Larkin told me, the Aboriginals had in times past lit fires and turned the surface to a form of glazed brick.

"You will hear nothing but good of the natives from Mr. Bonney at Momba," said Maurice. "My uncle says Bonney is taken with them. I think he's a student of them."

We saw smoke from a fire some way off. "That's them," said Maurice. Our path lay in that direction, and later in the day I saw the antediluvian people moving across their country. The men were tall and thin like the Aboriginal men on the wharf and wore cast-off jackets, no doubt given them by the Bonneys, with clouts of cloth on their lower body. The women wore mission dresses, but some were bare breasted, including a woman suckling a baby.

As we approached, an old woman advanced a way to look at us more closely, the sun glinting off a sort of halo adorning her head. "What is that?" I asked. "On her head."

It was a helmet of gypsum, as it turned out, which widowed women encased their head in after their husbands died. The gypsum helmet gave me my first impulse of fascination with the darks. By some mad loop of unreasoning, it made me think at once of Mama. She was not a widow, nor did I ever want her to be. But it had been ten years since she'd gone home to her parents. What helmet should she wear?

She had claimed she wanted to go and live with her parents. When she married Papa, he was a shorthand reporter and scribbler, but when she left his side he was a god. An impulse told me that had she worn a glinting helmet on her head it would have spoken and argued for her, and helped her move into the society of ordinary, ungod-like men and women, as she wanted to.

An impulse in me wanted Mama to be able to be as shrill as this dark widow now was, making a trembling plaint at her condition within Momba's great fence. Contrary to what the guvnor said, Mother got away from her turbulent children and husband the demigod to live in her parents' place, and then in her own neat little house in Gloucester Crescent. She had taken Charley, the oldest, with her, letting us all know she loved us before she moved there, weeping softly, making no loud gestures like this widow. Aunt Georgie, her own sister, stayed with father and us. Aunt Georgie, if widowed, would have raged like this dark woman. But mother was such a gentle claimant on our love. Perhaps she should have come to Gad's Hill after we moved out there to the Kentish countryside and wailed on the front steps as the old lady with the gypsum helmet wailed.

The melancholy of all this did not last long, for by late afternoon we entered the last gate and came to a homestead with a deep veranda not unlike the homestead of the unspeakable McGaw. But this one was not the sum of Momba, which was like a little village! There was a large store, a grand shed for the bullock wagon, a foundry, a sawmill, several cottages for drovers and carpenters, stables and a huge shearing shed with a fringe of sheep races and pens and yards. Larkin said it would be a wool factory once shearing began.

After opening the gate for Maurice's dray to roll through, Larkin and I rode in behind. I was nervous now about whether the Bonney brothers and Mr. Suttor would, if amiable, greet me with urgent questions regarding the guvnor. A proper demeanor quite rightly meant coolness, distance, until I showed I was aimed in the same direction as them—that I wanted to apply myself and be a lord of the fleece.

I was heartened when we went to the stables and Tom Larkin, who had not asked me labored questions, lifted the saddle off his horse's steaming back, and said, "Mr. Dickens . . . Plorn, I'd be pleased if when you get the chance you could thank Mr. Suttor, since he and his father stood up for us Catholic children of convicts while some would have had us in the pit. To think I was born in convict slavery while my mother still served her term, but here we are now, free men of worth, each with the universal franchise."

"But if that's so, Tom, you tell him yourself," I replied.

"Yes, but what a gift if you, the child of the great man, said it. In any case, if I told him, I would get stuck with the eloquence."

A handsome young dark boy, perhaps my own age, with sullen eyes and willing hands, took my saddle off me and bore it away to a rack. Then he turned and placed his limpid, huge eyes on me and said, "I brush him down, boss."

"Good Coutts," I whispered to the mare before I headed off. "Good Coutts."

I carried my fairly heavy saddlebags on my shoulder, knowing it was no good waiting around for a porter here.

❧

A tall man in shirtsleeves had emerged from the storeroom while we'd been unsaddling.

"Hoop-la," he said resonantly as he came towards us. "The boys from Fremmel's. Hello there, Maurice," he said before turning to me and saying, "I'm Willy Suttor. Which one are you, sonny?"

"Edward Bulwer Lytton Dickens, sir," I replied. "Sixteen years of age for five more days."

"Oh dear Lord," he roared, "you've not even gone to the homestead yet?"

"Not yet, sir. I wished to say a proper goodbye to Maurice, who has been very accommodating with me on the ride."

"Well, that is splendid of you, but you'll see him at dinner. And me, for that matter. A gala evening at the Bonney brothers!" His accent was a well-modulated Australian and the vowels as flat as the Momba landscape. He wasn't, like me, a "new chum," a "Pommy," the half-contemptuous terms the Australians reserved for newcomers. "Dear me, we've all taken a vow not to mention your father to you, since you must be sick of everyone doing that first off. But I have to say, young Dickens, it's astounding that you are the closest thing to the great magician himself! The dazzling civilizer of rough men like me! In the remotest huts he brings us to noble tears and evokes a sensibility we did not know we possessed. And, by heaven, you are flesh of his flesh, blood of his blood. We are delighted and a little discombobulated to have you here. But enough, I have already broken the pledge, but I shall be well behaved tonight. You should present yourself to Mr. Frederic Bonney, who is in a fever to greet you and has been pacing the veranda and drinking nervous tea. If you hang around here, Maurice will have you unloading the wagon!"

Suttor then turned his gleaming eyes on Maurice, saying, "I take it you have broached the subject . . . ?"

"No . . . No, there was not an opportunity . . ." Maurice replied, dropping his gaze.

"Oh well, up to you, old boy!" said Willy in a low, apologetic voice.

As they both looked at me, I said, "The blacksmith, Tom Larkin, who came with us, is a child of Papist convicts. He asked me to pass on his thanks to you."

"When I was young, I was of radical bent," said Willy, who still seemed a youngish man in any case.

I said then that if they would forgive me I would go and introduce myself at the homestead. When I told Maurice I would come and fetch my valise from his dray, Suttor said, "No, no. I'll get one of our young clodhoppers to deliver it. Also your saddlebags. Least we can do!"

As I walked toward the homestead I felt a sudden nervousness. The last Momba test now awaited, which was whether the Bonney brothers showed any malign echo of McGaw. The main house backed on to a stand of trees by a creek and was a little fortress-like, with a wing at either end, between which the veranda ran. It stood amongst a scatter of mulga trees and possessed no sentimental attempt to sport a trellised garden or the affectation of roses.

The veranda boards were pretty close to the ground, and as I approached I heard the sound of boots, before a sturdy little man with a trimmed moustache wearing a suit and a white pith helmet presented himself at the top of the stairs.

"Ah," he said, stopping there. "A good journey, Mr. Dickens?"

I told him yes and gave credit to Maurice and the new Momba blacksmith.

"Quite," he said. "Welcome to Momba. Must be deuced strange, but if you stay here awhile it will become the entire world. Please just follow me, young Dickens."

He was not quite as talkative as Suttor, and clearly English born, with a quite pleasant Midlands edge to his deep voice. He was also quite young, with boyishly plump cheeks. After showing me to my bedroom (a little too like the one on McGaw's station) he suggested I refresh myself and indicated the bath.

"Do tell me if you need anything at all," he urged me. Then he inhaled and added, "We are proud you've come to throw in your destiny with us."

As he walked away I pondered on how he had done the job servants did in England, the showing to the room, the information about the bath, the offer of help. My father's son, I was interested in this new version of man: master and servant in the one body— a combination required by the place we were in. The guvnor always put stress on the fact his grandparents had both been servants, his grandmother Elizabeth, a maid for one Lady Blandford, and his grandfather William Dickens, an old manservant to Lord Crewe, and later made valet. That was as far as the Dickenses were allowed to go in those days, the guvnor claimed. He said we must, being now gentlemen by the utter accident of his talent, see the human face in servants and waiters, in porters and boatmen.

A male cook, a ravaged-looking man, later came to my door with tea, which I welcomed. "Courtney, Mr. Dickens," he said a little wearily. "And I reckon the dinner'll be on the table by a quarter to seven. That sweet with you, Mr. Dickens?"

I told him it was very sweet.

As he turned to go he shook his head, chuckling to himself. "Little Nell," he said, as if remembering. "Little Nell. Can't believe it. Bawled my mongrel eyes out! Kill a person in a book, and they live forever, like!"

Here was a haggard cook who had read a book I'd never opened. He was clearly not part of the compact not to mention my father.

5

I left a film of red dust in the bottom of the bath. In my new role as desert servant, I washed and rubbed it away. Then I dressed in my slightly crumpled morning suit of modern cut. Even if it evoked knowing smiles that said "a newcomer," I felt I owed it to my fellow diners to wear it. By now I could hear an exchange of male voices from the dining room and walked towards it resolutely. Inside, Maurice, in a fresh shirt, moleskins, and cleaned boots, had been pressed into the business of offering sherry or brandy and water as an appetizer. Suttor, pretty much the way we had seen him in the store but with a canvas jacket and no tie, was drinking brandy. The *noblesse oblige* of running sheep on more than two thousand square miles of earth had put the Bonney brothers, both "bosses" of Momba, in suits like the habitual worn-in one Frederic Bonney had been wearing on the veranda.

Mr. Edward Bonney was older, stockier, and more matter-of-fact than his brother. He spoke economically with an accent that hinted of Staffordshire, where their father, a clergyman, had run a grammar school. It was an uncle of theirs who had come to Australia, caught the sheep bug, and made his fortune, returning to England a self-made man, to pass his leaseholds to his nephews, who had the look of made men. I meant to become as they were and thought it would be a fine thing to be the owner, like them, of two hundred thousand beasts.

For the moment, I was welcomed by every voice in the room and questioned about my colonial experience to this point. Then we sat down and drank a sturdy, beefy soup served by Courtney, whose nickname was "Squeaker." Squeaker was clearly named to honor his near-total silence. He occupied his silence as other men occupied their boundary riders' huts, and never wanted to confide in anyone or excuse or invite praise for his cooking. I am left to say little about a man with such an interesting surname except that he was very competent. After the soup he presented us with a roast mutton leg, à la Momba, which the elder Bonney carved up and served. During this, Frederic began to talk to me about the oddity of what we were all doing and hoping for at Momba.

"There is no way your English family can understand what you will go through here. Everyone here knows, but it is beyond the understanding of the best-intentioned scribe of colonial items in magazines and periodicals. Over there to the east, just to begin, there is a waterhole which is sadly drying up at the moment but may be redeemed for us by autumn rains. It is in fact a river course, the Paroo. I'd say it's a channel, for it prefers to flow underground. That is an oddity, first off."

There was assent around the table.

"No one quite describes this country as graphically as Frederic," said Willy Suttor. "He is of course a writer . . ."

Frederic smiled shyly. "Notes on ethnography, and thus only a shadow writer."

"He is the authority on the natives of the Paroo-cum-Darling," said Edward with some dry pride. "It is in his nature to be such."

"Seconded," cried Willy. "It is his nature. Anything to say in support of the motion, Maurice?"

"Nothing to say yet, Mr. Suttor," said Maurice, almost as a warning. "I will choose my time, thank you."

"Forgive me," said Willy before turning to Frederic. "Well then, Fred, give us your famous ruminations on the sheep, if you would."

"Indeed, I have often asked who has ever told a story about a sheep?" Frederic said. "Dogs, especially sheep dogs, have their library of tales; horses perhaps even more so. Bulls have a section of tales, even heifers. And as for calves . . . Then pigs and particularly piglets. The sheep, our chief beast here at Momba, has no volumes of humanizing tales apart from the story of the Golden Fleece Jason sought from the golden ram Chrysomallos, who is sadly lacking amongst our flocks. Apart from Jason, all else is manuals of sheep breeding. Now, my brother is an excellent breeder, but he has never been moved to poetry by a sheep. Or even by a ram. And yet . . . they are our staple, they are the animals of our dreams."

He was, I thought, the philosopher of wool breeding, but he had not finished yet.

"Sometimes at the stations further in towards the coast you will get an orphan lamb, and the station children will feed it on a bottle. But children are a luxury who have not yet come our way. Yet by far the richest man in Australia today is a baron of sheep, a role we aspire to but cannot claim, not even with all our square miles. And this baron has named not one sheep except for tracking and breeding purposes, as well as listing the rams in his stock book. And when drought strikes . . . well, there may be more profit in killing and boiling down sheep by the ton than cropping their wool. For the truth is we lack in these colonies sufficient mouths to eat the tens of thousands of sheep we stock."

This awesome idea hung in the air, and the other parties to this great sheep proposition looked at me as if I might have brought an answer with me.

"So it's wool we breed our merino sheep for," said Edward.

"And they happen to give us the best wool in the world. Ewe, ram, wether—they exist to have their fleece taken off once yearly—an exercise that takes a good shearer five minutes for each creature. That's our Golden Fleece and the reward we all seek. A suitably high wool price in London."

"But how curious," Frederic chimed in, "that we should have the Spanish merino breed, and that it happens to be exactly the right breed for wool-yielding in this country. How remarkable that the big, robust English sheep with their coarse wool should be out-fleeced—if that is a term—"

Willy cried, "Permit it, permit it, for truth's sake! It suits!"

"—should be out-fleeced by the smaller, robust merino whose wool is so fine and so desirable in the mills of Britain!"

They began to discuss then how the merino came to be here, in these giant pastures of Momba. Willy Suttor, as station historian, related that Farmer George, George III, was interested in them and, during one of his periods of sanity, bought merino ewes for his gardens at Kew through the Spanish ambassador, in exchange for two creamy coach horses Mrs. Ambassador desired. But how to get a merino ram?

"Oh, I think I know that one," supplied Maurice. "The ram was smuggled by English spies from Spain all the way to Hamburg and on a ship to England."

Willy nodded. "In defiance, mind you . . . in defiance of the Spanish king!"

"I think that story might be a romantic fiction," said Edward. "For one thing, the Saxons had the merino, and the Americans have merino relatives in Vermont."

"Ah," protested Willy, "let us have our deluded tales, Edward!"

And then, said Frederic, taking up the tale, an officer of the New South Wales garrison named John Macarthur, who'd been sent back to England for wounding his superior officer in a duel, bought merino rams in a dispersal sale of the royal flock at Kew and, after evading punishment for the duel, brought them back to Australia. And when the Blue Mountains outside Sydney were crossed . . . well, we had then the phenomenon by which merino fleece, in the hinterland of Australia, was worth more than gold. At least sometimes. In fact, frequently. Except . . . except for drought.

"But when has there been such a golden marriage between a continent and a species of sheep?" asked the poetic Willy Suttor, "and . . . *and* . . . between a species of sheep and the great British wool manufactories. People speak of angelic choirs. Well, the consonances of all this are like the harmonies of an angelic choir."

"Well said, Willy!" agreed Frederic.

My heart seemed to expand with the breadth of the vision these men were conjuring for me. I felt one in the noble fraternity of the fleece, and *these* were the men I had hoped to come amongst.

"Not that I have not had problems," Willy admitted. "I am for now the Momba storekeeper. We are rewarded in earthly terms with giant checks that come to us once a year. And sometimes our expenses . . . well, Mr. Dickens, you saw the front fence here as you arrived. Fencing is an enterprise . . . that matches the expense of building a pharaonic pyramid or a Salisbury Cathedral. And now I am fencing some hundreds of square miles of my own and need ready cash. So I come here as storekeeper to keep a shop and overcharge even the distinguished Bonney brothers . . ."

"My heaven, the beggar does so," said Edward, laughing. "Charges like . . . as the people say here . . . a wounded bull!"

There was widespread agreement and merriment around the table.

"I pass on only the costs already laid upon me by Maurice's avaricious Uncle Fremmel," claimed Willy.

"And he," said a smiling Maurice, "would tell you he passes on only the costs he incurs at the hands of the avaricious ferry captains on the river and bullock drivers from the Bogan."

"Anyway, I shall have my fence," said Willy, beaming. "And I shall have dingo shooters to protect my sheep from those mad native dogs."

"Sir," I said to Frederic, "Mr. Rusden tells me that you know the natives well."

"Who could know them really well, Mr. Dickens?" he replied rhetorically.

"Plorn, please, sir. It's what my father and family call me."

"Right," said Frederic, before pausing. Everyone, except perhaps Maurice, gazed at me as if adjusting to this unfamiliar label until Frederic continued on.

"The natives are in any case a study of mine. These people along the river are named Paakantji. Many of them are my dear friends. Some work for us as drovers. They are very reliable drovers and, despite not having seen a horse until twenty-five years ago, are adept at riding. Their powers of communication with animals are remarkable. Yes, Plorn, I could say I'm an enthusiast for the Paakantji."

"Indeed, Fred takes wet plate photographs of them," said Edward, as if he were uncomfortable with his brother's previously stated enthusiasm.

"That must be very difficult, Mr. Bonney," I interjected.

"It's true that setting up the colloidal plate takes some practice," said Frederic. "But none of them are shy of the photographic apparatus itself. I have heard tales of Africans and Red Indians being flighty about the camera, but not the Paakantji."

"It's because they trust you," said Edward as a compliment.

"And when I ask them to be still, they are stiller than the grave, for however long—forty seconds perhaps, while the device captures their image. It is true, I hope, that they expect no malice from my brother and me."

"Not from you, anyhow, Fred," said Willy, as if there were unstated history to this. "You are like one of them."

Frederic beamed as if the concept were delightful and said, "No, their openness is a courtesy."

"They have baptized you into their tribe," Edward insisted a little too much like a criticism.

"Again, as a courtesy. But the welcome thing is—from their long occupation of this Paroo Channel country—they know where every resource of water is."

"Oh, you have no heart, sir!" said Willy Suttor in mock protest. "We are back where we began. Water and sheep equal stock food growing amongst the pebbles, and stock food equals fleece. That is all it is with Fred Bonney!"

"Not quite all," said Frederic, smiling. They were each such good friends, knowing when to tease. "Indeed, I love the darks, I must confess. For both their loyalty and integrity."

"Mark that, Plorn!" Willy admonished me. "There are men who consider the Aborigine a form of malign vermin. But that is not the Bonney gospel."

"I would hope not," said Frederic, stifling a yawn.

It was ten o'clock already and no one had mentioned my father, I noted in amazement.

As the party broke up, Maurice asked me if I'd like a settling stroll before sleeping. I thought the idea excellent so Maurice notified Willy, who was his host at the store, that he would be a little late, and in no time we were out in an encompassing dark pricked with various campfires. I heard a few shrill utterances from native women off in the circle of the blacks' camp, which was more apparent now from their line of fires along the creek. The occasional female jokes and protests seemed from that direction of a different order from those of European women. I would have dearly loved to be party to their meaning. As we passed a drovers' fire, a few late-retiring men were holding pannikins—rum and black tea had graced their evening. I could see Momba's new, broad-faced, full-bearded blacksmith there.

"They are enchanted by wool, our hosts," Maurice remarked to me as we walked in moonstruck dust as soft as talcum.

"They speak well of it," I agreed.

"I am not so certain as they are that I want to give my life to it. I like Melbourne. I like Sydney, at least from what I have read of it. Adelaide seems too colonial altogether. But I fear I'm an urbanite. Do you despise me for that, Plorn?"

"I've lived in cities. In fact, the closest I've been to any pastoral project is around Rochester and the Medway River. And a farming school my guvnor sent me to. To me, all this . . ." I said, making an encompassing gesture. "To me, it is all astonishing. And such interesting men."

Maurice laughed. "Thank God they didn't get onto the topic of crossbreeding and the benefits of Border Leicester rams! What they did not tell you—though Willy did broach it—is that their wonder and poetic vision is as much subject to the cruel intrusion of vulgar cash as any merchant house in London or Melbourne. You can be sure that even the Bonney brothers are in debt to somebody, whether it be a bank or a stock and station agent. Even to my uncle. It is the suited men in towns and cities who would not know a Suffolk Downs or Dorset if it shat on their boots, who end up singing the alleluias of the wool business."

"What would you do if you left your uncle's business?" I asked.

He paused for a while and then said, "Look, Dickens . . . Plorn . . . that has been on my mind for the whole journey. It is why I chose to bring the dray rather than leave the Momba goods order to the usual drayman. The truth is I yearn for ink! I would like to be at the least a newspaper hack. I would write for any liberal-minded journal in any country town in the colonies. My politics tend to the liberal—my uncle would call it radical—side. I have written local articles under the pen name Juventas and I would not trouble you with them. But . . . I have a novel too. All written, though only a quarter or so viable. I would be so honored if you read it. If you halfway approved of it, I might then have the temerity to send it to your father's journal, *All the Year Round*. It would be wonderful to be published in the same magazine that, to its eternal glory, published the instalments of Collins's *The Woman in White*, and your father's 'The Signalman.'"

I thought of Wilkie Collins with his pixie-like face and full-blown whiskers. He'd long been my father's kindred soul on rambles, and they were all the time doing plays together. I paused, in something of a familiar panic, not knowing what to say. Maurice had done me the favor of assuming that I had a fragment of my father's literary discrimination in me. I had none. Alfred and I were notoriously backward readers, let alone writers—though we could manage letters. I was framing what to tell him, when I realized this young man, who could drive a confident wagon into the hinterland, was weeping.

"I'm sorry. I want to get away from my uncle . . . I shouldn't have presumed though," he said, after gathering his emotions a little. "It's not a simple matter. I don't like the stock and station business. Wait there if you will, Plorn."

He vanished into the store but was back quickly holding bundles of paper tied with red tape. He presented them to me as if giving up something sacred, tears still in his eyes and a pleading look.

"You hold my soul," he told me.

My hands, holding the pages, had an impulse to let go and hand them back.

But who can hand a man his soul back?

6

The first Sabbath of my education in the fleece industry was the next day, and the Bonneys, being the sons of a parson, observed it, but without fanaticism. By the fire site in the midst of the drovers' huts, Edward Bonney read a brief service from the Book of Common Prayer. As he did, I noticed the young Aboriginal boundary rider who had taken Coutts from me when I first arrived stood nearby frowning. Down the track a little, five Papists, including Tom Larkin, had gathered to recite their Rosary.

All apart from the native women were males in this enormous acreage, and that suited me fairly well at nearly seventeen, when the idea of a future beloved, a woman of vapor, had certainly arisen in me but with no urgency to see her in the flesh. I had decided that women in the flesh were a challenge to the callow, whether they represented an uncomplaining wistfulness like Mama, a sturdy and overriding competence like Aunt Georgie, or a jovial irreverence like my clever sister Kate. Papa had nicknamed Katie "Lucifer Box" for her capacity to flare, but she had married Wilkie Collins's sickly brother, Charlie, a fellow who seemed to have no fire at all.

As the service continued, I thought fretfully of the pages Maurice had thrust on me. I was pleased he was not at the service, and in a little while he would be going back to town, hopefully not to appear again to hear my verdict—I was incapable of aiding his ambition. I supposed I could tell him to send the pages to my eldest brother Charley at *All the Year Round*. The risk was that the guvnor might see them since he had an apartment in the magazine building in Wellington Street where he often stayed during the week. But he would probably be too busy with more eminent pieces to hear about Maurice's item unless it was very good, in which case my repute would shine a little.

Forcing myself back to the present, I looked at the worshippers about me, who were so sun-leathered that I had to judge their age chiefly by the color of their hair and beards. Some would head off tomorrow with their kelpie sheepdogs to spend a week patrolling the boundaries of some huge paddock as far across as Boulogne from London.

Many of these vast half-desert pastures were also inhabited by solitary hutkeepers. And in the really vast paddocks there might be two men living in a shanty keeping an eye on the stock, rabbits, the carnivorous intrusion of dingoes, the condition of wells and fences and all other matters. It was apparently important to visit these men, since sometimes their isolation bred an oddity of soul.

After the service and morning tea, Frederic Bonney asked me would I care to visit the Paakantji camp with him and help him with his photographic equipment.

Yandi was the name of the young Aboriginal man with brooding eyes who'd attended the service. When we arrived, he was waiting by the room in which Frederic Bonney kept his photographic equipment.

Frederic introduced us and spoke to him very casually in the Paakantji tongue, as if this were a daily exercise. The upshot was that Yandi waited in the shade while Frederic and I went into the darkly curtained room, which had just enough light for us to see each other.

"I make my own plates for now," he told me. "It gives me great satisfaction. They say in America they have ready-made dry plates, but one feels closer to whatever image ends up on them if you make them yourself. It will take me a few minutes to prepare them."

"Yandi would make a fine picture," I suggested.

He smiled warmly, as if I had complimented a relative. "Yes. He can be easily distracted though. I always send him out with older men, since he has a tendency to dream off. He's a fair enough horseman. He's also an artist. I gave him a copy of the *Illustrated Melbourne Post* and some pencils and he was away, sketching exactly, and handling light and shade. I pay him for his drawings which allows him to buy tobacco for the older men and thus be a hero . . ."

Frederic moved to a window and adjusted its black curtain to exclude some light so it was all at once hot and dim in the room. Now he put on cloth gloves, cleaned off a glass plate and very deftly poured some brown chemical on it, judging the amount expertly and pouring excess chemical from the plate back into the bottle.

"The brown fluid is collodion," he told me as we watched it dry on the glass. He then put the glass plate into a dish he had filled with another fluid, murmuring that it was "silver nitrate."

I looked on as Frederic continued his sorcery, explaining, "One can't do this too long before one goes out to make the picture. If you let the plate sit too long it won't achieve the effect."

"How did you learn all this, Mr. Bonney?" I asked.

"Please, since I call you Plorn, you could call me Fred."

"Are you sure, sir?"

"Certainly. It is the manner of the country. But still, to answer your question, I learned from manuals and trial and error. And—I must admit, a traveling photographer from Sydney who came out photographing homesteads. But otherwise I never had a master."

He waited some minutes, timing the process with his dimly perceived watch until I wondered whether, if I spoke, it would interfere with the alchemy. At last he said it was time. He extracted the plate and directed me to a wooden rectangular box into which he locked the plate away from light. Then he went to the camera apparatus and slid this box into a slot in it. "Safe now," he said and pulled the curtains open and then wrapped the black cloak of the camera cloth around him. Before I could get used to how elfin he looked in this posture, he emerged and asked me to carry the tripod. He then called Yandi in to fetch and transport the camera box. Yandi picked it up with a broad, worried smile.

"I believe, Yandi, you're an artist," I said to him.

"Say 'sketcher,'" Mr. Bonney advised me in a whisper.

"You sketch, Yandi."

Yandi's smile increased in breadth. "Too right. I'm bonza sketcher, mister."

"The Paakantji don't waste much time on definite or indefinite articles, or tenses," Frederic confided in me. "Wise of them."

"I'd like to see some of your work," I said to Yandi, more for the sake of sociability than out of desire.

The three of us set out in the spirit of perfect fraternity Fred had casually set for this small adventure. I inhaled the ancient dust—a profound, somber smell with an overtone of peppery eucalyptus.

The native houses were well made of a frame of hardwood boughs and shaggy accumulations of branches. Four of the older native women seated in front of them watched us arrive and help Fred set up his camera. Some men who'd been kicking a makeshift animal-skin ball in the air saw our arrival and gathered in to observe. The older men with their full gray beards also joined us. "Picture eh, Mr. Bonney?" one of them called, and the older women shrilled.

"Cultay, could I introduce you to young Mr. Dickens here?" Fred said to one of the older full-bearded men.

The man extended a mahogany hand, which I shook in the spirit of the equality Fred was keen to impose on us citizens of Momba.

"Mr. Cultay is my source on all important matters concerning the darks."

As Fred helped Yandi set the shuttered machine on top of its tripod, the Paakantji people took up positions very quickly, staring in all that vastness at the dark circle of the camera's barrel eye, even though Fred was still moving it about, finding proper ground for the whole rite of photography. When he'd managed that, I stood slightly behind him as he attached the black cloth to the frame of the machine and disappeared beneath it.

A few moments later he emerged to order everyone closer together. "Shoulder to shoulder, that's right," he said, and "Betty, closer in to Wonga, please." He also gave them some instructions in their own language. He was a serious practitioner, who could not have taken greater trouble with a set of important Londoners.

At one stage he paused in his work to ask about a particular man and woman he didn't recognize who'd appeared and seemed ambitious to be in the photograph, finding out they were cousins from a station northwards called Budda.

"They love to visit each other," he told me.

After Fred made a number of further darts into and out of the dark cloth to adjust the lens and check on how things looked, he cried, "Are you all ready?"

The Paakantji assented with a roar. Fred then removed a cover from the lens, and—coached to match his gesture—the subjects all stood still, those unbreathing, antique faces. It was as if even the desert oaks behind the native huts seemed to hold their breath, waiting out the necessary time for the light of the day to inscribe their images on Fred's glass plate. I had no need to, but I held my breath anyhow, and was beginning to find it a test when Fred placed the cap back on the lens.

"Thank you all so much," he called to great laughter and pride amongst the Paakantji.

~

By the afternoon, Maurice McArden had readied his sturdy horses to take the dray back to Wilcannia. It would be a lonely ride, but as he said goodbye to the Bonney brothers he showed no dread of it. Before he departed he asked me if I would walk him back to the store. As we neared the horses, Willy Suttor emerged from his residence at the back of the store to bid Maurice goodbye.

"Plorn," Maurice told me in a hurry, "forgive me for last night and pushing the pages on you."

For a moment I thought he was going to ask for the bundle back. Unfortunately he didn't, saying, "I shall wait for your word on the book I am writing."

I told him I was honored by his confidence in speaking to me and had kept his pages safe.

"I'll wait anxiously for your judgment on them," he replied.

I wished to say, came close to saying, "Maurice, I am a schoolboy. And not a clever one." However, I did not want to call myself a schoolboy in this country. It was an unpromising description of any fellow.

Willy and I watched Maurice drive the dray away, and a young drover open the homestead gate for him.

"I don't believe he's happy at his uncle's agency. He has a soul, though he'd be better without one in the stock and station business."

"What should he do?" I asked.

"Oh, he is there for his aunt, who has a great affection for him. He won't leave her to the undiluted company of Mr. Fremmel."

"Forgive my asking, but how interesting Tom Larkin's gratitude to you was," I commented.

"Ah," he replied, "gratitude to my father in particular. My father was educated by an Irish convict, you see, in the days before Catholic emancipation in the colony. He has since been vocal about Irish rights in the New South Wales legislature and is seen as something of a spokesman for Catholics. As for me, I lack sectarian passion too. My father had very fine Irish tenants with whose children I mixed in childhood. It is like Fred and the Paakantji. It is hard to pursue the hatred of the mass if you know one or two of their faces so intimately."

"But the religion, Mr. Suttor . . . ?" I meant Papism.

"It is strange and rich in frenzies, which is to be regretted. But it is not their fault."

I didn't say much more for fear of being seen as undemocratic in an age when democratic feeling was the norm of progressives. The guvnor had been a democrat and a radical and republican. He had some Catholic friends but did not like Catholics as a lump.

At dinner Fred showed me a thick cardboard print taken that morning. "The light is good and the images sharp," he told me. "I've written the names on the back so that it can be an *aide-mémoire* for the people depicted."

I felt that wherever Fred turned, light was shed. In his photograph it had fallen on the faces of the Paakantji by their huts.

❧

The next day, Fred helped me become more familiar with the station. I visited Tom Larkin, who was setting himself up in the blacksmith shop to work on the metal winding mechanism of a wool press. There were two men helping him, one of them working the bellows.

As I stopped at the door Tom called out "G'day, Mr. Dickens."

"Hello, Tom. Would I be intruding if I came into the shop?" I said, for though the fire gave double heat to the smithy I was willing to go in.

"No, sir. 'Twould be our honor," he replied, rubbing his hands on his leather apron as he came to meet me.

"Plorn," he confided, "I hope you don't mind my calling you 'Mr. Dickens' in front of my blokes. It's just as well to maintain the formalities with them."

I nodded and moved forward to be introduced to his two off-siders. The older of the two seemed to have some lung problem, having been a miner once.

"You passed my respects to Mr. Suttor?"

"I did. And he was very grateful."

"Ah," he said, "I knew you were the one to do it. I find by the way there is but one white woman on Momba as yet until my beloved arrives. It's the wife of Gavan and she cooks for the drovers. I hope my wife won't find it too strange here."

He was actually open to reassurance on this—despite me being a youth a couple of days shy of seventeen! I thought of children, which seemed a natural outcome from a hearty man like this. Who would be the midwife? Mrs. Gavan? Or a Paakantji woman?

After the visit to the smithy, Willy Suttor took me to meet the bullock wagon driver, a Mr. Piggot. He was a man of some worth on the station and ran the eighteen bullocks he owned on a stretch of pasture by one of the many streams flowing from the Paroo River. Today the bullocky was two miles out, and Willy rode with me to visit him and see his bullocks while he parbuckled logs onto the tray of his wagon.

Everything I had heard of bullockies had me expecting to meet a wild, solitary, cursing man bearing a whip in contest with his team of beasts. To get their bogged bullocks to drag a load out of the mud of the plains in rain time, I was told, they would light fires under their abdomens. It turned out that Edgar Piggot was a different man altogether. He kept his huge whip sloped on his shoulder and though we heard him cry to his team, "I'll see to you in a minute. I'll put the tape on you!" he did not move his whip at all.

Once the log was loaded, Edgar proved himself to be what the colonials call a "bush lawyer." He discussed freight rates with me and told me he had come to work for the Bonneys because working for yourself at four pounds per ton per hundred miles didn't make sense for him and had been making him poor. He talked about how he had been stuck at riverbanks with his loads for weeks in floods, saying, "That puts paid, Mr. Dickens, to the *sum-per-hundred-mile* part of the equation. Or rather, for me, it puts *not paid*. And in drought time an entire team can perish. I knew a man in Cobar owned three teams, but all of them died in the same season on the one track. If a blight struck my team here, Mr. Bonney would give me time and credit to restock."

I noticed that men liked to talk of calamities peculiar to this country, taking a perverse and sullen joy in the fact they could be desolated by mere bad luck. Wagon teams did not die of communal thirst in the English counties. Still, if bad fortune were not so malign, success such as that of the Bonneys would not be so delicious. But even success came in a form many men would not envy. There was no way you could tell your friends about it at the club for there was no club within a thousand miles. And you still lived in a womanless vastness, if the native women were discounted.

When we arrived back at the homestead, Fred asked me if I would ride out with him and Yandi to visit the boundary riders at Ullollie paddock, eighty miles out, in the morning. "There's something about the two chaps out there that bears watching!" he told me mysteriously.

Whatever it was that bore watching, the prospect of the journey filled me with exhilaration. There was no journey on the surface of the earth I would sooner make.

7

After saddling Coutts in the half light the next morning, I led her to the trough and then went to the drovers' kitchen with Yandi and Fred to have black tea and damper doused with "cocky's joy," a golden cane syrup ordinary farmers, or "cockies," used liberally in their meals. Magpies, the large Australian kind, were gargling from the branches of desert oaks around the homestead as we got ready. Fred told me a party of drovers would follow us in two days to muster the flock concentrated at Ullollie and drive them into Momba itself for a process called "drafting."

We walked our horses to the gate of the homestead compound, accompanied by three brown sheepdogs, and then rode through the Mount McPherson paddock. It would prove to be nearly thirty miles of saltbush and mulga and leopard tree across. I felt positively heroic and *applied* in that red soil country, fascinated by the unique vegetation that marked the landscape, sunken little pockets of trees whose crowns emerged stirrup high from natural pits. Only now and then did we see sheep as a dull gray rumor off to one side or another.

We rode in silence through that trackless terrain for long periods, and I noticed Fred had little yellow native finches that fluttered about him and ate grain from his hand. It would prove the darks called him "Yellow Birds" for his interest in attracting and taming those small birds.

We paused on the gravelly rim of a lake with actual water in it and drank tea and ate damper at lunch. There, in the company of Fred and Yandi I felt like a gallant figure on a quest. "Application" or lack thereof was no longer a problem for me here. One had no choice but to apply oneself in this country. For, as Fred had remarked in passing, Momba was the size of two Derbyshires plus two Staffordshires.

❧

We pushed our mounts on and came to Ullollie gate late in the afternoon. The first we saw of the area occupied by the boundary riders was a whim, a scaffold, and bucket, above a well. The hut was a haphazard one of hardwood logs, and only as we drew nearer did it look at all skillfully built. It had a skirt of rural debris or devices around it, a saddling rail, a knife sharpener, buckets sound and perforated, a wood heap. It also had a horse yard, with two horses in it, signaling the boundary riders were still at home.

Fred said, "The gentlemen you'll meet are Staples and Darnell. Darnell is young and quite a gent. Staples is an old soldier. You might hear the definitive history of the Battle of Inkerman from him."

The outstation dogs sighted us and chased each other to confront us, rounding us in towards the hut as if we were sheep. A man with a full beard emerged smoking a pipe, behind him a slighter man who looked a bit less hairy. They watched as we approached. I imagined traffic was rare in their world. There was a yammering of pink and gray galahs, instigated by the dogs, and parrots screaming like escapees. But the two figures were still in place as we reined in by their rail, eased ourselves down, and tethered the horses. They seemed to be judging the way we did things.

"Yandi, you black mongrel," the man with the full beard smoking the pipe called. "How do you stand with your God?"

"Pretty good, Mr. Staples," Yandi chirruped in return. "How the bloody hell you?"

"I am splendid, you impertinent child of Adam."

"I think we all child of that Adam, Mr. Staples."

"Ah, you have a good soul, Yandi, you sable devil."

"Thanks, Mr. Staples."

"But tell me, where is my bloody poor soul, Yandi?"

"It sit in trees there," Yandi told him, pointing. "It arguing with God."

"Ah, it does. What does God say?"

Yandi made a gesture as if the air itself revealed all. "I can do sketching for you. Sketch you."

"You're a bugger," said Staples. "This is what happens when you let buggers come visiting. Ah, Mr. Bonney? I do not include you in my general unease, sir."

"Glad to hear that," Fred declared.

"Mr. B-Bonney," said the younger man in greeting.

"Hello there, Darnell. Were you expecting letters from Home?"

I'd noticed the colonists called Britain "Home," with all the emphasis of a capital letter.

Darnell's stammer persisted as he said, "G-G-God forbid, Mr. Bonney. N-no one in Britain has cause to write. No one in the c-colonies knows of me. If a m-man w-wants to avoid the cost of p-p-postage, it's the best arrangement."

"I simply thought you might be expecting—"

"I t-think not, sir."

"And how is the flock?"

Staples said, "The thousands abound, sir, and their name is multitude. The well holds adequate water and the dams somewhat, the fences are in good order and the lambs are ready for their migration. Sir, put us out of our suspense like a kind fellow. Did you bring any Adelaide papers?"

"I have brought the Adelaide, the Melbourne, *and* the Sydney papers," Fred replied.

"Oh revelation," cried the old soldier. "It is all very well to converse with God, but there must be a topic, you understand."

"I'll give you a topic, Corporal Staples. Something other than the hubris of the Tsar's forces before Inkerman . . ."

"Oh dear Jesus, I never encountered men more convinced of success!"

"Yes, but for now, instead of them, may I present the youngest child of the immortal Charles Dickens who has come to learn the wool business amongst us," said Fred, pointing to me. "This is Edward Dickens."

Both of the boundary riders gawped at me. It was all right for them to do so where no one could see them.

"Charles Dickens of *David Copperfield*?" asked Staples.

"H-He of *Little D-Dorrit*?" asked Darnell, showing himself to be a more up-to-date reader.

"The great wizard himself," said Frederic, as he had forborne doing on the night of my arrival, "the archpriest of humanity, the supreme master of story, and the beloved friend of all English speakers! *That* Dickens! And here beside me is his son, Edward Dickens!"

"This . . . this is too m⅄much," cried Darnell, putting his hands over his ears as if he had come to Ullollie paddock precisely to do away with the chance of absorbing this kind of news.

"Please," I called out. "I'm just me."

No one seemed to take notice of this.

"Well," said Fred, "there's no escaping the weight of a name. Imagine if you had ambition now and your name was Shakespeare. How everyone would congratulate you on your name, and for nothing else! *A fortiori*, the genius of our own age! But Mr. Dickens here is not on some sort of regal progress through the colonies. He chooses to work with us here at Momba and is *our* very own Mr. Dickens!"

"This is a revelation in the desert," said Staples.

I shrank before this unwarranted exuberance.

Sensing my unease, Fred replied, "He's just working with us as a Momba gentleman drover."

"B-But," said Darnell, "my p-place in the hut is yours, Mr. Dickens."

"So we were not to be overwhelmed?" asked Staples of Fred.

"Edward would be appalled if you were. Put yourselves in his place."

"I can't," protested Staples.

"Then imagine yourself accidentally born into glory. Imagine yourselves the children of William Makepeace Thackeray!"

Darnell said, "There has not been, nor w-will there be, an equivalent to Charles D-Dickens in the annals of our t-t-tongue. Thus you must leave us some t-time for awe."

"Speak for yourself, Dandy. I'm bloody awed straight off," said Staples, giving me a military salute.

"It is his seventeenth birthday in a few days," Fred told them. "And I could not think of better men he should share it with, nor a more apt experience."

"Felicitations," said Staples to me. "Oh, to be still sixteen and unmarred!"

"And the s-son of a g-great man," declared Darnell. "Not a g-great man in the sense some of my uncles see themselves. But a g-great man who v-v-vibrates with the fables and t-truths of all peoples. That would be something, Soldier."

"By bloody jingo, it would be, Dandy," said Staples, grinning. "We rejoice for you, young Mr. Dickens."

"What do we have to eat?" asked Fred, for from the separate little cooking shed a warm redolence of meat cooking was seeping out.

"It will be r-r-rabbit this evening," said Darnell. "A change from m-m-mutton."

"I've brought you some good-quality rum to celebrate his demise," Fred told them.

"Oh, you are a fine master, sir," said Staples. "There will never be a trade union and revolt with men like you in the saddle."

"I am flattered, Soldier, by your renunciation of organized strikes. May it last even longer than the rum."

While the dinner cooked we all, Yandi and I included, sat on section-of-log stools drinking pannikins of tea and rum and water, according to choice. The sheepdogs rested around us in a protective formation as the day's heat contracted into the earth.

"You must sketch our goodly company, Yandi," said Mr. Bonney.

Yandi did not do so and indeed looked sullen.

"How are you at exams, young Mr. D-Dickens?" asked Darnell, who rose now and then to feed mulga branches into the outdoor fire. "First c-class, I'd guess. T-top notch."

I had drunk enough of the rum to be frank. "Not top notch, Mr. Darnell."

"D-Dandy," he said.

"Dandy," I said uncertainly. "Feel free to call me Plorn. My father does."

"P-Plorn."

I could not very well tell Dandy to call me that and Staples to continue calling me Mr. Dickens. Was this the familiarity of which Mr. Rusden had warned and which would bring me down? "Don't drink nobblers," he had also said, and here I was putting one down my throat, though with Fred's blessing. I suppose that was why men went astray in the colonies. The guidelines were obscured. Dandy and Mr. Staples exemplified that.

"I am not a gifted student," I admitted. "My brother Henry is. He's going to attend Cambridge."

"Ahhh," said Darnell. And then a little mockingly, "One of my uncles is a C-Cambridge man. But *you* . . . I cannot believe you had the pr-pr-oblems I did."

I was delighted to find another academic failure who could be frank about it here, in Ullollie paddock, where the sting of failure was mild, muted by light, distance and, it had to be admitted, nobblers.

"I failed Latin and chemistry at school in Rochester, near our house, where standards are not as high as Eton," I confessed. "Charley, my oldest brother, went to Eton, but Father surmised it would overchallenge me."

"Oh n-no, Plorn. I was sent to H-Harrow. It was never its b-being too hard. It was . . . it was too b-b-barbarous."

"What does your Charley do these days, Mr. Plorn?" asked Staples.

I refrained from mentioning Charley's China adventure, in which he'd attempted to start a tea-exporting business from Hong Kong to England and very quickly went broke, along with his failed printing business, and just said he had five young children and helped my father with running *All the Year Round*.

"The famous magazine," murmured Fred, reflectively.

"You will see we have two copies of *All the Year Round* in our hut, Mr. Plorn," said Staples.

How far did the reverberations of my father reach? Colonies of birds in the desert oaks were engaging in the last clamorous parliament of their day, but Dickens was in the hut at the heart of Ullollie!

At some stage in my second toddy of rum and water, Dandy took dinner into the hut and summoned us inside. As I passed under the lintel, I saw a handwritten note nailed to it.

Give me again my hollow tree, my crust of bread and liberty,
  Sufficient is this place to me . . .

A light was cast on our small, tin-topped table by a hurricane lamp hanging from a hook. There were tin plates, an uneven number of knives and forks, a fresh damper whose heat was like a scent, pannikins of black tea, and the steaming pot of rabbit in the middle. Fred performed an economical grace from the Book of Common Prayer and Dandy filled the dishes and passed them around.

As we savored the meat from the delicate rabbit bones, Dandy returned to the business of exams.

"Let me tell you, P-Plorn. As well as exams at Harrow too n-n-numerous to mention, I had the distinction to fail the India C-Civil Service e-exam, the army entrance e-e-exam, the Green-wich n-naval exam, the F-F-Foreign and Colonial and a d-dozen more. It m-made my uncles v-very happy to tell my m-mother how wrong she had been to . . . to m-m-m-marry my fa-fa-father."

He withdrew from that core grievance and drank some tea.

"Well then, Dandy," said Fred, "you are safe from all that here. There are no exams for boundary riders."

Dandy laughed gratefully and perhaps too much. "Only if you lose too m-many of the mob," he agreed.

"Oh," said Staples, "he is a beggar for that. If he hears a dingo at night he'll ride off hunting it."

"They will k-kill thirty head at a time. Rip their th-throats out. It's not appetite. It's d-d-devilry."

"And have you caught any?"

"I've shot two in mid d-devilry," boasted Dandy. "Just by f-following their calls."

Yandi rose at this and, beginning to sing something of Paakantji persuasion, left us.

After he was out of earshot, Fred explained, "You must be an initiated man amongst the Paakantji to kill a dingo. Hence Yandi steps aside."

Soldier Staples said, "In Highland clans they would kill a man for taking the wrong animal."

"Oh," said Fred, "the Paakantji are so much more sophisticated than that. They exercise dissent."

The two boundary riders insisted that Fred and I should have their beds, which in each case was a down-and-newspaper mattress spread on a tin surface supported by lengths of log. Dandy and Staples said they'd sleep on the floor in the space between us. Performing my ablutions, I saw that Yandi had laid out blankets some yards away from the house outside.

I fell asleep listening to Staples reading the newspaper while he lay on the floor. The last thing I heard him read was, "Mr. M. H. Chodder of Wangaratta claims to have extruded a tapeworm over six feet long after taking Dr. Dutton's Pills. Makes you wonder."

I woke to the sounds of dogs barking, horses whinnying, and boots. I looked up to see Dandy at my elbow with a pannikin of black tea. "D-damper and cocky's joy are on the t-t-table."

Through the open doorway I saw that Fred's roan mare was already saddled and he was conferring with Staples. I thought, I must apply myself to waking and to my work here as I drank the blistering tea. Then I put on my boots and went out to relieve myself behind the hessian curtains of their pit lavatory. The curtains provided privacy except to the west, from which direction Staples and Darnell were willing to risk exposure.

Fred had a map of the paddock and declared that he, Dandy, and I would reconnoiter northwest along a channel called Myers Creek. Meanwhile, Staples and Yandi would ride southwest along a chain of waterholes named Miriappa, looking for the strays and allowing for some further assessment of the country, and of how pasture and fencing were.

"When we get back," Fred told me, "the other drovers will have already begun their ride from Momba, and tomorrow we will begin the mustering!"

With damper still settling in my stomach, we rode off ourselves—Yandi having unhobbled and saddled Coutts for me. Dandy, more familiar with this great space, rode ahead easily on his wiry gelding. In the eye of this landscape, he had failed no exam, I thought. And nor had I. I rode beside and a little to the rump of Fred's neat little roan, Jenny, and three eager Australian kelpies followed us. The creek we picked up and followed was a channel of waterholes marked out with red gum trees and the gray-green trees called "coolabah." In the few Australian songs I had heard in Melbourne and on the ferry, bushmen preferred to die under the shade of a coolabah.

As two yellow birds gamboled and swerved around his figure, Fred imparted his knowledge of this country to me, telling me something of wool, or of sheep—the two being synonymous out here. He explained that merino lambs reached "puberty" (a term I'd never previously heard) later than the meat varieties of sheep like the Dorset or Suffolk. And we would need to emasculate the spring lambs in this great paddock. (The term "emasculate" another temporary puzzle for a young Englishman on the last day of his sixteenth year. Later, I found out its precise meaning from *A New English Dictionary* in the Momba homestead, and not without a prickling of embarrassment.)

We came to a cleft by the side of the track, surrounded by bushes and shaly rock. "This is Fiddle Glen," Fred told me. "Yandi's uncle Cultay told me it never dries even when the creek does in the sense you can always at least dig for water there and get it."

He took grain from his pocket and held it in his palm, the two little yellow finches came in, perching on his sleeve, and ate it, and were off.

"Is Staples still talking to God?" Fred called out to Dandy.

"Only when he has p-pain in his side from his old w-wound," Dandy called back.

"Does it worry you still?"

"N-no. Staples and G-G-God are harmless enough old fogies."

"What does he say to God?"

"He still d-d-discusses his brother-in-law being decapitated at Sevastopol and, above all, why the surgeons used c-caustic on the wound in his own side. 'Your son had a wound in his side,' he tells the D-Deity, 'and you didn't pour l-lunar caustic on that. You saved it for the Tenth L-Light H–Hussars.' That sort of thing."

"Odd," said Fred Bonney.

We came upon sheep by the thousand on the far side of a suddenly wide-open bank of the creek, in country that was rocky yet still full of vegetation. The English word "flock" did no justice to these great accumulations of sheep. Only the term "mob" suited them. The three dogs had been growling for some time and became instantly excited when whistled signals from Dandy and Fred gave them permission to unleash themselves. Even so, at first they approached the mob easily, as if the whistles contained a caution not to startle or stress the population of lambs.

"To the left with me, Mr. Dickens," cried Fred, riding to contain the mob and splashing through the waterhole.

I would never have imagined that a few men and three dogs could encircle and drive such a sheep's army as we did, all southeast towards the hut. The enablers were the dogs, and the joy with which they herded in response to whistles from my two comrades was something to behold. I could not tell these whistles apart, but Fred and Dandy could make the dogs run clockwise and counterclockwise, advance, retreat, go gentle, go hard.

At noon, whistled instructions had the dogs keeping the animals still while we rested and ate damper and mutton and boiled our tea. We brought them into the well by four in the afternoon. A half hour later, we saw the line of white and Paakantji riders coming in to join our party from the east. At that huge distance, and with no other evidence but the mood the day had put me in, I looked at them like brother knights. I could not wait to get back to Momba so I could write to Mr. Rusden and ask him to share my news with Father: the Bonneys were gentlemen and Plorn Dickens had achieved application.

8

That night, more rum was drunk by a vast fire the Paakantji stock-men shared with the white drovers. Tom Larkin, who'd been happy to transform from a blacksmith into a drover for the purpose of this muster, approached me where I sat near Dandy on a log.

"Mr. Plorn Dickens, is it rude of me to ask how you have liked the work here to this point?" he asked with what my first mug of rum and water made me think of as natural bush delicacy—so much more to be admired than the tortured manners of London.

"I could happily do this work forever," I said, surprising us both by beginning to weep, though they were the warmest, most delight-ful tears. If I had met the crassest of colonials in McGaw of Eli Elwah, I felt I had met the very cream of men here on massive Momba. Tom Larkin put his hand on my shoulder, causing a fresh rush of grateful tears from me.

After gathering myself, I introduced Tom to Dandy. I could not quite yet engage in full bush democracy, calling him Mr. Darnell, for I thought of Dandy as a gentleman.

But Dandy, knowing the rules and considering himself disqual-ified from my nicety by failed exams, held out his hand and said, "D-Dandy, Tom. You're new to M-Momba, no?"

"I am. I used to work for Brodribb on the Murrumbidgee. My

whole family have worked for Brodribb from the time they came to this country. I married and am the first to break the pattern."

"I have w-worked for the B-Bonneys since Mr. Edward, the older b-brother, came out on the s-s-same ship as me j-just six years back. Got treated with c-c-contempt as a new ch-chum."

"We don't mean anything by that," said the kindly Larkin. "It's just chaffing."

"All the same, thought it safest to be a b-boundary rider. In d-deuced vast paddocks!"

"Did this Brodribb fellow treat your people well?" I asked Tom, wondering if Brodribb was more of the nature of McGaw or Frederic Bonney.

"Oh," said Larkin, "my father and mother, who were—I might as well tell you—convicts, were assigned to him when he was in the Alps away to the south of Sydney. There he could not call on magistrates to discipline his convicts, nor could the convicts depend on magistrates to protect them from severity. As a result everyone had to respect each other, and do the same things and live the same life. Mr. Brodribb had the gift for managing that. His own father was a convict of the gentleman variety in Tasmania. Transported for some rebellious thing—a pamphlet or some such. He understood men, our Mr. Brodribb. My father considered him an honest man."

Whether I thought a convict was in a position to declare another man honest, Larkin had no doubt about it.

"A lot easier riding out here," Larkin continued. "There, up in the Alps, ground's steep and full of shifting rocks and wombat holes. We used to take the sheep and cattle up to the High Country, the Perisher Valley, in summer. My father and Mr. Brodribb and others many times drove sheep and cattle all the way through the Port Phillip Pass to Melbourne. The sheep sometimes became buried in snow and had to be dug out to continue the journey."

"Long b-bloody time," said Dandy, "before that'll happen here."

"After my father and mother got their freedom, they moved away but went back to work for him when he moved down onto the Murrumbidgee."

"Flat c-country that," Dandy asserted.

"Yes," said Larkin, "but did you know, Dandy, while we were in the Alps we discovered that if it snows the merino don't know how to forage for grass. They've never seen snow before. Mr. Brodribb had to have Suffolks, lesser though their fleece might be, to show the merinos by example."

"You are a t-true colonial," said Dandy, "and an edu—, an education to listen to."

That night everyone left the hut to Dandy and Staples and we made a wide camp in the open.

❧

The muster began at dawn the next day. I was again awoken by the shouts and stirring of men and the half-melodious complaints of horses in various stages of preparation. I retrieved a few bites of damper from a staunched fire and drank black tea from a pannikin. Yandi had saddled Coutts for me, and Fred Bonney's little yellow birds were drinking briskly from water he was holding in the palm of his hand.

Yandi came to me with a page of his sketchbook and said, "This is my country."

He had rendered the Momba country in great swirls with the ranges in fluid chunks. It was impressive and novel, and I said, "Are you sure you want me to have this, Yandi?"

"Yes. It's not your country. But you can see it."

I wondered, did Yandi see it this way, as a great ribbon of earth?

"I'll put it in my room," I said.

"Right-oh," he told me indifferently. "Big ride today, Mr. Dickens."

With a low command from Fred, hoots from drovers and whistles of command from dog owners, the riders galloped north and south to encompass and move the great sheep mob. Without directions I rode a little way from Fred. He whistled, and his dog circled behind me as Fred cried, "Cut in those stragglers on your right rear, Mr. Dickens!"

I rode off, wondering what noises to make and uttered a hoot that turned despicably soprano. Fred's dog was doing the task anyhow, compelling a stray knot of perhaps five hundred ewes and lambs towards the grand conglomeration of protesting animals with his speed and barking.

I was comforted, despite my own bleat, to have succeeded at my first task, and trailed the mob eating the ancient dust of Australia. Occasionally I was instructed to ride hard to cut off some errant stray, and did it, feeling increased mastery each blessed time.

The successful arrival of the mob at Momba's home pasture was at first a continuation of the pastoral idyll I lived in those early days, when the air sang with possibility. Willy Suttor came out of his store to meet us as we left the mob cropping the wide, dusty paddock and walked our horses back to the horse yards and stables.

"Mr. Dickens rides well for a kid bred in England," cried Larkin, and a number of men cheered.

This praise felt alien and succulent. Didn't they know that I was the academic despair of Wimbledon School and took up the same title at Cambridge Grammar in Rochester, where I was the despair of poor Dr. Sawyer, and went on to be little more accomplished at the agricultural college in Cirencester? Acclaim was unfamiliar meat to me.

"Not used to the stock saddle yet," a kindly voice added. "But when he is, make way for the wizard!"

"Bloody right!" cried another to more cheers.

The sun was nearly down as Yandi took my mare and unsaddled her before turning her loose. Willy Suttor walked beside me in the evening's violet dust, asking in a murmur, "Did Maurice McArden give you some writing of his, Plorn?"

At first, I was a bit hard put to decide who Maurice McArden was. "Fremmel, the stock agent's nephew," Willy reminded me.

"Yes," I said.

"May I tell you? Don't read it."

"Oh?"

"It is not appropriate. If what it contains gets around . . . people could be hurt. I beg you."

"Very well," I agreed, though in the light of the recent esteem I had won, part of me believed that no book should be closed to me.

I did not read anything that night. The day had been so intense that it had absorbed all other days and needed to be followed by oblivious sleep.

In the first clarity of a hot morning, Fred told one of his drovers to show me how to mark a male lamb's left ear by clipping a *W*-shaped segment out of it. We stood by a wooden cradle, as high as the fence in one sheep yard, while other men waded through the sea of moving wool in the neighbor yard.

"The ewes are all marked with a different letter," the drover told me in a thick rustic accent, maybe Lancashire. "It's Mr. Bonney's method. You can tell their age at a glance. Last year's one was a *V* in the right, you see, Mr. Dickens. If they see no marks, the fellers in the yard there'll lift them out to you, and you settle them on their backs in the cradle, and you give 'em the *W* on the ear. Then come down this end of the cradle when I say and hold the little bugger's legs!"

After the first lamb was lifted to us, I laid it on its back into the leather socket of the device and made the clip in the ear. Then I laid the clippers down on a narrow bench offered by the cradle edge and went and held its hind legs.

"Be firm with him, Mr. Dickens. Not tender!" the drover told me.

He had a knife in his hands and leaned over the lamb. I saw him make merely a small cut in the lamb's sac and put his mouth down on the wound to suck out with tobacco-stained teeth one testicle and its accompanying glutinous matter, and spit it on the ground, and then bend again to take up and spit out the second. He smiled at me with mucus-stained and blood-smeared lips. "You could get your father to write about that one," he told me and winked.

All other marking and, in the case of male lambs, neutering continued by knife, as if his first method using his teeth was a necessary opening ploy or rite. With marking and docking and, if necessary, castration, our yard filled, and my arms grew weary, and the clipping, docking, and castration went on with a rhythmic energy.

When we stopped for black tea, the nectar of the great stretches of sheep country, I sat in the shade of a tree with Dandy, who had ridden on with us, leaving Staples alone for now. Dandy was a fellow I felt I could confide in.

I said, "Despite the mutilating of the lambs, I feel I have found the only place on earth I can live."

"They are v-v-very un-unsentimental, the d-drovers," Dandy replied.

Wasn't it the way of things, though? I wondered. Unsentimentality seemed to be at one with the place.

"I must say it's p-pretty stunning, your g-governor being the Master N-Narrator," he said in a lowered voice.

For once I found this remark did not in any way make me flinch here, at the core of a dusty, uneasy mob.

"I think it shocks other people rather than us Dickens children," I told him flatly, without discomfort.

"If you were the child of M-Matthew, M-Mark, and Luke, I wouldn't be m-m-much m-more amazed. I don't m-mean you're not a p-p-perfectly civilized f-fellow. B-But . . . the oddity of it!"

"But it's not odd to us," I told him, "because we've never known it otherwise."

"But to have a pater who's home all d-day, inv-inventing tales . . . And s-such tales."

"Oh, he was away as much as most other people. He has an office at the magazine."

Before Charley had joined him, Father had felt he needed to be there to keep the magazine going. And he had rooms on the top floor that were well fitted out by his manager Wills to keep us children out. "He's got a Swiss chalet in the garden at Gad's Hill," I told Dandy. "At our home there, that is."

"Swiss chalet?" asked Dandy, fascinated beyond stammering.

"Yes." I was getting fascinated myself. "Charlie Fechter, the French theatrical, gave it to him and he put it together in the paddock beyond the railway embankment."

"B-but . . . you t-talk with him. He who talks with angels' v-voices."

"Yes," I conceded, "but we started doing it before we knew he was anything special."

"You m-must be a c-cleverer chap than you say."

"No. He sent me here because I'm not."

"B-but, how c-could you or anyone d-d-dare f-frame a sentence in f-front of such a g-god? I would be t-transfixed, Dickens. T-t-transfixed."

"Novelists are ordinary men," I assured him. "The guvnor liked everything tidy. We each had a peg for hat and coat and if we were not wearing them they had to be on that peg, or else."

"Or else," asked Dandy, "p-punishment?"

"No. His displeasure. And he was fussy about the library too. God forbid he inspect our rooms and find a missing book there."

"D-displeasure?" asked Dandy.

"The guvnor's tongue could be sharp. He hated a messy storeroom as well, and utterly deplored a messy cricket bag in the tack room—that's what we call the equipment room. We always had to make sure our pads and stumps and bails weren't hanging out. He clipped the ear of my brother Frank once after telling him his bags looked like disemboweled horses!"

Dandy was fascinated.

"They're all ordinary men," I continued, enjoying entertaining him. "Now, Wilkie Collins. There's an ordinary fellow. Likes a drink and a girl to tease. And my godfather, Bulwer-Lytton—"

"*The Last D-Days of Pompeii?*" asked Dandy breathlessly, as if he were nominating a divine text.

"Yes. Now he's a brain and a wizard. My father says of him, 'Lytton is a prince of words and a prince of powers.' He says to me, 'Plorn, you can be a prince of two countries as our friend Lytton is of two spheres, but I hope you've got better ears than him.' Lord Lytton, my godfather, he's quite deaf, you see."

It took two days to mark the lambs and castrate the male lambs then muster them out from amongst the ewes.

9

The night after we'd finished the sheep work, I finally undid the sturdy cardboard wrapping around the manuscript Maurice McArden had given me, feeling great anticipation now that Willy Suttor had taken the trouble to warn me off the thing.

I settled it on the desk in my room. The title, *Suppose an Aunt,* was written in a generously loopy hand and underlined twice. Immediately beneath it was: "Chapter the First: In which our hero bids farewell to his parents."

Oh heavens, I thought, how many openings were as plain as this? I must have read that same sentence in some dozen novels I had sampled and got only to the meat of the first paragraph before I tossed them aside and went out into the garden to bat a cricket ball around the flower beds.

There was something about Maurice's half-boyish handwriting that was suitable for my reading skills where print was not. I began and then, half to my own surprise, continued.

> *I think my parents were perfectly absorbed in each other and loved me as*
> *a creation of that love. My mother and father were not rich, but fashion-*
> *able enough that those who wanted to pay ten pounds less for a portrait*
> *than they would need to outlay on a full member of the Royal Academy*

were happy to use an artist almost guaranteed in time to become a bearer
of those wonderful letters, RA.

There was just a hint of rawness and newness in the passage to
keep me reading.

My mother was reconciled to the reality of the art world but frequently
joked that women painters, all of whom were excluded from the Acad-
emy, were employed by people who wanted their portraits done with skill,
either on their rise to eminence or on their fall, by women painters since
they were more economical. Between them, however, my parents made a
living and had the life they desired. And what they desired most was to
go to Italy in the autumn to paint landscapes. They loved the country of
the passes, the great St. Gotthard, the Simplon. They would take time to
sketch on the long, winding journey up from Andermatt, draw or paint
the Devil's Bridge, linger around the summit for the same purpose,
and then descend into the Tremola Valley and take lodgings at Ticino,
where they intended to turn their sketches into full-blown paintings.

I found I was embarked now as a reader of the narrative. It was
the right narrative for me at the right moment, perhaps, and for
unexplained reasons I was taken by this other man's two parents, as
a child from a lonely house might temporarily attach himself to the
parents of a friend and find them intriguing.

During the time of these expeditions I was a student at a North London
grammar school and lived in Marylebone with my retired uncle, Rever-
end Eustace Fremmel, and his young second wife, Livinia Fremmel. She
was the lively, twenty-year-old daughter of a withered-looking pair, the
father also a clergyman. It was in that house that, at about the age of
ten, I posited to myself the question: In what sense is Uncle Eustace's
connection to Aunt Livinia like that of uncle and favorite niece? And in

what sense is it not? I knew it was not the same because I sometimes
saw something like a sneer of judgment on Uncle Eustace's face when
Aunt Livinia said things like there was "a storm in the offering." A fond
uncle would find the mistake something he could tease a niece about.
Only husbands had that look, I somehow knew. So the connection was
something more profoundly personal. A solecism by the wife—

"Solecism," I learned in the dictionary on the stand in the hallway, was a "Noun, a grammatical mistake from the Greek *soloikos*
for speaking incorrectly."

I resumed reading:

—is an infliction on the husband. That was because, I supposed, that
as the parson says at weddings, they were one flesh. Thus an error in the
wife was accounted an error in the husband.

I knew what he meant for I had seen that same intimate disappointment on my father's face. It was disappointment at my mother
and her sons. Our solecisms! But I had never seen the whole business in the clever terms McArden used. My father was one flesh with
my mother, and so her lack of sharpness contradictorily stung him.

I knew there was a veil I did not care to discern, behind which Uncle
Eustace and Livinia, my sometimes playmate, withdrew, and where their
true life occurred. It was a life that could never be detailed to me. It was
meant to be holy, where they were on their mountaintop. But Uncle Eus-
tace's seaminess and paunch and tobacco-y reek and stained teeth did not
seem to be changeable into the truly holy, into the high and the mysterious
and the transforming.

Again, I understood. After the separation of the guvnor and
Mama I'd felt inexpressibly strange and even repelled by the idea

of my father and mother being one flesh and sharing somehow the
stew and the sanctity of that.

*My father told me about one time when they were returning to me from
Italy. The snow in the pass was still so high that their coach proceeded
down an alley of road cut between walls of white above the height of
the wagon. It was at this time, after late spring falls, that travelers were
at greatest peril. It was, however, on their way home in the autumn of
my thirteenth year that the calamity struck. For all that summer, while
they painted and drank their wine in Ticino, the slab of snow designed
to end their lives sat balanced on a ledge above the pass, acquired rubble
and boulders cracked off the great crags, and took on as the sun warmed
it and night froze it, some of the density and edge of ice.*

I knew what was coming. The terrible orphaning of Maurice.
And Maurice had the gift to make me feel the imminence of it. I felt
that chill of the implacable that others had assured me was one of
reading's joys. And here in this stranger's work I was finding it true.

*When that ledge of ice and snow and slush descended down the valley
towards the winding road from the pass, it broke into a number of huge
projectiles, and then splintered the coach my parents were in and tore
it away down the precipice until at a lower ground its indiscriminate
velocity overran farmhouses and devoured cattle as it had devoured my
parents. "What a mercy!" friends of both Uncle Eustace and Aunt
Livinia told me. "That my parents were simultaneously snatched by the
thunder of ice and did not for an instant need to mourn each other." The
pious were willing to give God the credit for smothering and shattering
and bearing away the bodies of my parents in the one instant, to be
discovered later and identified only through the fragments of clothing left
on them.*

My young aunt Livinia was my sole comfort during this time when

people said so many silly and kindly things to me. My parents, I was
assured by people who barely knew them, would not have chosen to
have survived each other. That it was up to me, now, to assume the
mantle of their cleverness and become a painter. There were gratifying
eulogies to both my parents in the main papers, which Aunt Livinia
read to me, emphasizing certain words she thought might be of special
comfort. On the one hand, she told me practical things—that the lawyer
had informed my uncle that the execution of my father's will would be
delayed a little because some claims on the estate had to be logged and
verified. "But you know," she told me, "your parents were not wealthy
people nor provident by nature or profession." Yet she had spoken to
Uncle Eustace and he was as determined as she was that I should not
need to leave my school.

For the sake of reading the obituaries, she pulled me close to her on
an ottoman. I felt the whalebone casings that held her tight, and from
within them could feel the beat of the generous blood of her heart. I
felt as well that she was a woman, and that in a sense she gave me her
breasts to lean against in a way which would not have occurred had we
not been reading these solemn memorials, had she not been determined
to convey them to me and implant each solemn syllable. I felt her as she
fervently embraced me and I felt in myself an answering enthusiasm,
a disturbance of the blood, and confusion of such marked delight and
enthusiasm and abasement that I knew I would seek it again.

Despite exhaustion dragging at me, I continued reading Maurice's account of his boyish excitement at his young aunt's embrace,
wondering if Aunt Georgie had ever held me so close when I was
little, since I was reputed to be a success as an infant, a charmer.
And Aunt Georgie was a woman separate unto herself in a way a
mother is not, without trailing the brawny tendrils that connect a
mother to her children. She had plenty of softness, a dreamy ten-
derness in her eyes but a housekeeping competence, too, that my

mother didn't possess. But she had already turned thirty by the time I was five and was a much more formed woman than this young Aunt Livinia sounded. In any case, discomfort with the question of Aunt Georgie and breasts and female mercy made me back away from it. It was the unseen Livinia who I dreamed of and ached for briefly before sleep took me and Maurice's manuscript slid to the floor of my room.

⁓

When I came down the hall to the dining room in the morning, I heard the voices of the Bonney brothers raised in midconversation. As I got closer I overheard Fred mysteriously assert, "My dear Edward, I certainly didn't take him off because I believed him in any moral danger."

"Yes, but you're a cunning one, Fred," Edward replied. "You take him away sketching. You take him away mustering. You use him on photographic expeditions."

I'd briefly thought they might be discussing me, but the "sketching" suggested it was Yandi.

"I don't criticize your predilection, Edward. But you must be aware the old men are delaying his initiation rite because of your enthusiasm for him. They are not fools."

"But as narrow-minded as a British clubman," said Edward, more forthright than he normally went to the trouble of being.

Fred Bonney said nothing, so I entered. Both brothers seemed in a mood following their argument, though Edward gazed at me with unaccustomed attention.

Over breakfast, Fred said to me, "I want you to take an annual job off my shoulders, Plorn. Cricket."

I nodded, smiling. "Cricket" was a word of instant magic for me as it was the family game of the Dickenses.

"We play an Easter game of cricket against the men at Netallie

Station. On the Saturday before that we'll have a practice match here, the drovers versus the rest as a guide for the Netallie game. I want you to get this practice match ready, now that you've had an experience of the muster. There are cricketers in the midst of many of them. Send a note to any boundary rider you think might have the talent and say they have permission to ride in for the game. And do not neglect the darks. Some of them have a natural aptitude that suggests Adam may have played cricket in Eden."

I beamed at both men, for I could not have been given any better task, and my days thereafter were filled with the democratic business of collecting men's names, letting all candidates know, sometimes by notes sent out by boundary riders, that they were eligible to play in an eighteen-a-side match in the home pasture with the prospect of being selected for the Momba XI.

After Fred told me to check the score cards of past cricket matches in the station ledger, I saw that Momba had been narrowly beaten before Christmas last by the town of Wilcannia, but it had meritoriously beaten Fort Bourke between Christmas and New Year. I also discovered that the game against Netallie was played for something called the Desailly Trophy, which had me wondering if it had anything to do with Mrs. Desailly, whom I'd met on the boat to Wilcannia.

I went and saw Willy Suttor, who had taken a trawl of wickets in each of the recorded games. To be able to tell a man of such character and age that in Fred's eyes he was as good as guaranteed a position in the final team felt like an act of colonial robustness, of male-to-maleness I had never been called on to exercise before. The thought that Australia might make a man of me quelled any speculation I might have had otherwise regarding the conversation I'd overheard between the Bonneys.

After we had discussed cricket awhile, Willy lowered his voice and said, "I am concerned that you may have begun Maurice's bit of rubbish before I warned you about it. He is a very strange and unsettled young man, though he will be all right once he leaves that uncle of his."

I assured Willy dishonestly that I hadn't read anything of Maurice before his warning or after, nor of course that I looked forward to returning to it.

"He would make a fool of himself if he submitted such a piece to an English magazine," Willy said. "I am a little angry at the boy for the idea he seemed to have that you were going to send it to *All the Year Round* for him. I believe it would put you in an odious position if you did, and an even more odious one if it were published. I doubt Maurice intended these results. But what a strange mixture of innocence and knowledge he is!"

I didn't want to ask Willy what he meant by this, for I wanted to drop the subject for fear of his discovering I had started reading it, though I did venture, "He told me it's to do with aunts."

Willy chortled knowingly for a minute but then confided in me, "You could say that. I tried to persuade him to go to Sydney or Melbourne and leave Wilcannia and his uncle's agency. But he feels he is his aunt's paladin—as if the Darling River were a venue for knights."

Now, more than ever, I wanted to read more of Maurice McArden's fascinating paragraphs.

"We might see the uncle and Maurice at the Netallie cricket," Willy continued. "But it's impossible to have a conversation with the uncle. He has no inner life at all."

Some caution prevented me from asking what kind of inner life Mr. Fremmel was lacking, and I changed the subject to a frame for Yandi's sketch. One I found in Willy's store turned out to fit it nicely, so I could put the fluid depiction of Yandi's country on the wall of my room.

I suspected that the blacksmith Larkin, who was so strong in the shoulders, might be a fast bowler or a hearty, agricultural belter of the ball or both. I decided he deserved a personal invitation on Mr. Bonney's behalf to take part in the selection trial game.

After receiving my invitation with gratitude he confided in me, saying, "Plorn, my wife is on her way here from Deniliquin. Would you consider gracing our plain but healthy table one night?"

This seemed to me, with everything that had befallen me at Momba, to round out my suspicion that Momba was doing much to invite me to apply myself, to find a compass within myself the guvnor said I lacked. This invitation from Larkin, child of convicts, was delivered to me without reference to my father and in Larkin's mistaken colonial perception that in calling me Plorn he was acceding to my wishes.

"Larkin," I told him. "Thank you, I shall not fail to find a night. I will bring sherry from Mr. Suttor's store."

"My wife is a Welsh girl and traveled to Peru and back on her father's wool ship," said Tom proudly. "She's a woman of wide experience. Dashed if I know what she saw in a rough bushie like me . . ."

But he didn't seem rough to me; rather, a spacious kind of colonial creature, educated in some hole in the bush by an enthusiastic teacher perhaps, benefiting from that schooling more than I had ever managed to do from mine.

"I told her," Tom continued, "that in particular lights this country and its long shallow heaves and its endlessness is like the Pacific Ocean itself. Except a Pacific stopped in place by God. As in a picture."

～

I gave the following day over completely to cricket and cricket speculation, making a table of batting and bowling averages of regular players in past confrontations with other stations as well as the towns of Fort Bourke, Louth, and Wilcannia. I knew I must play well enough in the trial game to validate my own selection, and thus make my Australian cricketing baptism.

I discovered that amongst the wicket-takers in past games was the old soldier, Dandy's hutmate, Staples. He was a spin bowler who took a steady three or four wickets per game, even with his wound thrown in. I would need to ask Mr. Bonney if a message could be sent to Soldier, or if, being a stalwart, he already had the date fixed in his mind.

～

When I arrived at dinner that night, Edward seemed to have drunk plenty of brandy, and to be flushed with it. Fred was easy to chat to concerning my researches, but Edward seemed downright sullen and left the table before I did.

When at last I found my way along the corridor towards my room, Edward suddenly emerged from his office. Indeed, it was once more clear that Frederic Bonney was the broad-ranging brother and the visible manager, and that Edward was the man of the office, of the order book and the ledgers. But he now stood in front of me as if he meant to do me an injury.

When I stopped perhaps flinching, he took me roughly—his hands around my ears—and kissed me inexactly on the mouth with great heat and pressure.

Stunned, I broke away from him and stepped back. I must have looked frightened and aghast because he raised his hands to his skull, like a man in a play who fears madness.

"Oh Christ, Dickens! You are not of that disposition. No, of course you are not," he muttered, then began weeping.

"I am losing the boy I love. Indeed, I never had him in the first place," he continued. "My brother tells me that. Oh God, it makes me demented. If I could I would flee with him. Perhaps to a kinder place. America, the West Indies . . . ?"

I presumed he was talking about Yandi and felt sick at him.

"Please tell me you forgive me?" he pleaded. "You wouldn't tell your father?"

"Not if it's the once," I replied.

"I wish I could annul the last thirty seconds," he muttered.

"Mr. Bonney," I began, losing all outrage in my pity for him. It seemed indecent somehow that he had to humble himself before me like this. "There is only you and me. Who says we can't forget the last minute or so?"

He looked at me with a long doleful gaze and asked sorrowfully, "Would you do that, Dickens?"

"I can forgive it all, Mr. Bonney. As long as further misuse is not on the cards."

He assured me of this. "Plorn," he told me, "dear boy. You really are a splinter off the noble block—by which I mean your father."

"He warned me of the chance of this sort of attack," I said.

"Oh, dear Lord," said Edward, "I would be abashed if he heard of my crassness."

"He will not, he will not," I insisted. "Please, Mr. Bonney, let me go."

"Yes, yes, of course, dear boy," he said, flattening himself against the wall to let me pass.

My face was burning again now. "When I see you in the morning," I murmured, "I want you to be the boss again."

I walked on then, not looking back at him.

10

Returned to my room I sat at my desk and, almost for comfort, and certainly to disperse the pungency of Edward Bonney's appetite for men, I sought Maurice McArden's manuscript.

At regular intervals, I would ask Aunt Livinia to read me the obituaries yet again, but always when Uncle Eustace was away. I felt a soft, warm excitement as I listened to the solemn words tolling like a bell over my parents' intact love and shattered bodies. "Britain has lost a splendid landscapist and future member of the Academy. . . . Her eye for the sea enabled us to see that universal medium of the globe in a fresh, feminine light. . . . Amongst his esteemed subjects were Lord Melbourne and Lady Ermenegilda Yeats. . . . Amongst her more popular portraits one must number her depiction of Bishop Grice and her rendering of Charlie Brinstead the jockey. . . . But her expansive canvasses of the Essex marshes, first exhibited at the Gallery of the Society of British Artists, enchanted as many visitors as did her paintings of the Alps exhibited at the Dudley . . ." I heard the august language not as a construction of polite grammar but as a warm pulse in my blood, which went with the feeling that derived from leaning on my young aunt's stomach or thighs or breasts. I was delighted to believe that the obituaries served some purpose of warmth and broad consolation to her as well. She needed a form of consolation, I believed, because her warm blood was called upon somehow by my uncle to console his old, cold blood.

During a dull Thursday morning in autumn, when Uncle Eustace was supposedly attending a meeting of the Biblical Translation Committee in Lambeth, I was at home in Marylebone with Aunt Livinia, reading pleasantly along in the rhythms of a eulogy, when the door to her day room swung open. Uncle Eustace's man, Guilfoyle, appeared in the doorway, but he stepped back instantly to reveal Uncle Eustace himself. Wearing a stricken, piteously extended mouth and an equally piteous gaze, his face was a terrible thing to behold. I have not used the wrong adjective. It was as if what he beheld put him in danger of fainting. He was not an angry god this time. He was a god easily hurt and thus in many ways harder to dismiss. In trying to stand to reassure this suffering and bewildered man, I slid not to my feet but on my back on the mat beneath the ottoman where Aunt Livinia and I had been reading the obituaries. Guilfoyle had none of the delicacy of Uncle Eustace's appearance. He came clumping across the floor, bent over, and grabbed my jacket lapels with two hands and raised me to my feet.

"Don't harm him," cried Uncle Eustace in his distress. "He is the bruisèd reed and the smoking flax. Do not break the child!"

"But he's a filthy little sod, sir," Guilfoyle complained, "and merits beating."

"For Christ's own sake," screamed Uncle Eustace, "let go of him, and get out!"

After Guilfoyle obeyed, Uncle Eustace approached Aunt Livinia and said, in a voice choking with disappointment that made my face blaze, "Compose yourself, wife. Arrange your dress properly. And rise."

Aunt Livinia gathered the obituaries scattered about the sofa and floor and reordered not only her dress but her hair. While she was applying herself to all this, my uncle turned sideways.

"To your room, sir! I will order Guilfoyle to lock you in while I decide how to dispose of you."

I wondered from his new harsher tone how he had so quickly disposed of "bruisèd reeds and smoking flax."

Within a day, very hungry and accompanied by Guilfoyle, whose bearing implied that at any second he would forget my uncle's Christian prohibition and beat the tripe out of me, I was sent to a cheap school in Lewes, where I was boarded for two years, including during holidays. I spent most of each Christmas Day alone until evening, when the headmaster, Mr. Pounder, invited me to Christmas dinner with his wife, one resentful son, and four generous but uninterested daughters. I felt I had been and was being punished for a relatively innocent infatuation. I had done nothing but succumb to an enchantment that, when heroes in novels suffered from it, was treated by famous authors as meritorious. I could not reconcile my guilt towards my uncle and aunt with the warm effusions of great men for women characters in works of art, and so I began to question those effusions.

Let me begin with Thackeray and his Henry Esmond, the latter an unfortunate Jacobite, a Catholic and supporter of the Stuarts, but no more immune than any other man to the delusions and mad enthusiasms of love. Thackeray writes of Esmond's feelings for Beatrix: "And so it is—a pair of bright eyes with a dozen glances suffice to subdue a man; to enslave him, and inflame him; to make him even forget; they dazzle him so that the past becomes straightaway dim to him; and he so prizes them he would give all his life to possess 'em."

He goes further than others, does Mr. Thackeray. He dares mention "hunger." He dares mention "desire." He dares mention "inflame." These are more appropriate than the descriptions of any other of the novelists of our day. But having let these three vivid verbs out of their cage, he quickly retrieves them and locks them away.

Charles Dickens's account of David Copperfield's reaction on encountering Dora, the childlike—or is it childish?—daughter of Mr. Spenlow:

"She was more than human to me. She was a Fairy, a Sylph, I don't know what she was. . . . I was swallowed up in an abyss of love in an instant. There was no pausing on the brink; no looking down, or looking back; I was gone, headlong, before I had sense to say a word to her. . . . What a form she had, what a face she had, what a graceful, variable, enchanting manner!"

More prosaic, more predictable, is Bulwer-Lytton in the unforgettable (yet not for the evocation of love) The Last Days of Pompeii, *in which Clodius describes Ione, the dancer, as having "the soul of Vestal with the girdle of Venus . . ." At one point Glaucus's reaction to seeing her is rendered thus: "that bright, that nymph-like beauty, which for months had shone down upon the waters of his memory."*

I could multiply examples. I knew from my experience with Aunt Livinia that the presence of a lovely woman is an ineffable experience for a man, but that it must then be somehow approximately described in tired language and half truths—goddess, nymph-like beauty, fairy, sylph, angel—words which fail to penetrate the mystery of human women, and which actually evade it.

What a fine writer Maurice was, I thought, in my first ever literary conclusion. I did not have the right to make that judgment, but for reasons I could not say the story enchanted me.

One great writer had told the utter truth and cut through the mesh of tired affirmations and affectations. William Blake asked the crucial questions and answered them without prose or cliché:

"What is it men in women do require? / The lineaments of Gratified Desire. / What is it women do in men require? / The lineaments of Gratified Desire."

That is, to observe gratified desire in each other's faces, and indeed, in each other's bodies. On reading that, I knew at once it was the sacred, innocent truth. That was what Guilfoyle had chosen to punish in me. He could see in my face the traces of Aunt Livinia's desire for closeness. And the answer came that in all Guilfoyle's exchanges with women he had not experienced that, that he had been a brute and was possibly incapable of seeing the said lineaments. So, as a means of reclaiming the limbs and form and body of Aunt Livinia for the cold blood and cold grasp of Uncle Eustace, he wished to punish me for having displayed even an echo of the aforesaid lineaments in my childish face.

After two years in Manchester, I received a letter from Uncle Eustace's younger and more secular brother Amos Fremmel. He and his wife, my education now being considered finished, were willing to welcome me to a remote part of New South Wales and give me employment in his business there.

I was willing to sign on to this eviction amongst unimaginable people in an unimaginable place, though I knew that as surely as Britannia ever sent a convict to Australia, my uncle Eustace was consigning me to the antipodean depths for the sake of his cold grip on Aunt Livinia.

And to the grand masters of the world of prose, I would say as Blake's spiritual child that we cannot venerate what we do not perceive. We can venerate only that which is declared in its fullness and without deception, the full woman revealed in spirit and flesh, removed from vagueness and the vulgar, from childish speculation over which infantile diminutives are pasted to represent the full mystery and holiness, and from the soothing but finally worthless imagery of even the best of writers.

Over the following days I carried Maurice McArden's half-perceived but high truths in my head, combined with a residue of resentment of him for questioning the limits of my guvnor's genius.

Finally the day arrived for the great trial cricket match in the vast home pasture of Momba. When I emerged from the homestead, I saw a crowd of Paakantji people standing on either side of a pitched tent on the homestead boundary, where men could pad up before batting, and ginger beer was kept cool in stone jars. Approaching the tent, I saw several sturdy-looking, bearded Paakantji men standing in lines behind chairs placed there for players. One held a hardwood club, and two others short spears with broad blades. No one present seemed to feel these weapons were held with any warlike intention—it was merely a case of tradesmen hunters absentmindedly bringing their tools with them on the chance of meeting some small, sweet-meated marsupial. The women sat in front of them, in full gowns. One old lady wore a widow's cap of gypsum. Babies in shirts but bare bottomed were scattered amongst the women.

Within a quite vast perimeter of home pasture marked out with flags, the day's eighteen-men-a-side game was to be played. I knew Fred had considerable command of what was to happen, and of who should be on which team. He'd told me that one team would bat for three hours or until all of them were out, and then the other team would take up the chase of runs.

Before play began, Fred said to the participants, "You had better give us your best, since the team will be chosen entirely on the day's performance."

Not far from Fred sat Edward Bonney, who was to be scorer and match referee. Seeing him, I was pleased to admit to myself, in my mood of expectation, that he had been an exemplary fellow since his strange assault on me. The two white women of the settlement were there to watch the match—Mrs. Gavan, a drover's wife, and Mrs. Larkin, Tom's recently arrived Welsh wife. Looking at her at closer range, I saw she had a round, comfortable face with striking dark eyes, a pert, neat nose, strong features, and lustrous black hair.

My team fielded first and I soon found out what a distance it was to chase a ball hit for four on that ground. It was in that sense like cricket in heaven, in which you hit a celestial four and then ran and ran till the ball was found, though here, you were credited only with four. There were a few surprises. Dandy was a poor cricketer, but his hutmate Staples was a hypnotically deceptive slow and deadly mystery bowler. That is, he bowled a ball which would break in an unexpected direction on Momba's hard earth. Who would have guessed he had the talent, except that cricket was a game of *who would have guessed*?

Yandi watched the sport like a dissenting schoolboy, but when invited to bowl he had a ferocious round-arm action. Larkin was, as I'd hoped, a wide-shouldered striker of the ball, his newly betrothed witnessing his success.

I heard the bearded boundary rider, Sydney Keogh, with whom Staples was to share a hut that night, tell him, "No bloody talking to God tonight, Soldier. Let poor bloody God have a rest. D'you reckon you could do that?"

This strange and profanely reverent idea, that God might need a recess from his children, tickled my imagination. I was delighted that Staples's friends could address his tendency to talk to the Deity openly, the way other Israelites might have mentioned Him to Moses.

In any case, when not fielding, Staples continued to show his wonderful tricks of bowling the ball out of the back of his hand and making it head in unexpected directions on the leg side. He bowled four men out and caused four more to nudge the ball to the wicketkeeper and the catchers in the slips close in. His experience of the divine had not harmed his clever and cunning bowling at all.

And each time he took a wicket, the man who spoke to God looked pensive and tenderly touched the site of his old wound.

The Paakantji bowled round-arm, and ferociously, standing still at the stumps and aiming their thunderbolts at the batsmen targets, who dealt with these deliveries with various levels of skill and evasion, sometimes simply avoiding their wickets and being called out. The natives loved nothing like a ball flattening a wicket, particularly if it was one of their own whose wicket was so flattened. If a Paakantji clean-bowled a fellow Paakantji, the hilarity was prodigious. But they liked Staples's magic, too, as did I.

At lunch Fred suggested that Larkin and I take the more fierce and accurate bowlers and give them training in the new and modern orthodoxy of overarm bowling, which we did.

After we returned to the field it was my team's turn to bat. Initially, the opposition bowlers sent down mad, wild, wide balls, and the drovers and Paakantji batsmen on our side made wild swings, launching the ball into the sky if they connected with it but incapable of guarding their wicket with a straight bat. The essential skills of blocking and nudging were just not in their repertoire, nor was the late cut or the full-bladed drive into the covers. Luckily for the batsmen on both sides, the fielding was agricultural. By the time it was my turn to bat, the bowlers had improved their line and length. I was anxious to show at least the form I'd had with the Higham XI in Kent and did my best to demonstrate a range of artful shots, making a respectable thirty-seven runs before I was caught at mid on by Tom Larkin.

II

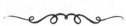

After the game, Fred and I discussed who should make up the team to play Netallie, Cultay observing us so closely I almost thought of him as an extra selector. By dusk we'd made our selections, with our team to consist of Frederic Bonney (captain), Tom Larkin, Momba Alfie, Willy Suttor, Soldier Staples, Edward Dickens, Momba George (whose real name, I had found, was Warnarka Willepungeree), Yandi (Wertie Coornbilla, Bonney confided to me), a drover named George Harbridge, hard-bitten boundary rider Sydney Keogh, and the wagoner's assistant and wheelwright, Brian Cleary. As had been the case in the past, Edward Bonney was to be honorary twelfth man and umpire.

Though exhausted by the cricket and the entertainments that followed, back in my room I picked up Maurice's story again. It resumed sharply, in an unappeased way.

I left the prevarications of Europe behind, perhaps forever, hoping I would find a more honest world in Australia. It was an inevitable hope brought on by the length of the journey, events such as an equator crossing, and the talk of fellow passengers about "the new world."

Three months' journey brought me to Melbourne—the golden glory of the Empire. From there I made a complex journey to Wilcannia, at the head of navigation of the Darling River. In any new place on Earth, people expand to take on the accustomed roles appropriate to any European principality. A sergeant of police is a man-at-arms; a lawyer like Malleson, in an office on a dusty street within the shade of river gums, an immortal jurist in the matter of such acreages. The princes were out there beyond the river, shaky in their sovereignty over their acres. But who had the true power in Wilcannia? Who was the person that no wise man and no prince chose to insult or slight and who thus, if he could not rise above all whispers, need never hear himself named without some honorific—"esteemed," "industrious," "well placed"—but Fremmel? The name of a stock and station agent and thus a wilderness god in Australia!

Imagine this, then: a robust and honest man from England runs sheep on a huge leasehold at Mount Murchison. As well as producing fine wool, he creates for himself and his family a tennis court packed with hard clay and marked up for civilized play and contained by a high wire fence. It is his intention that when other men and their families visit him from Momba or Toorale or Murtee or Yancannia, there will be friendly tennis tournaments. And imagine that on a picnic weekend the homestead offers hospitality not only to the leaders of other stations but even to a stock and station agent, Mr. Fremmel.

Mr. Fremmel doesn't have a history of tennis-playing, but he is confident that his civic esteem will somehow bolster him. During his sporting humiliation at the hands of the honest homesteader—who dares to laugh when Fremmel collides with the wire of the net—the stock and station agent decides that he has been subjected to an insult. On the Monday morning, returned safely to a town whose population is not aware that he plays laughable tennis, he writes to Elder Smith, the huge land agency to which the tennis-playing homesteader has some, until now, manageable debt, and to the English, Scottish and Austra-

lian Bank, ditto, suggesting that a recent visit to the man's huge pastoral holding has persuaded him that the place is not soundly run. And to the grief of the homesteader, the financial rug is pulled out from beneath him when both institutions decide on reliable intelligence that they want their debts paid instanter.

In my time with my uncle, I would see this happen not only to opposition tennis players but to others who offered my uncle a slight, perhaps even when they were not, in that rough country, aware of doing so. He had a capacity to offer them sympathy and to reduce his agency's fees when he auctioned their premises, their leasehold, their sheep. That is something I noticed of him. That there would be a particular set of ill will to his mouth, and the undermining letters were then written, his performance of finding the demands of the bank and the agency outrageous was so credible that men rode away to the larger towns saying, "At least Fremmel stuck by me."

Such is the man who, in return for my passage to Australia, made me undertake five years' service for bed and board and without further payment. But it was not only the matter of a tennis court in the remote bush that bespoke his tyranny. It was above all his rule over my French aunt, Mariepier, a tradesman's daughter whom he had first met during his trips as a commercial traveler to the English shops in Boulogne.

In the house on Reid Street, Wilcannia, and at his table, I found my uncle saw married love as an exercise of power. And if he had ever been enchanted and unstrung by the mere sight of Aunt Mariepier, he showed it as little as his older brother did in the case of Aunt Livinia.

What is it men in women most desire? I asked. And the answer seemed to be: the reflection of gratified power, and the shadow of their management.

As William Blake warned: "And priests in black gowns were walking their rounds / And binding with briars, my joys and desires."

I was fascinated by these passages. Because Maurice McArden had found in his aunts the fascination many of us found with girls more or less our age. There was something especially lush about aunts though, especially aunts misused. I felt guiltily about Aunt Georgie, neither to be pitied nor rescued and certainly not to be desired. Yet I was engrossed by the tale of Maurice and his aunts, even apart from the raciness of the text. I was close to suspecting that I was learning something to my advantage.

～

I was involved in further autumn musters from the southern paddocks with names like Kilkoosha and Tallandra, but also The Wells and Mount McPherson West. Tallandra was part of our strangely beautiful frontage on the Darling—I had slowly begun to refer to the Bonney leaseholds as if I had some ownership of them too. The splendid evenings along the creeks in the paddocks created intriguing effects of light amongst the huge columns of trees and over the deep alluvial riverbanks. Fred said to me, "Have you been raised, Plorn, to tot up the years in the Old Testament and the years of Christian history, and thus come up with the age of the earth? Perhaps six thousand years, as the pious say."

"I had heard the biblical theory. But my father has told many people that all the formations of the earth have to be, in the case of some rocks, older."

"Ah," said Bonney, beginning to feed his accompanying yellow finches. "Always the advanced man, your father. This . . ." He pointed to the deep-set riverbanks and the mirror surface of the river, "And all this looks older than six thousand years, wouldn't you say?"

It was easy to agree, since this earth seemed so ancient, and the balance of plants sagely wise.

"It is said to be Devonian. This catchment. This channel. Four hundred million years old. How venerable, Plorn, eh? How venerable is that?"

"That's pretty venerable, Mr. Bonney," I agreed.

Several boundary riders lived in huts along the Paroo River, some in twos, some solitary. Sometimes they were men accustomed to solitude—Scots Highlanders who you thought were welcoming you to their household in the old Gaelic language but which after a while you began to realize was English. Others were from cities and sought the paddocks as a gesture of their being finished with all that clamor and closeness. They papered the gaps in the timbers of their huts with newspaper stories which they would pause and read for a while, a frying pan in hand, perhaps, morning and night. We met a West Country man who was the boundary rider and hutkeeper in the southeasternmost paddock of Momba named Analarra, who would stop to read aloud an advertisement on the wall when bringing damper to the table for his visitors to eat.

One day I heard him read, "Matrimony. Spinster, middle-aged, lady-like, and affectionate with ample private means, feeling lonely, wishes to communicate with high-principled Christian gentleman, bachelor, or widower, of a quiet and sympathetic nature, with a view to marriage.—Address: Miss Henley, 83 Grosvenor St., London W."

He then shook his head as if he pitied the yearnings of Miss Henley, and said, "Such is the world, my friends. Such is the world."

We mustered and brought in and marked and drafted the sheep from the south. I was using an Australian stock saddle by now. And was to have one of a litter of sheepdog pups due to be dropped by the bitch Calpurnia. So complete a colonial gent was I becoming!

Back at the homestead in the evenings, when not flattened by fatigue, I continued to be drawn by fascination, by the very riskiness of Maurice's situation, to read more of his story.

My aunt Mariepier had a great reverence for my uncle Amos Fremmel. She frequently told me how she was an unworldly person who had been saved again and again from falsely misreading the world by his wisdom and savoir faire. She seemed absolutely convinced of her great good fortune in having him to set her right and to save her from silly misjudgments. She was a woman who had thus a complete explanation for the contempt with which Uncle Amos advised her on her behavior. She was discouraged by his mockery and code of prohibitions from extending any charity to Aboriginal people or smiling at hungry-looking Irish women with bruised faces. Yet I am sure she was the one who persuaded him to extend his version of charity to me, his nephew. "Mariepier," he told me, "would feed all the families of itinerant workers who live in those shacks on the flood embankment. Their men waste their pay in bush shebeens, but your aunt would feed all of them regardless of merit."

"That is the truth," said Mariepier. "I had no discrimination until I met your clever uncle."

Initially I accepted this theorem, because they both believed it so thoroughly and appeared to see it as constituting the nub of their marriage. As I observed them more, though, I began to believe that the truest instincts of Aunt Mariepier were more admirable than those of my uncle. Since he was often absent at night on committee meetings and other matters, I took my aunt aside and started to suggest that Uncle Amos was wrong to condemn her for childishness, and she could follow some of her natural impulses of generosity without seeming to be what she feared herself to be, a fatuous woman.

While I assured her of this I might sometimes take her wrist, which was strong and dimpled and robust, not at all like that of a woman who could not rely on her own instincts. As we discussed these matters more, some of the heightened emotions I was familiar with from my closeness to Aunt Livinia recurred. But Aunt Livinia had been a girl, while the woman I was advising to be less grateful to her husband was a woman of some years, a woman who in her movements did not seem as young and unaware as Aunt Livinia.

I said to her one night, "You tell yourself you are somehow simple-minded, all to convince yourself that your husband is moved by good intentions to you. But do you, in your heart, and before God, believe you should be so bullied? Do you believe that without him you would make mistake after mistake?"

One day, after much persuasion, my delightful French aunt grasped my upper arm. "Oh, Maurice, what does it mean if you are right?" I was by now reckless because of her closeness and her broad shoulders and beauty. "It means he is able to dismiss you and control you at every turn. You must open your eyes, Aunt, to who he is. He is not a great man. He is a small one."

There was something more frank and less restrained in my Wilcannia aunt than there had been in Livinia. Mariepier, I sensed, was more aware of the possibilities between bodies, and somehow aware also, perhaps from my kissing of her wrist, that I did not subscribe to the pious cant that the body is a lesser entity than the soul, but as William Blake declared, "the one being." For if it were not all one being, the soul would belong to God and the body to the devil, and Blake did not believe that. "Man has no body distinct from his soul," he said.

I paused in my reading after Maurice avowed that he had reached an age now when he wanted to possess a woman, body and soul, but asserted they were the one thing, and thus the soul could not be truly possessed unless the body was. The concept caused a prickling in my shoulders and thighs. I wondered how ordinary folk, me included, managed to find a girl to marry without asking such questions. I wondered, and did not want to dwell on, whether the guvnor had thought that way about Mama in the earlier days they were together. In any case, Maurice, who I was beginning to suspect of thinking too much, decided that his aunt had chosen to have a child's soul so that she could believe Uncle Amos's view of the world, and thus that she must be rescued from said uncle. I continued on.

Uncle Amos was at committee meetings many a night—jolly affairs such as the Wilcannia Jockey Club committee where race meetings were planned and motions were passed concerning programs and notification of meetings and the methods by which purses worth riding for could be created. Men drank nobblers at such meetings, and no one had a better time out of talking about horses and nominating a subcommittee to look into weights and handicaps than the committee of the jockey club did. He was also on the committee of the Church of England, whose meetings were a soberer affair, but some of whose members at least adjourned to drink nobblers or enthusiastic bumpers at the Commercial Hotel. One night I decided to stalk him after a committee meeting held on the lower embankment of the Darling River, where to my astonishment a wagon driver kept a shanty and sold his blank-faced young wife to my uncle. And to such crude structures of branches and seal cloth did I follow that exemplar of worldly wisdom, that source of good sense for my aunt.

One day when I was consoling and arguing with her, I yielded to the impulse to kiss her wrist, and as I did so her other hand descended on the back of my head like a benediction. I could if I wished to stop all connection there, for that is where the modern novelist would stop, or in any case the hand descended on the back of the head would be that of a supposedly chaste maiden and future bride. There was no exemplar in the writing of my age which could serve me or my aunt at this moment. And yet I knew that there must be many lovers like us, caught outside the railway lines of courtship and marriage, carried along with the same conviction and sense of inevitability that ever marked any marriage.

Where is there guidance for us in Dickens or Thackeray or Bulwer-Lytton or Wilkie Collins, who is said to be an extremely lively and modern man? Where did my beauteous aunt and I fit into this narrow equation of obedient wives and fallen women? For to call my aunt fallen in any way was an outrage of language and morality. Where then in our case was the joy of seeing a woman in desperate hunger expose herself not to the world but to her lover, as a privilege, and to gratify him and herself? Where was glorious interiority of woman and the fierce exteriority of man?

For the time being, the words "interiority" and "exteriority" evaded me, yet carried with them an unknowing and delicious pang. They were terms on which it was no use consulting the Momba homestead's dictionary.

And where is the weeping submission of the man and the sublime acceptance of the woman? Where do all the extraneous enthusiasms of a novel go, and what do they mean, without this? When Ham, the big lusty shipwright of David Copperfield, *throws himself into the sea during a prodigious storm, willing to rescue his fellow beings but willing as well to be swept under and consumed, he does so in part because he has lost his woman and has lost this specific and extreme joy. The joy which I now discovered with my aunt.*

Here I ceased reading Maurice McArden's confession, and his literary examination of my guvnor and his friends' failings. Not that Thackeray was a friend.

Lying in bed later I wondered, is this how the guvnor feels about the Irish actress?

Finally the day for our cricket match against Netallie arrived and we set off eagerly for the cross-country trip to the Outer Netallie homestead. Our cavalcade of vehicles and horsemen from Momba was led by the Bonney brothers in a light sulky, Mr. Edward having dissuaded his brother from packing his camera apparatus. Alongside their sulky rode Willy Suttor on a big robust Waler gelding. Looking around I thought that we were altogether the hordes of Momba on the plain, going to attack the hosts of Netallie. That was the way I chose to interpret it. A knightly ride!

I rode my mare beside the Larkins' dray, with Tom and his wife sitting side by side on the seat of the wagon. Inside the dray were perhaps as many as fourteen Paakantji women—young ones with babies held around their necks in blankets, and even two old women with their startling white headdresses of gypsum. Widowhood had not staunched their desire for a journey and a cricket match. Men might have yearned for them with all that dense feeling that was in Maurice McArden's manuscript. But they seemed to wear the loss of menfolk fairly easily beneath their clumps of white gypsum.

Parts of our way led between gentle hills and mulga wood and leopard trees and rugged grasses, which allowed me to talk to Grace Larkin. She was quick to praise Tom to me, saying, "My father once told me you might go a little way to find a gentleman amongst the wild colonials, but when you do, you'll find a real man whose manners are not based on the rote of etiquette, but upon his very blood and bone and convictions."

The state of mutual contentment between the newly married Larkins looked to me more humane and desirable than all the heat and argument of Maurice McArden's confession. It was hard to believe that in darkness or in light the gasping closeness Maurice wanted acknowledged in novels occurred between Tom and Mrs. Larkin, who had clearly taken her father's advice about what made an Australian native gentleman.

She went on to talk of my father's work easily, including me in her thanks for it in a way that did not cause me to squirm. She was especially taken with Little Nell, but also by all the French cruelty of *A Tale of Two Cities*, with which, having heard a little from other readers, I was able to make a vague and casual attempt at seeming familiar. She spoke in particular about the way Gaspard attached himself to the undercarriage of the Marquis St. Evrémonde's coach and assassinated the tyrannous Marquis in the night. I had actually seen the scenes reenacted, when I was younger, on the stage at the Lyceum Theatre.

Having heard some of Mrs. Larkin's early life from Tom, including her being the daughter of a Welsh captain, I asked, "Is it true you spent your childhood at sea?"

"It is true I spent all the ages between twelve years and sixteen at sea. I used to dream of living on the land. And every time I touched land the sea lost its hold on me."

"Yet it seems to be a wonderful dream," I said. "To travel all over the ocean with one's father. You must've been the mistress of the ship."

"For all the company I had, other than the rough seamen, I might as well have been. My skills at welcoming guests were rarely put to any test. I must tell you, Mr. Dickens, that I am more than happy where I am now, on old and settled earth."

Willy Suttor had by now joined us and asked Mrs. Larkin if she had known Tom's emancipist parents.

"Sadly," she said, "by the time my father and I decided to take up a holding in Deniliquin, both Tom's parents had perished."

Tom Larkin looked at me and smiled in a vague, pleasant way as if all the old history and chains had left him unmarred.

"The truth is," Mrs. Larkin declared, "that Tom was born of two convicts when they were still serving their sentences, yet if they were at all like him I know them to be noble people, whatever quarrel the Crown might have had with them."

Here I knew that she was putting paid to a sore point before it should arise. I'd learned that in Australia people of polite classes made a virtue of excluding the children of convicts from the field of marriage partners and friends. Yet she had fallen in love with a child not only of convicts but of Irish convicts, considered one grade down from English convicts. Even my fair-minded guvnor had never extended much of his tolerance in the direction of the Irish, except of course for Nelly Ternan and her family. I admired sturdy Mrs. Larkin for letting us know that not only had she admitted the child of Irish convicts to her heart but considered him to possess a native nobility.

After a brief stop, during which I put on my best hacking jacket, we approached Outer Netallie homestead and the informal village surrounding it while the sun was still at a good height. Some of the Netallie drovers and boundary riders, white and black, the latter Fred had told me were relatives of the Momba Paakantji, rode out yelling and hallooing to give us a welcome. Figures started to appear on the homestead veranda, including one who might have been Mrs. Desailly, though if so, she was not wearing her veil at this hour. As we got closer other women and gentlemen had come out and were watching us from the railing, across the flower beds of the garden.

Willy Suttor rode up close beside me and murmured, "I wish you well, Plorn, for you may be treated with an awe generally reserved in the bush for visiting British princes."

"I hope not, sir," I told him and I must have looked so alarmed he laughed.

"Don't worry. I am invited to dinner tonight, hard-up pastoralist though I might be. I'll keep an eye out for any potential gushers! I must say, Plorn, it speaks volumes for you that you simply wish to be treated as yourself."

He overstated my virtue. My fear was that I would be mistaken for someone particularly clever or wise.

12

The two Bonney brothers, Edward first as senior party, then Fred, ascended the homestead stairs of Netallie with me in tow. I realized then that we were the members of the party who were to be honored with accommodation in the main house. The master of Netallie, Alfred Desailly, came forward to greet us. He was a neat, wiry man of middle height, with a wide moustache and humor in his eyes.

His slightly taller wife loomed up behind him, declaring to me, "On the ferry, I thought you a mere boy who would soon leave again. I do abjectly apologize for here you are, in alliance with our enemies, the Bonneys." She had an admirable complexion, with fair skin and few creases in her chin or neck. I realized now what watchfulness it took for her to honor her vaporous complexion and avoid the ravages of the relentless sunlight and to mimic the dimness of Britain in this place.

"You thought a son of Charles Dickens could not survive the rough Bonneys?" asked Fred with a twinkle in his eye.

She laughed and it was quite musical. "To me you could have been a mere schoolboy from Melbourne or Adelaide. Why didn't you make a fuss of yourself?"

Fred Bonney said, "Oh, young Dickens doesn't stand on his pedigree, Mrs. Desailly. He stands, as a man in the colonies should, on who he is in himself."

"That is all sentimental rubbish, Fred," she announced, laughing again before turning back to me and saying, "Well, we are honored, sir. Indeed, at this hour we are perhaps the most honored house in the entire continental mass of Australia! For you are the son of humanity's laureate, of the person above all whom every Briton would be proud to call friend, or uncle. Or son, if it comes to that," she finished, to general laughter.

"We are honored to have you, Mr. Dickens," said Mr. Desailly, who seemed amused in the habitual, crease-eyed manner of a good husband appreciating the slight eccentricities of his spouse.

"My husband tries to staunch my eloquence. In any case, I second my husband's motion, Mr. Dickens."

"Indeed," said Mr. Desailly. "There is a prince of the royal household, a son of Queen Victoria, arriving just now in Western Australia and intending to come to New South Wales. He will be an apparition in the eastern colonies within a few weeks, but of course he will come nowhere near Netallie."

"Or Momba, by heavens," declared Edward Bonney, with his usual shy laughter.

"But even if we had a choice between you and him, we would choose you," Alfred Desailly continued. "An honest English stripling, over some wastrel prince."

"Don't say it," said Mrs. Desailly.

"Mr. Desailly is a republican," Fred explained to me.

"So is my father," I declared. "Though he doesn't believe in violent overthrow."

Everyone found this comment so priceless that I could hear the Desaillys' children standing around on the veranda joining in.

I was soon introduced to the two quite comely Desailly daughters, neither of whom looked as studiedly delicate as their mother.

No war with the sun for them. The elder one, whose name was Blanche, looked physically hearty, like a young woman who rode horses. The younger, perhaps sixteen years, was darker like her father with the same amused look in her eyes, though a little more reserved and watchful. Her name was Connie.

Everyone seemed very relieved that I'd renounced literary or other excessive grandeur. I even heard the older Desailly sister whisper to the tall young man at her side, "But he seems so normal." And yet I knew by their expectant faces they would want some exaltation from me, something my father always and routinely brought to his gatherings of friends, and to strangers, too, but something I had no gift for.

"Our other guests are already here and resting," said Mrs. Desailly. "Do you know the Fremmels?"

The Bonney brothers said of course they did. "The men are bolstering our team," said Mr. Desailly. "As are these gentlemen, Messrs. Brougham and Malleson."

I felt an immediate slump in joy, for the two of them somehow looked very fit as cricketers and suitors of the two charming Desailly girls.

"We try to field a team of white chaps here," said Mr. Desailly, as if it were an eccentricity of his. "A genuine Gentleman's XI. Quite an achievement so far out in the Australian bush! I don't have the liking for the darks that the Bonneys do. I treat them generously with rations while he behaves as if they are his brothers."

"Indeed they are my unspoiled brothers," Fred asserted. "They may have some challenging habits, but they had theirs before we had ours, so I do not judge. And when it comes to loyalty . . . We could not run Momba without them."

"Including those old ladies with clumps of white gypsum in their hair?" asked Mr. Desailly.

"If you like," Fred replied.

Mrs. Desailly let loose her laughter again, and it was the sort of laughter that set others off. "Don't expect me to wear a hat of gypsum should anything befall you, Mr. Desailly."

"I know from this side of the grave that there's no chance you will," said Mr. Desailly. "Unless you find out it's good for the complexion."

After a while a colonial maid showed me to my room, telling me in a strange accent—"Aye kin git yez warta for a barth enytoime yez'd loike it, serr!" I was grateful after I'd decoded what she'd said, for after the long ride a bath would be welcome. Before using the bathroom I felt I must speak to Willy Suttor, embarrassed as I would be to tell him I knew something of the manuscript. So I went out, still in my riding clothes, to find him. I knew he was staying in the Netallie storekeeper's house and chose the house most like his own— with a wide earthen veranda under a wood shingle house with a dark nugget of residence at its center.

I found Willy drinking black tea with the storekeeper on the veranda and he introduced me to his friend. I expressed the normal delight, then asked could I speak to Willy.

"You can speak here, Plorn," he told me.

"The Fremmels are here, and I don't think we expected that."

"Oh God," said Willy, "that man Fremmel has everyone on his hook. Even Desailly."

The other storekeeper laughed at this observation then declared, "You can be sure the very God you invoke, Willy, probably owes money either to him or to Elders Smith."

Willy asked could the storekeeper forgive us if he and I stepped out into the evening dusk to discuss the impact of this on our team and we walked a short distance away.

"So you read the mad Maurice manuscript, of course?" asked Willy leniently.

Despite sweating with shame at having plunged into Maurice's tale, I admitted it was so.

"I knew you would. I suppose, on reflection, there's nothing like motivating a chap to read a document or a book than by telling him not to!"

I was grateful to him for passing it off so lightly.

"So, you know now he claims to have had some questionable connection with his aunt, Mrs. Fremmel? Although that might be the literary imagination in him. I do hope so."

I must have looked wan for he shook his head and said, "I feel I must speak to him simply to avoid mayhem in that household. He is bound to the uncle for now, but there are plenty of places in Australia where a fellow can disappear—Tasmania, for example, or Queensland. My God, he'd probably be able to earn enough to take off to California or New Zealand for that matter, or across to Peru."

All this was delivered in such a man-to-man manner that I felt I should make an attempt to answer in kind. "I can tell him that I have read what is written," I suggested, "and that I doubt very much my father and Mr. Wills will publish it in *All the Year Round*."

"That is good," said Willy, doing the honor of thinking me his coconspirator for the good of marriage in Wilcannia. "I'm sure it's the truth, too. Such morbid stuff! I mean, it's not as if he tells us anything we don't know."

I didn't enlighten him of the fact that Maurice's writing had sent my senses running and for good or ill enlarged my map of the world. But as if I were a consumer not only of *All the Year Round* but of the *Quarterly Review*, *Fraser's Magazine*, *Punch*, and the *London Magazine*, I said, "I can't see any paper that would do Maurice any good publishing this. Many readers would be appalled, I think."

"Of course," said Willy. "No one would want boys your age reading this stuff. Yet I have to say Maurice seems to write it in such innocence. I will advise him to destroy it. As I said, the damage . . . doesn't bear thinking of, not least to Mrs. Fremmel. And I believe

Fremmel himself is a vengeful bugger, and I would not like to let him loose on his wife, Maurice, or any of us."

I nodded seriously but then Willy laughed and said, "As well as that, Fremmel is a stylish batsman and he'll be playing for Netallie, of course. There are two reasons for fearing him."

So we broke off our conference, Willy to go back to his black tea, me to go and bathe in some delightful hot *warta*.

∾

The dining room glittered that evening, a tribute to the British gift for remaking Britain on any margin of the earth. There were a great number of people at the table altogether, including Willy Suttor in his best if slightly worn jacket. I was delighted to find I'd been seated between the two beautiful Desailly daughters with Maurice on the other side of Blanche. He spent a deal of time engaging her and seemed in genuine conversation and not discussing any Blake-inspired ideas with her. I spoke with the young Constance Desailly and with Malleson, who was an articled clerk in a Wilcannia law practice. Constance had been learning shorthand in Adelaide and told me, "You must be aware by now, Mr. Dickens, that though living in Netallie makes us nominal citizens of the colony of New South Wales, we are actually closer to Victoria and South Australia."

Malleson agreed, saying, "Yes, we'll always be traveling to Melbourne or Adelaide until the government in Sydney constructs a railway to Wilcannia."

"Could you secede like the American states?" I asked. "It surely should not cause bloodshed here?"

They both considered this such a sally of wit that they repeated it around the table, and Mr. Desailly and both Bonneys praised me for having reminded them of the excellent concept of peaceful secession.

"Secession would be easy," Willy Suttor put in. "What would cause bloodshed is whether Fort Bourke or Wilcannia should be our capital!"

This was applauded, and bloodshed on such a basis was considered blood well spent.

I looked at Connie, who was laughing. She was wearing a burgundy dress with a black sash, though there was no mourning in her. She seemed such a pleasant, cheerful, sensible, calm girl—and pretty too. Were the machines and organs of desire in her? I wondered. How miraculous that beneath her shorthand and station exterior . . .

I blushed at my thoughts as her father rose and started to speak.

"I rise at the behest of my wife," he began, "who seems to believe the present Germanic House of Battenberg the appropriate rulers of Great Britain. I, by contrast, grieve for the defeat of the Stuarts at Culloden."

There were theatrical groans around the table and men picked up silverware and chimed it against the Desailly cut glass as if they were pretending to disapprove of him but wanted him to go on.

"Of the said House of Battenberg there is a prince named Alfred, son of the supposed Queen, visiting the Australian colonies now. He has already played cricket in Western Australia where, I am proud to say, his cricket team from the HMS *Galatea* was thrashed by the honest settlers!"

Boos, cheers, chimes. Looking across at Maurice I saw he was paying attention like a man not obsessed with his uncle's sins. His aunt, further up the table, seemed bewildered but bravely smiled. I felt a surge of pity for her, though why pity I don't know.

"So the wastrel Germanic son, trained in profligate habit, will make his way feasting and wenching through the Australian colonies . . ."

"Easy there, Dobbin!" men cried, and "Shame!" "How so a

wastrel?" "A Fenian in our midst!" And "Throw the Jacobite in the Tower!"

"All jokes aside, gentlemen," Mr. Desailly persisted, "I offer you, on behalf of my Loyalist wife, a toast to the health of said prince, the Duke of Edinburgh."

Chairs scraped back as gentlemen rose, and then pulled the lady folks' chairs out so they could join the toast.

"To His Royal Highness Prince Alfred," said Mr. Desailly, suddenly cured of his love of the displaced House of Stuart. "May his journey bring us all closer together . . ."

"And send up wool prices," interjected Fred Bonney.

We all drank and cried out our approval and went to sit down again, but before we could Mr. Desailly continued, saying, "Ladies and gentlemen, the toast is not yet complete. May I propose a toast with even greater enthusiasm to Charles Dickens, the Grand Master of the age, whose talents are based on the raw gifts of the human imagination and the unquenchable talents of ordinary British people rather than any blood inheritance. We are honored to have the son of the master here tonight, and so I give you: the great discerner of human hearts, Mr. Charles Dickens, and his son who graces our table, Mr. Edward Dickens!"

Shining faces turned to me and glasses were raised, even that of Mr. Fremmel, with whose limitations of heartiness and kindness I was now familiar.

"That is all," called Mr. Desailly to the company, to my great relief.

After we had sat back down, Constance Desailly said to me with a smile that was tentative but not cloyingly so, "I was so pleased when I read that David Copperfield learns shorthand in your father's novel. It made me feel very important and very clever. Do you have something that makes you feel clever, Mr. Dickens?"

I paused for a moment and said, "Horses. I feel I am fairly clever at horses. I certainly have a good mare."

"That's a good thing to be clever at in a country like this," she replied, further amused.

She was a most engaging young woman, I thought, but all such cultivation of new bonds was somehow in abeyance, and what weighed on me was that I needed to speak to Maurice.

"And how are you at cricket?" she asked.

"I'm a good scorer," I said. "I'm actually good at batting averages. It's the only mathematics I'm interested in."

She laughed again. "And are you a good batsman?"

I was tempted to fall back upon my small triumphs for the Higham XI, but I just said, "Well, we shall discover that tomorrow, shan't we?"

She also found this genuinely amusing.

I was disappointed when the time came for the women to retire to another room and I watched Connie leave with regret. The men remained, chattering amongst themselves.

"You have a rational relationship with your wife, Desailly!" I heard Mr. Fremmel boom.

"Rational?" laughed Mr. Desailly. "Why do you say that, my dear chap?"

"Reason seems to have triumphed over your eccentricities," said Fremmel. "And if I could say so, you seem equally matched in both. You understand each other's minds and each other's—if I can use the term—quirks. Such unions are I think rare."

Fremmel seemed to appeal to the room to back up this observation and a few of us, including Willy Suttor and the Bonney brothers, grunted sufficiently to satisfy him.

"And what do you think of the other sensation of the evening, Mr. Fremmel?" asked Willy Suttor.

"Oh, I have already had the honor of meeting young Mr. Dickens. I do not think I weigh heavily in his estimation, since he could not see his way clear to accept my invitation that he should address the Wilcannia Athenaeum Society and the public," Fremmel replied, turning to me with a penetrating glare that revealed a power to him I had not seen on our first meeting. It was as if he'd promised to deliver me like a live sacrifice to the Athenaeum Society and I had failed to comply with him. I felt everyone in the room had been informed by Mr. Fremmel of my rebuff and that I somehow had a debt to appease with him.

Fred Bonney chose to make a joke of Fremmel's statement, saying, "Young Dickens clearly couldn't wait to get to the Bonney brothers of Momba and discover the glories of the wool industry."

"Are you padding up for Netallie tomorrow, Fremmel?" Willy Suttor asked.

"Yes, both my nephew and I," Fremmel replied stiffly before relenting a little and saying, "In my case it may prove that the putting on of the pads will take longer than my time occupying the crease."

Though to me he'd made this statement because he knew he was amongst good fellows and must appear to be one himself, everyone rushed to say he was being too modest and that he would belt the ball around the paddock and be a thorn in the side of Momba's team.

As the men broke up into smaller groups, I approached Maurice and asked him, "May I have a word with you, later, Maurice, about your essay or story? Perhaps on the veranda?"

His eyes lit up. "Did you like the style, Dickens?"

"There is no doubt that you are a stylist," I told him sincerely.

"But you disliked the premise?"

"Let's talk later," I suggested.

"I would be very grateful to hear your suggestions, Plorn," he whispered, and I felt a kind of pity for him that he had betrayed himself by giving a record of his innermost thoughts to me since I was hardly a fellow for innermost thoughts.

Later, we joined the ladies, but because of my preoccupation with what to say to Maurice, I was not at my best with them. At last I went to see if I could find him. Out in the home paddock there were two hearty fires in the night, and the shadows before them, and that magnetic sound of other people's laughter. As I passed them I saw the drovers were celebrating their own society at one fire, and the Paakantji of our station were mixing with the Paakantji of this one around the other fire.

I caught a glimpse of Blanche Desailly in the veranda shadows and in the embrace of a young man named Brougham, who had told me earlier in the evening that an uncle of his, Lord Brougham, had known my father, adding, "My uncle is a terrible democrat and radical just like your guvnor, Dickens."

I admitted that I'd heard my father talking about a friend he called "Bruffam," but that I didn't think I'd ever met this gentleman at Gad's Hill. That made him laugh but not in a malicious way—he took my hand and wrung it, celebrating our British connection in this far, far away place.

The two lovers separated as soon as they saw me. What was one supposed to do, apologize or move on? I pretended not to have seen them and moved on. But I had destroyed their Eden for them, and they moved indoors.

Soon after Maurice approached me, saying, "Dickens? Plorn? Are you there, Plorn?"

"Here," I called from amongst the geraniums.

He hurried down the steps and came so close to me I could smell the sherry on his breath.

"So you read it?" he asked.

"Yes," I said, as if I dealt with manuscripts every day.

I paused, still unclear of how to give him my response, then said, "Well, it is indeed a superb form of writing if you take it on itself and on its own terms. But given that you attack both my father, the founder of *All the Year Round*, and staple contributors to *Fraser's Mag-*

azine, and thus Mr. Thackeray, I simply wondered on what grounds it would appeal to either of these gentlemen to publish it."

"Why, because they may very well be pleased to receive criticism? These are great men and thus, so I surmised, have great hearts."

"Yes," I admitted. "But don't you see they are as human as any man here tonight? As human as your uncle, say."

"I cannot believe that they are as squalid as that!" he hissed.

"They are honest men. But they have their limits. And I don't know what in your piece is imagination and what isn't, but I cannot imagine your aunt or uncle would benefit from its publication."

"I aim to set my fellow Britons free, as William Blake once attempted to do. I am aware of the extent to which people so used to enslavement resist freedom. But it is what my muse compels me to do."

I paused, not sure how to reply, then said, "Forgive me, Maurice, but I cannot pass this on to my father. Indeed, if I passed everything I was given on to my father, I would not have time for my own life."

Maurice appeared profoundly deflated. "You're a decent fellow, Plorn. I do understand your dilemma. But a piece like this would cause a sensation. Surely your father . . . ?"

"If he published this . . . it would be like jumping into a pit for no reason."

"I thought he was of a more courageous quality," said Maurice. "Such is his air of amplitude and generosity and goodwill. Does he want the writers of Britain to continue to represent love between a man and a woman in unreal and ridiculously staid terms?"

"He is only one writer, Maurice. He can only do what he can do," I began, before an uncommonly handy idea struck me. "Maybe when he and other authors write in such fervent terms about love, their adult readers know what is being suggested. But at the same time, authors keep their writing poetic so the young are not corrupted."

"That is old cant, Plorn," said Maurice in gentle despair. "There is nothing more corrupting than ignorance."

"Oh, your item is indeed artfully written—I must say you have the talent of narrating," I said. "And my comments do not mean it could not be published somewhere else."

"Well," said Maurice, sighing as if he was reconciling himself to the rejection. "I am quite disappointed."

"You have no need to be. For you write so well. It is merely the subject . . ."

He gave up then, settled himself, and thought not of defeat but of glory delayed and changed the subject. "And so . . . Are you playing tomorrow, Dickens?"

I was pleased that the conversation had descended back to the universal standard of cricket, replying, "I believe I am both bowling and batting second or third wicket down. Of course, it all depends upon my captain, Fred Bonney."

"I am playing, too, but at the moment I feel I've been ruled out of the most important team on Earth. However, Plorn, I shall do my best to clean-bowl you."

"I trust I shall be equal to your assault, but if you are successful, I shall applaud you on my way off the field."

With the literary part of the interview ended, I felt positively light-headed. At some stage I knew Willy Suttor would have the conversation with him about life and survival, and that would be the one he really needed to listen to.

When I returned to my room I was briefly detained by the memory of Constance Desailly boasting of sharing the gift of shorthand with David Copperfield. How charming, I thought, then was nearly instantly unconscious, around my shoulders the roseate possibility of plain cricketing glory on the morrow.

13

When I appeared at breakfast the older men were speaking of how their indulgences of the night before would be likely to inhibit their success on the field. I hoped so. I particularly hoped that Mr. Fremmel would be bowled out for a duck by a boundary rider like Tom Larkin or Staples, who would never be in need of credit and thus had nothing to lose. But cricket, I already knew, was a very inexact instrument of punishment, and was just as likely to make fools of good men as of bad.

Constance looked up at me in my cricket whites, her brown eyes sparkling as she said, "Good luck, Mr. Dickens, but not too much so."

I thought how delicious it might be to caress her by dark on the veranda. She was, after all, just a girl, fifteen or sixteen, still young enough to be unaware of her power over young males like me, and to carry it all casually.

In the midst of our brief conversation, I saw Mrs. Fremmel inspecting us with sharp eyes, as if admiring something between us, perhaps the artlessness of Constance. You could read doubt and goodwill in her expression. With any luck, it meant she had put an end to behavior that would only encourage her besotted nephew.

Fred Bonney came up to me wearing a red sash around his waist and a red cap. He was carrying a number of similar caps and sash belts, which he handed to me, saying, "Ah, my valiant lieutenant. Could you distribute these to our team, some of whom are gathered beyond the homestead gate? Mr. Desailly and I will toss a coin in about ten minutes. I believe his chaps are already marking out the field. Who would you say should open the bowling for us?"

I was conscious that Constance was taking a harmless account of our conversation and did my best to imitate the air of an aide advising his general. "I'm aware, Mr. Bonney, that you have a splendid record and that it would be suitable if you began from one end of the wicket, with the blacksmith, Larkin, from the other. Then maybe Staples and Mr. Suttor."

Smiling at Constance, Fred commented, "He is a scholar of such things, this Mr. Dickens."

I felt delighted at this first use of the word "scholar" and my name in the same sentence by this antipodean guardian of mine.

"You must have a turn with the ball though, Plorn. And I have you batting third wicket down. I hope that suits you." He lowered his voice. "Some of our openers may be brittle, so if they are bowled out cheaply I'd like you to be there to steady the ship."

I had batted first wicket down for the Higham team, but was familiar with the etiquette by which a gentleman coming to a new team should always be willing to bat further down the order than he was accustomed to.

Out in the full light of morning the limits of the cricket ground had been marked off with flags, and there was an atmosphere of a crowd, like a village fair. I suspect all the crafts and trades in the crowd would spend the day watching and drinking while engaging in the central drama itself. The Paakantji from both stations were milling around as if they had been accustomed to the English passion for cricket since the beginning of time. I distributed our red livery to Yandi, Tom Larkin, Staples, Willy Suttor, and the rest. Soon Fred Bonney and Mr. Desailly came out in glittering white shirts and their different sashes—blue for the Netallie team—and threw a florin coin into the air. Mr. Desailly won the toss to a roar from his team of station hands and gentlemen, and said, for the benefit of his side, "We'll bat first and then you chaps can drink too much beer at lunch and score abominably this afternoon. That way Netallie can have the victory!"

Taking the field I saw Blanche's beau, Mr. Brougham, whose face looked as transparent and empty of desire as an angel's be-neath his tan. He also looked like a competent cricketer.

Both teams now met and shook hands, witnessed by a crowd of men and women of perhaps unprecedented size on this ground.

"Will we allow round-arm bowling?" Fred Bonney asked Mr. Desailly loudly, to clear up the matter.

"My God, Fred. We are not Americans," Mr. Desailly replied.

"Yes, I must say I have a very handy round-arm bowler in Yandi. Could you not indulge us, Alfred?"

"Very well, we'll pretend it's Georgian times," agreed Mr. De-sailly to general laughter.

"No quarter!" called Fred Bonney for our team's sake and all of us red caps cheered. The Netallie storekeeper and Edward Bonney took up their umpiring positions, and Fred Bonney then set our fielding positions around the ground, consigning me along with the native named Momba Alfie to the slips positions near our padded and gloved wicketkeeper, Brian Cleary. We applauded the oppo-sition's two opening batsmen, the young law clerk Malleson and Brougham, as they came to their creases. They both looked like knowledgeable and stylish batsmen.

Fred Bonney opened the bowling with a polite and unthreat-ening set of deliveries. Brougham hooked one of them and it ran all the way to the boundary. Malleson did nearly as well, running three. Larkin then started his over from the other end. His first two balls were wild and wide, the third whistled past within a hair of the bat and then Larkin's last ball clipped the outside of Malleson's bat, and I managed to catch it in that wonderful way, without even knowing I had.

Ecstasy followed for me and the Momba team.

Yandi bowled a sullen round-arm and kept hitting batsmen very accurately on their bodies causing the white batsmen's tempers to flare. When not intimidating the batsmen Yandi smashed the wicket twice, the second time dispatching Maurice. As he walked back to the boundary a member of his team called out, "You should shoot that darkie, Maurice. But Fred Bonney won't let you."

There was a gust of laughter from the crowd, though it was pretty good-natured.

At last, Fred called, "I'm taking you off, Yandi, because you're just too good with that round-arm stuff."

Mr. Fremmel was a great success for the Netallie team, reaching his half-century and stylishly raising his bat to the people watching from the margins, including of course to his wife. Happily it was the fast bowling of Tom Larkin that got him two runs later, because there was little conceivable damage Fremmel could do to the amiable man.

Fred Bonney called that it was my turn to bowl from the northern end, and Staples from the southern. I had a quick success, spinning the ball that got the overseer of Mount Murchison Station out. When the Soldier came in to bowl, it was quickly apparent he was gifted in the art of that delivery they called the "wrong'un," so named for going the wrong way if one studied the bowler's arm. He bowled it once and took a wicket and bowled it a second time to the new batsman, clean-bowling him too!

Brotherton, the teacher from the Wilcannia national school, approached the stumps next to try to deal with Staples. He took his stance, patted the ground with his bat, and we watched as Staples made a short run-up to the wicket and then stopped abruptly, wrapping his arms across his chest as if he was stricken with the pain, and calling out, "Almighty Jehovah," to the cloudless sky. "I have been one with your Son and carrying an eternal wound on my side. I call on you, O Lord, to guard your servant in the end for no one else will . . ."

The manager of the National Scottish Bank in Wilcannia, who was the batter near him, said, "Come on, old chap, you can't talk to God here. This is a cricket match."

"Very well. I'd better bloody well bowl, I suppose."

And with that he ran and without interruption, delivered an absolutely unplayable ball which looked as if it would bounce towards the batsman's leg but veered to the offside instead, clipping the bat and going straight to point.

Now, from amongst the crowd, Dandy was running onto the field, stammering apologies to the two umpires. He reached Staples and called, "Is it p-playing up on you, old ch-chap?"

"Sometimes," Staples told him, "it happens for no bloody reason."

It was then we saw that the Momba red sash was saturated by Staples's blood and Dandy Darnell cried, "His w-wound! It's opened."

A sulky was quickly prepared and one of Netallie's nonplaying gentlemen raced Dandy and Staples off to be seen by the surgeon in Wilcannia, by good fortune a mere fifteen miles east.

Tom Larkin then took the last Netallie wicket with a sizzling delivery, leaving them all out by lunch for 137 runs.

During sandwiches and a cold beer, a passing Constance Desailly paid a small, wondrous compliment to my bowling and fielding, saying, "You look like a man who knows what he's doing, Mr. Dickens."

Fred Bonney leaned close to me and said, "Astonishing. The Soldier is a boundary rider, mounting, dismounting, repairing fences, and on some occasions doesn't even see Dandy for days. Yet it happens that today, when he is playing a game and with dozens of people, his wound opens. It seems to me that Staples has something of a grievance against the Deity. But he should be grateful for today."

14

The afternoon was as successful as Fred or I could have wanted. To the enthusiasm of the Paakantji people of both stations, Momba easily beat the Netallie total, having lost only four wickets. The native George, who believed in hitting only fours and sixes, was batting with me when it ended, to the shrilling of the native women.

There was a less formal dinner that night, very pleasant, and I learned that we would attend church in Wilcannia in the morning and say our goodbyes at the Commercial Hotel before we returned to Momba. We intended to visit Staples at the doctor's cottage hospital before leaving, with hopes even of collecting him, Fred Bonney telling me, "No more isolation for the Soldier. He must live near the station from now on."

I enjoyed a few plain and unsatisfactory exchanges with pretty, brown-eyed Constance, distracted a little by the question of whether Willy Suttor had spoken to Maurice.

There was a golden languor in my limbs from the day's exertions before I fell asleep recollecting the conversation with Mrs. Fremmel, which for some reason provoked memory of my mother. She wrote the fondest letters, without any of the tinge of worry that marked the guvnor's. She always called me "my darling boy." I doubted I could fail enough examinations to stop her doing it. She had said in her last letter that she was in part consoled for my loss because my brother Sydney was coming home on leave from the navy. She said it so plainly, as if no shadow lay over Sydney's name for his wild purchases in foreign ports, and his madness at cards. I fell asleep in the certainty of Mama's innocent love, a few instants' memory of what Aunt Georgie had told me, gushing, one day after combing my hair. She said, "You are the babe your mother had to console herself for the loss of her little Dora."

❧

From where I sat in the little fortress of Wilcannia's St. James Anglican Church, I saw Maurice and the Fremmels enter their dedicated pew, before standing for the entry of the Reverend David Rutledge, who had the sculpted face of an ascetic. Fred had told me Rutledge had brought a healthy wife to Wilcannia but she had died of a fever she'd contracted during a stay in the tropical north of Queensland.

During the recital of the introductory rites I wondered if Mrs. Fremmel was a Papist, like the French servants at Boulogne, and if Mr. Fremmel had persuaded her of the superiority of the Anglican rite. The three of them were attentive, as if they had all repented of the sins detailed by Maurice.

After the readings Rutledge rose to the pulpit and assessed us with a piercing gaze before intoning, "Dearest Brethren in Christ. On this bright morning, all over the Christian world, all over the Empire ordained for the care and governance of our race, the faithful like you look to the altar, to the symbols of Christ's presence, as if to see whether they are still the beloved of God and as if to assert the universal Communion of Saints meeting in sanctuaries from the North Sea to the Antarctic Ocean, from the rim of the Arctic to the southernmost remnant of Tasmania. God has given us this endless country fresh from the hands of the ungrasping Aborigine, and it happens that we receive it with gratitude and hope for the best from it. The British laborers who work to make textiles and clothing of what we send them are in their pews in Britain today. They are with you here in spirit. We are not a mere hundred or two hundred faithful here today. We are legion!

"And Christ's blood redeemed this country, so far from the customary places where Britons are found, as it redeemed the fields and copses and villages of Britain; as it redeemed Calcutta and the country beyond. In the geography of God, Wilcannia is as central as Jerusalem, and we must strive mightily and be righteous."

So he went on, and after a while there was a pause, as if he intended to add something further. But he seemed to decide he had said enough and descended to the altar for the Offertory prayers. We were strangely consoled by his vision of the English church binding us all.

As if sparked by the Reverend Rutledge and his invocation of distance, my mind turned to the little Dora business. I knew it had been terrible. Aunt Georgie and Mother had gone off to the Malvern spa because Mama was ill and pale, and needed rest and the waters, and she had left Dora with the rest of them. Dora was six months old. With my sisters Mamie and Kate doting and walking around the garden with her and pointing out flowers and birds, she was beginning an infant education. And my guvnor, "The Enchanter enchanted," said Aunt Georgie. He went out to give a speech in town and little Dora got convulsions during the evening and . . . It was unspeakable and so quick—a shudder and then life ceased. Father and two friends—big Mark Lemon of *Punch* was one—sat up with the dead baby girl all night, and the worst thing was still ahead, which was to fetch Mother home and tell her. He couldn't do it himself, he said. It could kill her or pitch her into madness, he was sure. He sent his Geordie friend Mr. Forster to collect her and Aunt Georgie, but to tell them only that the baby was sick. Only when the two sisters, Mama and

Aunt Georgie, got home did they understand Dora was dead upstairs.

And I was the child of grief and consolation. "They loved you for consoling them," I was told often enough for the idea to stick. And apparently I managed it without trying. The Enchanter himself, the guvnor, was enchanted again, and nicknamed me "Mr. Plornishmaroontigoonter," and other variations, the best nickname any child ever had. He took me on holidays to Boulogne and showed me off, and I smiled and uttered a few words and charmed English émigrés. And all without trying. It was when trying came into it—trying to do sums, trying to understand why a plus b equaled x under any circumstances—that trouble came.

In Wilcannia now, however, as I reminded myself, I was not subject to the accusations arising from algebra. I was in a country where batting well could liberate a youth from a great deal of aggravation.

In the churchyard, Willy Suttor approached me. "I have offered him fifty pounds to aid in his migration. It's about all I can afford, Plorn. Can you find it in you to top it up in any way?"

"I can certainly spare twenty-five," I confessed, feeling an instant desire to rescue Maurice.

"Hopefully between us we might save the poor boy's life," said Willy Suttor. "The trouble is that he thinks he's breaking ground for all of us. I said to him, 'Do you realize that this is *Wilcannia*?' and 'This is a country of sheep, not miracles.' But he has the delusion that he may break the mold of humanity here."

"The Reverend Rutledge seems a good fellow," I remarked to Willy. "Should we ask him to speak to Maurice?"

"Oh my God, Plorn, you are a brave one. How would we manage that?"

I could give no suggestion. Perhaps we could ask Maurice to give his written confessions to the good man. Without saying anything more we reserved the Reverend Rutledge for the most extreme necessity.

Our last call after the service and stocking up on various supplies was to the doctor's small village hospital, to visit Staples. Dandy was already there when we arrived, and the two of them were smoking together reflectively, as if they were at the door of their hut in the evening. The earnest young doctor, a Scot, appeared. The Scot explained that prior to Staples's old wound opening he'd felt a shifting or moving sensation in his side, which was due to a parting of the deeper wound layers, which then produced a series of further openings until a lesion emerged at the surface of the old wound. The wound was now resewn inside and outside and would, with any good fortune, heal. He added that he had told Mr. Staples his days as a boundary rider were over and asked the attentive Bonney brothers if there was work Staples could do at the main station.

Edward Bonney said there was ample work and that Staples could keep the stock books perhaps, and better organize the office.

Staples cleared his throat and said, "I can't leave the Dandy on his own. He wouldn't cope."

"Of c-course I could, S-S-Soldier. I'll be pleased of th-the quiet, I shall."

"Oh bugger me!" sighed Staples. "Who would've thought a man would become so bloody useless."

There were reassurances to the contrary, before we helped Staples into the same seat in the sulky as the Desailly Trophy. After putting a blanket over him we were off again on the Momba track, which now seemed a habitual route to me, as familiar as the road from Higham to Gad's Hill. In the dusk Fred shot some wild ducks and white and black cockatoos, which Yandi dressed deftly and cooked into a superb meal. As we sat down to eat, I said to Dandy, "Are you really content to lose the company of Staples?"

He considered the question awhile before replying, "I do not w-want to meet up with or t-tame another creature to share my hut. I am therefore b-b-better on my own."

After the stew, we rode into darkness and did not reach Momba until after midnight, still pleased with the success of our cricketing expedition.

15

Coming in from mustering the home paddocks one day, I found the bullock wagon had arrived from Cobar with a letter from Alfred.

Corona Station via Menindee
New South Wales
3 April 1869

My Dear Plorn,

I have received a letter from my friend Blanche Desailly, who I met at the Mount Murchison races. She sings your praises as both a man and a cricketer. Through her, I found out you vanquished Netallie Station, a hard task given their team is made up of cricketers from the colonial grammar schools of Adelaide and Melbourne, along with an occasional Eton or Rugby gent. Mr. Desailly obviously ignored a source of talent Fred Bonney doesn't—the darks, who can play cricket in a fierce way, lacking in nuance perhaps but very useful in social cricket. I have a chap here named Milparinka Sam whom I've taught overarm to, and he is a magnificent quick bowler. I had a chap from a bank who was clean-bowled by Sam warn me it was very bad form for me to allow a native to assert such dominance of white chaps!

In any case I sent Blanche's glowing praise on to the guvnor, just to
show him. I hope if you are ever in the rare situation of receiving praise
of me, that you'll do the same.

Recently we had a South Australian survey expedition over here. Do
you think they intend to conquer the eastern colonies? All jokes aside,
they were exceedingly astonished to find the son of the Illustrious running
Corona. It was to them like stumbling on a previously unclassified
wombat. The usual questions we both know so well arose: What was
my favorite book of the guvnor? Had I ever written? Would I ever write?
When I claimed my scholarly failures to prove why I was not a writer
they said, "But even your mother is a writer," referring to the dear old
cookery book she once put together. But a merciful God decrees that none
of the children of Grand Narrators inherit the same gift—otherwise,
we could have breeding factories for storytellers, and let me tell you,
that would be lunacy. As men of science and enlightenment, the South
Australian expeditioners accepted this.

I expect we will hear from the guvnor, Aunt Georgie, and the mater
soon. The sisters keep a correspondence too. The mail comes here
fortnightly. Do write to me.

If you are happy there, dear Plorn, then I rejoice for you. May
we both be happy and meet our colonial destinies. And surprise the
guvnor.

I address you in terms I don't always use. We are embedded here
now and possibly for a lifetime.

Your loving brother,
Alfred Tennyson d'Orsay Dickens

And what a wonder it would be, I thought, if my father could
tell people, "Plorn *has* applied himself."

～

As the winter came on, life was quieter. I traveled with Piggot, the bullock wagoner, to take supplies to the hutkeeping boundary riders. The Bonney brothers also had us weigh as many ewes as we could reasonably manage when visiting distant paddocks, as they were approaching or in the state named "estrus," that all-wise and all-profitable process that was the broad base of the grand pyramid of the region's wealth.

I met many other hutkeepers besides Dandy. Unlike shepherds in England, they were not all cut from the same cloth. I found that where two men occupied the same hut, they would not normally be men of similar background. To find a parson's son and a man from a family of Liverpool barge workers sharing a hut was not uncommon—indeed, such a pair supervised the huge adjoining paddocks of Perry and Bathing Spring. I could not imagine myself choosing to be quite so solitary. I noticed that the young ones often mentioned their families in an attempt to explain their remote location.

Fred Bonney sometimes took me to sit in the Paakantji camp to observe the people he talked to. Whenever we arrived, Fred, in his pith helmet, duck trousers, and collar and cravat, would walk through the camp crying greetings, more as a friend than as a visiting grandee. People would be sitting in the doorways of their grass and branch humpies whose clever architecture and sturdiness Mr. Bonney had convinced me of despite my initial prejudice against such questionable habitations. The women, young and old, would remove their pipes and greet him aloud and with sudden excitement and a kind of merriment. Some would stand up, but women weaving bags made of dyed grass, using their legs as a sort of weaving frame, grinned at the little man from a sitting position and shrilled at him.

The men were always pleased to see him, though on occasions we would find Edward there also, sitting amongst elders. When this happened Edward got up and left as his brother arrived and I had the sense that his going generated little regret among the elders.

By contrast, I never saw any man, in any circumstances, anywhere in the country, get a more thorough and unpretentious greeting from the natives than Fred. And I never saw anyone more interested in them, more reverent, more assured that they had in their possession secrets he believed he should become fit to know.

"People treat them somewhere between annoying fauna and ghosts, potentially lethal figures from the fringe of life," he complained to me once in terms I shall never forget. "But we, Plorn, are the ghosts. They think we whites are mere temporary phantasms."

He taught me the meaning of what at first sight seemed nothing, explaining once when we saw an old man wearing a hat of bark from a certain tree with leaves of a certain other tree, affixed with a cord around his head, that he was treating himself for headache, from which he regularly suffered. And near the women, within reach, were the broad stones of quartz basalt on which they ground grasses and extracted grain. The young men standing about in their station clothes and ready for work chewed sweet gum from the wattle tree, which I noticed afterwards as habitually as one would an alder tree along the Medway.

Fred told me the meaning of the Paakantji's true, subtle names. Yandi's elder brother Momba George's real name was Warnarka Willepungeree, which meant not only "lizard"—lizard was a favored totem and a favored food—but "lizard wintering in his den on a cold night." A woman dubbed Purnanga Nora had a true name that meant "ducks searching for food in a creek bed." The Paakantji only took their artificial names, made up, say, of the place they were born and a British forename, for station convenience.

I learned that Fred Bonney's Paakantji name meant "yellow birds about his shoulders." If by unlikely chance we ever became equal friends, I would nickname him "Yellow Birds."

On each visit two men of middling years, who seemed to have ignored Fred while the others greeted him, came up after a time and sat with him on the ground. These were his chief informants of Paakantji life. Policeman Danny (for he had once worked with the police) and Poondary Dick.

∽

I got a note from Willy Suttor on one of the winter days of lighter work saying, "Dear Plorn, some mail's come up to you from Cobar. And I have some news about Our Mutual Friend, if you will forgive that reference."

When I arrived, the veranda of the store was heaped up with new deliveries of tobacco, fencing wire, soap, and bleach. One of the young Paakantji was stacking it all away as Willy entered the number of items of each into his stock book.

Seeing me, he called, "A moment," before wiping his hands thoroughly against the leather apron he was wearing and going into the store. He emerged holding a letter delicately by the corners, asking with undisguised awe, "Do I really hold in my hands a written artefact of the Illustrious One?" I had never seen him struck with such reverence.

"Let me see," I said, moving in closer to look over his shoulder since it seemed unkind to shorten his enjoyment. "Oh, I'm sorry, the C. Dickens on the envelope is in the handwriting of my brother Charley. It's not my father's."

"But close enough," said Willy, gently waving it in the air a last time before handing it to me.

"And our friend? Maurice?" I asked. "Do you need the money I pledged you?"

Willy grimaced. "He says he won't go. He claims his aunt needs him for protection, though the opposite is true. But I can't reach him at all. Perhaps we should write to the Wilcannia parson. Though . . . let me ponder on the issue, Plorn."

Maurice's proposition, quoted from William Blake, on the images of gratified desire, possessed me again for a while. It was still a new idea for me—that even in daily life, in plain matters, men were looking for *that* in women, and more remarkably, women were looking for *that* in men.

I was pleased that Charley, so busily married, and thus preoccupied, I presumed, in the way Maurice suggested, had taken the time to write to me.

I opened the letter with the eagerness appropriate to an exile.

∿

"My Plorn," it read.

I hope you are contented in that far, fabled colony. Have you held off an attack by the natives yet? I trust you are in the bloom. I wanted to tell you in case you had not heard that I have now been given the full title of subeditor of the magazine but am also attending the guvnor on his outings and doing the effects some nights for his readings. I am very nearly transformed into a literary man and am being trained to substitute for poor Wills the subeditor who had that bad spill on his horse. I am grateful for this: I have five young mouths to feed, and Bessie is carrying a sixth. I recommend marriage, Plorn. I would be rudderless without it.

Pater is much improved, I think, but he has evinced a desire to perform the murder of Nancy by Bill Sykes in Oliver Twist. *When I took the children to visit him recently, he was raging around the garden, doing Bill Sykes, for it's never enough for him just to read with expressive hand gestures—he is still such a thespian. We came on him and he was murmuring in falsetto, "Bill, why do you look like that at me?" And then in basso, "You know, you she-devil!" I asked him about it, and he was of course determined to go ahead with the idea, even though a lot of us think it's far too tiring for him, the way he insists on performing it. In his more senior years, he has not got over the naming of children—he has pet names for all five, but he doesn't like them calling him "grandfather"*

instead having them call him "the Venerables" (yes, plural) instead. I
don't know where he gets plural from, unless he thinks he's the Holy
Trinity.

Later in the day anyhow he performed the whole thing for me, the
flight of Bill Sykes the killer as well, and he was so thoroughly in that
ruffian and in each victim that it was the most wonderful thing I've ever
heard or seen, and I said, "Bravo! But there's no chance you should be
doing it in the theater."

He laughed and said, "Everyone says that. Especially Dr. Steele."
Steele actually wrote to me about it, warning me to attend every
performance this coming autumn. So you see I've become the devoted son!
Speaking of devoted, Aunt Georgie is still in place and it's pleasing to
see how well she gets on with our fiery sister Katie now. And of course,
she and Mamie have always been close.

As for the mater—

After Charley had gone to Eton, where he'd been quite good at
Latin and Greek, he'd insisted on addressing the guvnor as "Pater"
and Mama as "Mater."

As for the mater, I visit her frequently and she continues to bear the
separation from the Dickens household and the daily separation from
her children bravely. Indeed, if there was a medal for that sort of thing
she would win it. Katie visits her a lot and goes so far as to tell her
she should be angrier. The mater resists it, as she resists all Grandma
Hogarth's fury about the schism between our parents. I think it was
a good thing that I stuck with Ma, though, at the time, telling Pater I
loved him but that Ma needed some company. It might be the best thing
I ever did in my life, apart from marrying Bessie—even though the
pater does not like Bessie's people, as you know. But in any case, I saw
that Mater understood all too well that all she had left was her dignity,
and she would lose that if she began to malign the guvnor. She actually

gets on with Bessie's people and dines with Mrs. Evans quite regularly still.

Pater is a man of reason, but he does tend to divide the world into His Side and Mater's Side. The only people who are permitted to be on both are me, Bessie, and our little ones, because he realizes that to be so is a condition of our very existence. Mater sees Mrs. Ingram too . . . you remember, the widow of that chap who started the Illustrated London News. *Pater's feeling for that journal is dubious. He says to me, "Ingram, when he was a humble shopkeeper, invented Old Parr's Longevity Pills. If he hadn't taken so many of them, he might have seen his fiftieth birthday." Big Mark Lemon and all that crowd are still on the outer with him, and on the inner with Mater.*

The upshot is, anyway, that the dear thing Mater is well and remembers you and Alfred so warmly and wishes you every success in that place of which, as Pater says, "No one can imagine it unless they've been." He still intends ultimately to visit you there, and he met up with the obnoxious Trollope the other day who boasts about the fact he's sent his son there, and says he intends to visit, give lectures there, and write a book about the place.

I write to you, dearest Plorn, chiefly because I feel I have entered the best phase of my life, and in coming to the magazine, have as it were come home. I hope things happen with you such as to make you feel the same about where you are.

Your affectionate brother,
Charles Culliford Boz Dickens

So, Charles Culliford Boz Dickens had also applied himself.

༄

Staples was working in the station office with Edward Bonney, who moved and spoke with a sad reserve I now understood. As Edward had promised the doctor in Wilcannia, Staples was working on the stock books, and questions of where and when and what rams were distributed throughout the great space, as well as the wages books of boundary riders. I did not know if the Bonney brothers made up this work for him, but Staples had writing and arithmetic, and skills of his own.

In any case, I visited him in the office one day in early winter, when the air was knife sharp and all the earth a golden, sculpted glory. "Mr. Staples," I said, looking about, pretending I'd come searching for Edward.

He gave me a broad smile and said, "Mr. Plorn, you see a man cured of cricket."

"Despite your deceptive bowling, Mr. Staples! And at such a good age, too."

"Yes, I am a good age. But there are good county cricketers older than me. Those Yorkshiremen, they play till they die, and they die happy."

"Well, who thought your bowling action would tear your old wound open? After all that mustering and boundary riding."

"Oh, it would happen out in the Ullollie paddock sometimes. But I would lie quiet until it closed again. God would seal it, you know. He is willing to seal it when it splits on proper business such as the muster. Not so willing when it's cricket. Vanity of vanities, you see. You watch, Mr. Plorn, I'll be back with Dandy, and carrying bloodwood stumps to help the fencers before you know it."

"Do you really believe that, Mr. Staples?"

"With every fiber of my being, Mr. Plorn! I wouldn't leave that Dandy on his own. He's too given to imagination."

"Forgive me, Mr. Staples. But did you ever have a family?"

The fibrous mesh of connections that Charles's letter had demonstrated meant families were on my mind.

"Ah yes. I arrived in Adelaide on a migrant laborer ship with my wife and our littl'un, but both have gone to God. There was little time to dwell on their souls out in Ullollie paddock, not much room for 'em here. But next to bugger-all room if I was in Adelaide."

He turned a page and started writing the names of rams in the rams column. He was engrossed in it.

Suddenly he said, without looking up, "Most kind of you, Mr. Plorn. But best to leave me out of the Momba XI in the future."

"That is a great loss of a genuine gift," I declared.

"Ain't so. There is some child within our vicinity with the gift of spin bowling. God is profuse with his gifts."

"If he ever tells you the name of the child . . . No, I mustn't be irreverent."

"Best bloody well not," Staples advised me.

As Charley had said, I was very little when the guvnor and Mama stopped getting on. There were the normal guvnor japes—a play after Christmas, an outing, but when Mama and the guvnor were in the same room, they looked past each other in a way I found odious. Later, carpenters mysteriously put up a partition in their bedroom at Tavistock.

I vaguely remember everyone coming home for Christmas 1857, except for Walter, who was in India, and that was the last Christmas the guvnor and Mama were together. Though I didn't understand why, I accepted it all as a given, as is probably normal when one is five.

When Mama moved out, she wept over us. And though I knew nothing of what was happening at the time of the separation, it seemed to activate everyone.

The guvnor was never quite the same after Mama left, and that was just the start. Thank God for the bright Saturdays and Sundays at Gad's Hill. That's when the guvnor was at his best. On the weekends with the visitors and us children—Alfred, Frank, Henry, me, Katie, and Mamie.

Before Mama left home, the guvnor made her visit and drink tea with a family of women named the Ternans, who the guvnor was helping. I didn't know why she must do it. I knew the guvnor thought the Ternans were good theatricals and that for some reason Mother had to be brought to agree to taking tea with them to make everyone happy and of one mind. I heard my sister Katie telling her not to go, but Mama insisted. Mysterious stuff. A household of actresses and my mother, alone, and not a thespian herself. What did that mean? And when she returned somber, recriminations from Katie. Why did you? What did you expect? And so on.

The following spring, when Mama moved out of Tavistock House, Aunt Georgie remained with us, getting me up every morning and dressing me in my clothes, and I thought that proper. But I came to know—I don't know how—that not all people thought it proper that Aunt Georgie stayed with us when Mama went. I caught it from the air perhaps, and from muttering people around us. There was a cleft in our world. People were cast to left from right and vice versa, and we needed to know who our new friends were. Then there was a letter published in *Household Words* and *The Times* and it had already been in the *New York Times* and it was in some way another divider of the world, and all at once I learned that people I had thought were friendly were vicious against the guvnor. Granny Hogarth was against him. Thackeray had said something "unforgivable" at the Garrick Club. So, he and his two lively girls couldn't be invited anymore on Twelfth Night, when we always had our plays. A few friends came to persuade him that Mr. Thackeray had not been insulting, but the guvnor seemed certain and couldn't be shaken. Mark Lemon, the guvnor's old theatrical friend, was to be spurned, too, and anyone who wrote for Lemon's magazine, *Punch*.

Father also argued we must all stay with *him*, because Aunt Georgie, Mama's very sister, had indeed stuck with us rather than going with Mama, and how ungrateful it would be for us in any degree to spurn that sacrifice, explained only by Aunt Georgie's love for us. She had done the raising of us, after all, because Mama was somehow deficient in the skills of mothering, he said, as we all knew. And now Mama was *estranged*—that was the word he used. At five or six I had not done a comparative study of parents, so I accepted the truth revealed by the guvnor. I knew Aunt Georgie wasn't estranged from us. Now, when we visited Mama, he told us, if Grandmother Hogarth or Aunt Helen appeared, we were to leave. These two women were not like Aunt Georgie. They would twist things.

When the guvnor was on the road, and in Ireland, doing readings, Aunt Georgie took us to see Mama and the two of them did not seem estranged. Mama said to me, with a watery smile, "You are still my affectionate boy, Plorn."

"Yes," I told her. "I am not estranged."

"No, you're not at all," she assured me, and nodded and nodded and then cried. I liked her familiar smell. The lavender. And a powder she used that was the very smell of motherhood. One day she took me to see Miss Coutts, a rich friend of hers and the guvnor's, but though that wasn't popular with him, he couldn't stop Miss Coutts.

So, life had changed. Yet it was tolerable. And the Gad's Hill house the guvnor bought just before Mother moved away was wonderful, and people came on weekends and Father was his old joking self. And Aunt Georgie was the constant. She was there, all the time.

Such was the state of my memory of my parents' separation that I brought to Australia. It was only now beginning to raise a few more questions that I couldn't answer.

16

The onset of winter in that half desert was sharp. You might wake and find the entire ground, the dust itself, and every plant, covered in frost. A freezing wind blew from the northwest, encouraging sheep to grow more insulating wool and us to apply extra layers of our clothing. It was normal to go abroad in the morning and hear drovers say, "I wore everything I own to stay warm last night."

One day a large letter in a heavy nap envelope, addressed to Fred Bonney and carrying the name and address of a London law firm, arrived amongst the other fortnightly mail from Cobar. And with it an even more spectacular envelope marked "Letters Patent" and embossed with a crown.

I heard Fred and Edward Bonney discuss them that night at dinner, with Fred saying, "I've received an inquiry from both lawyers and the House of Lords accusing me of knowing the whereabouts of one Alexander Darnell and pleading with me to find him. The Letters Patent tell me Dandy is the fourth Baron Yellowmead, and that if I know him, as is suspected, to tell him that he is summoned to the House of Lords."

"Dandy?" asked Edward incredulously. "But he can barely get a sentence out."

"Stammerer or not," said Fred. "I am *commanded*, nothing less, I am *commanded* to tell him to present himself at the House of Lords, Westminster."

"Well, I'll be deuced!" Edward declared, laughing. "I really will be deuced!"

Fred smiled. "As for the letter from the lawyers, they are inviting him to occupy Manston House and begin administering the Darnell lands in Cornwall, Devon, and Gloucestershire. All a little more complex than the mere paddock and sheep—however large in size and number—with which he has until now been burdened."

"And so," said Edward, "we are under obligation to let the poor beggar know?"

"Yes, poor chap."

"Poor chap? *Poor chap*?" asked Edward with a further laugh.

"He has chosen his life. It might be the most merciful thing to write back and tell them that though I once had contact with a Mr. Darnell, his present location is unknown to me."

"But you can't do that in response to Letters Patent," his brother argued. "You are bound to declare him. Any individual who becomes aware of Letters Patent is bound by law to comply."

Fred Bonney guffawed. "I can't quite see them setting up the chopping block in Momba to punish me and Dandy."

"You are bound, Fred, whether you want to or not, or he wants you to or not," Edward insisted, back to frowning now. "So don't chiack around and strike republican poses. He can probably renounce the title to some infant second cousin if he wants. But he can't get away without first presenting himself to the Lords. God Almighty, how many men would willingly take his place? If asked into the Lords, I would be there faster than a rat up a drainpipe."

He laughed creakily again, then said, "Take young Dickens with you, that'll cheer Dandy up, a thoughtful chap like him."

"If I took the cart, I could take the Soldier out there as well.

That would really give Dandy pause. But if he won't leave his hut and come back here with me, I won't make him."

"You can make him, Fred. You're his boss, after all."

"Poor Dandy," sighed Fred. "He is out there happy in what he thinks is his country, and we are going to disabuse him of it. It is reversed transportation, and distasteful. What have the Lords ever done for England except throttle progressive laws?"

Edward turned to me, our earlier awkwardness forgotten. "You didn't think you had a radical for a boss, did you, Plorn?"

"My father is a radical, Mr. Bonney," I replied, remembering my father's frequent cry that the House of Lords was "an institution that gives those who have risen by grand theft the authority to decide upon what pittances the rest of us are to subsist on."

"Ah, but your father is a sentimental radical, not as deep a one as my brother! He and his little birds twitter sedition to each other."

Though this assessment was meant by Edward to appear affectionate I wondered if the two of them were still secretly arguing, as I'd heard them that breakfast. I had the feeling that if they hadn't been brothers they might not have been friends.

～

Fred decided that a party made up of him, myself, the Soldier, and Yandi would ride out to Ullollie paddock where the heir to the Yellowmead baronetcy rode the fences and watched the Bonneys' mobs of sheep. A bed was set up in the back of the cart for the Soldier to recline on to protect his old wound. Yandi rode his stock horse. I still had my tough little mare, Coutts, but needed a second horse, for I'd learned that one should not travel alone and with just the one horse in this country. Never, I was sure, had such an expedition been put together in the Australian bush for such a purpose.

We set out at four o'clock in the morning, riding across bush pastures under frost, with all the earth looking silver and inky blue beneath the dense clutter of stars. I had by now acquired a jacket of sheepskin and was grateful to wear it. That hour was full of the signaling cries of dingoes, lugubrious and full of the desire for the blood of sheep. The Soldier chose to ride in the cart seat, with a determination that signaled he thought recourse to the invalid cot in the body of the vehicle would be a sort of failure on his part. The sun came up behind our shoulders and granted significant coloration to the red earth and all the subtle silvers and greens of the saltbush and mulga trees and the lines of river gums that marked out the streams and lagoons of water. The light seemed to gust Fred's three or four little yellow finches up into his company, where they chirped at him from the boards of the cart. We stopped only for a brisk breakfast of damper, golden syrup, and tea.

Despite his resolve, the Soldier started to get shaky, so we helped him into the back of the cart, and then Fred invited me to tether my mare to the cart and ride beside him. I did so, while Yandi roamed about on his horse, sometimes ahead, sometimes to the left, sometimes to the right of the cart, sometimes singing as if to himself. And under it all was the fixed sea of red soil, the medium of our travel and indeed of our hopes.

"What do you think of Yandi?" Fred asked me.

"I don't think he trusts me yet," I replied.

"Oh, he trusts you well enough. That casual air of his . . . is characteristic of them. I have seen wives seem casual to a husband they have not seen for weeks."

"To be frank, I believe he fears I might somehow take his place as your riding companion and aide."

"That doesn't worry him in the least. He believes, you see, that I am his maternal uncle reborn. And I am happy to fulfil that role for him."

I was confused but said nothing.

"His mother's brother, you see, was a small man, rather like me.

And when I came here and started making friends with the yellow birds—well, it was exactly what his uncle, the clever man, had got a repute for doing. The uncle was shot dead by South Australian troopers at Rufus River. Yandi and his mother believed me to be his uncle returned in another form. That is why I have Yandi as my aide."

He let this concept settle in my mind, knowing that it took an average Englishman a time to adjust to it, then added, "Who is to deny their perception, or would want to say in which of God's infinite minds this idea of Yandi's is invalid?"

"That is all very strange," I said.

"Yes, wonderfully strange," Fred agreed.

"So, to the natives, you are a shot man returned?"

"Yes, but if you find that outlandish, try to explain to Yandi that mere paper marks made by the powerful fifteen thousand miles away have made us take to the road hunting poor Dandy."

The Soldier revived in the afternoon and politely asked for his seat back. I gave it up willingly as I liked the freedom of my own mount. From my saddle I watched Yandi scout the country we advanced into. He shot and plucked some birds, but there was no time to cook them that night and we just had cold mutton and damper again. As we kept riding on in the aching cold of the desert night, I found myself daydreaming about being gallant for Connie Desailly. I imagined having my own run and inviting her to it and introducing my overseer who was—by the weight of daydream—Tom Larkin.

❧

In the darkness we approached Ullollie. We heard Dandy's dogs engaging in a spate of barking to warn dingoes away from their sheep or else warn of our approach. As the moon came up, we caught sight of the whim of the well, its upper structure with a windlass, fine etched against the night, and the flocks around the well. I'd discovered by now that moving sheep to water, then moving them on again before they grazed out and made a desert of the place around the waterhole, was a fine-edged proposition. They seemed to move on in any case, of course, as if by nature, in the pilgrimage for nourishment, but the shepherd or boundary rider was there to help them in their decisions.

As we got closer to the hut, the door opened and a figure emerged, delineated by the lantern illumination inside. Yandi began to hoot and emit a chirruping series of yells when he saw Dandy and went galloping towards him, reining in his horse and appearing to tell Dandy who was in our party. After he'd greeted us all, we helped the Soldier inside, not that he welcomed our care. Fred told Dandy that he and Yandi and I were fine to sleep in our swags till morning.

"But what b-brings you here?" Dandy wanted to know, suspecting the composition of the party indicated a special visit.

"Leave it till morning, my boy," said Fred. "Leave everything till morning."

"Do you know, Soldier?" asked Dandy of his old mate.

Not wanting to answer the question, Staples clutched his side as if it were under new pressure to open.

"What is it, S-Soldier?" Dandy asked, and Staples pleaded, "For God's sake, just let me rest, Dandy."

That seemed to work, so we put the horses in the yard and there was no more talk between man and man, or man and God, for that night. We were soon all abed, inside the hut and out, and the risk to Soldier's side and to Dandy's composure was for now averted.

An Australian bird that starts the dawn with a gargling sound woke me from profound sleep with confused dreams of classrooms and impenetrable algebraic and geometric formulae mixed in with Latin declensions. When we got up we had some more damper with sliced mutton and tea for breakfast, with Dandy's curiosity held at bay by his need to make sure the Soldier's plate was amply provisioned.

After we'd eaten, Fred Bonney took Yandi and me aside and asked us to start the mob of sheep onto the next waterhole at Myers Creek, saying, "I will simply acquaint Dandy with the news and then come on after you. That way, Dandy will have had time to digest his situation once we return this evening." Fred then spoke in Paakantji to Yandi.

We said our goodbyes to Dandy and Staples and—with dogs yelping happily about us, frantically enthusiastic to be of help—we started mustering the horde of sheep, doing work that Dandy would probably never do again now that he was Lord Yellowmead. Yandi, with neither self-consciousness nor malice, took over the command of the colonial sheepdogs, releasing them with one whistle round either flank of the large mob, and whistling in a different intonation to bring them back to the rear of the flock. The joy the dogs took in their ferocious energy was a wonder to behold. Larkin had been training me in the whistled orders for, blacksmith though he was, he had grown up on a sheep station and knew how to control sheep-dogs, though I doubted I would ever become as skilled as Yandi.

We made good, steady progress, and barely an hour and a half had passed before Fred Bonney caught up with us and spoke to Yandi a little while I took over the marvelous business of com-manding the dogs, who, remarkably, responded exactly to my set of learned and practiced whistles.

Fred rode up to me after a few minutes and said, "Dandy will take the day to think about his news." And he intoned, " 'Ill fares the land, to hastening ills a prey, Where wealth accumulates, and men decay' . . . Oliver Goldsmith. True eighty years back, true now. But a fellow could be just, I think. Dandy could be just."

From the west and into our path, a group of watching natives materialized. It seemed to be a large family group. There were a number of young men carrying two or three spears each, with many other implements tucked into their grass belts. In their midst was an older man with full hair and a beard. There was also a boy of perhaps ten, near naked and holding a club, and several smaller children, including infants in pouches of kangaroo skin on their mothers' backs. They were all standing, except for an older woman, wrapped in a blanket, who had taken the chance to drop to her haunches.

As Fred and I drew to a halt, Yandi rode up to the line of people and dismounted. He said nothing. At last the older of the two men raised his hand and began speaking.

"These are the Wanyawalku. They speak the same language as our people," said Fred, watching the encounter closely. "They're a shy people. The name of the old man talking to Yandi is Barra-koon. He is a purist and won't live on any station. His wife is from further west still. I think he might have got her from her people on a wife raid." At the same time as Fred informed me, two little yellow birds fluttering near him seemed to be informing him.

The old man now reached out for Yandi's hand and led him away from the others as they talked. Yandi talked back, his head bowed to the old man, only sometimes raising his eyes to him. Then the old man took hold of Yandi by both shoulders with the appear-ance of true affection and bent his head until it touched Yandi's breast.

"Hold my horse, and command the dogs to keep the sheep con-tained," Fred told me, handing me his reins then dismounting and walking in the direction of the old man. The yellow birds scattered about him, and the women began to shrill with the pleasure of this, very like people who'd heard of this trick before and were now hav-ing it confirmed before their own eyes.

As the old man greeted Fred there was something liquid about the way he spoke his language. After he'd finished, Fred laid his head down on the breast of the old man with the greatest solemnity. A necessary cycle had clearly been completed. More conversation followed in what looked like some sort of treaty-making, after which Fred walked over to the group and greeted everyone, taking out some grain to feed each yellow bird for the amusement of the party. Meanwhile, at what seemed the behest of Fred, Yandi walked over and slit the throat of one of the young ewe lambs, letting the blood drain and then carrying the carcass to the family. Everyone resumed their separate ways, with Yandi taking over the sheep again and Fred coming back to me.

"I offered them the hospitality of Momba, Plorn, but they have had a bad experience with South Australian troopers and want to make away northwards to be quit of them. They'll negotiate their way and camp amongst a people named the Karengapa up Wanaaring way."

As we began to ride, Fred ruminated on the ways of the South Australian police and their invasion of the border country southwards, saying, "They took one of the young men and his wife hostage for a day and the others believed they'd killed them. However, when the troopers demanded the return of a sextant that had gone missing and it was brought back by a native child, clearly not the thief, the couple were let go."

His certainty about what he said, the way the names and the motivation of the natives were so familiar to him and rolled off his tongue demonstrated to me yet again what an accomplished colonial he was.

After reaching Myers Creek, and watching the flock drinking, we left them there. Dandy's replacement boundary rider would move them on eastwards to another water source in time.

17

As we rode back to Dandy's hut, Fred's mind seemed as much concerned with the difficulties of the group of natives we had met as with the difficulty of Dandy. However, as we got closer to Dandy's place something looked awry about the wooden structure above the well, the whim, which looked far too solid, like a filled-in space.

Suddenly, Yandi stopped his horse and began to howl, crying, "Bad stuff, Mr. Bonney. Real bad spirit there, sir."

Looking at the whim more closely, I saw it was the body of a hanging man filling out the whim's framework.

We rode closer and saw that it was Dandy who had hanged himself, his face swollen and his neck looking absurdly stretched. As I dismounted and raced towards the structure, my dread mounted at the sight of Staples lying by the edge of the well. Fred rushed from his horse to Staples's side and frantically felt his neck.

"There's barely a pulse," he said grimly.

Looking down we both saw that Staples's shirt was saturated with blood. A long wooden staff was near him, which he must have been using to try to hook Dandy's noose back towards him.

"Get some water," Fred said, looking grim.

As I rushed back to my horse, Yandi was shouting and chanting in Paakantji as he rode around us at a distance.

Fred tried to feed Staples the water but he couldn't take it in. Fred sent me off to the cart to get the brandy bottle, but brandy and water didn't revive him.

"Lift his jacket and shirt," Fred ordered.

I gasped when I saw the wound, its lips torn asunder, mocking any idea of it ever closing up again.

Fred bustled into the hut and found a saddlery needle some- where. He threaded it with some brown twine, poured brandy over the wound, and asked me to drag its two sides closed. I did my best, but Fred was forced to give up.

As we realized our quest to save him was futile, I felt tears rising in me and tried to resist them. Sighing, Fred rose and went over to Dandy's hanging body, saying, "How will we get poor Dandy down?"

It was soon clear that Dandy had gone to the trouble of calculat- ing rope lengths to ensure he could dangle in the mouth of the well without being retrievable after he cast off. If we reached forward to where his feet swayed, one foot bare, that boot having fallen into the well, we would tumble in ourselves. At last, Fred hit on the idea of retrieving him with a stock whip, though he expressed regret that doing so would mark the corpse.

Shouting out to Yandi, Fred asked him to get horses into the shafts of the cart, which was some fifty steps from the well. Before Yandi did so he set fire to some leaves and ignited a whole fallen branch, which he waved over the cart, still chanting, smoking it and thus driving the demons out. Grabbing the whip from the cart, Fred gave it a powerful crack, which caught in a coil of strands around Dandy's lower legs. Fred gestured to me to haul it in using the handle, and we managed to draw Dandy close enough for me to mount the whim and cut the rope. Fred laid Dandy's body down gently, the noose still embedded in the flesh of his neck. Though Yandi showed no obvious reluctance to help lift the Soldier into the cart, Fred could not persuade him to handle Dandy.

Dandy's body was a great weight for Fred and me, and stank of urine and, I thought, already of death. We carried him past the pungent smoking branch Yandi had taken up again and deposited him in the back of the cart along the tailboard. Fred asked me to tether my horses to the cart and to sit in it with the Soldier and report any revival. He rode it at a good pace for the rest of the day and into the night, asking me at intervals whether there were any signs of life in the Soldier. I told him I thought the signs were diminishing.

Sunset evoked a new stint of chanting from Yandi. At some time after dark Fred stopped to inspect the Soldier. Then, still kneeling on the boards, he said, "You rest now, Plorn. It will be a long night and I may call on you to drive the cart later."

"Is he dead?" I asked him.

"If not, he's extremely close. It may have been apoplexy as well as the wound that felled him. Get your blankets, Plorn. You've applied yourself marvelously."

I was so exhausted I barely stopped to consider I'd been invited to sleep in the back of the cart with two dead men. I fetched my blankets and slept without demur beside the Soldier, on the edge of death as he might be.

When we reached Momba early the next morning, the Soldier was dead. Fred and I laid him down on a blanket in the stables and I helped Fred bathe his body from a bucket of water and wash his blood away. Dead, Staples's frame looked slight and undominant.

Drinking dense black tea with sugar, I listened to Fred inform Edward of the tragedy and saw a tear in Edward's eye as he said, "For God's sake, don't give the Reverend Rutledge grounds to refuse Dandy a Christian burial."

"We could bury them both somewhere a little way off from here," Fred agreed. "That won't worry the darks."

"Ah, the darks," said Edward, staring into his tea. "The Soldier would be at ease with that arrangement, I believe."

Fred nodded. "I believe he would see a certain holiness in a man like Dandy who died to avoid being anyone's lord."

"Silly bugger shouldn't have done it though."

"I don't know whether it was brave cowardice or cowardly valor," Fred mused.

"Was Yandi well?" Edward asked crisply.

"Yandi was alarmed and smoked everything, including the cart."

I was a little shocked to hear all this insofar as these were the sons of a clergyman, yet they appeared to accept Yandi's death rituals as appropriate and did not see the need to submit Dandy or the Soldier to the Anglican rites.

We all sat solemnly for a time before Fred remarked, "Poor Soldier died trying to save or at least cut Dandy down. In a sense, Dandy killed the Soldier."

"That's why I believe there must be some First Principle or Creator," said his brother. "Because only *that* personage could understand the motives of men."

It was hard to tell if Fred agreed or disagreed with this sentiment. He turned to me and asked, "Plorn, what do you think about all this? I hope you're not too shocked."

"My father would agree with you both," I replied, though I was both confused and grieving. In any case, that seemed to reassure them.

ॐ

Tom Larkin was sent to town to report the deaths. The letter Fred sent suggested against the coroner becoming involved for the sake of the family and the House of Lords. The story Fred relayed to

Dandy's family and the House of Lords did not mention that the prospect of being a lord had driven their scion to suicide.

The Paakantji kept away from the double funeral on Momba. I got the impression they considered the ghost of a suicide very dangerous. Fred read the Book of Common Prayer and then the Soldier and Dandy were buried in the Christian tradition off to the east of the homestead in a thicket where the mouth of Myers Creek and Natalia Creek split from each other. All these arrangements showed me that some things needed to be done in a different and even imaginative way in New South Wales. But mourning is universal, and even some of the station hands from Mount Murchison, having heard the real story, rode over for the burial.

18

A week after the sorry burial of Dandy and Staples, the greatest scandal of Wilcannia's history struck when Maurice McArden and his aunt vanished from town. It took a day or two for their absence to be noticed because Mr. Fremmel was in Adelaide on stock and station agent business at the time, and they'd left on horseback rather than taking a carriage. It was not known in which direction they'd gone and rumors about the two of them kept everyone on the trans–Darling River, including me, tantalized. One such held that Mrs. Fremmel must have been wearing men's clothes, since the innkeeper at the bush village of Gilgunnia saw two horsemen ride through the settlement early one morning.

As a reader of Maurice's manuscript, I was riveted by their disappearance, wondering if they'd decided to go somewhere they could gratify their desire in each other without intrusion from Mr. Fremmel.

There were men everywhere amongst the pastoralists who had taken loans through Fremmel's agency and now feared he would behave with universal vengeance for his humiliation. As a result, the committee of the jockey club immediately voted to award him life membership at a specially convened dinner, so they might be immune.

Not having any of their own business with Fremmel, the drovers and station workers of Momba cracked plenty of jokes. They were delighted that Fremmel's nephew had made Fremmel "wear cuckold's horns." As for me, I was astonished by the seriousness of Maurice's escape.

When Mr. Fremmel returned to Wilcannia, he behaved as if nothing had happened. "Oh, didn't you know?" he said. "I gave my nephew permission to accompany Mrs. Fremmel on a holiday." Everyone indebted to banks and larger lending bodies by way of Fremmel's agency made an effort to indicate they believed this tale. Or so Willy Suttor told me after he came back from a visit to town.

About a fortnight after their elopement I received a letter with Momba's address written in Maurice's assured hand, carrying the postmark of a town named Lake Cargelligo. It read:

Dear Mr. Dickens,

Confidentially and not for attribution

I have no grievances at all about your advice on the material I was thinking of submitting to your father's journal. I believe him to be amongst the noblest souls, but perhaps and understandably not quite noble enough to submit to having his limitations as a writer on the subject of physical attraction between characters in novels criticized as I have criticized him. Better, I think, that he should endure this limitation and be in all other ways who he is, for he is a prophet. Read, for example, chapter ten of Our Mutual Friend, *the diatribe against men who live by buying and selling shares. He excoriates them no less than Christ excoriated the Temple money changers!*

I felt I must tell you that we have not fled Wilcannia for the purposes you might have surmised. For beyond desire, and beyond everything intense and momentary, there is always enduring loyalty and enduring pity.

My aunt and I have fled Wilcannia for pity's sake. Our motives will be misinterpreted, but you and Mr. Suttor, to whom I send my regards, will accept that our escape was necessary and for motives your own renowned father would not disavow.

Both touched and confused, I took the letter to Willy Suttor. After he'd read it he looked up and said, "I don't think we have any obligation to tell Fremmel about this. He can spend money on private investigators, and let him do it!"

I was relieved to hear this. I wanted my sense that Maurice had taken a risk writing to me, and that his news should be cherished, confirmed to me by an older, wiser fellow. "In any case," said Willy, "from Lake Cargelligo they could be traveling anywhere— Melbourne or Sydney or a thousand private places in between. Or once in Sydney or Melbourne they might take a ship for New Zealand, California, or Valparaíso. We have nothing to tell Mr. Fremmel. He can go to buggery!"

So I got used to living with secrets and even to nurturing them. The mustering of lambs continued and then, throughout the winter, there were country races. I received a letter from my brother Alfred telling me he was bringing two horses to compete at the Mena Murtee Station races and could I plead with the Bonney brothers to let me ride there and visit him? No sooner did I mention it to the Bonneys than Fred insisted I must go and take this opportunity of a wonderful reunion of two sons of the immortal Charles in the heart of the new country.

19

As soon as winter ended, Fred began preparing for the start of the shearing season. Several weeks before the shearers were due to arrive he sent out messages to the back blocks of Momba Station ordering hutkeepers to have the different detachments of sheep marched in to certain places by certain dates. With two hundred thousand sheep to shear, regiment after regiment had to be shifted in lots of five thousand. If there were any delays in the moving in and out of one group for shearing, Fred would still have to pay the shearers and negotiate with "the boss of the board," as they called the overseer of shearing, the high priest in the huge, crude defleecing cathedrals and their shearing stands.

I rode out with others to the northeasternmost paddock named Wonkoo, from which we used our wise dogs to bring the sheep in to Momba, passing three great lakes of artesian water, Yantabangee and Olepoloko and Peery Lakes, then across the streams that flowed from them. We proceeded under the sage gaze of big red kangaroos, inspecting us from the breast-high creek grass.

Back at Momba, a battalion of shearers had started arriving in twos and threes, some on foot and others on horseback, swags full of their worldly possessions slung across the crop of their horses. The uncomfortable shearers' quarters they were to stay in were close to the great pile of the shearing shed, perhaps the largest structure of hardwood for hundreds of thousands of miles.

The women of the station, Mrs. Larkin and Mrs. Gavan, kept tea brewing to welcome the arriving men, and served them damper, cocky's joy, and other primitive refreshments from a rough table. Fred had signed up all the shearers with the one shearing contractor, and most had already shorn this season on other stations, the names of which rolled off their lips lyrically—Burrabogie and Billabong, Gilgunnia and Coolabah.

The shearing stands were great structures which stood on stilts and balks of timber above the ground so that sheep could be sheltered from any rain that came, since shearing wet fleece rendered the shearers themselves drenched and thus in danger of rheumatism. Wet sheep therefore meant that shearing had to stop. And when that happened, the rouseabouts, picker-uppers, sweepers, and the boss of the board had to go on being paid, but the shearers, who were paid per head, could earn nothing and still had to pay a share for their own food. I'd been told that when this happened they became restive and began to speak of the desirability of forming unions and taking radical action.

The day after we returned to Momba I went to see the army of shearers who'd turned up and registered themselves for a stand in the shed. I asked some of them whether they wanted to play cricket the coming Sunday, since we had a splendid team of our own, apart from the Soldier, of whose death they had all heard. They treated me with amusement and dismissiveness.

The shearing floor before the shearers took their stands was a place of august silence, its boards dark with oil from the fleeces shorn in previous years. As the shearers entered the shed and took up their stands, most of them wore red republican singlets, perhaps to honor Garibaldi, certainly to honor the dignity of the laboring man. From the yard outside, rouseabouts yelled and rattled cans to drive sheep up the chutes. Once the first sheep came up the ramp from the yards below, it sat powerless between the shearer's legs as he cut away. First, he would shear the belly wool off in one go and throw it on the floor, then he did the sheep's legs and face. In the rare case the skin of the beast was nicked, tar boys ran over to sheep with a cut and covered all slips of the shears with a mix of lampblack, kerosene, and tar. The rest, back and flanks, came off the animal in one sheet, like a big wool rug.

I was fascinated by how the shearer cut away the fleece at the neck, clearing the wool from wrinkles. As this main fleece fell to the floor the picker-uppers rushed in and lifted the whole thing as delicately as they could and carried it to the table at the end of the shed.

It was pure luck what type of sheep each shearer got. Generally old ewes were the easiest to shear, and the shearers called them "rosellas," while they called the sheep with the stiffest fleeces "the cobblers."

The shearing had its own established timetable, with two twenty-minute breaks for the essential black tea, as well as longer breaks for lunch, and "tea," which was what they called dinner. The name for everything they ate was "tucker." They invited me to have "tucker" one night with them at "teatime." Over a long day, interspersed with these occasional pleasures, a good shearer could get through more than thirty sheep, which was considered championship level. Alfred had complained under the influence of liquor of the disadvantage of being our father's sons, but I felt that these hearty, contemptuous men gave me a better time than they might most "new chums," in part, as the word got around, out of their bush courtesy towards our father, who was to many of them like a pontiff of the universal human heart.

I learned the terms of shearing with the rigor arising from my new spirit of application. I conveyed some of them to the guvnor in my letters to him. That, for example, rams could take three times as long to shear and counted double; young wethers were hard; and that if the shearer cut a sheep's jugular it perished and he had to bear the cost. The sheep being shorn at the call of "Time!" was named a "bell sheep" and could not be finished because the rouse-abouts and picker-uppers would not touch its wool, nor could the boss of the board nor even the Bonneys force him to. The man who sheared the most was acclaimed "the ringer." Some ringers achieved the same renown as jockeys and boxers.

During and at the end of the day, odd locks were cut from the legs which remained on the floor until they were swept up by boys and put in baskets. The fleece proper was always spread in one throw on the table, then its "points," shoulders, neck, haunches, were cut off by the classer's assistants and labeled "second cuts." Then the back of the sheep was rolled up and taken to the table of the ultimate connoisseur, the wool classer.

The wool classer at Momba that spring was a dapper fellow by the name of Wick, and he made it very clear he was a citizen of the city of Sydney who had learned the business there in the Australian agency of a big Yorkshire textile mill. Like most patricians, he did not get too familiar with the shearers, saying they were a rum lot and would take advantage if they could. I didn't want to cast any doubt on his high stature by asking in what sense they could take advantage. But in the red republic of the shearing shed, I was left in no doubt he was the autocrat.

He would sometimes leave his magisterial table and check what was happening at the tables of the piece pickers and wool rollers, ensuring the right wool was going in the right bin. He further divided the fleece back at his own table into "first and second combings," based on the length of the fibers.

The Bonneys had decreed that the first and second combings be labeled A and AA. The Bonneys seemed sure the wool classer could not live with the price of his first clothing falling by letting discolored wool be placed carelessly in the wrong bin. His reputation, like the reputation of princes or foreign ministers, was in his gradings. And if the wool of a first clothing could be used to make billiard cloths, that was the ultimate test, for billiard cloths signified the finest wool. Far away in Europe, or in the north of England, agents knew, year by year, what stations' first clothing was the one to buy. Momba had that repute, and the wool classer could not afford to let down its fame.

The wool taken from the sheep of Momba was greasy with wool yolk and had to be washed with soap and water in the creek behind Momba homestead. It was then dried in the sun before being pressed into bales, otherwise the Bonneys would have to pay hundreds of pounds for the transportation of grease.

That shearing season of 1869 increased my wonder at the Bonneys' great enterprise in this country beyond the Darling. And I committed all I learned to memory. If there was application available to me, this was it.

~

It took a little while to become used to the altered intensity of life after the shearing was complete, and as if to help me on the way Fred took me out chasing the large, stiff-gaited flightless birds called "emus," which Fred was very sentimental about and wouldn't allow to be hunted on Momba except by the Paakantji. We encountered a flock of these robust birds amidst the mulgas and the grass and saltbush. They stood over six feet tall and ran absurdly fast in ruthless straight lines, so to make them turn direction was a triumph, though when they did change course they veered faster than a horse. Fred told me to settle on one as my target and go after it. The one I chose led me on a cross-country ride of miles, all at a gallop, before it rounded on its track and turned at right angles.

During the shearing I hadn't had time to think of either the high question of that enchanting girl Connie Desailly, or of what course Maurice and Mrs. Fremmel might have taken. Now I wondered if Mrs. Fremmel had been able to take much money with her. And if not, how would Maurice feed them, given his uncle had not paid him? Or indeed, how would he be able to afford two ship tickets to distant ports even in New Zealand? I felt an occasional fretfulness for him, but it was combined with a bewilderment about what I could do. It was obvious that in one way or another he had taken fatal choices at too young an age, and that his intelligence and imagination seemed a blight on him.

And throughout this country either side of the Darling River, wherever there was cricket, racing, and debt, people out of politeness or dread went on subscribing to the belief that Mr. Fremmel's wife and nephew were on holiday.

❧

A somewhat delayed letter from Aunt Georgie told me the guvnor's younger brother, Uncle Fred, had died. I'd hardly known him, but I thought Alfred might have since Fred had been part of the family before he proved himself unworthy in many ways. Aunt Georgie outlined these in her letter, writing:

> After his unfortunate marriage to Anna Weller, a barmaid he got to know—which all of us predicted would be a disaster—he actually fled the country rather than pay alimony to her. And then on his return, of course he was arrested and put in the Marshalsea just like his father. But he gathered together enough money to get out by trading on your dear father's name. Terrible, terrible, and everything a true man should not be. The poor fellow was only forty-eight, and it was a burst abscess on his lung that asphyxiated him. Your father wisely and charitably said, "It was a wasted life, but God forbid one should be hard upon it."

She then went on to talk about the guvnor, saying:

Your father has not been in good health—he has had many trips to France, but they do not seem to have rested him—and the autumn has been severe on top of that, and so he sent young Charley to represent him at the funeral in Darlington, a bad enough place to begin with . . .

I knew that Uncle Fred had been rather like me when young but had never found his Momba, the place that concentrated the forces of his soul. I had a yearning to see Alfred, to receive Alfred's memory of the man. And yet Uncle Fred Dickens's spirit did not oppress me, for I believed I had escaped the family failure of many of my father's brothers, and even the failings of his father—the same lack of application from which Momba had delivered me.

I was going down to take tea at the store with Willy Suttor when Tom Larkin came to me through the dusk looking solemn. "Mr. Plorn," he told me, "my wife's persuaded me that you would want to see this. I don't know what it means. Nothing but good, I hope," he said and handed over a segment of newspaper, gave me what passed in the bush for a salute, and withdrew.

"My regards to your charming wife," I called out to him, and he raised a hand to acknowledge this greeting.

Following the letter from Aunt Georgie, the newspaper cutting had a wistfulness to it.

The announcement by Mr. Dickens that he would not this year publish a Christmas number of *All the Year Round* has been regretted by tens of thousands of his readers in this country. But it seems that nothing is to be lost in that an edition of his Christmas stories, containing the favorites of the past, *The Holly-tree Inn*, *The Wreck of the Golden Mary*, *The Perils of Certain English Prisoners*, *A Christmas Carol*, and *A House to Let*, will be published under the imprint of *Household Words*. Mr. Dickens has had an exhausting year involving a tour of the United States and is presently giving his acclaimed readings in Scotland and Ireland.

This was the intelligence, reprinted in the Melbourne *Argus* and taken originally from *The Times* of London, that Larkin had passed to me with the solemnity of a treaty between great powers. He had not known how it would influence me, since he could not imagine being in my place. In his natural grace he had managed to do it well. I am left home, I thought, and for the first time the guvnor has no child left to write a Christmas story for. That's what it was, apart from all the other causes. No child left.

20

When Fred Bonney suggested I should ride all the way to Alfred's station at Corona for Christmas, my first impulse was to ask, "But won't you need me here?" He replied that Cultay wished to visit his wife's people for some of what Fred called "law or lore" down there. Cultay would go with me and knew all the waterholes along the way. It should take a little more than two days' full ride, three at the most in severe heat.

I decided to go and inscribed two editions of *Our Mutual Friend* to Fred and Edward Bonney to mark the season. I'd ordered the copies through Willy Suttor thinking they were least likely to have read it, it being only a few years old according to my reckoning. I felt the usual fraudulence passing it on while barely having read a word of it. I knew it was a book that had influenced the brilliant and doomed Maurice. On that original ride into Momba he'd told me, "The most truly drawn of your father's characters is Bella Wilfer. You know, from *Mutual Friend*? She starts mercenary, then she identifies herself as mercenary, then she repents and cures herself, and then becomes a full moral being."

"Oh yes, oh yes, old chap," I replied before asking, "Why is Bella Wilfer the character that all those competent with print so admire?"

I gave nonliterary presents of chocolate and tobacco to Willy and the Larkins. The heat of the season sat most appealingly on Grace Larkin—a girl growing, it seemed, to become a woman of the house and a figure of bush authority so far from the sea. And then, a few days before Christmas, I set out with Cultay.

Fred Bonney gave me a present of four guineas and insisted I take an extra-sturdy Waler, as well as Coutts. Cultay was a magisterial fellow traveler, his attitude to the apparently barren country one of tranquil ownership. His father would have been the first of his forebears to see a horse—probably that of the exploring surveyor Charles Sturt or one of his followers—and yet he rode his Waler with an authority far more antique than that.

We traveled westward and along the creeks and rested amongst the trees from noon to three or later, before venturing on into the evening. On the first late afternoon we saw some prospectors' huts by hills of white shale but had no reason to trouble them this festive time of year. We also came upon a camp of Afghans and their laden camels, bound for the town of Packsaddle, and exchanged courteous greetings with them. Soon the plain opened wide on the straight red-dust way, with emus far off, rendered legless by the intervening waves of heat throbbing like a sea on our vision.

It was very late in the long day that we reached Packsaddle and came upon a great yard full of horses. Alfred had asked me to call in for further directions at the Packsaddle Inn, a shanty pub owned by former shearer Robert Norwich. Robert Norwich and his wife, who faithfully repeated the end of her husband's last sentences with editorial flourishes of her own, were not as pressed for company in this great vacancy as I'd expected. For Norwich supplied changes of horses for a weekly stagecoach from Wilcannia to the most distant of settlements, Tibooburra, with enough stations and possible mineral grounds in between to provide him with the sort of customers who might bring in their entire checks for him to cash or drink.

As Cultay made camp behind the hotel—for a lot of country

publicans did not like darks coming inside—I went into the main bar and found Robert Norwich alongside an old watery-eyed man in a brown suit that still declared its pretensions.

"It is him!" said Mr. Norwich, slapping the bar. "It is Alfred Dickens's brother! Likewise a gentleman and scholar, likewise a Dickens!"

". . . likewise a Dickens," repeated Mrs. Norwich.

"Expecting you yesterday when we had many passengers in the house, bound for Mount Browne."

". . . bound for Mount Browne for rumored gold, yes."

I told him Alfred had asked me to call in to get accurate directions to the Corona homestead, to which he replied, "But could I first supply you with a drink, Mr. Dickens?"

"A shandy, perhaps," I said, a "shandy" being half ale and half lemonade and the minimum a colonial publican could be expected to serve.

As Mrs. Norwich set to work to supply the shandy, I nodded to the man at the bar, of whom, Mr. Norwich said, "Our permanent guest, Mr. Gaggin. A long-term leaseholder in our district."

"Long-term leaseholder indeed," said Mrs. Norwich.

"I live here, on these premises," Gaggin told me like a boast, "and from here when I fall from my stool will be taken forth to my burial place."

I could barely help saying, "Do you have no relatives in other parts?"

"I have none, sir," said Mr. Gaggin. "If it were not for the shelter offered by the Packsaddle Inn . . . And yet it seems only yesterday, mind you, that I came to the West as a boy like you. Bad seasons, too much hope and reckless loans destroyed me. But I am lucky, since I have found a haven."

I thought him the saddest man I had ever met, somehow even sadder than Dandy Darnell, but said nothing.

"Now, you're looking for directions to the Corona homestead, then?" said Mr. Norwich, taking some paper from a drawer and beginning to sketch a map, which his wife seemed to examine in case of errors. Then, speaking very quickly, he said, "You take this left here, off from the coach track, get out there to this junction at Fowler's Creek—don't take the left, it's a really dry stretch to Menindee, but take this right one here to Euriowie."

Since he did not spell what he pronounced as *Your-irr-owy*, I was confused.

"At the fork of the road, the one you should take," he told me, "is marked with an empty can of cocky's joy on a stick."

"Can of cocky's joy right there," echoed Mrs. Norwich, "hammered to a stake."

Seeing my confusion, Mr. Norwich said, "Listen, bring your black fellow in."

So I went and got Cultay, who had started a campfire, and he stood up and listened to me, and then followed me in, where Norwich concluded the instructions to him and then gave me the map as a supplement.

Cultay said, "I know her, that road. I know Corona."

Mr. Norwich laughed. "That's right, you big mongrel. You'd have darkie relatives there, wouldn't you?"

Cultay nodded but said nothing, then left. Norwich insisted I accept a beer from him now, given the season and because he thought highly of Alfred. He also suggested I buy a bottle of the "dark lady"—port—for Cultay.

"Isn't that illegal, Mr. Norwich?" I asked. Influenced by Fred Bonney and stories of Americans weakening the fiber of Red Indians with firewater, I was ambivalent. Yet port is not as perilous as brandy or rum or whisky, I told myself. Hardly the downfall of a noble race.

"I think it might make you a friend, Mr. Dickens," said Norwich.

"I am not in the business of making drunks of the darks. But I know that one of yours, and he's a good drinker. Here, be my guest." And he put a dark-labeled bottle of sherry on the table. "Don't drink it yourself. I've got better stuff for you . . ."

"Much better stuff for a Dickens boy," echoed Mrs. Norwich.

Mr. Norwich asked again what I would take now and I ordered ale and sat to drink it.

"We are of course, as I say, honored, young Dickens, but in Mr. Gaggin you see one of the veteran pioneers of this country. What year did you settle out here, Mr. Gaggin?"

"I settled on Fowler's Creek in winter 1840," the old man replied. "The kangaroo grass was taller than my horse."

"They were still shipping convicts then," said Mr. Norwich with awe.

"They were," Mr. Gaggin agreed. "But not to where I was. South Australia I came up from as a young geologist. I thought I was made. Since the sandstones, dolomites, and quartz indicated the likelihood of iron, copper, silver, gold. I had a wife in Adelaide then who had not yet lost patience with me."

"And you found these treasures, Mr. Gaggin?" I asked as I sipped my mixed ale, wondering why my elders considered it a staple of life.

"Ore-bearing rock is not hard to discover, young Mr. Dickens. Oh, I sang to God amongst the low escarpments, I can tell you. I found chloride of silver in rocks the color of ginger snaps."

"Ginger snaps," said Mrs. Norwich. "I'm partial to ginger snaps."

"All I needed to be the Australian Croesus, young Mr. Dickens, was capital for someone to bring rock crushing and refining equipment, the smelters and mills, into the Barrier Range, on the many camels needed. All I require even now is still capital and a railway to—at the very least—Wilcannia. I have spent nigh on thirty years ranting at governors and politicians, first in South Australia, then in Sydney. The imagination of Sydney politicians dies at the Darling River, young sir, with the map in their brains not including this immensity. They are criminally deficient. Anyway, they tired of me, and I became a byword for the obvious they would not see. It all made me sour, my young friend, impossible to cohabit with."

Mrs. Norwich repeated the bit about the map of their brain. "Fort Bourke not on it either," she added.

Tears seemed to come into Mr. Gaggin's eyes, and he drank the rest of his brandy and passed the glass to Norwich to refill. Doing so from a bottle of brandy, Norwich said to me, "You see, young Mr. Dickens, Mr. Gaggin is a man before his time and lesser men have failed him. One day this area will be full of cities and the earth honeycombed with rich mines. One of the conurbations should be named Gaggin."

"Gaggin," murmured Mrs. Norwich. "I would be honored to live in a town named Gaggin."

"And so my last years are spent as a guest of the Packsaddle Inn," Gaggin concluded.

"You said you have a family . . ."

"I have a splendid daughter married to Justice Peter Bright of the South Australia Supreme Court. They kindly meet my modest needs. I am not too proud to tell you this, Mr. Dickens. I am immune to pride . . ."

With a surprising suddenness Mr. Gaggin took up his stick and brought it down on the bar, before intoning, "In the hideous solitude of that most hideous place, with Hope so far removed, Ambition quenched, and Death beside him rattling at the very door, reflection came as in a plague-beleaguered town; and so he felt and knew the failing of his life . . ."

He struck the bar again and said, "No one can say I do not know my *Martin Chuzzlewit!*"

"*Chuzzlewit*," chorused the amazed and delighted Mrs. Norwich, who was probably used to Mr. Gaggin's recitations. "*Chuzzlewit* puts it to the Americans."

Mr. Gaggin then pointed his stick at me emphatically. "Your father, sir! Your wonderful father!"

"My father would be honored to know that there is no Australian village where his words are not cherished."

"In Packsaddle, tell your father. In Packsaddle, sir!" Gaggin drank his brandy. Then he reflected further. "Born in London, and I'll die in bloody Packsaddle. There you go. A caution."

"Oh," I said, sympathetically, "you must understand that my father would rather write of men being saved by the colonies."

They accepted this and became thoughtful.

Though Norwich offered me a meal and room, I excused myself and headed out to my damper, mutton, and swag, for I favored that itinerant bed better than an uncertain bed in a colonial coaching inn. I said to Cultay, who had tea bubbling over the fire, "Cultay, I hope it is the right thing, but Mr. Norwich suggested that given it is Christmas I buy you some port wine. And so, thank you for being my companion! I feel safer with you. The port is a small tribute."

By firelight, the ageless Cultay's profoundly set eyes weighed me though he did not reach out from his kneeling position by the fire. I put the bottle by his knee, and he said, "Thanks, Mr. Dickens," and moved the sherry to his side of the fire. We ate dinner, and he had not touched the bottle before I washed in the creek and was ready for bed. Before I settled into my swag Cultay held out a wad of gum to me and said, "Mr. Dickens, you bite on that one and you get good dreaming."

"Really?" I stupidly asked.

"You need a good dreaming from that feller there." Objects were often referred to as "fellers" by the natives, as if everything had a soul. Ever polite, I took the wad of brown gum.

I was suddenly overtaken by a pulse of deep melancholy which perhaps Cultay had seen coming. Gaggin seemed such a sad creature, even in his fruitless knowledge of my father's writing. But I said, "I'm tired anyhow. I might save it for another night when I need it."

"Keep him by you," Cultay urged. "He's a good one. You travel easy with that feller. With him in you, you see the dead and they talk to you like mates."

I must have looked stricken by the waning firelight for Cultay chortled and said, "You see your missus before you meet her. You make friends with all the people in the dream place. You come back happy then."

"All right," I said, raising the wad of gum to prove it was on my agenda. "I'll certainly be into it if I have trouble sleeping."

He nodded and then sang to himself in a monotone and I went very shortly to sleep.

It cannot have been late in the night when I woke in a fright, thinking an owl, or a frogmouth, had been climbing on my face, eying me. I was sure I could taste feathers in my mouth, but the taste vanished as I became conscious and was replaced by a leaden weight of wakefulness. I thought of Alfred and felt dread. Why, I did not know, but it was as if I had risen from my mother's breast a blood-red hateful thing and could not be reconciled to the toil of becoming child and man, and that seeing Alfred turned me as a child to greater unappeased anger still. I was going to my brother for the sake of Christmas, for love's sake, and yet I felt I was approaching a well of venom, or taking my own poison to it, and not embarking in any way on an amiable exercise of fraternity.

". . . if I have trouble sleeping," I had said of the gum to Cultay, whose breathing and snuffling indicated he was asleep.

I took a segment of the mix of gum and ash, which had a heavy vegetable sweetness. As I chewed it, all the malice bled out of me and the hell in my head ebbed away. I felt an immense relief, for the alignment of all stars and all impulses was reversed, and the vast and star-crammed night grew kindly. This "feller" is a greater cure than port! I thought.

I started to have visions of being in some grand room playing a violin very fluently with Constance Desailly at her own instrument, a cello or some such, by my side. Over the music I said to her, "I never knew that I desired you. I thought you were a very ordinary girl." Connie found this amusing, but it did not make her pause in her music.

After that I saw Soldier Staples standing at the crease of the cricket pitch in Netallie Station with a cricket ball in his hand and his bloody side bleeding lustrously away over his red Momba XI sash. Mr. Fremmel was at the far batting crease, a man in despair, a condition to which our music had reduced him.

My mother then appeared at the fielding position of mid off, and she was as amused as Constance, the way women are in a conspiracy of amusement about men. Mama took Staples by the hands, and he dropped the ball and adjusted his arms to her plump body, saying, "Mind your dress, Mrs. Dickens."

"I'll send it off to those actresses," my mother trilled like a girl.

Constance and I were almost disappearing, united in one long curlicue of sound. "What a pity you don't know shorthand," Constance murmured. She seemed to think it would be necessary so that we could communicate further.

"I'll learn," I promised her.

From his batting crease the viperous Mr. Fremmel called out, "No one is bowling to *me*!" For some reason this was the most hilarious thing I had ever heard, and I bubbled with laughter down the skeins of music.

There *was* more, but it lacked the sharpness of the dream to that point. I know I was looking for signs of some sort in Constance's face. When I woke I was in the usual condition of boys my age. Yet though back in a kinder universe, I thought even then a little contemptuously of my dream self, who had been striving to achieve a single song with Constance Desailly and share her shorthand.

Against any further demons of night, I wrapped the remaining gum in paper and pocketed it.

"Christmas Eve, Cultay," I cried when I woke at dawn.

By the time we set off it was already fiercely hot and as we rode the sun lay on our shoulders like a weight. But we withdrew into ourselves and focused on the thought that we would reach Corona by dusk.

21

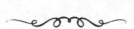

The village of Corona Station was not as large as Momba, but from the ridge above it looked prettily placed in a valley cut by a creek. The buildings were made of stones from the hills that seemed to bespeak quartz and, according to some, the possibility of silver. There was a well with a rise of sandstone behind it. As we approached, Paakantji children ran out from brush shelters by the creek to greet us, and two old men stepped up in shirts and canvas pants to stare at us. If they were relatives of Cultay, they gave no sign of greeting. A number of young drovers were building a bonfire in the dust of the home pasture. I could tell which of them came from a British city (London, Liverpool, Birmingham) to learn to be a squatter because I wore the same British-bought rig myself when I was working.

I saw Alfred emerge from the shadow of the store veranda. I called "Happy Christmas" to Cultay as he was escorted away by a crowd of his relatives, including shrilling women and reserved old men.

As soon as I dismounted, Alfred was beside me, crying, "Happy Christmas, Little Brother." As he embraced me by the shoulders, I smelled some warm spirit on his breath, possibly brandy. He had, I knew from old days, quite a taste for the hard stuff.

"My good Mr. Tom Chard, the storekeeper here, has been celebrating with me, knowing how easy it is to lead me astray on the eve of the birth of the Christ child. And when my brother is about to join me too!" Alfred said blithely with simple affection.

The storekeeper emerged from the shadows and stood a little way off, grinning amiably.

"Mr. Chard, Mr. Dickens, and the same in reverse," said Alfred. "You are becoming such a bush traveler, Plorn. I should let you know," he went on, "that there's a bonfire tonight. In the colonies we celebrate great heat by lighting bonfires. It's the only way to let God know we're still here."

"You're getting deuced theological, Dickens," said Tom Chard, not unpleasantly.

"It must be the season," said Alfred. "The mercury boils in the thermometer, so it must be Christmas in the colonies!" Then he whistled in his sporty, touty way—he had always been a jaunty person. And for all his scholarly disasters, his chin remained high and he kept that indomitable, cocky sparrow curve in his back.

"You brought that black man with you, though. That Cultay fellow?" he asked.

"Yes."

"I must speak to him. We have a few problems at Morphett's Creek. Thank the Bonneys for sending him."

I hadn't been aware until then that Cultay's visit had a meaning for Alfred. At Alfred's whistle, a young Aboriginal boy stopped running with his friends and came over to us.

My brother told him to take my saddlebags inside to Mrs. Geraghty and put them in my room, and then unsaddle and water my mare.

I pardoned myself and followed the boy through the scraggly front garden to the homestead, already trying to think of excuses to get out of too late a night of festivity, for in my brother's posture, his curved back, and his tidy set shoulders, I could see somehow, from seeing it in childhood, the intention to be festive. The boy led me into the homestead via a deep, low-roofed veranda, and we passed through a wet hessian curtain in the doorway and went into the dark coolness of the house.

We found Mrs. Geraghty sweeping in the back of the house. She was a strong-bodied woman, not very old, but very brown and gypsy-looking. She wore a long yellow dress on her full figure and boots on her feet without stockings.

As always with strangers, I felt the old rustiness and uncertainty. "I am Mr. Dickens's brother," I said, smiling hesitantly.

"Now I would say you would want some tea," she replied in a colonial accent.

I told her that would be very pleasant.

"Would you like it in the living room or in the kitchen?" she asked.

"The kitchen, please, Mrs. Geraghty," I replied, for I had a sudden yearning for the company of a woman of mothering proportions.

"All square, Mr. Dickens," she told me. "I'll get it ready. You just come along."

I was shown into the house and to my room, which was dark under a low-slung timber roof with big eaves and had for decoration only a report of a South Australian steeplechaser hammered by an enthusiast to the wall under the ornate pressed-tin ceiling.

After washing from a pitcher and basin, I put on a new shirt, and went out through the back of the house to the kitchen, which was a separate structure like we had at Momba.

Mrs. Geraghty had set up a little table with tea in a pot, a china cup, and a segment of tart covered by a doily. I was about to pour my tea when she came out, wiping her hands on a cloth, and demanding to perform the duty herself. She said as she poured, "It is a pleasure, of course, to be pouring for another son of—"

I presumed she'd refer to the guvnor, but instead she said, "—the great prophet of the kitchen and dining room, Lady Maria Clutterbuck."

I was confused for a moment, before I remembered the worn cooking manual Mama had written, which I'd seen Aunt Georgie occasionally peer into with the frown of a woman looking for an answer.

"That is, I believe," said Mrs. Geraghty, "the *nom de plume* of your own mother, Mrs. Dickens."

"It is," I said. "She wrote *What Shall We Have for Dinner?* when she was young, I think, before I was even born. It was said to be by a Lady Maria Clutterbuck. But that was my mother. It was really my mother herself."

"Yes, as I told you," said Mrs. Geraghty.

"And I think the guvnor, my father, wrote something at the start of it."

"How happy they must've been working, husband and wife, to make an entire book of recipes."

"Yes, they were very happy," I asserted.

But how did I know? I was not born. I asked again, was it Dora's loss that had made them unhappy? So sudden. The guvnor had played with her all afternoon, carrying her round the garden. And then she underwent a sudden baby seizure and died while he was giving a lecture. Aunt Georgie said that when the guvnor got home, he held the little corpse all night in his arms.

I decided to take a bet on Mrs. Geraghty, who carried whatever reading she had done without pretention, asking her, "Have you read much of my father's work?"

She weighed the question, then said, "I read a little bit of *Pickwick Papers* once. But it wasn't very useful."

I burst into laughter, feeling my burden of illiteracy relieved.

Mrs. Geraghty frowned. "Did I say something amusing, Mr. Dickens?"

"No. I was thinking how flattered my mother would be."

"I used her recipes time and time again while I lived in Tasmania, since we could get fresh fish there. Now your father's favorite, I believe, roast leg of mutton stuffed with oysters . . . I could do that with stewed kidneys as well, when I was working for a lady on the eastern coast of the place. But as for roast mutton here, I stuff it with a sauce-laden mince, which seems to suit your brother's taste. I make sausages as well, using a sausage-making machine the pastoral company set up for me."

I nodded politely, and she continued enthusiastically. "When it comes to poultry, we don't have it so badly here. I can generally send a boy out to bring in a few ducks. Now you can't find anyone in the bush to speak up for the humble brush turkey, but I catch them myself and serve them as fillets or in curry. I use your mother's pheasant recipe on them, too. As for beef and lamb, cutlets and saddles and sweetbread and legs, all of which Lady Clutterbuck recommends, you might have noticed we have no shortage."

"We have no shortage at Momba either. What we sadly lack is a cook like you."

Under her tan Mrs. Geraghty went red at this flattery. Mind you, I thought, our cook at Momba, the old fellow named Courtney, was not so bad at all.

"Now that tart there, on your plate, that is the desert fruit named 'quandong.' I use it in your mama's recipe for greengage tart. Taste that quandong while I watch."

I did and it was delightful. Seeing my expression, she said, "Now your brother, he said to me the first time he had that, 'Mrs. Geraghty,' he said, 'that there quandong is a revelation.'"

"I say it too," I told her, eating another mouthful. "Do you have a copy of the book there? The cookbook, I mean."

"Of course! I was given it in bound form by Mrs. Hare when my boy and I decided we must come to the mainland for the opportunities. The boy's about your age now and a fine son, who works as a drover at Poolamacca Station," she told me with a proud smile.

"Your Mrs. Hare must've been sad to see you go."

"Oh, I trained a girl up," said Mrs. Geraghty. "To fill my place."

She went inside and came back with a slim but large-page bound book which she handed to me before vanishing again. Knowing it was my mother validated in brown and red leather there, at the limits of colonial pastures, before the desert began, I started to weep, though I could not define why.

Seeing my tears when she reappeared, Mrs. Geraghty took my arm and said, "Of course, my dear boy, you must miss your mama."

"I don't know why I cried," I told her. "Don't tell my brother."

"Do you think your brother has never cried?" Mrs. Geraghty replied with a laugh.

"May I take this to my room for a while?" I asked, wiping away my tears.

She said of course and urged me to finish my quandong tart. I needed no command, thanked her, and went to my room, grateful for the moment that Alfred was settled in for a carouse. But it was not long before the boy who'd brought my bags in was knocking on the door.

"Please, Mr. Dickens, Mr. Dickens says would you like to come over to him and Mr. Chard there?"

"Tell him I'm indisposed for the moment but I'll see him in an hour," I replied.

"What's that, mister?" asked the young Paakantji.

"Tell him I'm a bit crook in the stomach, and I'll be there in a while."

"Fair play," the boy told me and left.

I sat at a desk by the window and opened the much-but-carefully-used cookbook, which was an 1852 edition. The year of my birth, that is. As women throughout the world bought the book, Mama was suckling me.

The title page declared the authorship as the fictitious Lady Maria Clutterbuck, and I knew, because Aunt Georgie had told me, that it was Father who wrote the introduction under the name Sir Charles Coldstream, who reflected on the enjoyment the late but beloved Sir Jonas took with these recipes. As for Lady Clutterbuck herself, she reflected (and I think here, too, it was Father reflecting for her):

> The late Sir Jonas Clutterbuck had, in addition to a host of other virtues, a very good appetite and an excellent digestion; to those endowments I was indebted (though some years the junior of my revered husband) for many hours of connubial happiness.
>
> Sir Jonas was not a *gourmand*, although a man of great gastronomical experience. Richmond never saw him more than once a month, and he was as rare a visitor to Blackwall and Greenwich. Of course, he attended most of the corporation dinners as a matter of duty (having been elected alderman in 1839), and now and then partook of a turtle feast at some celebrated place in the city; but these were only exceptions, his general practice being to dine at home; and I am consoled in believing that my attention to the requirements of his appetite secured me the possession of his esteem until the last.
>
> My experience in the confidences of many of my female friends tells me, alas! that others are not so happy in their domestic relations as I was. That their daily life is embittered by the consciousness that a delicacy forgotten or misapplied, a surplusage of cold mutton or a redundancy of chops, are gradually making the Club more attractive than the Home, and rendering "business in the city" of more frequent occur-

rence than it used to be in the earlier days of their connubial experience; while the ever-recurring inquiry of WHAT SHALL WE HAVE FOR DINNER? makes the matutinal meal a time to dread, only exceeded in its terrors by the more awful hour of dinner!

It is to rescue many fair friends from such domestic suffering that I have consented to give to the world THE BILLS OF FARE which met with the approval of Sir Jonas Clutterbuck, believing that by a constant reference to them, an easy solution may be obtained to that most difficult of questions— "WHAT SHALL WE HAVE FOR DINNER?"

Reading it I felt they must have still loved each other when he wrote that, passing himself off as the same person, my mother, who wrote the bills of fare. They were united in their publisher too as it turns out—Bradbury and Evans, before Father told us Fred Evans said nasty things about the separation and Aunt Georgie.

I turned to the recipes and began to read my mother's true prose. "The best part of the mutton from which to make good broth is the chump end of the loin, but it may be made excellently from the scrag end of the neck only, which should be stewed gently for a long time (full three hours or longer, if it be large) until it becomes tender . . ." The idea of her knowing that, of possibly talking about it to the cook as I slept in the nursery, was for some reason awfully sad and glorious at the same time and made me weep again for a good ten minutes. Then I closed the book, returned it to Mrs. Geraghty, and set out to see Alfred.

I reached the store where Alfred was now sitting with Chard in the veranda shade. "Here he comes, Mr. Chard," he called. "Pour my brother rum."

Chard regarded me with kind, dark eyes and asked gently, "Would you prefer ginger beer, son?"

After admitting I was still dry from my drive, Chard told me to go into the store and introduce myself to Mrs. Chard and ask her for ginger beer. I went into the dim store as ordered and called hello. A large, fleshy pale woman emerged from the residence behind the storeroom, which was a fair imitation of Willy Suttor's store in quantity of materials but, I thought at first glance, a little less rationally organized, and said, "Yairz?" like someone who'd arrived at that pronunciation of the affirmative by much practice and self-torture. I asked unnecessarily if she was Mrs. Chard and she said, "I em thet lady. Who warnts to noe?"

"My respects," I said quickly, knowing she might expect them for all the trouble she had taken with elocution. I told her I was Alfred Dickens's brother, and her husband had said I could get a glass of ginger beer from her.

"Aw, thet's awlrite then. I'll git you thet, no wauries et awl," she said in her tortured-sounding dialogue, then came back with an earthen jug and a pannikin, into which she poured the splashing, soda-y ginger beer.

"Does yuse thenk the gennelmen well desist frum the rurm and brundy suon?" she asked.

"I beg your pardon . . . Oh, I understand, the rum," I said before lowering my voice and asking, "Why don't you just tell them to stop?"

She said, "Ai kin tell Chard to storp. But nort Mr. Durckens. He's muniger on behalft of the Knew Sour Wails end Imperiol Pestoral Cumpny!"

"He's just my brother and too much is not good for him."

"Then you shud till im."

"Well, I'll do my best. He's older than me."

"Cingretulations on yure birth," she told me, giving me the pannikin. "I mean, yure being sun of Challs Deckens."

Who was I to argue with her? "Thank you," I replied, "though

I had no hand in it myself, Mrs. Chard." But as always people thought it had taken a certain cleverness on my part.

She told me confidentially, "Due whot you kin with the gennelmen. Poo-err Chard wull git very seck."

My brother was in fact so far gone in liquor that we had no further sensible conversation that night. While we were having a brief chat with Cultay, Mrs. Geraghty sent a message telling us that dinner was ready. Alfred let me help him to the table where we sat in shirtsleeves while Mrs. Geraghty served us soup with pearl barley and glazed mutton with excellent vegetables, both of which dishes were inspired, if she could be believed, by our mother's recipes. I would have liked to discuss our mother being such a phenomenon in Mrs. Geraghty's life and craft with Alfred, but I felt he was beyond that conversation. I also suspected that in his state the mention of our mother might lead us to discuss the guvnor's behavior towards her, a subject likely to make us melancholy at Christmas, especially in view that I was melancholy enough. With any luck Alfred might not drink so much tomorrow.

After Mrs. Geraghty had delivered us that main meal, Alfred asked me what I thought of her. I said I thought she was a kindly woman, and it was apparent she was an excellent cook, adding, "And she does marvelously with those quandongs."

Alfred got the giggles and repeated what I'd said. "She does marvelously with quandongs."

"She *is* an excellent cook," I replied, both because it was true and I hoped it would end his mockery.

Alfred lowered his voice. "If she'd only stop wearing her bloody boots like that." He then looked at his meal as if he was having trouble applying his knife and fork to it.

I was silent, not knowing what to say to him.

"Mrs. Geraghty is older than me," he added. "But of a fine figure, you'd admit. Juno would not sneer at her."

"Do you think you—?"

He stopped me, raising a hand that wavered in the air. "I speak as a detached observer," he claimed, then nearly fell asleep before reviving himself. "I do not have her stay in the house. That is the trick to avoid matrimony. We may think this is a huge country we're in, and what we do is not reported. But gossip makes a mockery of even the largest spaces, Plorn. If you have a woman stay in the homestead it's taken by the gossips of the entire region that the relationship is either one of concubinage or marriage. Besides, she spends much of her time looking after the ailing station wagoner named Clohessy, who's an old convict she knows from her days in Van Diemen's Land." He inhaled and breathed awhile, again seeming about to fall asleep. But he revived himself. "And under the mass of public opinion, a chap has to choose between being known as a husband or else a sensualist. That's what happened with my poor friend Chard. Have you heard his wife and her torturous speech? When he was managing a station, he made the mistake of having her reside in the homestead. And now she's his forever. A caution, my boy. A caution."

After this he did fall properly to sleep and, calling for Mrs. Geraghty to guide us, I helped him to his room, removed his boots, and put him on his bed.

Mrs. Geraghty whispered to me, "Your brother has great tolerance of the demon liquor. He'll come up bright for Christmas."

I felt my loneliness that night and thought of Cultay's lovely gum but did not take it. I wished I was back home in Momba.

22

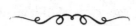

As Mrs. Geraghty had promised, Alfred was up the next morning and shook my hand solemnly as he wished me the blessings of the season. His gift to me was Mr. Wilkie Collins's novel *The Moonstone*.

I was relieved he wasn't giving me the book in any expectation that I would read it instantly. "Just the same," he said, with a smile, "I thought it was lively enough to make a literary gent of you." He smiled. "One other thing. Chard went to a lot of trouble to track a copy down, so I'd be obliged if you thanked him for his trouble if the chance arises."

I assured him I would. The book made me think back to how old joking Mr. Collins was always asking Aunt Georgie to run away with him, and she always replied no because he would leave her alone at home to go jaunting with Mr. Dickens.

Mrs. Geraghty brought in fresh bread she'd baked, with boiled eggs and bacon and the eternal black tea. She then wished us the joy of the feast day, and we wished the same back, Alfred asking, "Will you take your Christmas dinner with fortunate Mr. Clohessy today?"

"With him and young Mr. Levine," she confirmed.

When she'd gone Alfred told me Mrs. Geraghty went to Mr. Clohessy's hut to recite the Papist rite called the Rosary and they prayed together on the veranda in full sight of others.

"It's quite something to see a bullocky pray," he said, "for a bullock team on a muddy trail would make a profaner out of any saint, as you no doubt know by now. Clohessy did his time and got a conditional pardon. Just like that Abel Magwitch in the guvnor's book. The condition in the pardon being they can't ever go back to the British Isles."

We both laughed at the concept of our transportation.

"You think we'll get a conditional pardon one day, old chap?" he added. He laughed again, but with no rancor.

"We had a boundary rider hang himself rather than go back to England," I told him.

"Yes. I heard. Very strange, wouldn't you say? Something profound there. I mean to say, families are strange entities, but not to be able ever to face your own again . . ."

"And they were going to make him the new baronet."

"Well, even so . . ." And again he laughed. He seemed to have no pain from the night before, though he did drink a great deal of tea.

After breakfast I gave him a new briar pipe and a kangaroo-skin tobacco pouch, and we thought we'd done each other and the festival very well. Then, from nowhere, we heard someone with a fine voice begin singing outside, who Alfred said was a young Englishman who'd helped with the bonfire the night before. We went to the veranda with our cups of tea and there, in the home paddock of Corona Station, the young gentleman drover stood, his large hat in his hands, by the remnants of last night's fire. In purest tenor, he pierced the morning with the piteous nostalgia of the song.

The holly and the ivy,
When they are both full grown,
Of all the trees that are in the wood,
The holly bears the crown,
Oh, the rising of the sun,

And the running of the deer.
The playing of the merry organ,
Sweet singing in the choir . . .

Suddenly he paused, mid-verse, wavered and then walked into the shade of a river gum tree and was savagely sick.

"Oh, poor chap," said Alfred, before calling out to the singing drover. "Hayward, when you're well, come up and meet my brother and have some black tea."

Though probably a year or so older than me, Hayward seemed very boyish in his discomfort as he looked up and replied, "Black tea seems to be the ticket for me, Mr. Dickens."

Alfred and I went back to the dining room and Hayward soon came in, saying, "My appetite returns."

After making sure Hayward had washed his hands, Alfred said, "I have the pleasure to introduce my brother, Plorn Dickens, true name Edward, though he has rarely been called that. Plorn, I present to you Ernest Hayward."

"A Merry Christmas," I said. "You must've been the absolute joy of your choirmaster."

"My choirmaster could never afford the indulgence of praising me," he replied. "He was my father."

"Ernie is a child of the cloth and the parsonage, Plorn."

"I was praised by pretty girls though," said Ernie. "And in the public houses around Derby I have a repute for my version of the old song 'You Ain't Ashamed o' Me, Are You, Bill?'"

"Will you give us that at the Christmas meal perhaps?" asked Alfred.

"If still living, yes. If not, I demand the full honors of the Anglican rite of burial."

"Are you an admirer of the music hall?" I asked.

He sang, as if by way of an answer, *"'Tho' some o' your rich relations are as 'orty as can be, / Don't turn away, but kiss me, and say you ain't ashamed o' me.'"*

Then he consumed an entire cupful of tea in one mouthful and poured himself another. When he was half finished that, he turned again to me and said, "Yes, I belong to that corps of music hall wastrels, Mr. Dickens." This was followed by more singing:

I suppose she don't remember all the cash I said I'd spend,
When I walked 'er off to 'Ampstead all the way,
I suppose she don't remember 'ow I used to pawn 'er watch
And promise I would take 'er to the play.

"Well," said Alfred, laughing, "I think you're a total disgrace to the diocese of Durham and the Durham School itself."

"Thank you, sir," said Ernie Hayward. "To be a disgrace to one's school is an honor reserved for a few privileged souls, but to be a disgrace to an entire British diocese—that demands the special endeavor of a person."

Alfred told him to go and rest and be back at noon, which was when the Chards were coming.

As Hayward left, Alfred summoned the young Paakantji boy and asked him to draw a hessian blind on the veranda and drench it with water to temper any hot air coming through its pores.

After that we sat in easy cane furniture in the veranda shade, Alfred smoking cigarettes and talking about the breaking in of his new briar pipe.

He said, "I hope Kate and Mamie visit Mama today."

I assured him they would or may have already been yesterday.

"Good old Katie would have seen to it, of course," he agreed with a laugh. "Lucifer Box," he chortled, using our father's name for fiery Kate. "And just as well she is a Lucifer Box, standing up to the guvnor."

"I wouldn't mind dropping in to Gad's Hill for an hour or two," I said, liking this version of my brother.

"We'd be so suntanned they wouldn't know who we were. And Pa would be outraged by our boots."

I liked him calling the guvnor "Pa" as well.

"She was 'Lucifer Box,' and Mamie was 'Mild Glo'ster.' Tells you something, eh? Ma told me once that when Katie was five years old and they were on a tour of Italy, she got an abscess on the neck and ordered Father to look after her, insisting he change all her dressings for six months. Just as well, because Mama was carrying the noble *moi* at the time. Katie was the one always saw through the guvnor, but they really loved each other . . . Changed all her dressings. Can you imagine? And she gave him hot mustard in return."

I let him go on elaborating on beautiful Kate, our mediator with the august guvnor.

"D'you remember her falling in love with Ed Yates? I think you were a baby then."

Indeed I was, if born at all. This was exactly the sort of inside knowledge I could receive from my seven-years-older brother— what all my brothers and sisters did, indeed what other people did, before they had a Plorn in their lives.

"Ed Yates was one of Father's young friends. Stuck with the guvnor through a lot of thick and a deal of thin. Our beautiful Katie, she would stand there twisting a hand around a balustrade or a column or anything that presented, looking enchanted with Yates. He pretended not to notice, but Katie nearly wore the varnish off furniture, longing for him. And he was already married then, to Miss Wilkinson—but Katie saw only him, Adonis, and to hell with the wife."

I did remember seeing the guvnor weeping and exclaiming over Katie's wedding dress when she eventually married Charlie Collins. A nice man, who everyone said had a strange penitential streak,

Charlie was nothing like his brother Wilkie. And nothing like Katie for that matter.

"Did you know Charlie Collins has been ill the last year or so?" I asked.

"He always was ill," said Alfred, as if that was somehow an endearing trait.

"Well, Katie got very thin and worn down from nursing him, and then she got sick and demanded the guvnor's presence just like you say she did when she was little, and the guvnor sat with her through the whole fever."

"Poor Katie," Alfred murmured. "I doubt Charlie Collins ever fulfilled the role of husband for her—you understand what I mean, Plorn?"

I didn't know whether to nod knowingly or blush. It was easy to believe Katie hadn't seen the features of gratified desire in the case of Charlie Collins. On top of everything else, they were poor, because he took so long to make paintings, so these days he'd taken to writing pieces in *All the Year Round*.

"Did you see much of Katie's painting before you left?" Alfred asked.

"I did. She does children a lot. The guvnor says if only she were a man she might be raised to the Academy one day. He says she has to be bolder, and that her husband isn't a good example to her, leaving most of his paintings unfinished and despising the ones he does finish."

"But what do you think of her paintings yourself, Plorn? Not Father. Yourself."

"They look splendid to me," I said. "I don't know how she does it. Drawing is beyond me, let alone oils."

"And of course no sign of a child? A little Dickens-Collins prodigy?"

"I . . . I don't think so."

Alfred nodded grimly but not as if it was anyone's fault.

The rest of the morning passed pleasantly with discussion of family members, and gossip that did not wound, to the extent that I totally forgot it was Christmas, here or anywhere else. Alfred drank nothing hard—all we had was tea as the hessian dried out and the conversation parched us.

At around noon Alfred announced we should go and shave and put suits on. As I shaved I considered whether it was a good idea not to have told Alfred about overhearing Aunt Georgie talking to our sister Mamie about something to do with Katie, I suspected, and another painter called Prinsep. They were speaking in that voice women adopt when they're certain they're saying something no child can overhear. They'd agreed Prinsep was "very manly" and a doer of things, who finished paintings, no fuss, no excuses.

Mamie had said, "How can you blame her? A virgin for ten years of marriage." To which Aunt Georgie had replied, "Well, Mr. Prinsep may have seen to that problem."

Later that day, I entered the dining room, where Alfred was serving sherry and whisky. Hayward was there wearing a riding suit of splendid cut of a similar style to my own suit of brown checks brought from London. When Mrs. and Mr. Tom Chard arrived, Hayward was attentive to them in a very gentlemanly way and made no sport of Mrs. Chard's astounding accent.

Chard looked fresher than he had yesterday and shook my hand with new enthusiasm, saying he was sure I was more of a gentleman than my brother, for no gentleman liked to see another man reduced to insensibility and raving. "And my poor wife had to put up with me and find some surface on which I could sleep off my beastliness."

"I believe I owe you thanks for the work you did on tracking down *The Moonstone*," I said. "The author is a jolly friend of our father."

"I've heard that," said Chard almost as if he didn't believe it. "I must keep reminding myself that you passed your infancy by the light of planets and potentates and grandeurs beyond our ordinary imagining."

Inspiration struck me and I said, "But my dear Chard, they did not speak to me as planets and potentates and grandeurs. They spoke to me as men speak to a child asking me what my favorite toy was, and whether I knew the alphabet. You must not overstate our experience when we were younger."

"Well put, well put," said the storekeeper, nodding his head, and looking suddenly very much like what he was—an Englishman far removed from his home, and somewhat lost.

I could hear Mrs. Chard speaking to my brother in the background. "Pu-er Mester Chard, he wuzz thut suck lest naight, Mester Deckins. Et wuz too badd alttugutha of yue!"

"I am chastened, dear lady," Alfred told her with apparent earnestness. "I will myself tell Mr. Chard to reject my future offers of hospitality, and for your sake I shall not press . . ."

"Yezzir, dun't you priss 'im anymower, Mester Deckens."

Chard lowered his voice now. "My darling there," he said, nodding at his wife. "She is a pearl. And the wonderful thing in the colonies, you can marry anyone who takes your heart. Juries of aunts and uncles don't have to sit on the girl and test her suitability. And so I have my love, no matter what anyone thinks. Oh . . ."

Almost in a whisper he added, "She has this voice modulation which is a little strange, but that is for my sake. She feels I've married badly and would love to pass as a stage Englishwoman . . ."

"Oh," I said, enlightened, "that's what it is."

"Yes, that is what she is attempting. It is altogether poignant, isn't it? But it will pass." He paused and coughed. "I wished to tell you actually, Dickens, your brother has done great things here. We have peace. It is hard to believe that only two years past, Gow, the manager before him, had to fight off the Cooper's Creek darks. Even the local Paakantji fear them. Gow and four of his men shut themselves up in my store, hammered up great bulwarks of hardwood, and turned it into a fortress. A dawn attack took place, like it would in an American novel. But with some help from the Messr. Bonney, Alfred changed all that because he refused to live as if he were under siege. There are some Cooper's Creek men back here now, and I believe Alfred means to visit them tomorrow."

"Are you praising my supposed statesmanship?" called Alfred.

"Indeed I am, Alfred," Chard replied.

"That's an old song," said Alfred, before going back to talking to Mrs. Chard.

Chard whispered to me, "Remember your brother's wisdom when you get a place of your own, Mr. Plorn. Let the darks take a few sheep. If they have permission, they'll take fewer. Punishing every infringement will merely make them bitter and they will secretly kill many more. In Gow's day, the Cooper's Creek darks retreated over paddocks in which they left hundreds if not thousands of dead sheep."

Alfred was clapping his hands now to alert us to the onset of the Christmas feast, announcing, "Lady and gentlemen, Mrs. Geraghty would like a word with us."

Mrs. Geraghty appeared behind him in a white dress and large boots, with a handsome slick of sweat on her cheeks, and said, "For your Christmas meal, Mrs. Chard and gentlemen, I have prepared everything from recipes supplied by Mr. Alfred and Mr. Edward Dickens's mother in her famous cookbook, doing my best with Australian conditions."

"Splendid conditions they are!" cried Alfred.

"So," continued Mrs. Geraghty, "I will start you off with Mrs. Dickens's menu for six to seven people, it being more promising for our purposes. We begin with Murray cod freshly extracted from the Darling River itself."

"Or a mud hole thereof," my brother interjected irreverently.

"This will be accompanied by my dry-land version of oyster sauce."

"Very dry perhaps," said Alfred, enjoying himself.

Mrs. Geraghty did not pay attention to him, saying, "This will be followed by roast loin of mutton and boiled fowls with bacon, accompanied by colcannon, minced collops, spinach, and mashed and brown potatoes."

"Boiled fowls, Mrs. Geraghty," Hayward interjected. "Are these fowl, or brush turkey impersonating fowl? I simply asked for the elucidation of the entire party."

"When I serve brush turkey I never pass it off as fowl," said Mrs. Geraghty. "I have never done it in your experience, have I, Mr. Hayward?"

"I do not believe you have, admirable Mrs. Geraghty."

"So I would be grateful if you asked only the questions that needed asking," she said, to which Hayward imitated a man impaled. There were cries around the table, even from Mrs. Chard, along the lines that Mrs. Geraghty had got him between the eyes and it served him right.

"For your dessert," Mrs. Geraghty continued, "there is the normal pudding of the season with a brandy sauce, and cabinet pudding made from our lemon trees, accompanied by cream from our few dairy cows. I will leave you now with wishes for a happy Christmas and a reminder that I have tried to give the Messrs. Dickens a memory of their childhoods, and to introduce the rest of you to that memory. May God bless us all."

"Thank you, Mrs. Geraghty. Don't forget to take that Christmas bottle of rum to Clohessy's with you. You mightn't miss it, but I can tell you Clohessy can't say the Rosary without it."

At table we drank the white wine with the fowl and fish, and the red with the beef. The cod was wonderful, and as we broached the fowl and beef we paid further compliments both to Mrs. Geraghty and to her prophet, Mrs. Catherine Dickens. This induced a sadness in me as I was reminded that today my mother would miss the lively Christmases Father could still produce at Gad's Hill, with presents, games, charades, and plays.

Shaking off my sudden melancholy and grateful for the company, I said, "We have here at table five people of whom only one is colonial born. I think we would all love to hear any details of your story that you are willing to share with us, Mrs. Chard."

"Oh yue doen wanta hear abite me, Mester Deckens."

There were cries from all of us that we wanted to. And so she began the story in her strained accent, telling us she was only colonial born because her mother was delivered of her on the shores of Holdfast Bay three days after landing in South Australia. Her parents lived in a cabin on the Isle of Skye, but the kelp trade had given out so they took advantage of the colony's offer to pay the passages of sturdy Highlanders and islanders. After their arrival in Adelaide on a wagon, her people had traveled northeast along the Murray River, and then to Menindee in New South Wales where she'd grown up and where Chard had first seen and recruited her as a maid or housekeeper.

"And I was struck by her totally and at once," said Chard.

I did envy him at such a time as this, wondering when I would be struck totally and at once, and rendered incapable of worrying whether she was Imperial Sterling or Colonial Currency; nor how her opinions lay. When would I find all someone's frailties enchanting, as Chard had found his wife's? He had been very determined to identify as lovable quirks what others might regard as outrageous eccentricities. But that was his good luck, and the triumph of his generous heart over the more limited views.

"What was Lola Montez doing at the Royal Theatre in Menindee when you were ten, Mrs. Chard?" Alfred said, as a tease.

"Oh, Mester Deckens, yue know there weren't enny opera in Minindee."

"I thought Lola Montez was in love with the pub owner there," said Alfred, winking at the rest of us.

"Oh, Mester Deckens, yue are thet wucked!" cried Mrs. Chard. "My fether drove boolock teams, a humble Scot but greatly acquinted with the Scruptures, bitter then menny a Prisbytarian pastor!"

"But isn't it true he was a notable Caledonian highwayman?" asked Hayward.

"Mester Hayward," she cried. "Mye yor fibs choke your goud and trulley! Nun uv the Scots were cremenels. None! It is hour boust! The Englush and Irush are the cremenels."

And so she went on, galloping through thickets of diphthongs, searching—I was sure—for the sound that would not disgrace her husband, and failing at every turn.

෴

By half past two we were all in a merry condition, and Mrs. Chard was beginning to slip into her true colonial accent. "Orright, Chard. No more trouble from you, Sonny Jim!"

Mrs. Geraghty came back to serve the pudding, receiving quite a respectable volume of amazement and acclaim from the company of just five. Rosy with wine, I looked forward to my Momba prospects and found for the first time in my conscious life that the prospect of the coming year held no terrors. I knew what to expect from the curriculum of sheep, as I never had from the school curriculum. As if to crown that awareness, Hayward was prevailed upon to sing a music hall song called "Our Lodger's Such a Nice Man" and then, egged on by a tide of applause, "The Lay of the Very Last Minstrel."

The pudding was long eaten and the light was at last declining when the homestead clock announced it was five o'clock. The

Chards were suddenly on their way out, with Hayward calling mischievously, "This time next year there might be three Chards."

Not long after, the couple came back to the homestead with Alfred to fetch his tobacco. Finding myself alone on the veranda with Mrs. Chard, I felt a general goodwill, and not least to this lady. I foolishly said, "Mrs. Chard, you don't need to try with pronunciations. He is enchanted by you and would be happy however you spoke."

She astounded me by leaning across and kissing me. "You're a lovely boy," she told me in an unstrained Australian accent. "But, see, I'm just keeping him interested with all the pronunciation stuff. Our secret. Orright, Sonny Jim?"

"Indeed," I told her, consumed with admiration.

Soon after, her husband and my brother returned, and Alfred and I saw the Chards out into the still heat of the late afternoon.

"Why are you smiling?" Alfred asked me.

"They are an amusing pair," I told him.

"Yes," he said, "poor old Chard."

That would always be his version of events.

23

Later that night, on the veranda, with Alfred drinking brandy and smoking his pipe, we lazily discussed our brother Sydney at sea aboard some ship of battle, before moving on to others of our family. Talking about Frank, the young inspector in Bengal, we wondered what brigands he might be pursuing. Then we discussed the sisters, and Charley's work with the guvnor, and how Henry would be down from Cambridge for the holiday. We also remembered our deceased brother, Walter, dead of a paroxysm in the military officers' hospital in Calcutta while talking about going home.

But in the turn of a second, some unhappiness started to emerge in Alfred. It began casually, with his remarking, "Mother had a day of glory at Corona with Mrs. Geraghty's cooking, eh?"

"Yes. We must write and tell her," I said.

"She'd be gratified, yes. She's been transported like her sons. Have you ever thought about Father transporting people to Australia in his novels?"

"Does he send many?" I asked, hoping that in discussing numbers we would not go deeply into the question.

"Look, if he wants to get rid of someone in his books, he either kills them or sends them to Australia."

"I wasn't aware of that," I said, devoutly wishing yet again I'd read more of the guvnor's works so I could put up a defense. "But it's only his imagination, isn't it?"

"He sends quite a few people to Australia in *David Copperfield*, you know. Hopeless Mr. Micawber and Little Em'ly, who has lost her virtue. And all her relatives, her uncle Peggotty and so on, to keep her company. It seems fallen women un-fall themselves when they get to Australia. That's what Pa seems to believe anyhow."

"Well, it is a fresh start, isn't it? Look at us!"

"Ah," he murmured. "Exactly. Would you like some brandy, Plorn?"

"Tipsy enough on wine from lunch, thank you, Alfred."

Alfred poured himself more.

"It's not his sending Micawber to Australia—you really must read that damned book, Plorn! It's another thing. There's a place in the book where David is married to his beloved Dora, close to the silliest woman Pa could invent, and he thinks he's happy about that, and doing well enough to employ a page boy. So he does, and this boy-child is the sort of person who wipes his nose regularly with the tip of his handkerchief, after which he folds the handkerchief neatly for its next use. And any hint his services might be dispensed with fills him with terrible grief, which upsets David and Dora and makes them feel bound to him. And wouldn't you know—and how *convenient*, as a number of the guvnor's characters often pronounce that word— that the boy has been thieving food and valuables and clothes all the time. And how does the guvnor get rid of him? Why, he's arrested and transported to Australia. You see, death or Australia, that's the equation, Plorn. And he's already got death in childbirth awaiting Dora—has to get rid of her so that David can marry his real love, Agnes. Where would our father's plots be, I ask, without death and Australia? The pit at the end of the world you toss useless folk in."

I tried to interject to ask him about Corona, but he was speaking heatedly now, and at a pace that brooked no interruption.

"Do you think then, Plorn, that you and I are that clumsy boy with the corner of the handkerchief? Do you think that for the guvnor Australia was the sentence short of death?"

"Do you actually hate Father?" I asked, tired of this line he was pursuing.

"Don't be fractious with me, Plorn. I'm not saying that. The guvnor's a god, anyway. There's no future in hating gods. But did you choose being here by yourself? Or were you driven in this direction?"

"Well, I was happy at home. And am happy to be here as well. I wasn't *driven*."

Though it had never occurred to me before, for a second I wondered if I had been because there was such certitude about it in Alfred's eyes.

"I chose to come," said Alfred. "I'd had my failures at trying other things. But my being here . . . the guvnor used that as a reason to drive you here. Unlike the rest of us, you weren't tried at other things. You were sent straight here after school. And even your schooling was truncated."

"But I'm happy here, Alfie," I asserted, or perhaps pleaded.

"Did you ever hear of Urania Cottage when you were younger?" he asked.

I had, in fact. It was a place for disreputable young women; somewhere my sisters and Aunt Georgie and Mama thought was good and brave for my father to attend to, but not good enough to be talked about in full voice in front of me.

Alfred shivered suddenly with the effect of the brandy. "Do you know Urania is some sort of goddess of astrology, but it seems she is also the polite version of Aphrodite. Aphrodite in a bloody mission dress."

I felt that he was somehow intent on undermining the guvnor now. And that in the process his use of unaccustomed language and colonial bluntness was meant to jolt me, since he knew I would support the guvnor's honor.

"I knew it was a place for young women and that Miss Coutts was somehow in it," I said.

"They were in it together. Miss Coutts put up the money and bought the house in Shepherd's Bush, and Father put up his well-known imagination. Miss Coutts was such a bluestocking, such a pious, dry old tart, though Mama never minded her."

"I liked Miss Coutts," I said, as if to warn him. Mama had told me once that Miss Coutts was an example of the humble being exalted. I'd kept the table at Momba enthralled one night with the fairytale-like story of Miss Coutts, though I hadn't mentioned anything to do with Urania Cottage.

Mama had told me the story like this: a little girl, the youngest of six children, grew up in a house where her father (the radical member of Parliament Sir Francis Burdett) was wise and loved her greatly. Soldiers shot people dead (the Peterloo Massacre), and the father told all the world that those who shot innocent people dead must be punished. And for saying that, he was put in prison! Here we were then, with the necessary components—a princess, a seer, and a dungeon.

The princess (Miss Coutts) vowed that if God would let her father free, she would always be a just woman. One day she saw him brought back, and walking to her door as a hero, cheered by ordinary people who knew he was their friend. Later, when her wealthy grandfather died, his wife received his cave of treasures. But then, while the princess was still little more than a girl, this wife also died. The wife's lawyer gathered the family together to tell them what the second wife had decided should happen with the cave of treasures. It emerged from the lawyer that the woman who'd recently died had noticed how loyal the princess had been to her father and had decided that she could have the cave (as long as the princess did not marry a foreigner, though that was an item that did not quite fit the story). So now there was only one woman in the kingdom richer than the princess, and that was the Queen.

And to help her, the princess called on the greatest wizard in the land (the guvnor) to ask him about some of the things he would advise her to do with her treasure. And the wizard said, give some of the treasure to the ragged schools that teach the children of the very poor, and make the schoolrooms bigger, and build a bathhouse where the ragged children can wash themselves. And next the wizard advised her to do something for unfortunate girls, having spoken to a wise woman (Mrs. Chisholm) who had told him that the outer kingdoms in Australia and Canada were such blessed places that an unfortunate girl could remake herself there after she was prepared and reformed in a London house.

That was how the princess and the wizard came up with Urania Cottage, which Alfred was now bringing up to buttress his argument.

"The idea of Urania Cottage," said Alfred, "was to be a house of reform for poor women, even prostitutes. It used a points system for good behavior, and when one of the girls had scored enough points, what do you think the reward was?"

"I know that they were sent away with a sum of money to start a new life."

"And where were they sent?"

"To Canada. And here. Australia."

"And so why, Plorn, were they sent to Australia?"

"You know why, Alfred. To remake themselves."

"There you are, my boy. There you are," he said, beginning to blink, with tears appearing on his lashes.

It was foolish of me, but I could not help asking, "What are you trying to make of that, Alfred? Are you really trying to tell me—"

"Apart from Henry, who is such a clever chap, the guvnor sent

Walter to India, Frank to Canada, and us here because he saw us all as unfortunate boys, in the same way he saw the girls of Urania Cottage as unfortunate girls. What else am I to think? The issue has nothing to do with the fact of flourishing here, as we clearly have. The issue is that he weighed us as he weighed the lost girls, and found us wanting, and in need of a new heaven and a new earth."

"You make it sound as if he abandoned us, as if he threw us into a pit. But he wrote letters ahead and he made inquiries about Melbourne and the bush. He did it carefully and for our own good."

"As he did for the tarts," Alfred drunkenly insisted.

"It's Christmas," I protested, "and you sit there full of brandy and judge Father in that way. I hate it, Alfred. I'm going to bed."

Alfred blinked at me with those watery eyes. "Don't do that. Don't cut me off, Plorn, there's the boy!"

"Then don't insult Father."

"For heaven's sake, who else can I sit and reflect on him with? Besides, Plorn, do you really understand love? All love in the world is the love of imperfect people. Imperfect children love imperfect parents. It's easy to love someone who's never put a foot wrong. And you want me to believe the guvnor, despite his gifts and difference from all us other humans, never put a foot wrong? That is delusion, not love, Plorn. To *know* . . . and then to love anyhow . . . that's the trick!"

I was still in a fury and wondered later whether I was distressed because the way he spoke about our father might distract me from applying myself—for the guvnor's sake—on Momba. "Yes, but the trick isn't to slur everything the guvnor's ever done for us. And for others, whoever they are. That stuff with Urania Cottage . . . that's the work of a good man!"

"Oh, Plorn, he's just a man. Only to everyone else is he God bloody Almighty! Look, when he was starting his magazine he went and saw that Chisholm lady, the famous one who shipped boatloads of ragged young girls here from England and from the Irish bogs. First issue of his magazine, of *Household Words*, there are five . . . yes, five . . . articles on how Australia is heaven for the lower orders."

"Perhaps I ought to begin with the magazines and then get on to the books," I suggested, to distract him. Even the text of magazines seemed as dense as jungles to me.

"Listen to me," he advised. "Pa doesn't need you to read his books, so don't think not reading them is an insult to him. It's just that it's handy to read them because every bastard in the colonies seems to have done so. And to want a discussion, you understand."

But it mattered more to me than that, and neglecting his works still felt like an insult to the guvnor, so that redressing it went along with applying myself on Momba.

"Anyhow," continued Alfred, "the guvnor parodied this Chisholm woman in *Bleak House*, calling her Mrs. Jellyby, and though he gives her a great cause, she also has a slovenly home, uncared-for children, and a beaten-down husband. He didn't even like her, you see, but he *believed* her. The problem was she implanted this bug about Australia in his damned ear and it wormed its way into his brain. And who's better in the end? Mrs. Jellyby, who doesn't notice when her little'un gets his head stuck in the railings on the landing. Or the guvnor, who sent them to India and Canada and here?"

I wanted to stop him. I cried out, "I'm here by my choice."

"No, you're not. You're here at parental direction."

"Of my own choice!" I yelled, furious that Alfred was embroiling me in childhood again, and so in failure.

Thank God he said nothing, and the resultant silence stretched. We had reached an impasse and perhaps an end, though I still itched to say more. I had felt I'd somehow got into wool as Henry had got into the law at Cambridge, its own strange outstation of England, and that we were both now equally successful sons, Henry, Alfred, me. Alfred refused to believe it, as it seemed I needed to if I was to go on breathing.

"I must go," I told him, rising, and feeling soured wine in my gorge.

He said, "I want the same thing as you, Plorn. I want to understand."

"But you look at the bad. Never the good."

He belched briefly and contemplated this accusation with bleak eyes, then said, "The whole damn world utters the good for him. Ten years ago, ten years, he pitched Mama out of the house! And he told us we were not to trust Mama's family except for Aunt Georgina. That's what I can't forget, my Little Brother. And yet still his authority is absolute."

"Not to everyone," I told him, remembering McGaw. "Some ask questions."

"So few," he sniffed. "So few."

"Not many good ones either. I must go. I'm feeling sick."

"Go then, Little Brother. For Christ's sake, go!"

He continued to look fixedly before him.

"You'll be all right?" I asked, suddenly full of brotherly sentiment.

"As ever," he said. "But let me tell you, without you to raise these matters with, I think I would go mad. When do you start out for Momba again?"

"Morning after next."

He held out an arm towards me, the gesture nearly unseating him. "No one I can say these things to, these things that I feel must be said. Except for you. And you're two or three damned days' ride away!"

I called good night.

"We have an excursion tomorrow, out along the creek," he promised me. "You'll enjoy it. We'll take your man Cultay with us."

I went back to my room and locked myself away, feeling the weight of his propositions. I thought I had applied myself, but according to Alfred I'd applied myself in the realm of the fallen, where it meant nothing. I was unable to lie on my bed, unable to do anything, and in the midst of my furious tide of indecision, I thought that Mrs. Geraghty's quandong tart might rouse me or be the final joy before my moral extinction. Quandong tart.

I made my way to the kitchen in my shirtsleeves. It was still hot in there from the endeavor to reproduce my mother's recipes. I found the wonderful tart beneath a wire canopy and began to shove handfuls of it into my mouth. Then, hearing a noise behind me, I turned and beheld Mrs. Geraghty, wearing a white nightgown which encompassed her from the neck to below her knees, beneath which her large white feet stood on the beaten earth floor.

"Mr. Dickens," she said in bemusement.

I was not in a position to explain myself. If I'd been eating her quandong tart like an adult, I could plead late-night hunger. But I had been eating like a greedy child, and she had caught me.

She came over, took my elbow, and said, "Sit, Mr. Dickens."

I obeyed her, still swallowing the last of what I'd shoveled into my mouth. "No," I protested. "No! I . . ."

She said as if it were a secret, "I heard your brother arguing with you."

"Well, brothers do quarrel," I replied tersely. Then, to my shame, I began crying.

Mrs. Geraghty pulled me against her body, and I felt her abundant life beyond that one layer of cloth. She said, "You poor little fellow, what are you doing here?"

"I am splendid," I said, unable to cease weeping. "I am applying myself. I am making my way."

"As is Mr. Alfred," she replied.

"I wish he would not drink," I said, feeling a great relief to be weeping into her breast, too distressed with Alfred to think of Maurice's advice on all this.

"You argue about your father, I think. You certainly don't argue about your mother."

"Yes. My guvnor's the complicated one."

"Very well," she said, releasing me.

I lunged at her as if I could not bear to be separated.

"Please, Mr. Dickens, it is not proper," she said.

And with a great reluctance, I let her go.

"Ah," she said, "it is a matter of wonder to me that whoever we are, we are all the one lost baby. I would dearly like to sit by you until you were asleep, Mr. Dickens. But there would be gossip, deadly gossip. Please, sit down, and I shall cut you a slice of the tart."

Like a child I did sit and waited for that measured slice, that polite ratio, which was all I was entitled to.

24

Through all this, Cultay kept his own festival, if for him it was one, with his relatives. But on Boxing Day, Alfred and I set out with Cultay and Alfred's native escort, who was also Paakantji. Alfred had woken with an astonishingly clear head, and I felt aggrieved with him for his treacherous night binges and morning serenities.

After passing Corona's handsome stone woolshed we followed the creek northwest. It was very different country from Momba, fewer hardwood trees, more quartzite rock. We were on our way to meet a chap Alfred described as an exceptional fellow, a man named Sparrow, who was a boundary rider in a paddock two to three hours' ride up the creek, in the direction of the South Australian border.

I felt that, between them, Soldier Staples and poor Dandy had exhausted my interest in hutkeeping boundary riders, and as we rose up the ridge to the north of the station homestead, I clung sullenly to that proposition. Oh, if I could just sit at Chard's store and listen to Mrs. Chard mangle the English language, what a happy young Briton I would be!

I asked Alfred why Hayward was not with us for this holiday excursion, and he explained that Hayward was not yet presentable after the festive carousels. However, he would meet us at dinner that night and had promised to perform one of the guvnor's favorites,

"The Dogs' Meat Man," with which the guvnor himself had entertained guests at Gad's Hill.

My thoughts turned to the previous evening and the outrage I'd tried to commit on Mrs. Geraghty. Could I ever forget it, or ever face a quandong without being reproached by it? And yet the rhythm of horseback, the canter, the careful rein-work on the descent on the far side of the ridge soothed me for the present, and the terrain and my Waler's passage over it absorbed me, and half convinced me towards contentment.

Corona had an undulating succession of these ridges and gullies. Finally, beyond one of them, by a creek delineated by river gums, we saw Sparrow's hut, which had a horse saddled by the door. A jaunty little fellow emerged flanked by two sheepdogs. He was carrying a rifle and wearing a striped shirt, newly shaven behind his whiskers, his hair combed.

We descended to his house and as we got abreast of it Alfred got down from his horse and called to Cultay, "You will talk to your brethren, sir, will you?"

As I dismounted, Cultay and the other dark rode a little further to confer with some natives I now saw, who were camped amongst trees along the creek.

"These are the Cooper's Creek blacks?" I asked, remembering what Chard had told me.

"Yes. Bonney's sent me Cultay to deal with them. Cultay is a powerful man and a magus, and the blacks over here have been waiting for him."

"Cultay is a powerful man and a magus," Alfred told me, "and I need him to talk to some traveling blacks who are camped out there."

"Gentlemen," called Sparrow cheerfully, stepping up. He did not seem to have any of the reclusiveness, the air of the hermit, which had marked Staples and Dandy.

Sparrow shook Alfred's hand and greeted him with a slight frown, then greeted me in the same manner. I thought he might mention the ocher-seeking travelers along the creek, but instead he said, "You picked a furnace day to come riding, Mr. Dickens."

Alfred said, "You are my most remarkable boundary rider, Sparrow, and I could hardly let my brother go back to Momba without meeting you. Did the darks trouble you last night?"

"I slept soundly, Mr. Dickens. Depended on my dogs to warn me, and I had the horse saddled. The darks don't concern me."

"Sturdy man. I half thought I'd come yesterday but the note you sent seemed so admirably calm . . ."

"Yes," said Sparrow. "They're just staying here a long time, that's all. It might be the heat."

"Cultay will read them the terms," Alfred said blithely. "He is the pacifier and has kept the Bonneys free of any attack all these years!"

Fred Bonney had told me that Cultay was adept at the use of the *yountoo* and *moolee*, the items of potent vengeance which in hands less wise than his might be used recklessly. Fred, as close to a member of the tribe as you could get and still be white, explained that the *yountoo* was a small bone taken from the leg of the corpse of a friend, a fellow clansman. It was then wrapped up in a small piece of dried flesh cut from the thigh of another deceased but friendly body—friendly at least to a man of power like Cultay—before or after burial and dried in the sun. The string for the package was made of the hair of yet another deceased friend. The *yountoo* was taken to the place where a lawbreaker was sleeping, warmed in the ashes of his fire, pointed at him, and then a small flake of bone was thrown at his body, the subject remaining unconscious through the whole procedure. As the lawbreaker came to sicken, he would no doubt call on his own doctor to try to suck the killing flake of bone out of him. His survival became a contest between curse and cure.

The *moolee* was a rough piece of white quartz two inches long, with a length of possum hair, which was dipped in human fat from a further dead clansman, pointed at the victim, and then left to warm in or by fire. As it blazed, so did the curse within the victim. Cultay was the high priest of both of these rituals, ponderous with symbols and significance, and in that country, amongst native stockmen, his rites somehow seemed as authoritative as the rites in the Book of Common Prayer.

"I have brought you some cheer, Sparrow," said Alfred, producing a bottle of rum from his packsaddle and waving it in the torrid air.

"I hadn't realized it was actually Christmas yesterday," said Sparrow.

"By the common agreement of the Anglican Church and Western Christendom," Alfred told him as I watched Cultay and his kinsman moving amongst the visiting Cooper's Creek natives along the creek.

"I didn't think it was till the day after tomorrow," Sparrow told us with a short laugh. "Just shows a man! You must come inside. I've got wet hessian on the door. We'll drink your gift, Mr. Dickens."

Worried now, I followed them in; it was a little cooler in the half darkness. We sat down at a small table covered with newspaper items pasted in place, exactly the same as the one in the hut Staples and Dandy had occupied.

Sparrow fetched pannikins for the rum, but I asked if I could have tea instead, which he made for me outside on the fire, bringing me back a jet-black brew. Then he served himself and Alfred rum. I felt an admiration for Alfred's capability with liquor, and his air of command. So we all drank, and Alfred reached out and took Sparrow by the wrist, saying, "Do your tricks for my brother, if you'd be so kind."

Sparrow showed an amount of reluctance, arguing that his unstated skills were not of much merit and that he was in any case rusty at them.

"No, no," Alfred insisted. "I won't abide that. I'll start off. Let's see. Here's one! How many rivers are there in Scotland?"

"More than in this damned Western Division of New South Wales, I'll tell you that."

"Yes, yes. But how many are there?"

"How do you know I am right if I tell you how many rivers there are in Scotland?" asked Sparrow, letting the rum reside in his upper throat and choke him a little.

"You insult your own honesty, Sparrow. Besides, Plorn knows the answer." Alfred winked at me.

"Very well," he said casually. "Do you mean rivers or waters?"

"Let's keep it to official rivers."

"In that case it's two hundred and nineteen bodies of water named as rivers in Scotland *and* the isles. This would include rivers of the same base name but normally divided by the annotation North and South, as in North Esk River and South Esk River."

Again a wink to me from Alfred. "Tell me, Brother Plorn, is that correct?"

"It sounds credible to me," I admitted, deciding to join the game. "Though I thought it was only two hundred and eight."

"Well done, Mr. Sparrow," cried Alfred. "And please confirm to my amazed brother that you used to do this for a living at the Alhambra and Britannia theaters in London. Now tell me, Omniscient Wizard, how many feet is the length of the gun deck on the HMS *Victory*?"

"One hundred and eighty-six, sir. As paced by myself as a boy."

"And while we're at it, with sail fully set, how many square yards was the canvas the *Victory* could carry?"

"Why, sir," said Sparrow in a suddenly enlivened voice, "that is a favorite question of patriotic Britons and the answer is six thousand five hundred and ten square yards."

"Why, I do believe," said Alfred, "based on our own educations, that my brother and I concur."

"You are wise to do so when faced with the infallible Man Who Knows Everything," Sparrow cried, then held his mug of rum up, and drank it as Alfred clapped and shook his head and murmured, "The Man Who Knows Everything."

"You were on the stage?" I asked him. "The Dickenses are mad for the stage."

Alfred nodded. "I told him that. I told him. How the guvnor had a theater room in Tavistock House. And the Queen wanted to see one of his productions there. *The Frozen Deep* it was called, a title that rings pretty ironically in this place." He sounded proud now, to be the guvnor's son. "But ask him something, Plorn! Anything! They used to accuse him of having a man with a gazetteer back-stage whispering the answers to him, but there's no one here. Ask him then, for God's sake!"

"Could you tell me the height of the Crystal Palace?" I asked.

"In its original structure in Hyde Park or its present one at Sydenham Hill?"

"You see, you see," said Alfred, as if the point was already proven.

"When it was opened," I specified.

Sparrow's eyes were bright but had a certain sadness, as if he was not entirely happy to show his act or actually wished he could be less forward about it.

"Its interior height was a hundred and twenty-eight feet, and I'm willing to solicit from you a more difficult question, concerning, for example, the square yardage of glass used in its construction. No, sir? You do not bite on that? Then ask me another unrelated question."

"Tell me, if you will, the names of the builders of the new London Bridge."

"Jolliffe and Banks of Merstham in Surrey."

And so we went on for a while—Sparrow answering all manner of questions including the number of rivets in the *Great Eastern*.

Fascinated, I asked him what happened if he did not know something, for after all no man could know everything. He told me that since his childhood his father had him sitting down learning the *Penny Cyclopaedia* and the *Imperial Gazetteer of England and Wales* and had told him that if he knew enough about the major monuments of the kingdom to be right most of the time, his occasional error, even if noticed, would be forgiven. A woman worked with him—a girl called Mariella, who was eighteen years old when she began. Sometimes he would seem to be stumped by the answer and Mariella would whisper it in his ear, to the hilarity of the audience. At other times she would convey written questions from the crowd to him which he might put away for a moment, and as the crowd protested, implying that he did have someone backstage, he would groan and tell them the answer anyhow, seeming reluctant about it, and Mariella would confirm the answer by knowingly shaking her head. They were engaged and married. He respected her with a holy respect, he said, and he knew her parents, who were comedians. On Sparrow and Mariella's honeymoon, when she was just twenty-one, they were persuaded to visit India and perform. Sadly, Mariella died there of some sort of brain swelling that took her away in three or four days.

And now, in his hut in the Barrier Ranges, melancholy recurred. Finishing his pannikin of rum, he said he had no stomach for performing, "Except for your brother."

We were interrupted at this stage by a mannerly knock at the door from Cultay. Alfred and Sparrow went to meet him, and there was a muttered conversation in which I heard Cultay say, "The ocher men going tomorrow."

"And they are happy?" asked Alfred.

"They are happy."

"You're a wonder, Cultay."

But I doubt any of us had any idea how Cultay's authority had appeased the Cooper's Creek men, and by what means he'd allayed any danger from them. In midafternoon in baking heat we began the ride back to Corona where, as promised, at the end of this day of unlikely performances, Hayward charmingly sang his doggerel.

Near the old Fly Market, not a long time ago,
An old maid lived a life of woe;
She was past forty-three, and her face was tan,
When she fell in love with the dogs' meat man.

Yankee doodle, doodle dandy,
Turn right round in the bottom of the gangy,
An Injun puddin' and a pumpkin pie,
Lord! how they made the whisky fly.

I was not cheered. I found Sparrow's tale had enhanced my puzzlement and melancholy. The question of whether I could spend time with Alfred and be safe from an assault on memory and respect worried me. He wanted me to join him in pity for the two of us, to number ourselves amongst exiles, and to condemn the guvnor. And he wanted that to happen when he was least in his senses—when he was drunk. I knew in my blood I could not allow him to do it.

And yet he had given me Sparrow as a gift. Playfully, just like the guvnor. At Momba we'd had the wounded sage, Staples, and the

Lord of Stammerers. At Corona, they had the omniscient wizard. Was every boundary rider in Australia an escapee from strange and soured talent?

∽

On the ride home I daydreamed in the saddle and used the remainder of Cultay's gum. The weather had grown cooler for our return. It was as if Cultay had parlayed the sun as well. My thoughts were on everything in my father that contradicted the callous transporter; the man who Alfred wanted me to believe in when he was drunk. I cursed myself for not having been quick-witted enough to remind Alfred of our father as the lord of revels. We'd had such endless, exorbitant fun at Gad's Hill between Christmas and Twelfth Night, which was Charley's birthday. The house was always full of guests, and the guvnor even rented a nearby cottage for the bachelors.

Something Mama had told me once—in her admiration for the man who had broken with her—was that one night during the summer when he was courting her, Mama, Aunt Georgie, and their mother were half expecting a call from the guvnor, when a Franco-Spanish sailor jumped through the French windows, performed a hornpipe in front of the amazed and affrighted ladies and, after a while, vaulted into the garden again. Then, a few seconds later, the guvnor presented himself properly dressed via the front door. It was he who had impersonated the sailor. The lord of illusion! He was like that. The generous impulses of humor rose in him and he obeyed them thoroughly, costuming himself for the amusement of others.

There'd been exuberant fun too when he tried magic after he and Mr. Forster bought out the entire stock-in-trade of a conjurer. Some of the tricks allowed him to conjure the watches of the company into tea caddies, cause coins to fly from one pocket to another, and make handkerchiefs seem to burn while not burning them. I remember a doll that he would make appear and disappear and give messages to the children. That was my favorite. He'd taught Mamie the tricks as well.

The guvnor always gave up work for the week of Christmas, and we'd go for long walks down into the woods of Cobham House. Then, when we got back, there were games of proverbs and charades and the guessing game dumb crambo. One year when we were going to do charades with costumes he decided to invite an audience, and afterwards served mulled wine to the neighbors who had watched and applauded. Then there was the time, two or three years back, when he organized some field sports on courses laid out by flags in the open grounds behind the house and invited all the neighbors to take part in the contests. He bade the landlord of the Sir John Falstaff down on our corner to have a drinking booth on the grounds, and the sport didn't finish until darkness fell. He gave a speech at dusk, and the people who were there that day behaved with absolute propriety and departed leaving no mess behind as a token of their respect for him. That's what Alfred did not speak enough of—how adored the guvnor was!

One Christmas when we were isolated by snow, he'd set the bachelors of the party to work assembling the Swiss chalet the actor Fechter had given him, which he would ultimately favor to work in. As I helped the young men I felt important, and my father winked at me. Yet this generous host and game player, this cultivator of surprise and wonder in children, was submerged by the grim and punishing father Alfred seemed determined to have me believe in.

25

At the end of summer, when I'd been at Momba the better part of a year and was approaching my eighteenth birthday, a Belgian priest by the name of Father Charisse arrived at the station on a scraggy gelding. He was a skeletal man, wearing a dusty white habit and sandals, who drank wine hungrily and enjoyed his mutton dinner as he told us about the crimes of slave dealers on the island of Zanzibar, where he'd been sent by his order of monks. He recounted how the archbishop of Sydney had asked the superior of Father Charisse's order to send an apostle to the Australian natives, and he'd come from Zanzibar to Sydney by way of Louvain in Belgium.

It was fascinating for me to converse with a Papist, and to see a man of enlightenment like Fred Bonney allow him to pitch his tent by the Paakantji camp. My father would have said that native people would be ill served by Papism, that it was a matter of barbarism speaking to barbarism. But Fred Bonney was probably impressed by the man's goodwill, as well as by his broad knowledge of the Aboriginal peoples' religion and of what had befallen the Paakantji, in particular since settlers had brought livestock to the Paroo.

"I have seen homesteads which are fortified positions," Father Charisse told us. "The white visitors have no intention to yield up the land again to the natives."

"Indeed," said Fred, whose own best intentions towards the Paakantji did not include the yielding up of Momba.

"And whether the natives attack the newcomers, or extend gestures of cooperation," said the monk, "they can still be misused or slaughtered."

"Is it not inevitable that men will use the scriptures in Genesis to justify their seizure, Father?" asked Edward Bonney. "I do not agree, but I've heard Jehovah's exhortation to humanity to make the earth fruitful in Genesis cited in the churches of the pastoralists."

"There is no structure of law to cover what prevails in Australia," said Fred. "Not when it comes to the natives. It suits me to say so, you will no doubt say, but it is also true. Thus, I try to make Momba a haven for the natives. I am sensible of the fact that Edward and I, as young Dickens will in turn, are making our fortunes here. It's only fair for us to provide the natives with asylum."

"You would agree, however, Mr. Bonney, that justice endows them with the land?" said Father Charisse.

"That it is really theirs is self-evident," said Fred politely, while Edward raised his eyebrows but said nothing.

"And there will come a time when that fact of ownership is reflected in the laws . . ."

"And when the law is made," Fred asserted, "I shall obey it."

"But in the meantime," said the priest, "the situation weighs upon us and I cry out for wisdom."

"We pray too," said Edward. "Our father is an Anglican priest. But in what sense can they be said to have a conventional title to the land?"

"In every sense, I would say," declared Father Charisse.

Fred smiled that shy but seraphic smile he had. "It is not obvious to all lawmakers, or even to ministers of religion."

The priest looked at me, half smiling. "And to you, Mr. Dickens?"

"I don't know," I told the priest, a little panicked. "They understand the country. Is that the same as owning it?" I was not comfortable and wanted to make a point of my ignorance. "They seem to think it is somehow theirs, and they are not evil," I struggled to add.

The priest adopted the kind of oratorical pose I was familiar with from people who wanted to recite my father's work back to me. But, I thought, surely not. For he is a foreigner.

I was wrong, for he continued, saying, "Remember what Mrs. Boffin said in *Our Mutual Friend* about the indignities inflicted upon the poor in workhouses."

Do I never read how they are put off, put off, put off—how they are grudged, grudged, grudged the shelter, or the doctor, or the drop of physic, or the bit of bread? Do I never read how they grow heartsick of it and give it up, after having let themselves drop so low, and how they after all die out for want of help? Then I say, I hope I can die as well as another, and I'll die without that disgrace.

Absolutely impossible my Lords and Gentlemen and Honourable Boards, by any stretch of legislative wisdom to set these perverse people right in their logic?

He dropped his hands and adopted a more conversational posture. "Such a writer as your father is not far from God, Mr. Dickens, and in fact, the Spirit who breatheth where he listeth is not far from the soul of such a man as your father!"

"Yes," said Fred, nodding, the boyish smile in place, and without literary affectation. "*Our Mutual Friend* must be very close to my favorite."

"Yes," said Father Charisse, "the Jew Riah, and Jenny Wren."

"And Bella Wilfer," said Fred.

I remained silent, for though I was the son of the true maker of all these fabled beings, I was caught in the middle of the kindly barrage of cherished names I had not yet encountered.

"Do you know of a man commonly called Barrakoon?" the priest asked Fred with such suddenness that I thought they were still discussing characters from Father's novels.

"Why, yes," said Fred. "He has often camped on Momba. Normally in the north, around Lake Peery."

"I believe he tries to persuade his clansmen against working on stations," the priest observed.

"Yes," said Fred with a broad grin, as if Barrakoon was an eccentric he had affection for—which may very well have been the truth. "He is a purist. He will not use flour or drink tea because he thinks they will cause him to submit. Some of the people in our camp would know him well because some of them go and spend time with him, rather like a retreat to a monastery."

"And it sounds as if one were to find him," said the monk, "it would be in the north?"

Fred nodded and added that sometimes the old man crossed into Queensland.

Edward said, "There are no boundaries with these people. Tribal boundaries perhaps. Colonial boundaries? They don't understand the concept."

Fred seemed genuinely amused. "The Queensland troopers and the South Australians too—they suffer from the same problem. And they behave much worse than our colonial police in New South Wales."

"Who are a mere two hundred and fifty miles to the south," said Edward.

"Indeed," Fred admitted. "Not conveniently placed for our purposes."

"That might be a good thing," said the monk. "Police are a blunt tool, wherever they're from."

"Welcome when essential, though," challenged Edward.

The priest said nothing at first. "The lack of police has put you to the trouble of being just men. In the matter of ocher . . ."

"Ah yes," said Fred Bonney. "But you may be too kind in assessing us, Father. It is hard to be a peacemaker. You see, the Cooper's Creek darks have not had to accommodate fleece enthusiasts like us. I'm not sure their area is even gazetted for lease. And they come down the Paroo channel each year to visit relatives and fetch back their ceremonial ocher, which is essential to them."

"Yes," the priest agreed solemnly. "It is their sacrament. Their bread and their wine. I see that."

"When they come through this area on their way to South Australia to get ocher I have let them know through one of my wise men here that they are free to take ocher from the hill by Lake Dick, and thus cause no problems further south."

"A gracious idea," said the monk.

"Yes, but it did not serve," Fred told him. "Other people down in the south travel north to take ocher from Lake Dick. But the Cooper's Creek people believe they must have ocher from over in the South Australian desert for their ceremonies. That, you see, is the ocher their ancestors used. Lake Dick won't serve."

"It is complex," the priest admitted.

"But they keep peace with us. I let them have their fill of lamb, which is wiser than opposing. If I treat them in terms of fair dealing, then they behave civilly to me, and on top of that I do not need to barricade the homestead."

I suppressed a yawn as the discussion continued, with Fred saying, "I have a weapon they fear."

The monk frowned, as if Fred were about to mention some armament and nominate its caliber.

"I have a great Paakantji priest, as I said earlier. He has many spiritual sanctions he can employ, including the imposition of curses and ritual debts."

"Which of them is he?" asked the priest.

"Why, I sent him down at Christmas to Corona, to young Plorn's brother, to ensure a peace there."

"Cultay?" I murmured.

"Yes," said Fred.

The next morning I watched Father Charisse saying Mass at a table in the midst of the black stockmen's camp. He was wearing his Romish vestments, and though I knew I should disapprove, they seemed to suit the shade beneath the vaults of river gums. I do not for a moment say that it was a Mass recited in the cathedral of nature. There was something about Australia and the Paakantji that didn't offer these easy comparisons. Tom Larkin attended him as an acolyte and rang the bell when he needed to, but the dark stockmen's women and children did not take much notice of him. The natives wandered past, treading softly—that being the extent of their reverence—and regarded him with curiosity, not piety. The only two people to take Communion were the monk and Tom Larkin.

I stayed awhile out of mere politeness. Tom caught me afterwards and asked would I come at last to dinner at the hut he and his wife lived in, boasting that Father Charisse, of whom secretly I had now seen enough, would be there.

The blacksmith's marriage seemed to me like a kindly and loving business, however, and there was a certain fascination in that. Whenever I saw Mrs. Larkin she strode the earth like a proprietor, and I suspected this was because she had Tom. How Maurice McArden's image of gratified desire fit into this connection I did not know, but the obvious picture was very gratifying. I told Tom I would come to dinner.

∾

I decided to write to my father, given that he was so implanted in my mind by the argument in Corona.

"Dearest Father," I wrote.

I know how busy you have been and so have sent most of my news for you in letters to Aunt Georgie. But Aunt Georgie too is not a great writer—even though she is a great friend and aunt to us all, of course— so she cannot be critical of my style as you are entitled to be. I should have written hah-hah! at the end of that sentence.

I wanted you to know that Mr. Bonney allowed me to ride all the way to Alfred's station at Christmastime. Naturally, the conversation between me and Alfred turned to you and our desire never to disappoint you here in Australia, even if we might have done so already on occasion in England. It is only a few years since moving in small parties was a dangerous thing here, especially since the natives thought they might be able to make us leave the country. But now that they know we are staying they've settled into it with us and are making a genial fist of it. In any case, the owner here at Momba, Mr. Bonney, who has great admiration for the people, had one of their most noble men travel with me to Corona, knowing I would be safe in all respects with him, including of course not perishing, which an uninformed man could easily do in this area where it is so far between wells and bores, and where in the Christmas season many creeks lack water.

While we were on our way back home, the native man told me how the country was made by two snakes who were brothers. The snakes were rainbow colored and were the ancestors of the Paakantji. He sang a song beneath his breath about the country they had made. I must say I found it fascinating. It wasn't at all like Anglicanism. Part of the time these great serpents were joined at the tail by an older woman who lived in the treetops, and their struggle to be separate made many of the watercourses and secret places around Momba Station. That is not the purpose of this letter, to tell you this, but I know how you are interested by all the peculiarities of humans, whether they are boatmen on the Thames or, I would imagine, the ancient peoples of New South Wales.

I wanted to let you know how well Alfred is doing at Corona and how much the people there respect him. He and I spoke about the old days of course, and so much about you and Aunt Georgie, and how you would not believe how well known you are in these colonies. We meet people who can recite whole passages from your work. We meet people who think we are clever just because we are your sons. When I told Alfred I would write to you and praise him for his success, which I know will make you very happy, he said, "Don't do that. He'll think we're in a plot together." But I decided that you would be kinder than that and you would indeed be proud. Alfred has made peace in the area where there was war only eighteen months ago between the earlier manager and the natives who came down from the north. By the way, and I hope you don't mind my saying, the housekeeper there cooked the Christmas meal out of Mama's cookery book that she wrote when she was young.

In any case, everything about Corona speaks of good management and Alfred's great competence. He is a colonial man on the way up, and I hope that within a few years you will hear similar things of me. I know from Aunt Georgie that the American tour was very hard on you and I think you should stay at home and let Aunt Georgie feed you up, then have the Higham cricket team there to play games once the spring comes. I would love to ride to Gad's Hill, up the Gravesend Road and past the Falstaff, for a Saturday game of cricket, but there is much to do here, and you would not believe how many interesting people come our way. There is a stock and station agent in the town of Wilcannia whose nephew has run away with the man's French wife and, in this country where there are so few people, has managed to disappear. And nobody knows why he did this nor where he has vanished to. Stock and station agents are something like a nobleman here, and a lot of people owe him *money, and so there is the pretense that the aunt and the youth are just on some form of holiday. It strikes me that these are the sort of puzzles out of which you make your great books, and that if you should visit here, as you have sometimes said you might, you would find yourself not without stories.*

I send you all my affection from Momba, and I hope you are pleased to hear of Alfred's great success and that your foot gets better.

Signed,
Plorn

I had thought too of the extraordinary story of Dandy, and of Mrs. Chard's tortured, knowing diction, but was too tired to include reference to them.

~

Unlike the dinners the silent cook Squeaker Courtney prepared, breakfast at Momba was a relatively slapdash affair. It usually consisted of mutton and damper, though occasionally a few refinements were drawn in like porridge and cocky's joy and preserves, even marmalade, to eat on our damper. Sometimes I ate alone and sometimes I ate with the Bonney brothers, though any conversations at the morning table were usually urgent and short.

One morning I was just about to enter the morning room when I heard the brothers in eager debate.

"It is the time for his initiation and I'm asking you to relinquish him," Fred was saying.

"You mustn't think my enthusiasm is not reciprocated. And I can't see how you have decided I should be governed by the demands of a barbarous ceremony," Edward replied testily, "and one you would not choose to go through yourself."

"But it is a necessary ceremony for *him*," Fred argued. "And you can see how he's stuck uncomfortably between childhood and full manhood."

Edward replied that this was so much cant, and it was in the nature of young men to be surly. Then, suddenly, he came out of the room and saw me.

"Don't flee, Plorn!" he called. "My brother. He is such an absolutist."

I turned to him and said, "It is all right, Mr. Bonney. I wasn't listening, and in any case . . ."

"My brother will no doubt tell you what you may have guessed. I am made in the narrow mold, Plorn: I like men. I have been taken by one in particular . . . But I am a rational man. I am not some predator."

"Very well," I told him, which I would have said to any confession he made, and he'd made this one so frankly that I wished to disappear. "There is no need—"

"There may be . . . because of my earlier excessive behavior to you."

I realized then they were still debating an attachment Edward had to give up so that a rite could take place. I decided to retreat to my room until they had had it out.

"Well, I am going," I began.

"No," he said, "you were on your way to breakfast. Keep on, keep on, Plorn."

So I did and found Fred abstracted, and still I had no firm idea who or what they were arguing about.

26

Over the following few days the Bonneys returned to what I considered normal discourse, to the extent that I wondered if I'd dreamed my exchange with Edward.

But I got a glimmering one morning when Fred excused me from the day's mustering and asked me if I'd like to join him for what he called Yandi's "man-making" ceremony.

"I have the honor to be invited," Fred told me, "and I know you have always shown sympathy for them and would be instructed by what you saw."

I agreed somewhat hesitantly and walked with Fred to where he said the ceremony would be taking place. After we'd passed the huts of the Paakantji, we saw a group of older men, including Cultay, waiting for us wearing kangaroo-skin cloaks, with throwing sticks and boomerangs in their belts. One of the old men, Hughie, real name Boolingooroo, wore a cap of leaves, and had branches and leaves tied around his head to ease a headache: Fred had explained to me that these were the leaves of the snake vine, and its milky sap was considered a sovereign remedy. The red fruit of the bush and its yellow flowers smelled of urine, but its curative powers made all this acceptable to Hughie.

These older men started moving southeast to the Momba water-hole, and we walked a little behind, ignored but accepted.

"Do you notice how sullen Yandi has been?" Fred asked. "He was fearful the old men would capture him and take him off to initiation, which is something many of the young think of as involving terrors. But he was also in fear they wouldn't do it and would leave him a child forever."

"In two minds," I suggested.

"Yes, being left as a child forever would be the worse outcome," Fred told me. "I haven't seen Yandi recently and when I've asked the men where he is I've been getting only mumbles. Now I understand his absence. I think he's been moody lately because after they tell him the reality of the world, and death, and all the rest, they leave him alone to contemplate it on land surrounded by ghosts. And Yandi has a mortal terror of ghosts. Remember how frightened he was of the stammerer?"

I would find out in time that if a woman or a white stockman stumbled upon the place where a newly initiated boy or man was enduring his isolation, the ceremony and the mysteries and the bewilderment the older men induced in the young needed to be started all over again. And so the young initiate was given an implement Fred told me was known as a *moola-uncka*, consisting of a piece of flat wood with a hole in it which the Paakantji could whirl through the air on the end of a thong to make a monstrous whooping sound like a huge predatory bird or a booming, guttural monster.

After a mile and a half we followed the old men into a copse of trees where we found a group of youths sitting in a very small open space with Yandi amongst them looking barely recognizable, in that he had white clay all over his body. I was impressed by the strange and unexpected augustness of this and realized it was the most graphic way the natives had of letting people know that Yandi was a new man; and indeed he looked remade. Sitting on a bed of bush fuchsia branches—which must have meant something too—he had a majesty to him, and his hands were splayed serenely on his upper legs, which were bent under him.

In a line in front of Yandi sat a number of younger men with their backs to him, each carrying a narrow shield decorated with ink and ocher and carvings. Like a council of some sort, the old men sat and faced these young men. This was followed by an extraordinary scene in which the young men rose to full height and seemed to abuse and insult the older men, making dismissive gestures with their hands, as though complaining about their folly and tyranny. The old men grew slowly enraged, and they too rose and consulted each other with angry eyes and gestures and sneers, theatrical yet awe-inspiring, though they said nothing. After a while the insults seemed to reach a climax, and the old men began throwing their fighting sticks and boomerangs at the younger ones, who bounced them away contemptuously with their wooden shields. When there were no more digging sticks and boomerangs to throw, the old men rushed forward as if to punish the young, but the young men grasped them and threw them to the ground. After that the old men got up, acting disgruntled, and left the clearing singing an ominous chant.

Fred and I followed them doing the same, except for the chant. I was thoroughly confused by this Paakantji ritual. As they retired up the creek, the old men chatted happily to each other, not at all aggrieved by the ritual in the clearing.

As if Fred knew the ceremony exactly, he went up to one of the retreating old men and spoke to him softly in Paakantji. After the discussion, Fred came to me and told me we would all be returning to Yandi and his friends soon. Ah, I thought, that's when the older men will show them who is in charge. But in fact I couldn't have been more mistaken, because as we followed them back into the clearing again, there were no loud noises of the kind you would expect, say, of schoolmasters reimposing order amongst the young. The old men were still jovial and took up their positions to watch the end of the rite in which two of the young men crouched down by Yandi on his bed of brush. The two men had ligatures tied around their upper arm and had cut a vein on the upper side of their wrist, the blood from the wounds streaming into a wooden bowl. Yandi, on his knees, knelt forward, his hands locked behind his back, and drank the blood as might a stooping deer or even a dog. Fred told me later that this was all Yandi was permitted to drink or eat for some days, till he was cleansed with smoke.

Yandi and another young man, a sort of sponsor, stood wearing long kangaroo cloaks, only their heads uncovered, then sat again on a heap of green boughs of the fuchsia bush. Spread out beneath them were heaps of dry grass with sticks at the bottom which were lit. The result was not flame but a thick smoke that enshrouded the two figures, penetrating their cloaks and rising around their shoulders and throats. Both men placed a finger in each nostril to save themselves from suffocation.

Then Yandi and his sponsor raised the kangaroo cloaks up over their heads and the smoking continued, and the two youths remained there, almost obliterated by the sacramental vapor. I was concerned enough to look at Fred a number of times, but he merely widened his eyes and nodded his head, acknowledging my bewilderment as if in part he shared it himself. Then at last the older men began to call to the two young men at the center of the rite and to coax them forward. When Yandi walked off the smoking ground and presented himself, the hair on his head was cut short with an edged stone, the locks falling to the ground. Yandi did not flinch as the old men then filched out bristles from his face with their fingers. This was followed by the smearing of red ocher over his body, before a necklace of twisted possum hair was placed around his neck. About now one of the young men who had earlier staved off the throwing sticks and boomerangs with shields went darting from the scene. He had the tooth one of the men had knocked out of Yandi's mouth earlier, when his initiation was still lonely and unobserved except by old men. He would hide it near some source of water. What happened to it then was an omen, apparently, for how Yandi's life would unfold.

Fred and I left before the ceremony was fully completed, feeling privileged to have seen it this far. On the way back to the homestead he told me that if Yandi chose he could marry a girl in another skin group to whom he'd been betrothed as a child. But he might choose instead to wander for a wife. It was at once clear to me that it was no simpler to select a wife and be sanctioned to marry in Yandi's society than it was in ours.

"You'll find he's a much happier lad now," Fred told me as we reached the house.

Edward was abstracted at dinner that night, confirming my suspicion that it was Yandi whom he had been reluctant to relinquish.

I was pleased when I found out that Willy Suttor was also coming to dinner at the Larkins', not only because he would serve as a buffer against the earnestness of the Belgian monk, but also because he'd offered to advise me on the purchase of a racehorse or two, which I could run in the jockey club meetings around the region, now that I had some resources.

When I reached the Larkins' house, Suttor was already there, sitting at the set table drinking rum with Tom.

"You do us a great honor, Mr. Plorn," said Tom, rising to meet me, his face shining. He then turned to his wife and said, "Who would have thought, eh, Gracie?"

"In New South Wales!" she agreed, cleaning her hands on her apron and nodding at me.

Before anything more could be said, the priest arrived in a cassock that looked harsh woven, unlike the normal clerical cloth. Wearing such stuff, he seemed worthier of attention, even apart from his interest in the Paakantji, whom I now believed had adequate sacraments of their own without needing the Christian ones. I would have liked to see some of the clergymen I'd met in my childhood, including the late sainted Dr. Sawyer, going through or putting his parishioners through the ceremony of smoking that Yandi had survived.

The Larkins went into a different form of exultation with the priest. I'd supposedly brought literary glamour with me, but Father Charisse brought the tenor of the saints, and might be one himself. They bowed their heads, and Willy looked solemn as the priest uttered his benediction in Latin and very exactly quartered the air to make a cross above the company's heads.

The Larkin cottage seemed a civilized nest, from its fabric curtains to its neat little wall lamps. There was a white tablecloth and silver cutlery, probably a wedding present. Its glint of comfort and solace mocked not only the makeshift nature of the boundary riders' huts but the austerity of grander places. Tom had that shiny look of a man who had scrubbed himself thoroughly after demanding work, and when Mrs. Larkin entered the room from the kitchen the glances and touches between herself and her husband bespoke that comfort and solace. It was hard not to believe that this was what marriage was for. This ease and affection did not seem to me to come from the same place as the orphan hunger that had marked Maurice's story about aunts. Ease and hunger could be at war with each other. What did people do when that happened?

When one posed a question like that, admittedly the question of a youth, one did not apply it to one's own family. I did not then, as I might later, look at how my father had sent Mama back to her family, and though he'd provided her with her own good house, had never again admitted her to his or visited her in hers. My mother's face had seemed bruised and bleak when I caught her unawares during visits to her new house in Camden Town, and it would take some time to creak itself into her lovely full-featured smile.

I turned away from these thoughts as we sat down at the table. Mrs. Larkin had clearly put a lot of careful thought into the composition of the meal, which began with soup. Tom Larkin produced a bottle of French white wine—very likely it was a gift from Willy—and Father Charisse agreed to try a glass.

The main course was roast lamb with a fine array of baked vegetables and niceties such as mustard and mint jelly, obtainable by special order through the shopkeeper. This was accompanied by a fruity bottle of red wine.

As we ate I attempted to imitate Willy Suttor's easy manner with the priest. "Yes, I know Barrakoon, Father," Willy admitted, "but I doubt you should have ambitions to visit him. It's unlikely he would perceive a difference between you and the crassest of boundary riders or even the prospectors one finds dragging their way to Mount Browne on the rumor there's been gold found there."

I remembered the day Fred and Yandi and I had met Barrakoon's party out in the Ullollie paddock.

"My order was founded, Mr. Suttor, to seek out the rejected and outcast," the priest said. "I sit tonight with genial people and at a sanctified hearth. It would be very pleasant if my place was amongst you people on whom God has already smiled. But, you see, it is an inevitable impulse of vocation to be a witness on the furthest edge of things. The fact that everyone believes that one day the Mounted Police from Queensland might pursue that outcast group means that I must number myself amongst Barrakoon's people. It is a clear mandate, you see. I wish frequently that it were not so, and my nature hankers for a simple shelter like this and an honorable trade. But—"

Larkin interrupted, saying, "My mother said that when her transport lay in Dublin Bay, Two Sisters of Mercy came aboard to visit the women on the prison deck. And all the prisoners thought it good of the nuns to visit them for the day, yet when the ship . . . the *Whitby* . . . heaved itself out into the Irish Sea, the two nuns were still on board, willing to travel with them all the way and minister to them . . ."

"I can believe it," the priest said, himself a little chastened by the grandeur of the nuns. "For some souls, there is only one home—at the side of the despised."

"I understand what you say, Father," Larkin declared. "But you won't stop what has happened all over the land already. My mother and my father saw the Ngarigu driven from the high plains of Monaro. I can't say whether that is God's work or not. My parents felt some pity, though, for those darks driven off. And yet, kindly or not, it happened. Now, if you went to see this Barrakoon man and he harmed you in any way, the New South Wales troopers stationed near Wentworth would be called out. Or the Queenslanders, if it happened anywhere near Queensland. You could be the provocation the powers of the earth seek, Father."

"Being raised Protestant myself," Mrs. Larkin said swiftly, "I wonder that you would try to order around a priest, Thomas."

"I speak merely as a man to him, Gracie. I do not want to see good Father Charisse come to damage, since priests have always been thin on the ground in New South Wales."

"I accept what you say to me, Thomas," the priest declared. "But what if I came to you tomorrow and said no more smithing, you are to make barrels from now on. Would not this cause a rift in your nature?"

Larkin did not answer.

"I hope you have a good horse, Father," said Willy.

"It is a better one than it looks," said Father Charisse, like most normal men better impressed with his own mount than other people were.

"Forgive me, Father, I'm just a Protestant like Tom," said Willy. "But surely your order cannot expect you to court martyrdom? If they did, they would soon be reduced to small numbers."

"You are a sensible man," the priest told him, "but there are reasons that exceed reason."

"Anyway," said Mrs. Larkin cheerily, "let us eat up."

She held out the hope that food would raise us to the priest's level of reason, or else tame him back to ours.

"Your father, anyhow, Mr. Dickens, is a just man," said the priest through a fairly lusty mouthful of mutton and potato, which he swallowed prematurely to embark on a recitation. "'Now these tumbling tenements contain, by night, a swarm of misery. As, on the ruined human wretch, vermin parasites appear, so these ruined shelters have bred a crowd of foul existence that crawls in and out of gaps in walls and boards; and coils itself to sleep, in maggot numbers, where the rain drips in . . .' This is your father on the place named Tom-all-Alone's in *Bleak House*. Christ spoke the truth of the poor. Your father has written it as no one else has, not Shakespeare, not Voltaire, not Lamartine. Your father is like an extension of the Gospels! You must be so proud of this."

"My father would be proud to hear the claim from your lips," I said. "But I doubt that he would feel in any way parallel to Christ."

My father had enjoyed plaudits in his time, but he would have been astounded to know this priest in New South Wales was partnering him with the Gospels.

"But he always had a great sympathy for the poor," I lamely concluded.

"And that is the Second Commandment," said Father Charisse.

I did not tell him of course that my father deplored Papists.

The dinner proceeded pleasantly, and I even had a chance to tell stories of some of the rowing expeditions the guvnor and we boys undertook on the Medway.

～

I was to see Father Charisse celebrate one more apparently futile Mass in the camp of the station darks. When he elevated the Host, a few of the old widows sitting in the doorways of their gunyahs with gypsum on their heads could tell that something solemn had happened, the moment being accompanied by a small handbell rung by Tom Larkin. The women shrilled as they had shrilled when Yandi returned to the camp from his great smoking.

And then the priest was gone. Cultay went with him at Fred Bonney's request. After a number of days Cultay returned to Momba, and everyone assumed he had somehow managed to make introductions between the priest and the purist group around Barrakoon.

27

The Bonney brothers, like all the other pastoral folk, were still experimenting with the best blends of wool for the terrain and climate of Momba. As part of my training, and an exercise of my usefulness, Fred asked me to ride to Wilcannia with an open check in my possession, enabling me to buy a lot of two hundred White Suffolk sire rams at no more than four pounds a head at an auction run by Mr. Fremmel. Jemmy Clough, one of the Bonney brothers' most trusted boundary riders, would come with me and apply his jaundiced eye over the sheep's gums, staple length, hoofs, and rumps. If all seemed well, we could proceed. But I had to hand over the instrument of payment, and it was an honor of which I was acutely aware. I had also been instructed to make the bidding. I had never had any such transaction laid upon my shoulders before.

At the close of a long desert winter's day, under a sky of scoured and streaky clouds, Clough and I camped near the Wilcannia saleyards with a number of other purchasing parties from around the district. I moved easily around the camp, without much terror that any stockman or boundary rider would recite my father's work to me. A number of boundary riders and bullock cart drivers had gathered around a large fire, and a concertina and a fiddle were playing with an accompanying voice I recognized as Hayward's. His cheeks, already richly glowing from the heat, seemed further aglow with rum as he sang in a plaintive, accented tenor, and the men around the fire were in an ecstasy of hilarity.

In lodgings my brother Jim used to be,
He lived in a little back room,
His landlady, she was a widow, who used
To walk in her sleep in the gloom.

Oh! Oh! It's a terrible tale,
She walked into Jim's room, I vow.
He got such a fright that he left the next night.
That's the reason I'm lodging there now.

When he finished, to tremendous bush acclamation, he raised a pannikin and emptied it. Men called for more songs from him but he told them, in a stage Irish accent, "Bejaysuz, I've been singing for yez all the fookin' night."

A number of men tried to grab him as he walked away, wanting to be his friend forever. But when he heard my cry, perhaps because it was a rare sober one, he turned around.

"Well, I'll be buggered," he said, his face lighting up. "It is Plorn Dickens, is it not?"

He came over and shook my hand, saying, "The fellow I was going to write to but now don't have to. I have left your brother on amiable terms and am on my way to take over the management of Toorale Station on the Warrego River."

"Oh," I replied, a little envious, although he was a couple of years my senior.

"In eighteen months I reach my majority and would like to go into partnership with a friend to purchase a homestead freehold and take up a pastoral lease, the management of which I would undertake. I wondered if you would be that friend, Plorn? Do you think that on further acquaintance you could work with me?"

Secretly delighted, I nonetheless pleaded that I had three years to go to my majority.

"If there were anything you could borrow against," he said, suddenly serious, "and you really wanted to join my station, would that be a possibility?"

"Indeed, it might well be. I am very flattered."

"Come, Plorn, that's what women say when they knock a chap back for marriage."

"But I *am*. I will write . . ." I was going to say "to Aunt Georgie," but that might have caused Hayward's derision. "I will write home and make inquiries."

"Good, and by the way, my dear friend, this is just an initial proposition, a sounding out. I'm aware you need to hear good things of me in the coming times. But though a troubadour, I am capable, old chap, of deadly seriousness when it comes to making our pastoral mark. Shall we drink on it?"

I thought about this. We were a few hundred yards from the Commercial Hotel, where many of the pastoral gentlemen were staying. I agreed.

We set off together, Hayward trilling,

At Trinity Church I met my doom,
Now we live in a top back room,
Up to my eyes in debt for rent,
That's what she and heaven sent . . .

"You have a vast store of songs, Hayward," I remarked, not utterly in admiration.

"Thank you, sir, though many are of the vulgar kind." As if to prove the point he sang:

I once went to a country fair,
The fattest girl on earth was there,
She was ninety-seven inches wide,
And we all rushed in when the showman cried . . .

A sneezing fit interrupted him. "Ah," he continued when it passed, "my guvnor sayeth to me, 'Why can you remember low doggerel and not your theorems?' Had I been able to answer him I might have been Hayward of the Foreign Office or Lieutenant Colonel Hayward of the Royal Engineers."

I said, "I can remember cricket scores but not theorems. I *understand* the cricket scores."

"Exactly, Plorn. I understood the doggerel. We'll make excellent partners."

A roar of conversation was emanating from the Commercial's public and saloon bar, but one could also hear much politer songs than Hayward's being played on a piano—indeed, "Green Grow the Rushes, Oh!"

As we approached, the pianist took up "The Low, Low Lands of Holland" and a soprano voice pierced the night.

"Yon lassie can sing," remarked Hayward.

At that, I thought, How can I go into business with you? I rarely meet you fully sober.

Surprisingly, as we got closer to the hotel the general hubbub of conversation seemed to make the soprano's voice dimmer, but it still penetrated with its needlepoint sound. Hayward led me into the crowded public bar where he was obviously well known and well liked.

"Here he comes, the bloody minstrel boy!" men called out and he was shoulder-slapped in the direction of the bar, where he ordered rum for himself and ale for me. As we drank, his eyes darted from admiring face to admiring face. It was a wonderful thing that he was the acclaimed oddity of this party; that, for once, it wasn't me.

"Who is yon lass with splendid voice?" he asked of the company.

"Jealous, are you, Hayward?" called one of the drinkers.

"Desirous of an introduction," declared Hayward.

"It's old Desailly having a party for his chums in one of the parlors," one man said. "The singer must be one of his daughters. Or one of their friends."

"Hey," called one, "isn't that the young Dickens boy you're with?"

"Boy? Boy? He's as good a man as any," Hayward declared.

Some besotted soul thought it was time to cheer. "Thinking of writing a book, are ye?" another called, and for some reason everyone thought this sidecrackingly funny.

I didn't like the way this was going, but I was excited by the idea that Constance Desailly might be in the hotel, and the voice told me infallibly that it was hers. I have to make some serious investment in her, I thought. I grabbed Hayward by the arm and told him, "I know the Desaillys."

"Do you think you can take us both?" he asked.

I finished my ale without replying and moved off towards the sound of the piano. The singing had stopped now but the piano was still being played.

A man cried, "There goes young Dickens! Some girl's in danger!"

I grinned as convincingly as I could, for in Australia I'd discovered it was better to go along with the joke than be the butt of it.

I reached the corridor and turned to find Hayward was still with me. We followed the sound of the piano to a door, and I knocked. I was nervous but pleased to be in charge of Hayward, who seemed chastened for once and was holding his broad hat by its brim. It was Malleson, the law clerk, who opened the door. I thought that of course he would be there, paying court. But he behaved with warmth and courtesy. "Dickens, how good to see you."

"I felt that I must come and pay my respects to Mr. Desailly," I replied.

Malleson turned to the room and announced over the piano, "It's young Dickens and another gentleman, come to give their respects."

Alfred and Mrs. Desailly walked across the room to greet us.

"We are not well dressed for polite company," I said.

"Of course that doesn't matter," Mrs. Desailly fluted. "But come in and bring your friend." She and Mr. Desailly were just as they had been at the time of the cricket encounter, amiable in an openhanded, colonial way. Hayward seemed quite stunned by the welcome I was receiving from the Desaillys.

Across the room I saw Constance looking amused. She was standing by the piano wearing green and appeared ampler than she'd been at our last meeting. Her sister was at the piano, and not far from Blanche was her Mr. Brougham.

Alfred Desailly said, "The girls were just giving us some tunes."

"Some tunes?" I protested. "Sublime melodies," I insisted.

Mrs. Desailly clapped her hands and everyone in the room ceased talking. I caught sight of Mr. Fremmel and the Reverend Rutledge with his wife. "May I introduce a gentleman you might already know, Mr. Edward Dickens and his friend, Mr. . . . ?"

"Hayward. New manager of Toorale," said Hayward, nodding smoothly around the room.

A few ladies clapped. Toorale was a pastoral property most would have heard of, and its owner was a popular Ulsterman named Sam Wilson.

I regretted that Hayward and I had distracted the company from the singing. I saw Constance move away from the piano as if she were about to embark on conversations around the room. So I

was grateful to Mr. Brougham for stepping forward and announcing he was sure the newly arrived guests and others in the room
would be happy if the Desailly sisters proceeded with the third of
their selections. Hayward and I rushed to say we'd be delighted to
hear them. There were coughs and snifflings in the company as it
settled, then Blanche began playing a short teasing introduction
to "Wild Mountain Thyme," which Constance began to sing, her
brown eyes ablaze.

This was an almost unfairly inveigling song, a true love plaint,
and melodic to a fault. And I heard Connie Desailly's crystalline soprano cutting into me like a knife. It is a song supposedly sung by a
man, but as she sang "*Will you go, lassie, go?*" I was struck by a desire
to dare anything, to ride to the ocher pits of South Australia and
bring that red preciousness back to her. Wherever on this continent,
or at least beyond the Darling, "*the wild mountain thyme grows around
the blooming heather,*" I was willing to quest for it.

"Extraordinary! Who is she, Dickens?" Hayward whispered.
"She is enchanting."

I did not answer. He knew who she was anyhow. She was Euterpe, muse of song, reborn somehow on the banks of the sometimes bounteous, sometimes grudging Darling. And if my father
had never sent me to the colonies, I would not have been aware
that, with the dew of the divine fountains she had risen from still
fresh on her, she had fetched up there.

The song ended and, after a stunned moment, the room erupted
to handclapping and lusty cheers from younger men as Brougham
cried, "The muses of Netallie Station, ladies and gentlemen!"

I saw Fremmel applauding as if it were just another song, while
the Reverend Rutledge seemed distracted. Were these people even
alive? I wondered.

Hayward beat Malleson to Constance's side, begging the honor of introducing himself. I felt vacant with enchantment. What I feared most was that he would manage to sing something like the exquisite "Holly and the Ivy" he'd sung at Corona. If they sang together, it might be apparent to all that the charm of one complemented the other. They would be somehow fused.

28

While I stood bewildered by this question of Connie and other men, I found with a shock that Mr. Fremmel was by my side.

"How is life at Momba, Mr. Dickens?" he asked.

"All is well," I replied. "The water has fallen in the creek system, Natiola and Momba Creeks are down on what they were when I first arrived, but Fred Bonney's hoping for late winter rains."

"*Fred* Bonney," he said with a raised eyebrow.

"Mr. Bonney," I corrected myself.

"You find the Bonneys good masters?" asked Fremmel distractedly, as if he didn't care how I found them.

"I don't know if my father bred me to acknowledge a master, Mr. Fremmel, but I'm very happy working for the Messrs. Bonney."

"You have not been assailed as yet by Mr. Edward Bonney?" he asked.

"No," I told him, a little shocked he'd used the word "assailed."

"He is a sodomite, don't you know?"

"I don't think it's proper—" I began.

"Oh, come, Dickens, don't be prissy. The fact is widely known. And I wondered if he had importuned you, by any chance."

"I assure you he has not, Mr. Fremmel."

"Then do you know if he has received a letter from my nephew Maurice?"

"I don't believe so."

"The new postmaster says one was delivered to Momba. And I know Maurice and the Bonneys are correspondents. That's all."

"I wouldn't know," I replied with half an eye on Constance trilling with laughter at every second sentence Hayward uttered.

"You're here for the stock sales?" Fremmel asked.

I admitted I was.

"You have a commission from Mr. Fred Bonney to bid for certain stock?"

"I'm honored to say that I do."

"A delightful man, Fred," said Fremmel joylessly. "Compared to his brother, who lacks distinction."

"Both have been very kind to me," I replied, as a warning.

"What is the commission Fred Bonney has favored you with in this case, young Dickens?"

I did not like that "young Dickens"—it smelled of classroom condescension.

"I believe that is confidential between Mr. Bonney and myself," I declared.

"I would reckon that it's the white-faced Suffolks. Ever the experimenter, Fred, ever the Enlightenment man. Well, let me tell you, I can get those Suffolks to you for two pounds, fifteen shillings a head, which I surmise would cause Mr. Bonney to declare you a wonder-worker."

"Well, that would be a reasonable price, all up," I agreed.

"All I would need is for you to find that letter from my nephew."

"But I couldn't do that, even if it existed."

"When the time comes, and it seems to be coming faster than slower given Fred Bonney's trust in you, you will find I can be very helpful in getting you started. For one thing, fencing is expensive and yet the government will demand it of you, and so will the circumstances."

I wondered if I pretended to be willing to collaborate with him, which on one level seemed a wise idea, I could cross the room and by some ploy disrupt the conversation between Hayward and Constance. I even betrayed myself into contemplating a collaboration with this malign being. "You are trying to make me your client?" I asked.

"It would not hurt you if you were."

"Amongst all the correspondence Mr. Edward Bonney receives, why would he keep a letter from your nephew?" I asked.

"Because he was in love with the boy, that's why. He seems to have made his overtures to Maurice, which I think were largely rebuffed. The letter would probably be in his keeping somewhere close to him and can't be hard to find. Please listen to me and don't look around like that. I would like to know where Maurice is."

"You don't know?" I asked with false innocence.

"I don't. Nor do I have the time to devote . . . I would pay you for that letter, though. If it came with an address, however vague, I would pay two hundred pounds on top of the special price for the Suffolks."

I gave him my full attention now. A sum like that would be very useful in my venture with Hayward. But having Fremmel for an associate would also be terrifying in its way. "No, I cannot do it," I told him. "Momba is my home. I won't go creeping about."

Fremmel grinned and shook his head in a measuring kind of gesture, saying, "Oh, I think you will go creeping about, and I think you will search for that letter now, just out of boyish curiosity. I bet you do. And when you have found it, I'm here. But I believe my nephew is fairly nomadic at the moment and so the information would only be good for a week or so. Don't tell the Bonneys or any-one else I approached you. No one will believe you, in any case. But remember that I'm here. I'm going home now. I hope the prices don't go too high on the Suffolks for you and Fred Bonney."

Love had been on one side of the parlor and malice on the other, and now I saw Hayward, Constance, and Blanche all leaning over the piano, trying out a few bars of this or that melody. Sud-denly Blanche sat at the keyboard and Constance and Hayward began singing "Widecombe Fair" together, and I could have cried for the plainness with which Hayward willfully debased the pure crystal of Connie Desailly's voice. I said unsatisfactory and wooden good nights to everyone, including the Desailly sisters, who seemed barely to notice as they listened to the *sotto voce* lyrics of some of the music hall songs Hayward was rehearsing for their amusement. Hayward had grabbed Euterpe from the divine spring and dragged her down to the factory canal. It was his way. I could never think of entering a business with him I decided as I returned to the spot where Clough and I were camped.

The next day at the saleyards a popular, jaunty fellow named Dun-can was auctioning livestock for Fremmel. When it was time for the lot of Suffolk to attract bids, a fellow in the crowd wearing a heavy military-style cape began by bidding one pound ten shillings. My bid drove it to two pounds ten, and though the man in the big cape seemed dubious he raised the bid to three pounds. He kept on my tail until he had raised it to three pounds fifteen, and when I raised the bid to four pounds I both feared and half hoped he would out-bid me, since bringing the rams home to Momba at that price was a fairly ordinary fulfilment of my mission. But the man in the cavalry cape seemed to have vanished.

There was no time to lose if I wanted to deliver them to Momba by next day, so Clough, the dogs, and I drove the rams off a little way to graze near the peppertrees that favored the river and shaded the town.

"That bugger in a cloak was a plant," complained Clough. "We would've had 'em cheaper without him there."

Dismayed, my disquiet only increased as I saw Fremmel approach us from beyond the melee of the yards. He was wearing a suit of brown checks and a little tout-ish hat and looked a man on top of the world, all the more so because I wasn't on top of mine.

"You see," he told me frankly, "you could have had them for cheaper and been Fred Bonney's hero when you got them into Momba. And what harm would that have done anyone?"

I was too defeated to reply before he continued, telling me, "You must know I am the broker for a number of pastoral investment companies. There are benefits I can send your way in future if you accommodate me with that letter . . . Reasonably enough, I want my wife back, Mr. Dickens. That is a greater and holier imperative than a letter from Maurice to that *sodomite*."

Again, he relished the solidity and age of that word, and the load of contempt it could carry.

"I trust you'll find your wife," I replied, though I didn't trust it at all. "But I won't get you that letter, Mr. Fremmel."

Fremmel looked away and muttered, "Your brother's done well at Corona, I hear."

"I'm proud to say he has."

"And he has an ambition to buy into a stock and station agency in Hamilton, I believe."

"I'm . . . I'm not aware of that."

"Well, I told you I'm a broker and I keep on top of things. There has been an application from one Alfred Dickens for a loan of four hundred and fifty pounds to enable purchase of a partnership and goodwill in Robert Stapylton Bree and Company, Stock and Station Agency, as well as an interest in Wangagong Station near the town of Forbes. I do not have universal powers to grant that favor, especially given the interests involved are not located in the Western Division. But I certainly have power to influence the *rejection* of the application, given that Corona is in my bailiwick."

"So you can keep my brother in place!" I challenged him.

"Or let him be favored, Dickens. Get me the sodomite's letter, and I shall also foster your career."

I was getting a head of contempt for him and asked, "Why not simply ask Mr. Bonney yourself?"

"He despises me," Fremmel admitted frankly. He had nothing to hide from me since, in weightier places and with weightier folk, he could deny everything he had told me. "I am sending a man out to Momba next Tuesday with a wagon of wire. Kindly give him the letter, sealed in a new envelope and addressed to me, when you see him."

Our sheepdogs were running around, yelping at Clough and me, willing to start the rams moving to Momba.

Fremmel turned and was leaving without the pretense of normal good wishes.

"I won't have anything for your man," I called after him.

"I think you might," he said, not turning.

Indeed I was myself full of curiosity to read the letter, and perhaps I could by secretly tracking it down in Edward Bonney's office or bedroom. But it would be terrible to give it then to Fremmel because he would use it to set private detectives on Maurice's track, and I wanted to save poor, tender Maurice that peril.

⁓

We drove the rams to graze on the large common, where a number of men were buying and selling horses. A trooper was patrolling the area, looking at bills of sale and other instruments and making sure the horses being offered were of legal provenance. I was too young to be wary, and my eyes lit on an Arab-looking gray mare. I felt a man with a horse like that could never be regarded as despicable. Not a butt of Hayward's merry nature nor of Fremmel's plans. I had joined the Wilcannia jockey club and needed only a Thoroughbred (or a horse tolerably related to a Thoroughbred, as this obviously was) to participate. Now that I was being paid by the Bonneys I finally had some reserves to purchase one.

The mare was tethered to a central spike in the ground and being ridden in circles by a red-haired little girl wearing a red-spotted white dress and boots so big they seemed to constitute half her mass. The child's wiry father was wearing a dusty red-striped suit and the sort of hat Australians called a "wideawake." He simply contemplated his circulating daughter and horse.

It is possible for foolish men, even ones older than me, to become infatuated with a horse on an instantaneous basis and to read fantastic properties into it. I thought, of course this man had trouble selling his superior horse, since people did not necessarily want a horse as biddable as this—so biddable the man's daughter could ride it.

I told Clough to take the ever-enthusiastic dogs and rams out along Woore Street, past the desert gardens of the houses and in the direction of Wanaaring, and said I would catch him up. He was a man of few words, though he had introduced me to some in his time, most notably, in my memory, to the idea that rams were possessed by continuous libido. He could probably tell that I was going to talk to the horse dealer but had nothing to say to me on that perilous matter.

~

Feigning nonchalance, I rode over to the dealer and cried, "Your little girl looks comfortable enough there."

"That is the categorical truth, mister. It was her favorite from a foal. She gives me tiger, I assure you, at the idea of me selling it. But there you are. It is a categorical necessity, sir. After all, it is not a work horse. Too much aristocracy in this little mare for that!"

"Have you raced her, sir?"

"I've only raced her once when she was second in Cobar in a race for yearlings. But she is nearing two years and I think she is categorical ready for it now."

"If I could put her through her paces I might be interested," I called back to him.

The slight man held up his hand to the child, who reined in the tethered horse and bounced off it.

"Oh mister," said her father, "you look like an honest enough bloke, but I've been stung before. The faster the horse, the harder to get it back should you run with it."

It was no use being offended or saying, "Sir, I am a gentleman."

"But I will leave you my horse as guarantee."

"All respects, mister, your mare is not up to the price of mine. Yours is a stockhorse, mine a categorical Thoroughbred."

"Dada," asked the child, strolling up wide-eyed and a-tremble to her father. "Do you think this gentleman is a thief?"

"I would say not, Susannah. It is simply I don't know him from a bar of soap."

"You want me to buy a horse I can't take for a run?"

"Mister, you can ride her as my daughter does. Her name's du Barry. As for the rest, I'd argue her lines and demeanor are visible to the world from where she is."

Mr. . . . ?"

"Delahunty. My serenity is one with that of my Maker. If I don't sell her here, I'll just ride her down to the sales at Louth. Some people buy yearlings and docile two-year-olds without even taking the trouble to ride them."

"Oh," I replied. "Well, I'm not one of them. Please let me try her, Mr. Delahunty."

He agreed, and the little girl told me, "Be well mannered with her, sir. She's so well mannered herself."

I tethered my own mare to a tree and mounted du Barry in the prescribed, well-mannered way. When I prodded her she made a number of circuits, and, at the canter, I believed I could feel the speed coiled within her. After a while, given the limits involved in making circles, I got down and, feeling worldly, made a few negative, price-reducing remarks.

"A little fine-boned, isn't she?" I suggested. "And the chest . . ."

"Mister," Susannah told me, "she's tall, fifteen and a half hands. That makes her bones look small."

There was some truth to that.

"Out of the mouths of bloody babes, mister," said Delahunty, his eyes gleaming.

The upshot was that the mare was mine for forty pounds, and I gave Mr. Delahunty an order on the Bank of New South Wales. Whispering endearments to her, I took du Barry and she walked behind my mare, attached to my pommel by a rope tether unworthy of her heritage and a very plain accoutrement to my dreams of jockey club renown.

The rest became something of a story, at least for a few weeks. Soon after I caught up with Clough and the dogs with the flock of rams, du Barry began rearing and plummeting and threatening to drag me and Coutts back towards her previous owner.

"She's full of magnesium, I'd say," declared Clough professorially, riding near, "or at least was. You can tell a stallion that's been overdosed to make it look calm. Its donger doesn't look right. But mares . . ."

I reinforced the rope tie I had on du Barry. Coutts had bravely tolerated du Barry's occasional rebellious drag as well as her attempts to charge and bite Coutts's rump, but we had miles of this to tolerate together yet.

"Did you suspect it would be troublesome back there, when we first saw it?" I asked.

"Well, I wouldn't've bought the beast myself, Mr. Dickens."

"Why didn't you say so?"

"Wasn't my business. We all learn the horse trade by buying bad 'uns."

I said nothing further, but sure that if I'd had Cultay with me, he would have warned me.

I discussed the question of riding back to search for Delahunty, but Clough said, "That fellow's on his way somewhere now, you can be sure. Get some of the dark boys at Momba to work on her, Mr. Dickens. That might go well enough."

I felt dismal and remembered Fremmel sickly, as well as that other usurper, Hayward.

29

My wild horse became the joke of Momba Station for the better part of that year. Yandi and a string of other young black stockmen attempted to take the devil from her. Their confidence in their horsemanship was supreme, they rode her bareback with just a rope halter, though they had to blindfold her to get on, and when they were thrown they got up howling with laughter, except for one who suffered a concussion. White stockmen tried to tame her, and any traveling horsemen who came through, including two lean prospectors with the hollow eyes of Old Testament prophets.

"Having a go at du Barry" became station talk for testing valor. "Mate, he's game enough to have a go at du Barry."

At last Willy Suttor took me aside and told me to try to sell her after giving any prospective buyers warnings about her nature. "You should get fifteen or twenty shillings, I think—twenty shillings for some reason doesn't sound as extortionate as a pound even though they are the same amount. Not that du Barry," he continued with a smile, "does not hold a high place in all our affections . . ."

But I delayed, partly out of pride at getting a fiftieth of what I'd paid. I came close to off-loading her to a surveyor who was short of a team. I tried to forget her. There were more important lessons to be learned that year.

It struck me early that I should approach Edward Bonney, without acquainting him with the insults Fremmel had directed his way. But Fremmel had ill will to us all, and Edward did not.

Two days after I got back, I went to Edward Bonney's office, which was, as befitted the elder brother, more spacious than Fred's, its bookshelf stocked with nearly as many blue leather-bound, gold-leaf entitled stud and stock books as a solicitor's office might be with red-leathered books of case reports.

"How is that disastrous horse of yours?" he asked.

"Still disastrous, Mr. Bonney," I admitted.

"You acknowledge it like a true man, Dickens," he assured me. "We've all been fooled by horses in our day. That's why we take such delight when it happens to others. Have a seat."

I was cheered by his consolation, which was amiable and brotherly.

I told him I must speak to him because I had been approached by Mr. Fremmel.

"Oh," he replied. "Yes? And what is that priest of Mammon up to?"

"He is convinced you have a letter from Maurice, his nephew. He offered me inducements to get hold of it, together with its postmark. I told him, and it is the truth, that I did not know one way or another if Maurice had written to you or if you are friends. Then he went on to—"

"He told you he could help you in so many ways and he may have even extended the offer to your brother," said Edward, finishing my sentence.

"He said he could even thwart my brother Alfred's plans."

"The man thinks he's the Holy Roman emperor."

"To have him and du Barry in the one day made it a bleak journey home," I admitted.

"But he does have the power to help you," Edward declared. "And to harm you. This is Lilliput on the Darling, where giant dreams can be impeded by minute men. Where dreams that are vaporous and big can be brought down to earth by little creatures like him, carping on interest payments."

I nodded, surprised by the depth of his abomination for Fremmel. "I can pay him no heed, but I fear what he might do to my brother," I admitted.

"Yes, I understand that," he said, thinking. Then he looked me in the eye. "I realize I am lucky that you came to me instead of searching for the thing and perhaps finding it and passing it to that slimy being. You don't boast of loyalty, Plorn, but you possess it."

I was flattered. Such a speech directed my way was unaccustomed.

"I am a friend of Maurice, and he is the best of young men, if overenthusiastic," Edward continued. "I have confessed my tendencies to you. My friendship with Maurice was above all that. He is now embarked on a journey of honor and compassion—over everything else, it's that. I wouldn't like at all for his uncle to know where he is."

All very well, I thought, but . . .

"And I know that's all very well," he said as if in echo. "Look here, Dickens, I think we may be able to satisfy everyone's hopes and at the same time protect everyone we would choose to. Have you met Heatherley out in the Cobrilla paddock near Peery Lake?"

I told him I hadn't.

"Heatherley did fourteen years in Van Diemen's Land as a forger. Take Yandi or anyone you like to fetch him in. We are in need of him."

I noticed how he had said, "Yandi or anyone you like . . ." As if Yandi was no longer an essential person to him.

I found Yandi, who did seem a happier soul now that his initiation was accomplished. He called cheerily to other darks as we left, saying, "Mr. Dickens and me are off to find that Heatherley feller."

Yandi was a useful guide. Fred Bonney had boasted, like a proud uncle, that the Paakantji did not have maps but they had songs, and as they traveled they mentally recited the song and compared it to hills and watercourses or sumps round about to find out where they were. He'd told me, "If you ever hear a Paakantji say he knows the song for the country, you can be at ease. You'll never get lost."

The country over which we rode on the way to Cobrilla was undulating, with revelations beyond most low ridges and now and then a treasure—a waterhole, or mulla mulla grass with white cones of flowers, or the vivid purple blooms of the parakeelya desert bush in the midst of red soil. For I too was acquiring a map of this country. I could tell a clump of cow Mitchell grass from Queensland bluegrass and from neverfail, the grass that defied droughts.

We got to the gate into Cobrilla paddock late in the day and advanced into a basin full of saltbush to Heatherley's hut. He was not there but rode in at last from inspecting Cobrilla's western boundary. He was a man in his late thirties, I would say, tall but with an apologetic stoop and amply bearded. He didn't seem surprised when I told him I'd been sent to fetch him by Edward Bonney.

It was getting cold in the manner of this desert country, and he invited us into his hut to eat dinner. Several crayon sketches of the countryside were pinned on the walls, along with a watercolor of what looked like the Lake District back home. It looked recent so was possibly done from memory. When I praised the drawings he'd done of the Mutawintji mountains and the Cullowie artesian springs, all he replied was, "Learned a mite of draftsmanship once."

After dinner, Heatherley offered me his bed for the night, but I liked my swag, the glint of my own fire, and the southern hemisphere sky thick with so many constellations.

The next morning we left early, when the hills were pure fawn edges in the clearest early light. Whatever the day came to deliver, this country looked newborn each morning and in winter, with frost or condensation, glinted forth promises it might not keep.

I asked Heatherley if the priest or Cultay had come through Cobrilla on their search for Barrakoon.

"I wouldn't have objected to seeing a priest," said Heatherley, "my old mother being of that persuasion. But no."

I delivered him to Edward Bonney's office a little before noon and waited in the dining room for a glimmer of enlightenment as to why Edward had sent for him by way of voices overheard through the closed door.

After a while Edward emerged, his manner secretive but jovial. He thanked me for fetching Heatherley and said, "This is to be a confidential matter between us. Are you happy that it be so, Plorn?"

I said of course, and he said I had always been a properly discreet chap, and that since I had come to him with news of Fremmel's machinations, I deserved an explanation. "Come here and have a sherry with me at five," he suggested. "Willy Suttor's got the right materials for Heatherley, so he'll be over there by then. I'll tell you all in confidence. Very well?"

Naturally enough, I agreed, believing Edward Bonney had no interest in me in terms of his "tendency." Meanwhile, I went over to the blacksmith's shop and found Larkin and his assistant crafting a metal gate frame.

Larkin, child of convicts, carried that quietly intoxicating air of a man who had found precisely his time and place and companions.

"Have you heard from the priest?" I asked Larkin.

"I don't think he'll ever send me news, Mr. Plorn. But one of the Afghan camel drivers who was here recently saw Father Charisse trailing behind Barrakoon's people on the road up near Mount Browne. I asked did he have a horse, and the Ghan told me, 'No horse, sahib.' Walking, he said, and looking thin. Probably had gut problems from some of the food."

We let our minds play on this image of the cassocked monk keeping up with the ruthless pace of a clan of darks on their travels.

"A strange choice for a priest to make," I said.

"If I were him, I would stay with my own people," Larkin replied, "which is certainly the way things are normally done. But he has a different wisdom."

We thought about the monk, and of how far from the normal exercise of clerics like the Reverend Rutledge in town he had strayed. It was a strange comfort to know Anglicans were not tempted to anything as extravagant as Father Charisse was chasing.

"I hope they give him a second kangaroo skin against the cold at night."

"My wife gave him one of the quilts," said the blacksmith. "The thing is, he can claim to be the apostle to the Paakantji . . ."

It struck me that it was midsummer in England and I wondered if the guvnor had enough time to enjoy himself at Gad's Hill. Falstaff's Hill just by it. The Medway behind, the Thames before. A place not far from where the guvnor had grown up, in Chatham. It seemed Father had always wanted to live on that hill. We were required to memorize Poins's speech to Falstaff and Prince Hal from Shakespeare: "But, my lads, my lads, tomorrow morning, by four o'clock early at Gad's Hill, there are pilgrims going to Canterbury with rich offerings, and traders riding to London with fat purses. I have vizards for you all; you have horses for yourselves."

Aunt Georgie said once, casually, that this speech from *Henry IV* added hundreds if not thousands to the value of Gad's Hill as far as Father was concerned. The guvnor seemed, every chance that he got, to call it Shakespeare's Gad's Hill, and he would not have been as proud of Gad's Hill had it been the scene of a tragic event in Shakespeare as he was that it was a sportive one, in the spirit of the place.

I couldn't remember much of my childhood before he owned it, and it was associated with those particularly rich, full times of which I wanted to remind Alfred; when it was full of people and we children all ran mad in the garden. And Uncle Henry Austin helped him build a wonderful tunnel under the road into the area we called the Wilderness, on the other side, where he had his little chalet.

In the spirit of these memories, I wrote to Aunt Georgie to find out how the summer was progressing, and then to Mama at Gloucester Crescent, boasting a little of my colonial accomplishments.

By the time I'd finished writing to Mama it was nearly five o'clock. Edward welcomed me into his office and poured us each a glass of port, saying, "Heatherley's labors kept him late into the day and he will rest tonight with Willy Suttor and be off home to Cobrilla paddock tomorrow. It is fortunate for my brother and me that British society, combined with the penal history of the colonies, generates an army of reclusive men, and Heatherley is yet another of them."

He paused briefly and then said, "I did receive a letter from Maurice. It is a confidential letter between him and me. But now, Heatherley is a remarkable fellow with remarkable gifts who was transported to Van Diemen's Land for forging elegant bills of exchange and promissory notes. He arrived in Tasmania on the heels of some Canadian and American rebels who had taken part in an uprising in Ontario. Our consul general in New York warned the government that an American plot was afoot to rescue some of the rebels by having whaling ships rendezvous with them. Letters to the prisoners from the conspirators—friends, that is, of the prisoners—were intercepted, as were replies from the American convicts. So the authorities in Van Diemen's Land promised Heatherley his ticket-of-leave if he forged new letters, which he did. These caused a number of the prisoners to be arrested for attempted escape when they arrived at the wrong point on the coast to be picked up by their rescue ships, while the whalers likewise hove to at a false meeting place and ultimately continued their voyage without a single escapee to their credit.

"So I've asked Mr. Heatherley to use his magic with Maurice's letter, interspersing what Maurice wrote with false information. He has also aged and marked an envelope with an Adelaide postmark, since postmarks are one of his skills as well. I hope you get the same small thrill of subversion from it as I do."

I smiled.

Edward told me I could use one of the drovers to deliver the revised letter to Mr. Fremmel with a note to him saying I'd found it inside a copy of *Palgrave's Golden Treasury* in Mr. Bonney's office. The envelope prepared for it by Heatherley had the slight furriness around its edges that oft-handled and specially stored envelopes have. When I came out of the office again Edward Bonney winked at me, in a modestly triumphant frame of mind. "It's dangerous to cross Mr. Fremmel, but it's dangerous to cross the Bonneys too," he said. "I'll always be grateful to you, Plorn."

Beneath my excitement I did feel a little like a man on a rock ledge, fascinated by the prospects before me but uncertain of how secure my footing was. But one day, when the time was ripe, I would have a splendid story to tell Alfred, perhaps in his stock and station agency in Hamilton, Victoria, should that come to pass.

Next morning, just after Clough turned his horse to town with the forged letter and envelope, enclosed in a larger envelope still, I saw Heatherley move out from the store, grateful to be returning to Cobrilla.

30

One crisp day in late June, which would turn out to be a momentous month, I received a letter from my brother Frank on embossed letterhead saying: SUBINSPECTOR F. J. DICKENS, BENGAL MOUNTED POLICE.

I was impressed by "Subinspector"—it seemed to sit on the page like a promise of greater things still.

Dearest Plorn,

I'm conscious that I haven't written to my favorite and youngest brother to wish him a happy time in the colonies. I've hesitated for fear that my interest in doing so might be a bad omen because after the guvnor got me a post here, I was expecting to meet up with dear old Walter in Calcutta, just as you were hoping to meet up with Alfred. And to think that he died just weeks before I landed! At least he died in an hour of happiness, looking forward to home.

Poor Walter indeed. Dead at twenty-one before the New Year pealed.

All I ended up seeing of him were his bills for the officers' mess, the regimental store, the billiards room, and a few merchants. Little more than a fairly modest pile, but more than I could deal with, given my uncertainty about my own future expenses. So I sent these invoices on to the ever-reliable Aunt Georgie. Anyhow, because of the fit that killed poor Walter, it was not to be a conquest of Bengal by the Dickens brothers. I got over it, of course, and have made sure he has a neat little grave in the military cemetery at the camp in Bhowanipore. Please tell Mother you heard as much when you write to her. Brother Charley tells me she still takes Walter's loss pretty hard, poor woman, and knowing we keep Walter's memory green between us is a comfort to her.

Indeed, such is the potency of the guvnor's name that a number of the powerful here have suggested Walter be moved to South Park cemetery, the chief one here, as if it is to be Walter's duty in death to console passing mourners on the basis that if a Dickens is there people will know that even the great wizard of tales has given a son to the Indian enterprise!

There is a certain amount of routine in the work here. I am often sent with a troop of native police just to seize a debtor's assets. But the place is colorful. All cloth, all spice. And no one could say I was overworked. The guvnor could do what's required of me and still have time over to write in the long evenings. There is no shortage of servants and my villa is charming in a plain sort of way, with filmy curtains all through it that sometimes give a sense to me that it's built out of air. We are all quite safe. Walter and others did excellent work suppressing the mutiny, and I doubt anything like it will happen again.

Even so, I think I might like Australia or New Zealand or South Africa perhaps. Yes, it is all very colorful here, but not with the colors of my soul, I don't think. Yet I do feel I owe it to the guvnor to achieve rank and merit here, and I am pleased it is within my power to do so. By the way, the other day I was in the regimental library of the Black Watch and there was a thin bound volume of the guvnor's letter to fallen girls going to Urania Cottage. It is a wonderful letter, written without any *false piety from a grand soul to souls in the abyss, and my heart burst with pride in it. I think I can say it was Christ-like. I've determined to keep a copy close to me, to remind me how to behave towards others.*

I believe Alfred is near you in the bush, which must be very pleasing and a solace. Give Skittles my fraternal love when you see him. I imagine you are both dazzling the colonial maidens with pavanes and the monologues of Mayhew? Here there are many girls, but their targets are the regimental chaps and we police are chiefly approached by widows whose standards have slipped. If your forlorn brother Frankie is ever to find a bride, I think it must be during home leave if I can persuade some innocent girl she will love Bengal. And indeed, if you saw some of the parasitic fevers chaps from the remoter stations catch, Calcutta can seem a desirable center with every convenience. Of course, should I ever be promoted to Inspector, I will be posted to one of those outer places like Ghaihab amongst the Moslems or Jhargram amongst the Hindus. I am sternly determined, let me assure you, to live through with daily ingestion of malt whisky chota pegs.

With brotherly affection,
Frank

I felt an exquisite pleasure at Frank's assessment of our father and went looking for his letter amongst the bookshelves in the living room of Momba Station homestead. The titles of a number of my father's works chided me here, but at least I could pretend I was approaching them through the foothills of the guvnor's shorter works. I searched in some bound copies of *Household Words*, then I looked at a volume of essays and found his *American Notes*, written long before I was born, as well as a piece on the Anglican Church and *A Child's History of England*. But not the letter Frank had mentioned.

31

Very early one morning I was woken by the sound of movement and horses, and some loud shouting in the homestead paddock. When I rose and shaved, the house seemed serene again. It was only when I walked into the dining room that I saw an extraordinary and flamboyant man sitting sideways at the table drinking tea through an assembly of mighty moustache and beard. Slung over his left shoulder was the type of short jacket worn by a Russian or Hungarian hussar. He was also wearing blue pants with gold piping and large knee boots. On the table in front of him, in the place of the plate, was a revolver.

Both Fred and Edward Bonney tried to catch my eye, signaling me to be careful.

"Ah, Plorn," said Fred, "may I introduce you to Mr. Pearson? Mr. Pearson is in charge of us for the time being, it seems."

"It is *Doctor* Pearson, if you don't mind," the visitor told us in a West Country English voice, quite melodious.

"Dr. Pearson," Edward murmured, as if he were trying out the name on the tongue.

"Dr. Pearson arrived early this morning and has command of the station," Fred told me.

"Starlight," I murmured. "I have read about you. You're Captain Starlight."

"I never claimed that nickname," he told me. "I am a doctor. Learned thereto by doctoring horses in the Russian army. But I am not a captain, you must understand."

"You and your associates are captains of Momba at the moment," observed Edward Bonney with a sniff.

"Well, we will bring everyone in here soon, and then we'll see what captaincy is about. What is your name, young man?"

"I'm usually called P-L-O-R-N, Plorn. It doesn't mean anything. It's a family name."

"And what is your family name?"

The Bonney brothers semaphored frantically with their eyebrows.

"Simpson," I told Captain Starlight. "S-I-M-P—"

"I can spell it," Dr. Pearson informed me as I saw the relief and small nods of approval from the Bonney brothers.

"Well," he continued, "I've heard that this station is huge, you run it sweet as a nut, and I've been wanting to visit for some time. During our stay, all will remain sweet, Messrs. Bonney. We have no animus against anyone here, and take pride in how we treat our guests, and all in fun. Yes, Mr. Bonney and Mr. Bonney both, fun!"

At that he picked up the revolver and went to confer with his lieutenants outside. For Captain Starlight was holding up our entire station, remote boundary riders excepted for the moment.

"By the way, my associate Rutherford is a cultivated man," he said, stopping at the door. "Do you have newspapers, books, et cetera?"

"Indeed," said Fred.

"D'you read, Simpson?"

"I'm sure Mr. Rutherford would enjoy *The Moonstone*, Wilkie Collins's latest, which I have."

"I want you to put together newspapers and books. Don't stint. And you, Mr. Bonney, come at your convenience, but without too much delay, and tell your darks there'll be no station labor today. No one will ride out of Momba either."

Fred nodded. "As you say, Doctor."

And off Pearson strode, holstering his revolver as he walked into the hallway.

"Well, my young friend Simpson . . ." said Edward Bonney, dryly amused. "We are bailed up by bushrangers. That's a new colonial experience for you. But who do they think they are, striking such poses?"

"Pearson thinks he's a surgeon, obviously," said Fred. "And he thinks Plorn's called Simpson. Let's maintain that. We don't want him writing to your father for a ransom, and in the meantime Plorn will have to bucket round the countryside with Pearson and co. until it's paid. I'll go out and talk to the dark people. Plorn, put together a parcel of perhaps half a dozen recent books, none of your father's, and any newspapers around the place. By all means, go into my office."

I got the printed matter together, including newspapers from Sydney, Melbourne, and Adelaide from Fred's office—he liked newsprint—as well as *Australasian Sketcher* and a recent copy of the guvnor's mag, *All the Year Round*. I left them all in the hallway for Rutherford, the literate desperado I had not yet met.

Since Dr. Pearson had left the homestead, I took the opportunity to go out onto the veranda and watch the scene, if scene it were, from there. I noticed that a husky man in a kangaroo-skin jacket and cavalry pants like Dr. Pearson's carrying an elegant carbine was on casual guard at the homestead's pasture gate. Perhaps a hundred paces from where I stood, a man I presumed to be Rutherford was supervising a number of his armed confederates, who were escorting members of Momba village—including Willy Sutton, the

Larkins, the drover Clough and others—into a knot of hostages. No one looked scared. In fact the chief visible emotion was amusement. Two of the gang emerged from one of the drovers' huts with a sack, presumably containing hard-won valuables. They had also heaped what they desired from Willy's stock—a pile of tobacco, cocky's joy, a brandy flagon, a few notebooks and ink, and three saddles with their accompanying tack—on the veranda of the store.

I felt a certain anger. It was not as if drovers like Clough had limitless possessions, and the cost of wagon transport from Cobar meant they could certainly not be cheaply replaced. Fred Bonney appeared from the direction of the darks' camp, reassuring his people and speaking to Dr. Pearson and the man I supposed to be Rutherford. Dr. Pearson was standing to one side with a tall Aboriginal member of his group, who laughed frankly whenever anyone in the crowd showed any sign of discomfort. Perhaps he was pleased to see white people incommoded, given some of the things his people had suffered at white hands. His occasional amusement seemed to annoy Dr. Pearson, who sent him off, probably to keep an eye on the darks' camp.

Rutherford, Dr. Pearson, and two of their lieutenants, young and bushy bearded, started shepherding the white population of Momba towards the homestead. I stood by and watched them pass me on the veranda. As they did, Fred called to me loudly, saying, "You had better join us, too, Mr. Simpson."

"Yes, sir," I replied promptly, and it was apparent to me that Fred had signaled my change of name to the group. Clough said to Rutherford, "It wouldn't be happening like this, mate, if I'd got to my rifle under the bed."

Rutherford, carbine in the angle of his left arm and a gun at his waist, said in a robust and amused native-born accent, "It's not your rifle anymore, son, but you can acquire another, eh? And next time we're in the area, I'll drop you a line so you'll be ready for me."

We were all taken into the sitting room where, under the watchful gaze of Dr. Pearson and Rutherford, we disposed ourselves around the room. The station hands were reluctant to sit on the good furniture and many slid to the floor or to their haunches, then the younger of the gang brought in some extra chairs from the dining room for the two ladies.

When everyone was settled, Dr. Pearson addressed us.

"My name is Dr. Pearson and I am the son of a Mexican woman and a Yankee Irishman," he announced in a voice entirely from the environs of Plymouth. "I was trained to doctor horses in the Twenty-Seventh Imperial Guards of Russian hussars. My associate is Mr. Charlie Rutherford, and my two lieutenants Mr. Blacker and Mr. Thompson. We will all remain in this room together till first light tomorrow, while my associates assess our needs against your possessions."

"Then you will depart with all we own," cried Tom Larkin, "and consider yourselves just men."

Dr. Pearson sighed. "My friend, I would advise against such outbursts. We all know what is happening, and we don't need it defined. But I hope that when you measure what we leave, as against what we take, you may think more kindly of us than the Angles did of the Danes. Isn't that so, Mr. Rutherford?"

"Our needs are modest, ladies and gentlemen," confirmed Mr. Rutherford from the other end of the room. "And besides, in most towns shopkeepers are only too anxious to help us out. I spent the early hours of the day with your shopkeeper, Mr. Suttor, and found him a trump and an utterly amiable chap."

"Speaking of amiability," said Dr. Pearson, "we have a literal day to occupy ourselves. Thank God for the piano here. The two ladies in this room will be treated with every courtesy and this evening will be allowed to retire to one of the bedrooms under guard. Until then, I must depend upon you to entertain us and yourselves.

Who has a favorite song? A comic recitation perhaps? Even a solemn one, if you must, as long as it doesn't take too long."

As we captives looked at each other questioningly, Rutherford continued the instructions. "We are not hostile to a recitation of Psalms, if you must, for some of them are quite beautiful, as I learned from my mama. But please do not think that by reciting the Psalms you will improve the doctor or myself because the two of us are all square with the Deity, who likes our spirit and is willing as a father to forgive us our childlike crimes which hold no parity with the crimes of our betters. So, entertainers, come forward."

When there was no response, Dr. Pearson smiled at Rutherford. "Isn't this always the way with people?" he said. "It's as if they don't believe in our sincerity. A man who was trusted by tsars and tsarinas, in my case, and a consummate gentleman of the bush in yours, Mr. Rutherford. As always I must call on you to start things off." He now changed himself to a recitative music hall mode. "And so, ladies and gentlemen, I present my friend, the incomparable intellect from the inkiest interstices of the bush, the brave and battling, bold and unboastful behemoth of boisterous and bosky beatitudes, Mr. Charlie Rutherford. And what is it to be today, Charlie—a Mayhew monologue, or a verse by Robert Burns? But please, please, not that saucy devil Lord Rochester! Perhaps that immortal verse 'The Pig'? Or 'Whisky in the Jar'—recited or sung?"

"No, Doctor," said Rutherford, "today I intend to recite from *The Pickwick Papers*."

Everyone in the room tried not to look at me, but did, as if now I was definitely given away.

"I begin, Dr. Pearson, with the oft-quoted and universally cherished speech of the prosecuting Serjeant Buzfuz against Mr. Pickwick in the case of Mrs. Bardell versus Pickwick, she having sued that gentleman for breach of promise."

He composed himself and began in his idea of a fustian British accent.

The plaintiff, gentlemen, the plaintiff is a widow; yes, gentlemen, a widow. The late Mr. Bardell, after enjoying, for many years, the esteem and confidence of his sovereign, as one of the guardians of his royal revenues, glided almost imperceptibly from the world, to seek elsewhere for that repose and peace which a custom-house can never afford.

Some time before his death, he had stamped his likeness upon a little boy.

There were a few tentative laughs around the room.

With this little boy, the only pledge of her departed exciseman, Mrs. Bardell shrank from the world, and courted the retirement and tranquillity of Goswell Street; and here she placed in her front parlour window a written placard, bearing this inscription—"Apartments furnished for a single gentleman. Inquire within."

"Apartments furnished for a single gentleman!" Mrs. Bardell's opinions of the opposite sex, gentlemen, were derived from a long contemplation of the inestimable qualities of her lost husband . . . "Mr. Bardell," said the widow. "Mr. Bardell was a man of honour, Mr. Bardell was a man of his word, Mr. Bardell was no deceiver, Mr. Bardell was once a single gentleman himself; to single gentlemen I looked for protection, for assistance, for comfort, and for consolation; in single gentlemen I shall perpetually see something to remind me of what Mr. Bardell was when he first won my young and untried affections; to a single gentleman, then, shall my lodgings be let."

I could see that some of the drovers had become quite engrossed in Rutherford's flawless and practiced recitation.

Before the bill had been in the parlour window three days— three days, gentlemen—a being, erect upon two legs, and bearing all the outward resemblance of a man, and not of a monster, knocked on the door of Mrs. Bardell's house. He inquired within—he took the lodgings; and on the very next day he entered into possession of them. This man was Pickwick— Pickwick, the defendant.

Rutherford's gifts were such that no one was paying me any attention now. They were engrossed in the drama of Sergeant Buzfuz's oratory. But the most enthusiastic supporters of Rutherford were his own bushranger crew and, above all, the doctor himself. Rutherford continued into Buzfuz's examination of Pickwick's letters to Mrs. Bardell.

They are covert, sly, underhanded communications . . . letters which must be viewed with a cautious or suspicious eye—letters that were evidently intended at the time, by Mr. Pickwick, to mislead and delude any third parties into whose hands they might fall. Let me read the first: "Garraways, twelve o'clock. Dear Mrs. B—Chops and tomato sauce. Yours, PICKWICK." Gentlemen, what does this mean? Chops and tomato sauce. Yours, Pickwick! Chops! Gracious heavens! And tomato sauce! Gentlemen, is the happiness of a sensitive and confiding female to be trifled away, by such shallow artifices as these?

I saw Mrs. Larkin look at her husband and laugh despite herself, shaking her head. I didn't hear the end of the speech as recited by

Rutherford, daydreaming instead of the fact that my father's hand gave even Australian outlaws the chance to shine before their fellow beings.

The concluding applause startled me back to the present as Dr. Pearson stood up and said, "I thank my brother in arms, Rutherford, for breaking the ice amongst us, ladies and gentlemen, and for demonstrating the good intentions of those who presume to keep you captive for a mere day. What brave soul will follow with song or utterance? Please don't be shy . . ."

Already a young stockman called Tallis was rising, cheered on by his mates. The doctor asked for his name and when that was given asked him if he had something suitable for the ladies for—so the doctor said—he was aware of the rough humor of men of the bush. On that proviso, Tallis sang a complaint song called "Oh! Angelina Was Always Fond of Soldiers" with a snarl on his face. It was one of those songs for which frowning and disgruntlement and a harsh voice were better than being a smiling tenor. *"Oh! Angelina was always fond of soldiers, / When I think on't, I can't restrain my tears. / She was once so very kind, but I've lost my peace of mind, / Since the visit of the Belgium Volunteers, tum, tum."*

Once the applause died, Dr. Pearson reminded the company that there was a piano in the room and how celestial it would be to hear the gallant Tallis accompanied. I saw Tom Larkin urge his wife forward, willing her to shine even if he disapproved of the company. She did so, sitting at the piano and performing a very creditable version of "Für Elise." Through all this I kept my obscure position on the floor, my back against the wall, knees up level with my cheeks. Then one of the drovers said he was a poor hand at the piano but he had a squeezebox in his hut "if it hain't been stole" and if one of the doctor's friends would accompany him he would bring it back and perform.

In the meantime, comic and not so comic recitations abounded.

Mathews's *Patter versus Clatter* and *Alone I Did It*, and then the beautiful Mrs. Larkin sang and played "Who Is Sylvia?" The squeezebox
man returned, and a prospective singer came forward and con-
ferred with the piano and the concertina over a song that perhaps
they all knew, and Mrs. Larkin frowned but committed herself to
the task, and soon we heard a fine rendition of "When the Corn Is
Waving, Annie Dear." The young lieutenants left the sitting room
as Willy Suttor performed "The Wreck of the Hesperus," and returned with a great kettle of black tea and a canister of sugar, and
all we captives took grateful part before returning to the midst of
the floor-sitting men. Later, as noon rolled around, they took the
cook out to the kitchen to make a mass of mutton sandwiches.
In between items of entertainment, the captives chattered about
remembering the first time they'd heard that song, or when their
auntie had taken them to the fabled Eagle in City Road, London,
to see Charlie Mathews. Dr. Pearson went so far as to admit that
his mother had been a dancer in the music halls of Texas, and we
could see people nodding and reflecting on his non-Texas accent.

There were special rounds of applause for the gifted Mrs. Larkin. Tom, sensibly enough, seemed gratified that within the population of the station she had become a musical legend and sat at an
apex of refinement.

After lunch the women were escorted to the homestead out-
houses, and the male captives were permitted to urinate amongst
the gums and peppertrees in the direction of the creek behind the
homestead. All seemed quiet except for a normal sudden outcry or
incantatory-sounding speech of a woman in the Paakantji tongue,
calling out to a child or recalcitrant man. As we buttoned ourselves
and returned inside, a number of the station men took a hushed
glee in calling me Mr. Simpson.

32

After returning to the sitting room after lunch, we were required to stand up and defeat drowsiness by playing a game proposed by Dr. Pearson. "To play this game," he told us without irony, "you must first stand honestly, then give up and sit down when you can no longer think of a town. Remember, you are on your honor. We will play one game devoted to the cities and towns of the old country, and one game devoted to those of the Antipodes. The last one standing is the winner of the game."

The game involved Pearson calling out "*A*," at which if we knew an Australian town or city that began with that letter, we clapped our hands vigorously above our heads to increase circulation and signify our cleverness. Each clapper was asked what town he had in mind and remained standing if the answer was right. But when Pearson called a letter for which we could not think of an answer, we had to sit down defeated. "On your honor as Britons," he warned us again. And so we began, and the whole room obviously got Adelaide, and then Brisbane, clap, and the guesses became diffuse at *C*—Cabramatta, Caloundra, Cuppacumbalong, Clovelly, Coburg, Cootamundra, Cobar, of course, Coopernook. It was easy to cheat if you were not the first asked, but we *were* on our honor as Britons, after all. Dungog, Dunedoo. It was quite a pleasant if temporary release from tension to clap our hands above our heads. At *E*, some of the players began to sit, while the mind raced ahead to speculate whether there was any town or city in the colonies beginning with *Z*. In any case, I speculated that if I was still in the game by *W*, I knew of a Wallerawang, an inevitable Wellington, a Warrabri, and a Wollongong.

A considerable number of us were still standing by *O*, but a lot were defeated by that letter and sat. Two of the station hands near me got into an argument when the town nominated by one of them was Ongerwrong.

"Where in the name of God is Ongerwrong?"

"It's in Western Australia, mate," came the reply.

"That's bloody bulldust and you know it."

"So, have you ever been to Western Australia?"

"I haven't, but neither have you. And if there weren't ladies present I'd call you a bloody liar."

"And if there weren't ladies present, you mongrel, I would be grossly offended to the limit of uttering bloody curses at you, and calling you a blackguard, and an insulting wretch, as you are—and one who has cheated at euchre as all your mates bloody well know!"

Charlie Rutherford whistled and called for peace before Dr. Pearson said, "This is not an arena for hostility."

But a bandit whose chief tools of detention were fun and games lacked the authority to cut into the dispute as the accusing stockman took the other one by the shirt. The champion of Ongerwrong tore himself loose and shot out an arm at the other man, who staggered back. Having myself bowed out at *O* I felt shamed by this petty behavior—in the end, it was no matter whether Ongerwrong was a functioning township or a fiction. But these men were unduly exposing themselves and possibly their fear to the bushrangers and disgracing the company of their fellow captives. And there *were* ladies present—Mrs. Larkin and Mrs. Gavan.

Since I was so much closer to the two men than Fred or Edward,

I rose to make peace and suggest they both disqualify themselves from the game.

"Gentlemen," I said, placing a hand on the shoulder of the one who had nominated Ongerwrong. "Let's not betray ourselves in front of our guests."

Sadly, the man accused of being a euchre thief, a large accusation amongst bush folk with whom euchre was the supreme game, again attacked the other man's shoulder, who was sent stumbling into me, and cried, "My Christ, sorry, Mr. Dickens."

A silence followed in which a solitary magpie could be heard singing a long song that seemed to say, "We're for it now."

"Did you say 'Dickens'?" asked Dr. Pearson.

"My mistake, Doctor," said the man who'd barreled into me.

"Isn't his name Simpson?" asked Rutherford.

I could see Fred Bonney half rising to intervene, but unsure about exactly how to do so.

"Why do you call him Dickens? We're very interested in that name," asked Rutherford.

"I'm sure you are," declared Fred Bonney. "But may I warn you, at the moment the authorities in New South Wales seek your arrest. If you do any wrong to Mr. Dickens, or even offer him insult, you will bring the entire world down upon your neck."

None of the gang seemed to quaver at this warning. Rutherford said to me calmly, "Are you Dickens, then? Are you the son we have heard rumors of?"

"Yes, I am," I confirmed, suddenly feeling no fear. "It was entirely my idea to conceal who I was."

"Mr. Rutherford and I must speak to you," Pearson told me sternly, and gave instructions to the two junior bushrangers to hold the crowd securely while I left with them.

Fred Bonney declared, "I must be there too. I am the boy's guardian."

Rutherford and Dr. Pearson exchanged looks. "You can be present, Mr. Bonney, yes. Come, young Dickens!"

I moved to the door with the outlaws and dear old Fred. People stood back to clear a way for us, as for two men on the way to the gallows. And then the two fabled bushrangers and Fred stood aside to let me out into the corridor. On this raw desert day, the hallway was cold.

"Is there somewhere we can confer, Mr. Bonney?" asked Dr. Pearson.

"Yes," said Fred, resolute. "We can use my office by the kitchen."

He led the way to the back of the house and into his office with his pictures of Paakantji on the wall. On entering, the two bushrangers were taken by the magic and science of this.

"How do you get these, Mr. Bonney?" Pearson asked.

"It is just the impact of light on certain chemicals coated on a glass plate. Surely you've seen photographs before."

"It's not your work, is it?"

"Yes. I am a photographer. But it is only science. The science of light."

"It is more than that," insisted Pearson. "Let us all sit."

Fred took his seat behind his desk, Pearson pointed me to a chair across the room, and he and Charlie Rutherford sat together on a settee by the wall.

"So," Charlie said, "what's your name?"

"My name is Edward Bulwer Lytton Dickens," I said defiantly. "I am the son of Charles and Catherine Dickens."

"Tell them who your godfather is," Fred urged me.

"My godfather is Baron Edward Bulwer-Lytton, formerly Secretary of State for the Colonies and a very famed novelist," I replied.

"You see, gentlemen," said Fred, "you are playing with fire. Princes and principalities and more will be ranged against any malign act you commit here."

"You misjudge us, Bonney," declared Rutherford, "as your type always does."

Pearson asked, "It is the world-revered author who is your father?"

"Yes. I'm the youngest in the family."

"We thought you would have beams of light shining from your forehead," said Pearson.

"As you see, apart from my father I'm an average English boy. And I was not even good at school."

The bushrangers looked at each other, frowning and, it seemed, a little bewildered.

"Yet," interposed the ever-loyal Fred, "he is naturally gifted for the life of a colonial pastoralist. And I suggest you let him continue in it."

"You have already made that point twice, Mr. Bonney," said Pearson.

"We admire your father as reverently as any citizens in the world," declared Rutherford.

"And it is our honor to greet you, Mr. Dickens," Pearson assured me. "Bewildered as we are by the fact you chose to hide yourself from us as if we were Corsican banditti."

"What do you expect?" Fred asked them. "After the newspapers have finished laying out your history of raids and depredations!"

"Grossly exaggerated," insisted Rutherford.

"What do you expect?" Fred challenged them again.

But instead of taking offense, Rutherford and Pearson seemed to be exchanging consultative glances.

"It is my sad duty—and Mr. Rutherford and I have concluded it to be a grievous duty we cannot step back from—to let you know that your eminent and esteemed father . . . has died," said Pearson with a type of fraternal mournfulness.

I blinked, feeling panicked and bewildered. My skin prickled and I felt as if I were bursting out of a chrysalis, turning into a new, unwelcome kind of being.

"We held up the pub in Mount Manara three days ago," said Pearson. "There was a gentleman there who'd come posthaste from Sydney to inspect a station and he had on him a *Sydney Morning Herald* only six days old."

Charlie Rutherford said, "It's a new world, you see, young Dickens. There is now an undersea cable all the way to India, so they knew about the death almost as quick as folk in Britain. Then a steaming ship brought the news to Sydney, and our gent brought it to Mount Manara, and that's how we learned the grievous fact."

"You are confusing us," Fred complained. "What exactly are you trying to say?"

With a bowed head, Rutherford withdrew a sheet of newsprint from his breast pocket and slowly unfolded it. The page he held up had a heavy black border with the headline, CHARLES DICKENS DIES IN KENT. I was able to take in a further line, EXPIRES IN HIS DAUGHTER'S ARMS AT HIS BELOVED GAD'S HILL PLACE.

I wanted to stand and fight the proposition, but with the words "Gad's Hill Place" quivering in my brain, I lost all power and plummeted to the floor. I have fled, I thought in the instant I fell, a counterfeit world.

I came to with the taste of acrid brandy being poured past my lips, which took my breath and set me coughing. I saw Fred's concerned face, and the brandy bottle he was holding, and Rutherford still standing there with the black-bordered page of newspaper. Dr. Pearson was kneeling by me, his fingers on the side of my throat.

"Well," said Pearson, "we did wonder if we should forget it and let you discover in time. But that seemed to smack of bloody cruelty."

"The ignorance that is not bliss," supplied Rutherford. "I am sorry, young'un. I am sorry for all of us, but for you above all."

"A terrible business," agreed Fred as he and Pearson helped me back on my feet and into the chair. "May I be the first, Plorn, to offer my sincerest condolences. If the world has suffered a grievous loss, I cannot imagine the depth of your own grief."

"But it can't be true," I told him in a panic of loss. "It is a lie they are trying to put in place, God knows why."

At that I heard Rutherford whimper with genuine grief and I thought that maybe he believed the black-edged lie himself rather than being its perpetrator. Dr. Pearson whispered in my ear, "I would give my life at this moment to make it untrue."

"You can't believe it's a fact, Mr. Bonney?" I appealed to Fred.

"It is the *Sydney Morning Herald*," Fred assured me, as if that organ was the closest thing to divine writ.

"Of course, we will depart immediately, Mr. Bonney," said Pearson. "We will not prey on a house of grief. We will take from the store only what we need, since it is a long ride between provedores in this Western Division."

Still taken up with the question of veracity and the reliability of his word, Rutherford was reading from the printed page now.

It is not only the *Bengal Gazette* and a number of other Northern Indian organs that announce the sad news, but they quote directly from cables that include the very report of *The Times* of London, and indeed further accounts of the modest ceremony of the interment in Westminster Abbey of the greatest British storyteller since Shakespeare. We are therefore left with no options of denial and feel bound to announce to the population of New South Wales that this death of a man of irreplaceable spirit is now certain, and that we should mourn it as other children of the English language from Toronto to New York, from Africa to East Bengal mourn it, and even as it is mourned at the court of the French emperor and that of the Czars . . .

He looked up for confirmation that his breaking the news had been well intentioned and was not fatuous.

Miss Georgina Hogarth, aunt to the Dickens' children and faithful housekeeper of Gad's Hill Place, declared that Dickens, on the day of his collapse, Wednesday 8 June, had been at the office of *All the Year Round* magazine, in Wellington Street, 41 Long Acre, Covent Garden, but was at Gad's Hill near Rochester, Kent, by the middle of the day. Miss Hogarth reports that he rested and had a cigar and then went to work in the small chalet in the grounds of his house, returning to the house in the late afternoon to write letters in the study. He entered the dining room at 6 o'clock looking unwell. Miss Hogarth asked him if he felt ill and he replied, "Yes, very ill. I have been very ill for the last hour." On her saying she would send for a doctor, he declared that after dinner he needed to go to London. He complained of toothache and held his face, and asked that the dining room window be closed, which she complied with. When she suggested that he lie down, he declared, "Yes, on the ground.'

"These four words were to be the last uttered by that great engine of invention. With them, he resigned from our lives and collapsed to the floor."

"I know that floor," I wanted to yell. The parquetry. All the paintings on the wall, the long sideboard. The big domed mirror rising amongst them. The fluted legs of the dinner table. And all the gleaming fine-cut cruets of a successful life. But the man sinking to the floor would not be unstopping them again.

My grief became a well now. It was *my* grief, no longer carried by the bushrangers as an item of plunder. It had lodged mercilessly in me. I began to sob. In fact, I would find from my later reading of the report that he had lived, barely conscious, another day.

"Oh Jesus Christ, sorry, laddie," said Rutherford above me, as Dr. Pearson kneaded my shoulder in sympathy.

"So it has happened?" I asked Fred.

"I would say so," he replied mournfully.

"We'll ride away now, Mr. Bonney," offered Dr. Pearson again. "I do ask your word of honor that you will not send your men on our track."

"I will give you my word. As for honor . . ."

"Good enough," said Rutherford, as if not wanting to hear the rest of the sentence.

"Spare a kind thought for us when we are hanged," suggested Dr. Pearson. "And I may still take a few horses. I'm trying to be square with you."

33

The Starlight gang vanished from the environs of Momba homestead within an hour, having released all captives to return to their dwellings. Dr. Pearson and Fred Bonney explained to them that my father was reported to be dead and they were not going ahead with their planned robbery.

Still, on reflection, I could not believe the guvnor was gone. I believed in the sincerity of the report; I mean, as far as it had been read to me by Rutherford. I possessed the printed report of it and took it to my room. But I did not read it at first. I thought that if I delayed, another cable would come along the undersea wire and news of it would travel then from Bengal to Australia, and the tale would be reversed, my father being declared healthy. There had been some mention of interment in the Abbey, but it might have grown purely from the mistaken assumption of his death.

During the night, however, I could not prevent myself reading the rest, and I felt a panicked impulse to scurry to Alfred in Corona, though in that vastness scurrying was not a choice.

"Alfred," I said. "Story's over."

By the giant act of expiring, my father would in time reduce him, surely, to simple grief.

I read more of the black-bordered page.

I found that Dr. Steele had ordered the sofa be brought into the dining room over by the window that looked out to the field behind the house, the field that produced a few acres of hay and many days of delightful sport. As the patient was lifted onto it, Steele believed my father was past help. Katie and Mamie were summoned by telegram and arrived about midnight. Mama wasn't summoned at all, it seemed. My two sisters and Aunt Georgie sat with him all through the night, placing hot bricks at his feet. Charley arrived from town by morning. I yearned to have arrived myself. I believed, despite my inelegant vocabulary, that I would have had the words to awaken him, and besides, he would want to awaken and ask me how was Australia? Dr. Frank Beard, his old friend, came in answer to a telegram from Aunt Georgie and declared there had been a brain hemorrhage.

Father died, according to this account, at six o'clock in the evening. Henry came down from Cambridge, beside himself since he had been told by a porter on Rochester Station. The guvnor's sister, Aunt Letitia, came too. Mamie took a lock from Father's head. The girls had red geraniums, the guvnor's favorite flowers, and blue lobelias, brought in from the beds at the front of the house and arranged around the body. The next morning, said the *Herald* per favor of *The Times*, Katie went up to London to let Mama know the sad news.

The Queen sent Mama a telegram. John Millais, Katie's good friend, came to draw the guvnor's face in death and a sculptor took a cast. George Dolby, the guvnor's tour manager, also came, bleary with grief.

Had the young Irish friend of Father's been there at any stage, I wondered. We children received a mention in the report, even me. But Miss Ternan was never mentioned, being—if she *was* there—more than a guest yet not counted amongst them. Beyond the death itself there was nothing left for the plain grocery of the human emotions, little items such as jealousy. If I hated her, it was because she lived and he didn't, and his time being finite she may have somehow received more of his true nature than Alfred and I did. More than a child could.

Some four days later, his body was transported for interment at Westminster Abbey. Pa's useless brother Alfred's son, Edmund, had been in one of the three coaches that followed the body. The guvnor often said he wanted to be buried in the old churchyard at Shorne, the village just down the road from Higham, with lozenge-shaped little limestone markers for the graves of infants. The cathedral at Rochester had made a bid for his coffined body, though, and now the Abbey did, too, and of course the Abbey won.

As Father had decreed, there were not many mourners. His body had come up early in the morning from Higham to Charing Cross, along with his mourners—Katie, Mamie, Charley, and Henry were there—on the same train. He was always on that line, back and forth. And now he was traveling it dead. It couldn't be! The resurrection of Christ was easier to believe in than the death of Charles Dickens. Aunt Georgie traveled with him, Wilkie Collins, Pa's brother Alfred, Katie's husband, Aunt Letitia, Frank Beard, and John Forster had also attended. Who else? George Sala, who worked at the magazine. Fred Ouvry, who had given me a lawyerly talking-to before I left home. Had the girl been there, too, in the coaches? At the Abbey? The newspaper article did not mention her. Mama was not mentioned. Had he gone to the trouble, the guvnor, of saying she shouldn't be?

The Abbey bell tolled and the dean and canons were waiting inside the main door as the coffin and the mourners arrived. They processed up the nave and the doors were closed behind him. Even the organ was muted. No funeral oration was given, no choir sang. The guvnor had wanted it that way.

The *Herald* had the grace to quote Longfellow, who said, "Dickens was so full of life that it did not seem possible he could die. I never knew an author's death to cause such general mourning. It is no exaggeration to say that this whole country is stricken with grief."

And this the Americans, whom the guvnor had accused of too much spitting and boasting!

～

I did not easily recover from the idea that casual friends like Dr. Beard and the guvnor's nephew and George Sala had been at the guvnor's interment. I envied all who had been allowed to attend, while still believing the guvnor was alive.

Even before a letter from Aunt Georgie arrived confirming the fall, a Wilcannia policeman came riding into Momba with a summons from the colonial government of New South Wales. The governor, the Parliament, the people of the state were to mourn the death of our father in Sydney, and Alfred and I were called on to be central to that. They knew of the death and it seemed dreadful to me that they did. And that to powers and potentates and people it was a settled fact.

～

A civic reception to mark Father's death was held at the Commercial in Wilcannia, before Alfred and I set out on our pilgrims' route to Sydney. When he and I met in a private little room there, he seized me fiercely and began to hack and choke with tears himself and said, "It's terrible. No letter from anyone that we love to tell us, Plorn, old son. I want, in my hands, a letter from Aunt Georgie or Mama before I believe it fully."

His grief was an extraordinary thing to see, and I have to say that I felt somehow it came from exactly the same well of bitterness as all his earlier complaints about the dear old guvnor. As I held him, I could see that we were more equal men than we had ever been. Even on the simple physical level I was nearly as tall as him, and he looked to me like a trim little man, with his swaybacked straightness, his head raised in a way you often saw in men of medium height, a cock sparrow look, ready for the tall of the world to do their worst.

We were under a duty, however, to compose ourselves and go to meet the citizens of the Darling River in that very same parlor or ballroom where I'd heard Connie Desailly and Hayward sing together. I was shocked by this fierce display, by the scale of it, in Alfred. It was a given that English people faced the death of loved ones with restraint and whispers and resignation. All the etiquette books said so, the ones we studied at Wimbledon and Rochester. Italians railed at God, demanded a resurrection, and refused to be consoled. But it occurred to me that something Alfred got from the guvnor himself was more along the Italian lines than the British. The large gestures of grief for my sister Dora were the guvnor's. And when I met Alfred in Wilcannia, he wept with a passion for a solid quarter hour, and I was the comforter. No ordinary writhing, his, and at last I had to ask him to try to settle for Father's sake.

He did, and we went into the ballroom, where speeches were made by the mayor of Wilcannia, and readings were given from the death of Little Nell, by the local theatrical company. "She seemed a creature fresh from the hand of God, and waiting for the breath of life; not one who had lived and suffered death. . . . So shall we know the angels in their majesty, after death" was beautifully delivered by a woman from the Wilcannia school. Then a bank clerk read a section of *A Tale of Two Cities*, in which Charles Darnay is preparing for death, and Sydney Carton would redeem him as Christ redeemed us all in the believed-in long term. This performer strove for relevance by means of volume.

I realized, though, that these good people had done their best to find and rehearse death scenes in Father's books. And then, without my knowing it, Connie Desailly was there on the stage, beyond the banks of flowers. "Connie Desailly," I told Alfred in a whisper, in case he had forgotten. She recited a poem by Alfred Tennyson, Alfred's godfather, and he watched her intently and, I believe, with a form of consolation. It was beautifully odd, a girl reciting from *Le Morte d'Arthur*. "So saying, from the ruined shrine he stept / And in the moon athwart the place of tombs / Where lay the mighty bones of ancient men . . ."

It all sounded exactly right in her unaffected mouth. Oh, it became apparent to me then, I simply loved her, vowels and all. But there was Hayward. She and Hayward were destiny's duet. You could see it. She would stop him from being brutishly drunk and studiedly vulgar! She had arisen in a geographic locality that was a harsh place for hues and subtleties and hints. But I loved the way she said "athwart."

Suddenly she was on "In Memoriam."

Meanwhile, I muttered it to myself as an experiment. "Athwart." And reflected what a disaster "In Memoriam" would have been on an overpious, breathy tongue.

"Did you say something?" asked Alfred in a whisper as his god-father's august rhythms rolled on. I bumped my fisted right hand against my lips to convey I had coughed. But "athwart" I had said in enchantment.

"Awful time he had as a child," the guvnor had said of Uncle Alfred Tennyson. I think cocaine and lunacy were involved, and a wretched mother and a father who, though a clergyman, was as malignant as any other fellow.

Connie continued: "I held it truth, with him who sings / To one clear harp in divers tones / That men may rise on stepping-stones / Of their dead selves to higher things."

I liked the way she then recited, "Let love clasp Grief lest both be drowned . . ."

I wanted to say, "Love clasp Grief" aloud, as I had said "athwart."

After Connie yielded the stage, Reverend Rutledge took it and recited Psalm 23, and then people joined a queue to express their condolences to us and, as the Reverend Rutledge had said, to console themselves by looking upon the flesh and blood of immortal Dickens, amongst those in Wilcannia more obviously than anywhere else on Earth in Alfred and me.

It was true that a genuine awe hung over the occasion. The condolences were not facile. They were, in a wonderful sense, communal.

At last the Desaillys appeared in front of me. It was soothing to see their frowning ceremoniousness. Mrs. Desailly parted her veil to deliver her feelings. Alfred Desailly was more brusque, of the school of thought that death was so enormous a beast that there was no word crafted to penetrate its hide. Connie said, "There are no words, Plorn, for your bereavement. If anything happens to my dad—"

I suppressed an urge to ask her to say "athwart."

Inevitably, in the line we needed to face the bland condolences of Mr. Fremmel, who appeared soon after, very anxious to introduce himself to Alfred, whose loan had apparently been approved. There was subservience in the way Fremmel made his speech to Alfred. His oratory was started with "If I can ever be of any help." And "Should you require any service it is within the compass of Fremmel and Company to deliver . . ." If Fremmel came to suspect any chicanery of me, Alfred would be far away in a year or so, and unassailable.

It also seemed obvious to us—though Alfred had a better eye for it than I did—that some of the tradespeople were looking to our inheritance. I had not until then thought of the family spoils arising from Father's death and would have parted with the lot to buy another mortal day for the guvnor.

Afterwards tea was served, and I sought out the Desailly family again, gradually maneuvering myself to Connie's side, whereupon she did me the enormous honor of speaking in the plain daily bread of words, saying, "Why did you leave that night we were all singing?"

"I thought the Desailly girls had found the right company for the evening."

"The right company? Hayward?"

"He's a very good tenor. He's good company." I smiled, as if at ease. "I felt entitled to go off to my swag, seeing you were so well set up."

"Well, I don't want you ever to do that again," she told me in a lowered voice. "I mean it. I might be a rough girl from the Western Division but I require things to be done properly. I do hope you understand that, Plorn. The appropriate ceremonies."

I said I was sorry, and she extended her hand to my forearm. I could see the lines on it from handling saddlery and reins. And though her mother went to such trouble to avoid the taint of the sun, Connie's own hand was olive. She must have taken her complexion from her brown-domed father rather than from the cautious, veiled mother.

I said, "I will be very pleased to perform the appropriate ceremonies from now on. Even though I'm not a tenor and can't sing music hall songs."

She shook her head and said, "Out of respect for your father, I must suspend your further education until you return from Sydney."

I smiled. In the midst of ashes, she had made me happy, and the idea of a future series of educative contacts was joyful to me even in bereavement.

34

Alfred and I spent some days on the road to Sydney in a coach provided by Cobb and Co. Local newspapers announced the time of our likely passing through the towns or hamlets on the way, and if they had a church, the bell tolled our passage past the storefronts and the façades of the hotels, and the guests watched us earnestly from the upper verandas. Sometimes cheers were raised from the footpath, since, on top of the story of our family's loss, garbled tales abounded about my saving Momba from the Starlight gang.

Since Sir Charles Cowper, the premier of the self-governing colony of New South Wales, had summoned Alfred and me to the week of state mourning there, both of us now traveled not only under the beneficence and care of this august version of a young state—NEWLY ARISEN HOW BRIGHTLY YOU SHINE! said its escutcheon—but with an escort of four troopers to discourage other wandering banditti from afflicting us, since newspapers were simultaneously attributing the departure of Dr. Pearson's gang to Queensland to the dignity of the grief-inspired courage I had displayed to them.

"Do you think," asked Alfred as we rolled through Dubbo on the fourth day, with schoolchildren, police, and public officials lining the road, "that the guvnor knew it would be like this? Australia, I mean?"

"Athwart," I let my mind sing as ever.

I told him the story of how I had bought du Barry in a fit of purchasing lunacy and how, perhaps in a brief period when du Barry was amenable, or perhaps when she was notably rebellious, Dr. Pearson had taken her out of admiration for her lines, possibly with a belief he could manage any horse by craft or physic. The fact that the great Pearson had stolen du Barry exempted me from my own folly and transformed the horse from a source of shame to an anecdote, which I told with flourishes to distract my brother.

The *Herald* said that the guvnor's works were being read in all schools in New South Wales, so that those who had not known him were drawn into the great worldwide ring of grievers. As we came through Nyngan, the girls and boys in overcoats lined out in late light, their breath steaming amidst the streaky sunlight falling through giant eucalyptus.

⁓

Conversations Alfred and I had during the journey were influenced by the convention that no bad should be spoken of the dead. Certainly nothing bad had been said in any newspaper report to titillate the McGaws of the world. The Australian newspapers had mentioned that Father had considered a tour some years back and had said that he meant to write a travel book named *The Uncommercial Traveller Upside Down*. Australia, through the voices of its citizens, seemed to mourn the fact that the great narrator of the age would now never read here, as he had in the United States. Nor would a great novel of Australia emerge from that creator. How I would have loved to have told the guvnor about Pearson and Rutherford. The bushrangers would, I think, have appealed to him as table talk, and might, perhaps, have made their way into a novel.

Sometimes as I sat at the window passing through townships, being gawked at as a Dickens incarnation, I felt the fraudulence of my state intensely, that until I steeled myself to encounter the books, I was impersonating a son.

I found I wanted increasingly to mention Father's Irish girl to Alfred, but hesitated since it might spark undue reflections on the guvnor's character. Something about my certainty she had been there at the death troubled me, especially given that our mother had not been there. The girl who was Father's friend above all friends. And I had my grievance that she'd seen the guvnor laid in the Thames soil beneath the Abbey.

I felt at last it was my duty to bring up the girl. "By all reports, Mama wasn't there at the end, I said."

"No," said Alfred. "He had grown utterly away from Mama. He should have realized, however, that there was no way we could grow apart from her."

I knew that this was nothing but fair comment. I asked, despite the risk, "Do you think the girl was there?" And then having begun I could not stop. "Do you think she was there at the end?"

"I think it's very likely," said Alfred, almost matter-of-factly. "She is the engine who drove his past years. And that's . . . That's all we can say."

I was disarmed enough to add, "If she was at the Abbey . . . I wish it was me instead."

"Yes, yes," said Alfred gently, graciously not taking up the bait. "Look, Plorn, the truth is that our parents fell out of love. And even then, not Mama. But it seems the man's privilege to do so. Everything changed then. I have to say it: if he'd stayed with Mama he would have lived five, ten years longer. Perhaps the Irish girl is not to blame. But whether she chose to be or not, she was poison. Total poison."

And of course it was inevitable that in our time together we should talk about inheritance. Despite our differences on what sort of man Father was, we knew he would have left us a solid legacy. And his death, which we would not have wished for and even now didn't truly believe, had changed our prospects—as Fremmel's behavior towards me had shown.

The question of whether Father had left the girl anything proved to be part of Alfred's musings, and many people would have said, why not? As for our own condition, when letters arrived from home we would know more. But amongst what Father, in his conscientious way, would have applied himself to was the issue of what each of us needed, of what his two daughters Mamie and Katie needed, Katie being married, Mamie a spinster. And then Aunt Georgie, who deserved the guvnor's generosity. And then the children, Alfred and me included. And then, Mama. And last of all, whether we liked it or not, the Irish girl.

There were also practical considerations. I was eighteen and might not be able to take control of what I had been left until I was twenty-one. Alfred, however, was twenty-five, and would have direct access to any beneficence of the guvnor. Thus Alfred's plans to move across the Murray River and settle in Hamilton were as good as realized.

"Would you care to join me in Hamilton?" he asked suddenly at one point in the journey. "We could even share a residence," he suggested tentatively. Alfred thought it an attractive idea, the Dickens brothers living in a pleasant and verdant town with a view of mountains which some Scots settler had sentimentally named the Grampians.

I said I was very flattered to be asked, and indeed I was. I felt pleased Alfred considered me fit to aid him in the making of his colonial fortune. But I said that I wanted to make my own mark in the pastoral industry before retiring to a friendly town somewhere. Fred Bonney was paying me a good though not sumptuous wage, but with nothing to spend it on it had accumulated wonderfully. I had to wait, I explained, until I came of age and could then take any patrimony Father had sent my way and use it in the country I so admired. I also wished, amongst other things, to have my camp of Paakantji or of whatever tribe. I wished to deploy my hundreds of thousands of sheep in the vastness, though someone like Connie Desailly lay in that destiny—someone who had the hands of a colonial horsewoman and could say "athwart" with an unrehearsed directness.

And, in any case, I needed to postpone all decisions about my future until after the memorial events and eulogies in Sydney.

We left behind our ceremonial horsemen at the rail terminus to the west of the mountains. And it was there that another gentleman about Alfred's age entered our railway coach. He was sun-tanned and had piercing eyes beneath a curled black forelock, and a full beard. "Alfred, Edward," he said solemnly, seeming to understand that he was part stranger and part visitor. "I too have been dragged in by the authorities to represent my father at the obsequies. Forgive me. I am Fred Trollope, Anthony's son. Will you accept my condolences? Our family all remember your father with great fondness."

Yes, this man had once come for a weekend at Gad's Hill as a boy. And the guvnor sometimes mentioned that he'd seen Anthony Trollope at the Garrick or Athenaeum clubs. But he and Fred's father had never been close friends because he was too much of a Tory masquerading as a Liberal for the guvnor. He'd actually stood for Parliament as a Liberal, and the guvnor had sworn frequently and bitterly to my godfather and others that he himself would rather go to hell than try for a seat in the Commons.

Fred Trollope sat down in apologetic mode on my side of the railway compartment, facing Alfred. As they exchanged pleasantries I noticed that Alfred was a little restrained in his welcome, calling Trollope "old man" in a way I could tell from growing up with him was not sincere. I asked Fred how far he'd traveled to join us and he replied that he'd ridden from his station near Forbes, which was called Mortray, to the rail terminus. He went to some trouble to tell us that he'd tried to plead he was too busy with work at his station to come to Sydney, mainly because he thought it was a bit simple-minded of the colonial government to lump together other novelists' sons with the Dickens boys. But Sir Charles Cowper had insisted it would be a salutary and exemplary thing, and he had given in. "I hope you chaps don't mind," he told us frequently.

Our train brought us through mighty hills to the great sandstone bastions on the inland side of the Blue Mountains. The bush above the rail track was full of points of snow.

Fred asked me about my time as a hostage of the bushrangers, making it clear that the episode had grown into a three-act drama in the popular mind. In some versions I had nonplussed Pearson and Rutherford by pure artifice and valor, routing them in Momba by a form of Dickens bushranger-outwitting genius.

I asked him about his station, which he was very willing to talk about. He told me some of it was mountain country, from which a number of good streams descended. The highest point of the mountains was called the Pinnacle, which attracted gold prospectors. Abounding either side of his up-country fences were families of former Irish convicts with very loose attitudes to stealing livestock, damaging fences out of spite, as if he were a tyrannous landlord in another country and not a fellow toiler. Along one of the creeks in the lower land on its northern side a speculator had selected 680 acres under the Selection Act and was waiting there for Fred to buy him out again. But it was obvious that, like us, he loved the prospects and freedoms of the business, despite its demands— the troubles of selectors, the hill-sheltering Irish; its prospects and freedoms, and the fact you did not need Greek grammar to negotiate it.

After a time he excused himself, probably to go for a reflective smoke at the end of the carriage, and to use the convenience.

"You do not warm to him," I observed to Alfred.

"He would have been right to refuse the premier's invitation. He should have gone on doing so. His father is fat and well in Britain and ours is under the floor of the Abbey."

"I do think he was caught coming and going, and didn't know what to do," I pleaded.

"Besides that, his father made a parody of the guvnor."

"But not Fred."

"Not Fred," he conceded, a little short with me. "His bloody father did, though."

"When did that happen?" I asked.

"In some novel or other. Of the old man, old Trollope. *The Warden*, I think. He called the guvnor Mr. Popular Sentiment."

"I didn't know," I said, turning myself a little against Fred Trollope.

"The guvnor laughed at it," Alfred insisted, having become my father's champion. "But the guvnor is dead and the mocker is still alive. And, I would say, an inferior novelist by comparison."

"But do you think the guvnor would want us to embarrass his son? He's clearly not his father. He lives the same life as us."

Alfred took a flask out of his pocket, consumed a mouthful of spirits, then shook it in my direction, inviting me to partake as well, though I refused, and he put it away.

"Still," said Alfred, unreconciled. "*Mr. Popular Sentiment*."

When Fred Trollope returned, I smiled a welcome at him. After that, there was a long silence as we looked out the windows as shacks and then terraced houses began to appear—the suburbs of Sydney. Some fine, tall houses in Burwood and Petersham stood as the country estates of the grand folk of Sydney, which we approached through the factories and squalor of Redfern. As we got down at the station, feeling numb and uncertain, a militia band began to play the "Dead March" from Handel's *Saul*, unleashing my grief. I wept as rarely I had since the news of our father's death. As Alfred laid a hand on my shoulder and fraternally guided me along, I noticed poor Fred Trollope looked more chastened and doubtful than ever.

35

We had rooms at the Australia Hotel, and were invited to dine there after our days of travel. I felt bound to ask Fred to join us, and was relieved when, after a few whiskies, Alfred seemed content to accept him as not a bad fellow who was trying to fit in, and who in any case had none of his father's pretensions. The chef also cheered us up by telling us he had cooked leg of mutton stuffed with oysters, knowing it was our late father's favorite dish.

A waiter made us a wonderful punch in Father's style, and we sat into the night drinking it by the cup and discussing pastoral matters. The brotherhood of the bush, after all, united us. Fred asked us whether we thought it might be worth his while to take his cattle and sheep westwards for sale in the South Australian settlement of Adelaide.

The next morning, we were driven a few blocks along Macquarie Street to meet up with Sir Charles, who our coachman told us everyone called "Slippery Charlie," yet who seemed too ordinary a man for such a romantic nickname. I was ready for someone arduous and loud, but Sir Charles was dressed in sober morning suit and black neck cloth. He announced his grief at the guvnor's passing quite elegantly, and then invited us to join him at the breakfast table. He wanted to persuade us that had our father ever visited

New South Wales he would have agreed that it had a much saner and companionable balance than the neighboring colony of Victoria, with its Customs Houses along the Murray River to gouge revenue out of anything, from a cowhide to a jug of milk to a shovel the New South Welshmen might try to export across that mighty barrier. He told us we would be meeting the New South Wales governor, one Lord Belmore, whom he described as an Ulster landlord, but not a bad chap. He also confided that Lady Belmore was sickly and wanted to be back in Fermanagh at the family estate, and that Belmore himself wanted to pursue his political career. Lord Belmore would preside over the memorial service at the Anglican cathedral later in the day.

We were asked by Sir Charles of the tractability of the natives, and I spoke of the reliability of the Momba darks as Fred Bonney would have wanted me to, but only when invited. Fred Trollope spoke about the fact there should be some legal sanction against selectors who took up good acreage, not because they intended to farm it but to make the original leaseholder—him—pay them out. It was, opined Trollope, a form of legalized blackmail. That sort of thing had not yet occurred at Momba, I said—when pressed by Sir Charles—but it was bound to. It had happened at Poolamacca Station, said Alfred, where a notorious duffer had claimed six hundred acres of creek-front land in full knowledge that he could not sustain it as a farm but was waiting to be paid off so that he could do it again somewhere else.

By the way Sir Charles leaned forward, we began to get that elation the innocent too easily acquire when the powerful so much as listened: that we had a hand in changing grand policy.

After conversing with the premier, we were taken to the splendid drive of Government House and ushered into the sandstone mansion by a young subaltern of the Inniskilling Fusiliers. I thought of the photograph we had of Lieutenant Walter Dickens looking solemn and boyish, his neck emerging thin from an ample gilt collar as if the uniform was borrowed, and desperately grasping his undrawn sword by its handle with his left hand.

The youngish governor was tall and good-looking, with a casual rather than official polish.

"Oh, my heavens, how I wish this meeting were occurring on less sad terms," he said to all three of us as he wrung our hands. Then, addressing Alfred and me, he added, "When your father fell to the floor, British letters fell! Nations lie hostage to his loss."

So much for Trollope senior's Mr. Popular Sentiment!

"I saw your father read his Dombey material one night in Belfast just—well, confound me, it was all of four years ago. He left nothing unexpressed!"

Though Alfred and I had been predisposed to suspect this Ulster landlord, having been raised in the household of a radical, he seemed a thoughtful fellow, without superciliousness. He praised Australian claret to us and said we would be drinking it at dinner, as a fine substitute for Bordeaux.

We went for a walk on open sward above the brilliant harbor when Lord Belmore said suddenly, "Of course, both you Dickens children will say a few words this afternoon? Just a memory or two of your father. I am sure the colonials will be delighted, as many read your father's books as a cure for homesickness and will feel his loss very severely. Even the most ordinary household memory of yours will console them."

I was overtaken by a rush of panic which revealed itself in a stupid blush. Knowing what a test speaking would be for me, Alfred tried to excuse me from the burden, saying, "I will certainly be able to accommodate that."

"And Mr. Edward?" asked Lord Belmore.

"I . . ." I began, but could not find a verb to follow.

"Remember the day you and I went rowing with him and he stole my hat," suggested Alfred. "Just tell people about that."

"That's right," Lord Belmore chimed. "Just an anecdote. As if you were talking to one person."

"That's right," Alfred assured me. "As if to one person."

"I . . . I suppose I can do that, sir," I told the governor, though I wondered if I could.

&

Before the memorial service we were fitted out with morning suits and silk hats of the kind the guvnor despised as funerary pomp. After gathering with parliamentary and civic notables in the bright afternoon sunlight, we progressed into a vaulted church behind Belmore in his governor's rig with sword and gaiters and cocked hat, and the bishop and attendant clergy. As Alfred and I walked towards the front of the cathedral, worthies in the pews craned to see our father's face living on in ours. Here, it struck me that this was a far more intense funerary ceremony than the guvnor would have tolerated in the Abbey.

I averted my eyes from those faces avid with solemnity. But I felt a sudden tremor when I saw Connie's neat and pretty face turned to me from one of the pews, her sister and parents arrayed beside her. Her face meant more than the multitudes of features. Her gaze was straight and had no whimsy in it, and her mouth was appropriately pursed. These good people must have traveled the week to get here and would need a week to travel back! They had traveled as far to this memorial service in fact as anyone on Earth should be required to. People were grateful to relatives who came a day's journey to an English funeral. *Athwart*, I felt like singing. *Athwart! Athwart!*

After the organ stopped, as always the air felt shocked into silence broken only by the scuffle of feet. Then, in his great cape and miter, the bishop declared that the Lord was the resurrection and the life, that none of us has life in himself and none becomes his own master when in doubt and in death. "Oh God of grace and glory, we remember before you this day, our brother Charles. We thank you for giving him to us, to his family and his friends throughout the world, to know and love as a companion on our earthly pilgrimage."

We, in our seats in the front row, answered responses and listened to the reading from the Book of Lamentations. The choir sang a plangent old dirge magnificently, and then as the bishop read from the Gospel of John, "In my father's house there are many mansions," the imminence of my having to speak drummed in me like a pulse.

So now, without mentioning the fact that the guvnor had been a lackluster attender of the Anglican church, the bishop dared compare the many mansions in heaven to the many mansions of the mind from which the immortal Mr. Dickens had made his work, giving us tales and characters that were exemplary of all that was noblest and basest in humanity, and angels sang in his work, and what was demonic in the hearts of men and women was brought low. He expressed the hope that we should tell people in England that the Anglican Communion in the distant colonies of Australia were unanimous in their applause of and grief for the death of our irreplaceable father. Alfred looked across at me and winked improbably and punched his fist a little like an exhortation to courage.

It was now Governor Belmore's turn to speak. Tall and courtly in his black and silver uniform, he declared that Australia was made up of a number of congregations, that as divided as it might recently have been by the sad attack upon Prince Alfred, it was united in admiration for the late Charles Dickens. He had seen the great writer *sub specie* perform a reading in Belfast four years before, and as immediate as were the characters and illuminations of his books when read, incidents when recounted and acted out by Dickens convinced the audience of the depths and color of the novels of Dickens the writer. He was the inheritance of all peoples, and in the great universal equality of death still shone with the constancy of a great star. Lord Belmore said it was his duty to signify the commiserations of the people of New South Wales to the Dickens family, and in particular to the two sons who were present, and to call on Mr. Alfred Dickens to express some sentiments about his father's death.

I watched Alfred as he rose from our pew and stepped forward into the echoing stone spaces before climbing up the marble step of the choir. I wondered, would I be able to do that? As he scanned the assembled crowd his face seemed to fill with blood and he frowned. Was he about to complain that no one mentions Mother? I wondered nervously. Worse still, might he say, "No one mentions the girl"?

After acknowledging His Excellency and His Lordship the bishop, he said, "I am the sixth child of Mr. Charles Dickens, and of my mother, Mrs. Catherine Dickens, who, through God's mercy, has been spared to grieve her husband. My brother Walter, born four years before me, died as a young man after serving to suppress the Bengali mutiny. My little sister Dora perished at the age of ten months, suddenly and without warning, and my father held her in his arms all night. But now he is reunited with Dora and with poor Walter, so Walter has now enjoyed the reunion that death previously denied him."

Alfred nodded and committed himself to what people wanted to hear, talking about how Father used to like family and friends' plays, especially on Twelfth Night, our eldest brother Charley's birthday. He would devise parts for the children, and Alfred remembered a play in which he was required to be a page, and come onstage to say, "Ladies and gentlemen, I have been sent ahead by the emperor to ask you to ready yourselves for his arrival." Instead, Alfred said, he walked onto the stage and, seeing family and friends, including Mr. Thackeray, Lord Lytton, and Mr. Wilkie Collins, all there and silently looking at him, he believed the warning unnecessary and walked over and sat on Mr. Collins's knee. The congregation laughed at this enchanting tale, and I felt a surge of brotherly love. Alfred's auburn sideburns and neat auburn moustache looked like a hope rather than an assertion of success and, in the light of his story, were poignant.

"If God's Kingdom grants our loved ones that which they most desire," he said, "then Father is now directing a play, you can be sure, and is taking a substantial role in it, in an even nicer theater than the one behind Tavistock House, where he had some of the greatest painters of the day, Millais and Maclise and Clarkson Stanfield, come by and paint the scenery for him."

After he'd concluded he came and hunched beside me, whispering in my ear, "Tell them you're frightened, tell them you are terrified of talking. They'll forgive you anything."

I heard my name called by the clergyman who was acting as master of ceremonies and rose like a prodded beast might rise, empty of thought, with each nerve vibrating in a key of alarm. Like Alfred going to Wilkie Collins's familiar lap, I contemplated standing right there, my back to the faithful, looking to the western rose window which, at the moment, was engorged with robust winter light. I spent a while contemplating it, like the crater of some friendly volcano I could pitch myself into. I made myself turn, and looked for Connie's face, but realized I had no time to search the file upon file of human countenances raised to me.

I forgot to nominate all the dignitaries and then began, "I am not . . ." pausing as I saw Alfred make a "louder, please!" gesture with his hands. I raised my voice. "I am not a good speaker, ladies and gentlemen. You must not think I am just because my father could speak and read to beat the rest of the world. Some gifts are not passed on."

There were actually a few kindly chuckles at this, and I did wonder for a crazy second if I said it again it would double the sympathy of the cathedral congregation. "The Medway . . ." I continued, then paused again and saw a few people glance at each other as the silence grew. "It is a river that flows close to Gad's Hill.

"My father was a boy of Kent and liked to say he was a Kentish man since Gad's Hill, the home he settled in, was north of the Medway."

There were nods and smiles from those with their own Kentish background. North of the River Medway, "Kentish men and women." South, "men and women of Kent."

"My father greatly enjoyed taking a boat from Rochester Castle to Maidstone," I continued. "He would come home and say he had rowed it himself, so one day Alfred and I asked him to take us. We were given a set of oars each and Father acted as our cox. I remember as the sun grew strong he took Alfred's boater away and claimed it as his, declaring he had seen Alfred's blow overboard."

There was now reverent laughter in the church, and I began to wonder what I'd feared about facing an audience. "Seven miles down that lovely river and seven miles back. Then, as we landed, Father handed the boater back to Alfred, pretending he'd fetched it from the water."

Franker laughter still.

"Alfred and I will always remember that day, and my father's criticizing our rowing in the quick, humorous way he had. My father might be a great writer to you, but to me he is the man who took us on adventures, whether they be on the water of the Medway or on the home stages of Tavistock House or Gad's Hill. He was father and sometimes playmate to us. And for both, we are eternally grateful to him."

I could not think what else to say for a second but then declared, "I will tell my mother that you were all here and were so generous in your feelings. I know she will be amazed and grateful to you . . ."

I remembered where we were then and said, "And to God."

36

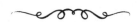

After the ceremony I did not see the Desaillys, though I'd hoped to be greeted and indeed congratulated by Connie. It gratified and consoled me that everyone we spoke to said we had done our father great honor. Alfred and I were in a positive mood as we dressed in frockcoats for that night's dinner at Government House, where the three of us were greeted by Lord and Lady Belmore.

Alfred sat beside Lady Belmore at dinner in the long dining hall, and a wan Fred Trollope was to her left. She conversed well with them, asking them questions about their Australian careers. I heard her confide that she and "Dick" had done eight circuits of New South Wales but had been advised by the ministers of the state government not to go to the Western Division. Both Alfred and Fred Trollope reassured her that all appropriate viceregal comforts were available along the Darling.

I was seated next to Mrs. Charles Cowper, who spoke with an Essex accent and had made Sir Charles the happy father of seven children. On my other side was an extraordinary and sumptuous woman in white silk who introduced herself as Mrs. Wivenhoe, and told me her husband, Captain Wivenhoe, who was secretary to the governor, was away finding and organizing the fitting-out of a suitable house in the Southern Highlands where Their Excellencies could spend their summers away from Sydney—Lady Belmore suffered from the heat and humidity acutely.

There was a trace of Sheffield in Mrs. Wivenhoe's voice, and she told me that in some ways she saw herself as an ordinary woman from an ordinary household of raucous children. She was not an innocent being like Connie, and was older by some years, but seemed permanently young, black haired and blue eyed and sweet of feature with an active intelligence in her eyes. She could see through me, I had no doubt, and I liked the fact that I was transparent to her. She placed a long-fingered, beringed hand of pure ivory on my dinner jacket sleeve when she spoke. One of her rings was a ruby. It was large enough to declare "I am here, and I glow."

She said, her eyes on me and wanting me to believe her, "I hope you understand how proud your father would have been of you two boys. It is easy to commemorate him as a marvel. But you and your brother commemorated him as a man."

From other lips this would have been a handsome sentiment. From hers it was close to intoxicating. I said thank you, and turned to Mrs. Cowper, when she asked me, "You must surely be a little impressed by our harbor, Mr. Dickens?" I would soon discover this was nearly always the first question out of the mouths of Sydney-siders, as the citizen-denizens were called. I would also discover that you could not be too eloquent in praises of this body of water. Sydney folk were like the children of an exquisite mother and expected to be congratulated on their good fortune. But it being the first time I was asked, I answered all the more ponderously, because I wanted to get back to talking to Mrs. Wivenhoe, though I politely tried to hide the fact. I wanted to provoke her to tell me things, so when I had the chance, I asked, "Your husband is seconded from a regiment in India?"

"Yes," she replied, sitting upright like a sensible woman and squaring her shoulders. "We were stationed in Calcutta."

"My brother Walter died in Calcutta." It had been a matter of a second's spurt of blood in his brain. It could happen to me. I could fall from my horse like a sack of potatoes. The sudden brain-burst had killed Dora, had killed Walter, and now Father. I would probably go that way. Not yet, oh God! Not while there were Mrs. Wivenhoes to sit beside.

"I heard your brother say that," she told me, "and a pang went through me. There are so many young officers lying in Park Street cemetery—young mothers, too, who died during childbirth. Some of the young men there don't have a wife to see to their health. My husband has occasional fevers, but I take on the supervision of nursing and call the doctor early rather than late."

"Your husband is very fortunate," I said gallantly. Beneath the table, I was aware of her hip and upper leg being close to mine and could sense a movement in my blood. It was delightful. I felt wise and worldly and capable of chat.

"That is very kind of you. Perhaps you could remind him occasionally—husbands are known to overlook these things."

Could Mrs. Wivenhoe be overlooked?

"You know . . ." she began. "No, of course you don't know what I was going to say. What a silly usage! What I was going to tell you is that I believe my favorite of your father's books is *Bleak House*. I love Honoria Dedlock, how she writhes to avoid the scandal of her youth. And of course, like other women of humble origin, I love Esther Summerson. I do not say for a moment that my origins are tainted with disgrace as Esther's are. But your father is telling us, 'Look at this girl, for she is better than those who despise her.' It is a very daring and new and very kindly thing to do."

I thought it might be time for me to mention Urania Cottage and my father's attitude to those girls. But before I could, she looked at me intently and then smiled and said, "You haven't read it, have you, young Dickens?"

"Not yet," I admitted. For some reason I was not ashamed to tell her. "Not yet. But I am pleased that I will have time to read all his books."

"Yes. Between you and me, the capacity to deal with books is something that comes with years. I was an idiotic little thing, let me tell you, when I was at school." She lowered her voice further. "Forgive me for suggesting it, but it might be politic for you to speak to Mrs. Cowper."

I agreed, and turned to do my duty, even though Mrs. Cowper was talking about predestination to the bishop on the other side of her. I sat looking towards her and waited for the honor of my turn for her ear. When she looked at me, I said, "You must thank the premier, Mrs. Cowper, for all he has done for my father. I am sure that today was a finer ceremony than the burial in Westminster Abbey, for my father did not want much fuss there. He'd be delighted to know how he was honored, and indeed missed, here in Sydney."

She thanked me and asked me questions about Gad's Hill. "Ah yes," she said pleasantly. "Kent. I come from a little north of you, in Colchester. You would have eaten our oysters."

"My father was very partial to them indeed," I told her.

"He was such an Englishman," said Mrs. Cowper. "Such an Englishman!"

"He ate them, even with mutton," I told her.

"What a good colonial he would have made," she said, laughing.

The bishop leaned forward and said, "I was ordained a deacon in Rochester. It's an exquisite town. And the Medway, as you say, is also wonderful. But my work was carried out in Liverpool chiefly, and I had just been inducted into a new parish—indeed, one formerly occupied by my brother—when I was called to Sydney."

I had the impression that the bishop was not an easy man, that he had tolerated the near levity of the memorial service because it was Charles Dickens, but that it would take the death of another equal figure for him to let the churchgoing multitudes back into his cathedral.

At last I was able to turn back to Mrs. Wivenhoe and wait for her to notice me. Eventually she herself turned and examined me with her dark eyes. "When did your father speak to you last?"

"I think it is nearly eighteen months past," I admitted, a little surprised myself at the passage of time. "No, nearly two years. We caught the train together from Higham to Paddington and then he said goodbye. My older brother Henry saw me as far as Plymouth."

"Oh, so sad," said Mrs. Wivenhoe. "And, as it transpires, so final."

"It was," I agreed and my eyes filled with tears.

It was as if she was searching for something in her lap, and I could not be of assistance to her. With a lightning little dab of her left hand she placed a small card on my knee. As if I knew we were conspirators I covered it.

"The place and time, Mr. Dickens," she told me, with a nod.

Like a polished intriguer I put the card in my side pocket. Soon after, dessert was served. I spoke some more to Mrs. Cowper—pious stuff about Father. Finally, the governor and Mr. Cowper rose as one, and men began to leave the table for cigars and brandy. I said a regretful farewell to Mrs. Wivenhoe and a sincere one to Mrs. Cowper, and when I entered the drawing room I noticed that Alfred and Fred Trollope were standing together happily discussing the challenges of their situations.

~

The Midlands accent of the famed New South Wales orator Henry Parkes dominated the after-dinner conversation. He did not drink much and had a cigar in hand but no brandy. He was all at once addressing Alfred, saying, "If I asked you whether you might enjoy a snifter, Mr. Dickens, I hope almost certainly you would tell me, 'Barkis is willing!'"

Everyone thought this sidesplitting and Alfred was not averse to the suggestion. "Barkis is willing indeed, as it happens, Mr. Parkes. But I wonder which of you gentlemen knows the origins of that saying."

"Why," Henry Parkes objected in artificial dudgeon, "you should know that I have a substantial library as well as being an habitué of the Sydney Mechanics' School of Arts, and there was a list run by that library to register readers for your father's novels, of which the one featuring Barkis, who is willing, is I believe his gem, his superlative. To protect your challenge, Mr. Dickens, I will say only that it is a book published in the 1850s and so famous that it's almost vulgar to ask its name. I could say also that a fine friend of the chief character is actually a lawyer, but another character is a vain and empty-headed politician."

This caused the men around him to show how entertained they were by Mr. Parkes's teasing out of the matter.

"Yes, what is the title of this book then, gentlemen?" he called.

"They all blur," a colonial gentleman complained. "Excellent reading. But they all blur."

Indeed, there were cries of *"Oliver Twist,"* which Alfred and Henry Parkes derisively rejected. There were further cries of *"Pickwick Papers"* and then *"Barnaby Rudge"* and *"Nicholas Nickleby"* and *"Martin Chuzzlewit."* It was a classic case of people, half-inebriated, avoiding the obvious answer because it *was* obvious. As well as that, this little quizzing seemed to me to show how shallow literary fame could be; how, as the gentleman said, "They all blur." A quiet young man, half-tipsy but reverential, restored the guvnor's credit by saying, "It is the deathless *David Copperfield.* And Barkis is proposing to Peggotty by way of David Copperfield—or Trotwood, as his aunt insists on calling David."

"A scholar," Henry Parkes cried, "and a reader and retainer! I did not know I had one in my entire constituency—I had only heard rumors of the mythic existence of one, rarely sighted. But here he is, Mr. Dickens! He redeems my electorate of its vacuity."

But then Parkes grew sober amidst the laughter. "Please forgive me—I do not mean to be frivolous in the light of your dear father's decease. I have read he was a sociable fellow and enjoyed a joke."

"Yes, sir," said Alfred. "He abominated people who were falsely solemn in the face of death."

Parkes's eyes surveyed the room and found mine. "And you, young Mr. Dickens? We are aware a great light has gone out, but that, thanks to your father's works, it has not faded."

I bowed to Mr. Parkes to show I was not offended by his little joke. The truth was my mind was possessed by Mrs. Wivenhoe and the message she had given me.

The young reader said, "And the lawyer David Copperfield approves of, by the way, is Tommy Traddles."

"Yes," said Alfred as if in a public house. "Tommy Traddles. Drinks are on me!"

Everyone laughed and Henry Parkes remarked, "I read a story in one of the scandal sheets concerning a great creation of your dear father's. I was telling the company . . . Now, Miss Havisham, *Great Expectations*. Miss Havisham, the woman—above all women—left at the altar and living amongst the ruins of her marriage feast and its ornamentations! I have heard it sworn that you and your brother told your illustrious father about our permanently jilted Miss Donnithorne in Sydney, not three miles from here, who famously still keeps the marriage cake and all the nuptial appurtenances in place in her father's house in the suburb of Newtown and has never left the house since her failed wedding fourteen years past. Now is that the truth or not that you two gave him that story?"

Alfred and I looked at each other with amazed smiles.

"My brother and I have never heard of Miss Donnithorne, Mr. Parkes," said Alfred, to which I agreed.

"*Great Expectations* appeared in 1861," Alfred assured the orator. "I did not come to Australia until four years later. And my brother arrived only in the last few years. So, we could not have contributed the Australian version of Miss Havisham to our father."

"Oh desolation! You are stripping our colony of its literary status. I accept what you say, Messrs. Dickens," said jovial Parkes with another bow to each of us. "But I am devastated and, like a true colonial, will simply go on repeating the story."

We all laughed, and I know the guvnor would also have laughed. "I rather regret it myself," I suggested. "I need a little literary credit."

Alfred said, "When *Great Expectations* appeared in volume form, it was dedicated to Chauncy Townshend, who taught my father how to mesmerize people."

"Your father is indeed a mesmeric writer!" one of the men called out.

"Father was actually to mesmerize people in the flesh," said Alfred. "He had a gift for it but seemed to give it up because it made my mother uneasy."

"I should say so!" the man said with a guffaw, but then looked about him, unsure of what the joke was supposed to be. It had not been a joke with Mama. I somehow knew it was an area of shadow.

"The thing is," said Alfred, "Chauncy Hare Townshend died before I left England. I mention that as proof that I could not have sent my father notes from Australia to contribute to a book dedicated to a living friend who was already dead when I got here. I'm sure, Mr. Parkes, you get the point."

I thought, even in my impatience, that Alfred had done a wonderful job of debunking.

Dear old Alfred even winked at me then, stalwart in the face of rumor.

~~

While milling in the paneled hall of government waiting for our carriages, Alfred approached me, eyes shining from his social success, and ready for a wild time.

"Fred and I were settling on the Australia Hotel bar," he said. "Let's go together, brother Plorn."

I was beginning to color before I replied, "I can't be there for a time."

Alfred raised an eyebrow, and I fell back on the best lie I could find, saying, "The bishop's grandson was injured in a riding accident, and I thought it was only polite of me to visit him at Sydney Hospital."

I knew it sounded ridiculous.

"At this hour? The bishop's grandson?" said Alfred.

Alfred looked towards Fred Trollope. It was as if Alfred intended to invite Fred in to mark what I had said. I lowered my eyes. But then it was as if some worldliness and mercy entered Alfred. "Very well, old son," he murmured. "You have your own arrangements, I understand. Simply be careful though. I can't risk losing my brother to someone like Mrs. Chard." He lowered his voice further still. "Do you have precautions?"

I looked at him, bewildered, as he reached inside one of his pockets and dropped a small, flat package in my hand. "Put it away."

I swiftly did so. He winked in his normal jaunty way and whispered, "Actual rubber not sheep guts. And later, we'll either be in the Australia Hotel or a short walk away in the bar of the Pioneers' Club, should you want to say good night."

He left so immediately and graciously that I felt a surge of love and gratitude for him. He knew I was marching to some drum or answering some fixed idea that had come on me. I hope he didn't guess the drum in question was Mrs. Wivenhoe's.

When my coach arrived I asked the driver if he could take me on a little spin around the city, explaining I was new to Sydney and hadn't seen it by night.

"Sir, without offending you, I do not let streetwalkers enter the coach."

"Oh," I said, "nothing like that. I have an address I want to be dropped at after we have had a little . . . a little spin."

The driver said he'd take me to Mrs. Macquarie's Chair first and we set off. It turned out to be a handsome rock outcrop where, the driver explained, the wife of an earlier governor had sat and yearned for home. After that we headed down towards the Circular Quay and along to George Street, where the public houses were still rowdy. Then across to the stores and emporia of Pitt Street, up around the park, and by the Papist cathedral. By now I had read the card Mrs. Wivenhoe had put on my knee. It gave an address for a house in Elizabeth Bay, and a further number, twenty-three, which I presumed and hoped was a room number. So now I tapped on the window and opened the communication flap and asked could the gentleman take me there.

He said he would, and that it was less than a quarter of an hour away. I was convinced that a quarter of an hour away lay, therefore, the resolution of the arc of wanting that had built between me and Mrs. Wivenhoe. Arriving at the address, I gave the driver ten shillings to wait for me and went up the stairs of a quite elegant house.

A well-dressed old man in the lobby asked for my room number, and then a boy about my age led me up the stairs to the door of twenty-three, which he opened and then gave me the key. I went inside. Somehow I thought it had promising wallpaper, thick and blue and gold. But the space lacked Mrs. Wivenhoe.

I consulted the card and amongst the other figures it declared 12:30, so I was half an hour early. At twenty past the hour, the young man arrived with a bottle of chilled white wine and two glasses and politely asked me if there was anything else I needed. My need was not to have a seizure before my expectations were resolved. I am ashamed to say that the memory of Connie did not distract me nor did it even as yet arise. I wanted the lineaments of gratified desire, as improbable as that seemed, given I had never had them before and could not imagine what said lineaments resembled.

At thirty minutes after midnight there was a tap on the door and before I could frame words Mrs. Wivenhoe was there, compellingly present in a jaunty, forwards-sloping silk hat and a fur stole about her shoulders.

"Mr. Dickens," she said, slightly short of breath. "What a worldly young fellow you are to interpret my note."

"I am not worldly," I told her, though I felt that her arrival had increased my level of worldliness threefold. "But I am pleased I did not misunderstand you."

"Would you like to open the wine?" she asked. "I ordered a muscatel rather than fizz. Fizz is a rather flippant drink, isn't it? And I don't intend to be flippant."

Setting to work with the corkscrew, I wondered what such an assertion could mean, that I was in for some level of instruction perhaps, a duty she had taken on herself.

I noticed as I worked on the cork, that she was removing long gloves. I poured the wine in two glasses and took one to her. She accepted it and took a sip, then dragged me to her and kissed me in a way I did not know women of her kind ever kissed. It was an oral experience which seemed almost sufficient in itself, even as prelude to nothing more. And yet I knew by instinct and ache that there was more intended.

She suggested we go to the bed, and I moved there quickly, as if it were not my baptism in the matter.

"Do you know what this place is?" she asked. "It is a house of assignation of great benefit to many ladies."

I was amazed by that. "Of great benefit to many ladies" was a statement of female desire. Of the desire of wives! "Athwart" was swamped—at least for now—by the scale of what she said, the world that was opened to me.

"Please don't think, though, that I make flippant use of it. And, please can you help me undress?" she asked.

I kissed fervently every area of flesh as it was revealed. She then helped me out of my courtly garments, even out of the expanders which kept my shirtsleeves up. I produced the small sachet Alfred had given me with the device inside and, seeing it, she said, "How thoughtful you are. You know more than a colonial young man your age!" She counseled me how to put it on my trembling body and told me with stern humor not to give way yet. And so when I lay on the bed, and she lay by my side in a shift which exposed most of her legs, I saw her strong thighs, her solid-ankled legs poignantly like those, I imagined, of a farm girl. She was rid of the shift soon, and her upper body seemed a confection of desire and her breasts a miraculous and ample haven open to me. Her generosity was affecting to me—I felt an impulse to weep, though I was distracted by the chief lineament of my desire, heavy and gravid as it was, and demanding to be appeased only by her. She lifted her hips and told me, "This is where it goes, dear Edward Bulwer Lytton Dickens."

Afterwards, my body seemed to have been wounded by its contacts with and invasions of Mrs. Wivenhoe. It seemed to bleed away deliciously from the divine damage it had received. It cried out to be wounded and subdued again. But she had already stated as a necessary fact, "We will not meet like this ever again. You have had a grown woman and I have had my Dickens."

I did not know what she meant by that. Nor did I wish to in-quire. "I will be an old lady before you are forty," she said. "There is someone young awaiting you. So please don't come chasing me," she warned. "I have a husband."

I had told her I loved her. I'd even told her I could not stay away from her. I told her of Maurice and the French aunt, in the mode of escape together somewhere in the world. No wonder he had run away with her.

"Listen to yourself! Will you take me back to Momba? No thank you."

So that was the rule. Her mercy, her pedagogy, extended once, would never be extended again. But if not, what was I to do with the world of sensual desire now residing inside me?

37

The next day Sir Charles provided us with a soothing cruise on the harbor. We traveled its charming reaches and saw the mansions amongst the bush of the eastern shore. The premier told us we were going to a small version of Brighton named Manly, which had been built on the northern shore of the harbor, under a great headland open to the massive tug of the Pacific Ocean, bright, choppy and un-Pacific today, its entering waves topped with spume.

We landed at Manly, at the beach where the first governor had been speared by "manly" natives, and drank a toast to Father. Alfred and Fred were a little fragile from their drinking session and seemed melancholy as the ferry reached up the harbor towards Sydney Cove, or perhaps it was my sadness at not being permitted the self-forbidden Mrs. Wivenhoe. Where was I to take my aching blood?

"I'll be pleased to be home," Alfred confided to me.

When we got back to shore, the premier bade us farewell and a carriage took us to the Pioneers' Club, where we made desultory plans to meet in the bar before dinner. As I was about to follow the other two upstairs, a page came up to me, passing me a card and saying, "This gentleman asked would you kindly meet him outside?"

On the card a name was inked. "Maurice McArden."

"Where?" I called to the page, who said, "Outside, sir, on the street."

As soon as I went out and saw Maurice, I could see why he hadn't wanted to come inside. He wore a battered-looking Eton cap, his shirt collar was open, and he looked stark around the eyes. There were cuts on his cheeks and jawline from imprecise shaving. But he also retained an air of earnestness and purpose.

As I walked up to him he said, "Forgive me for intruding, Plorn, but I read in the *Herald* that you are visiting the city. I hope you'll accept my sympathies along with all the rest."

"Of course I will, old fellow, and happy to have them. But how are you? And what has happened to Mrs. Fremmel?"

"We don't use those names," he told me with a small smile. "I have honored your father by calling ourselves the Rokesmiths."

I guessed this was the name of one of the guvnor's notable characters.

"The Rokesmiths have the struggle at the moment that Mrs. Rokesmith is far from well, I fear," he said.

I expressed my regrets.

"I trusted, you see," he told me, "that a man like you, a man of your lineage, was someone I could safely declare myself to. So I wanted to see you. It was a powerful impulse. I'm sure when we fled Wilcannia everyone said it would not be long before Mrs. Rokesmith would be back, or before I left her. I wanted someone to know that this is not the case, that I am devoted to her still." A thought arose in him. "If you had a moment, I could take you to see her."

Of course, I said I was amenable to seeing the good lady again. It was a carelessly uttered sentiment, but Maurice took up the possibility feverishly, as if my seeing her under his devotion and care would be a sort of vindication of their escape.

"I could take you very quickly and have you back, Plorn. It's a short ride by omnibus."

I felt I was obligated to visit Maurice and his French aunt, so it must be now. I had my education in the lineaments of desire to which Maurice had introduced me in his not quite crazy essay. What happened, though, when the lineaments sickened? I had of course seen wives with sickly husbands, husbands with sickly wives. And now it was to be Maurice and his sick aunt.

"I must be back within an hour," I warned him. "And I must excuse myself from my brother and Mr. Trollope. Give me a few seconds, please, Maurice."

He granted that with a new vigor and a wintry smile. I went back into the club and found Alfred by the bar with a whisky. I said, "Would you and Fred excuse me one more time?"

Alfred frowned. "A man deserves his secrets, Plorn, but this is getting ridiculous."

"Can you keep a secret, Alfred? A serious one."

He began to smile. "What is the name of this secret? Is it the dark-eyed tart from last night's dinner?"

"Don't talk that way," I demanded with a sudden sternness. "It's Maurice McArden—Fremmel's nephew who ran off."

"With Fremmel's wife, I believe."

"This is an absolute word-of-honor secret, Alfred. He wants to see me. I won't be long."

"Fremmel is not a good enemy to make," Alfred murmured.

"He'll only know if you tell him."

So I left Alfred with an undertaking to be back in time for dinner and went out into the street, where Maurice led me to a corner, telling me that I was very good to do this. We got onto a two-story omnibus just like the London ones, with an outside staircase to the top compartment. After paying the conductor, we continued through the city, whose multitudes milled at street corners and darted onto the roadway just like city folk anywhere. After five minutes or so we entered a street named, perhaps for the sake of familiarity and solace, Oxford Street. The fronts of shops were continuous awhile, and then gave way to mean wooden and brick buildings which seemed older in their poverty than the city was. We got off near a public house named for the three weeds of Britain, the Rose, Shamrock, and Thistle. As we went down a laneway by the pub, Maurice said cheerfully, "This is a hill, you see, Plorn. The drainage is good here."

He took me into a square building with two stories and an attic. "There is no danger from her to you," he assured me in a solemn voice as we climbed the first two sets of stairs. "In many ways you will find her condition very sad. But it is my uncle's fault, as you know. He initiated the disease."

I entered one of the two attic rooms. "*Tu*, Maurice?" cried Mrs. Fremmel, staring at us from a dowdy but comfortable-looking seat of Turkish upholstery. There was indeed a strong medicinal smell in the room, camphor predominating. Mrs. Fremmel or Rokesmith was straining in her chair to turn.

"I have a guest," Maurice boasted, and motioned me forward so that we faced her.

She was veiled like Mrs. Desailly in sunlight. "Oh my God, it is the son of Dickens! I am a sad picture, Mr. Dickens," she told me. "Maurice told me you were in the city for the memorial services. I am so distressed for you and your father, young man."

I thanked her, and then, seeming a little fevered, she told me there were nuns who ran a hospice for people like her, not far from there. "I have told Maurice to drop me there and be free. This is a disease passed between one human and another either in ignorance or treachery. In my opinion, no one but the sufferer should be forced to attend to it."

"Don't be ridiculous, Mariepier," said Maurice then turned to me and explained, "She is a model of patience. I have a job as a messenger for the Department of Lands. She sits here all day reading . . ."

At the mention of reading, Mrs. Fremmel said, "Your dear, dear father. The name we carry now, Mr. Plorn, is intended to honor him."

Maurice lit a lantern on the table. Beyond her veils I saw something like a grid or a rash across her face. At first it looked like a visual delusion, but then I noticed a few red pustules. I did not want to see any more than this, and mercifully could not possibly see more anyhow.

"The work of the monster," said Maurice.

"But Mr. Fremmel doesn't appear to have any visible illness," I protested.

"He has had it all along," said Maurice, "and Mariepier has caught it. But it has gone dormant in him and may remain that way for ages."

"*Mon dieu!*" murmured Mariepier, justifiably enough. "Imagine it!"

"I am with you, Mrs. Rokesmith," Maurice reassured her, smiling through his razor scars. Then to me he said, "The devil genuinely has looked after his own son in the case of Uncle Amos. Meanwhile, the mercury treatment causes Mariepier great anxiety and pain. But if everything goes well, it may become dormant in her as it has in the fiend himself and life will be normal."

"Normal?" I asked.

"As close as we can get."

And yet the lineaments of desire to whose existence Maurice had alerted me were diseased in her. Perhaps in him. He had made such a fuss about all that, and now must give it up to become an attendant, a doser, and an anointer. I wanted to understand how he had made that journey, from longing to a sort of brotherly love. But he seemed so happy to be with Mariepier that I could not question him about it.

It was soon time to return to Alfred and our final Sydney dinner. Maurice shook my hand thoroughly and thanked me. I took him aside and said, trying to imitate a sage dispassion, "Don't be offended, old chap. But do you need money?"

He was offended. "Do you think I tracked you down for *that?*" he challenged.

"No, no. But . . ." I gestured towards Mrs. Fremmel, implying her case must be a drain on him and that a friend might help.

"The Sisters of Charity at St. Vincent's Hospital take excellent care of our needs," he told me. Then he lowered his voice. "It is handsome of you to offer, Plorn, and I should have foreseen your generosity. But as I said, I am working. And perhaps I can write. I have a suspicion though that my sensibility might better suit French than English publishers. English publishers are like English diners, they like meat and potatoes." There was a pause. "Oh my God, I didn't mean of course your . . ."

I laughed. "I know," I assured him. "I know."

"He, in death as in life, is the exception to all rules."

So I said good night to him and to Mrs. Fremmel, who had set her sights on the view from the window and sounded distracted. I felt ashamed at how grateful I was to leave Maurice and his stricken aunt and return to the meat and potatoes of Oxford Street, where I hailed a hackney.

⁓

The next day the train that would take us home was to leave at noon, away from the city of the most succulent Mrs. Wivenhoe and the stricken Rokesmiths. But the bookstores of the town, we had noticed, were displaying and seemed to be selling only the guvnor's work, so I went to one in Pitt Street and began looking for editions of what Frank had recommended to me as proving the guvnor's nobility of soul. I thought it might be worthwhile to have it as a defense against Alfred, in case his drinking in the great port city of Sydney had brought out the melancholy son in him. I asked the clerk to direct me to Mr. Dickens's essays and he accompanied me on the quest. "Any particular essay, sir?"

"Just some of the shorter ones. From *Household Words*, for instance. I'll just look through a few tables of contents."

He left me to the search amidst a thicket of my father's dimly perceived creatures—Pickwick and Sam Weller, of whom I'd heard, through David Copperfield to Sydney Carton, and of course Mr. and Mrs. Rokesmith, whom I'd never met except in the form of Mrs. Fremmel and Maurice McArden, engaged on their serious escape by the use of names that were in many senses *noms de plume.*

I found what I was looking for in the form of a thin bound volume, similar in shape and size to Mother's *What Shall We Have for Dinner?* It was entitled *Charles Dickens' Proposal for a Women's Asylum,* together with "An Appeal to Fallen Women," and "The Tale of Urania Cottage" by the Right Reverend Cooper. It was precisely what I wanted but I hoped the bookseller who wrapped it up for me did not think my interest was prurient. I was grateful for the Doctorate of Divinity after Cooper's name.

Again we had an entire carriage for our use, but this time our return to normal life was symbolized by the fact that a number of other carriages occupied by customary passengers were attached to the train. In our spacious compartment, Alfred slept, and Fred Trollope talked drowsily to me, confessing an interest in a police magistrate's daughter in Forbes.

"A police magistrate?" I asked. "Handy for tracking down cattle duffers."

"Not always so," Fred told me, yawning, his eyes dreamy, possibly from the memory of the girl. "The miscreants of Australia are always able to steal better horses than the government provides to the police magistrates. It was something I meant to bring up with old Cowper. So many matters to bring up with him!"

After crossing the mountains we reached the terminus near the town of Bathurst. The colonials did have a tendency to name things, towns, and rivers after the worst of recent Tories. Bathurst had been a monster in my father's eyes, and so was Castlereagh. Darling had apparently been a high Tory governor of New South Wales, authoritarian and cramping, and his name was on our western river.

These were the sorts of disconnected musings that were not as delicious as the memory of my companion from two nights before, through whom I felt I had entered a new plane, losing old confusions and acquiring new ones.

The next morning, after we had all slept soundly, recovering from the excesses of the capital, Fred said goodbye to us and we pledged to each other that we would meet up again if his father came to Australia, as ours had always thought he might but now never would. Fred Trollope seemed to have no divided feelings about his father. The father and mother were still together, though Mrs. Trollope was believed to be something of a shrew. But there was nothing sharp edged about Fred.

Alfred and I took to the tedium of our carriage and passed through towns at a trot with nothing processional about our passage, just two gentlemen drovers on their way back to the outer stations. Alfred put down a copy of *Australasian Sketcher* with a cover illustration of a bushfire and fleeing cattle and settlers. He had the sort of moodiness that I feared might lead to his carping.

"They say a drought is on the way. And as charming as Corona might be, I'd rather wait it out in a tidy little town like Hamilton— that is not eight days' ride from Melbourne, either. Do you know they call the country around Hamilton 'Australia Felix'? Sweet enough, eh? A jockey club! And a railway on its way. And you could work for me and start your own branch when you turn twenty-one."

But the abiding problem was that his drinking made him moody and brought him to the issue of our family, and in that matter I could be his only responder whenever he might return to the guvnor issue.

"You would have been very young," he said suddenly. "But do you remember the maid named Anne?"

"Yes," I said. "Of course. Mama's maid Anne."

"Yes, that's it. He got her to put up the first partition in their room. Mama's own maid. Do you remember?"

"Vaguely," I replied. "When you're five years you know there are reasons, but they are like the reasons of Greek gods."

"Inscrutable," suggested Alfred.

"That's the word."

"But it isn't inscrutable now, is it? You're old enough to know what a partition means."

I did not answer.

"So Mama never complained to you? About that?"

"No."

"Or try to turn you against the guvnor?"

"No, she never did."

"Nor with me," he said. "It was her gentle way."

I said nothing. If I had agreed, I could not predict where he would take us.

"He never sent you to the Boulogne school," said Alfred. "I went the same year the partition went up."

I felt guilty relief to have been saved from the Boulogne school and its two clergymen-headmasters. I had only been to France for holidays, and I remembered a wonderful kite the guvnor flew outside our villa, which had a marvelous name like Villa du Camp de Droite or some such—the Villa of the Camp of the Army of the Right. I was three and on the watch for flamboyantly uniformed French soldiers. Whereas for my brothers Boulogne meant a stern curriculum (though you could learn to fence) and the freezing dormitories the brother clergymen thought good for boys. The cold was all French and the cooking all English, my brother Henry had once told me. A bad mix.

"He could have moved away himself," said Alfred. "But he was too selfish. He wanted the house and the staff. And wanted to keep Aunt Georgie running it. How do you think Mama felt?"

"Whatever the man's sins," I argued, "surely his death atones."

But his eyes were pinpointed and he did not seem to hear me.

"And then there was the engraved bracelet business."

I had heard rumors of the bracelet but had not quite understood when I was little. Apparently it was delivered to Mama with some message for the girl. It seemed to me at the time to be part of the higher wisdom of adults to take offense at such things. Now I realized what a bad business it was. But I had an inspired thought and said, "If you admire how Mother bore these afflictions," I argued, "why are you not willing to imitate her now? No large complaints from her have appeared in the newspapers. No word against anyone. So please calm down, Alfred."

"But you see, Plorn. Sending us away to Boulogne—it cleared the house of anyone who could reproach him."

"Katie and Mamie were there. And Aunt Georgie, Mama's own sister! They were with him and could reproach him. And Katie did it."

I knew this somehow, that he was reproached by Katie.

"That's when he took up his public readings with a vengeance," said Alfred, as if that were a plot to escape Katie's ire. "And at the end of the winter, poor Charley had the indignity of meeting the guvnor and that Ternan girl by accident on Hampstead Heath."

Alfred shook his head as he stared out of the carriage. "There's so much shame. We don't even talk about that train crash! You tell me Frankie called him Christ-like. Did Christ send jewelry to the wrong woman? Did he send a wife back to her mother, and then masquerade as the Christmas storyteller above all others?"

I was silent, just wanting him to stop his tirade. He reached a hand out to my shoulder and his anger gave way to pleading. "Remember, if you and I cannot look at these things, who else will?"

"All right," I said testily. "But talk about him like a man with faults, not like an archvillain. I will never believe in the archvillain."

"You won't?" he challenged me. "How many thousand miles then are you and I from Gad's Hill?"

"He did it from love, Alfred. From love!"

We were quiet for a while, despairing of seeing eye to eye. "He certainly loved us when we were little," he said then. "He adored you. The Plornishmaroontigoonter. Absolutely enchanted! He had us calling you 'J. B. in W.,' which stood for the Jolliest Boy in the World. 'Has anyone seen the J. B. in W.,' he'd ask us. It was later in our childhoods he got frustrated with us. Except for Henry, who was a brain. Once he told me I'd got my lack of application from Mama's family, by which he must have meant Mama and Aunt Helen, because he had respect for Aunt Georgie."

I admit that I was subject to similar reflections from the guvnor. I realized by now that I had been mistaken in trying to silence Alfred, because he would not be silenced. He might become a different man if I let him finish the story his way, and then perhaps he would not need to go through it again and again—it might all take on the quality of a settled difference between us.

38

As we were approaching the crossroads at the town of Nevertire, one of the troopers came to the carriage window and told us there was a line of barrels blocking the road. He and his colleague were riding ahead to see what it meant. We watched them ride on, our discussion of the guvnor suspended.

We were relieved to see a New South Wales policeman and a number of men with firearms over their shoulders emerge from the barricade and begin to spin the barricading barrels on their side so we could pass. The troopers returned and one of them explained, "Gilbert's gang were heard to say they would take the town of Nevertire prisoner, so the people have barricaded the town against them. It's up to you, gentlemen, whether we go on."

"I vote to go on," said Alfred. "My little brother can deal with the bushrangers."

So we passed through town and into the bush beyond. Gilbert's mob, like Starlight's, had a reputation for bush urbanity, and if they saw the black crepe of mourning on the coach they might just let us go, surmising we were those Dickens boys and—as Dr. Pearson had discovered—more trouble than we were worth.

Alfred returned to the guvnor, though, saying, "So, listen to the argument, Plorn. Now you haven't gone to the novels yet, but you'll have to. The convict Magwitch is transported to Australia after Pip shelters him. And in Australia he makes his sheep fortune, but he has to creep back into England because he's forbidden by law to return. The guvnor's saying that a condemned person in England may be a great man in Australia!"

"That's stretching it," I protested, "and in any case, he's not talking about us."

"Hold hard. Then there are all the people he sends to Australia in *David Copperfield.*"

This reminded me of how, before we parted, Mrs. Wivenhoe had said, "You must read *David Copperfield* if you want to know anything. Go and read *David Copperfield.*" Her command made it possible I might.

"So who does he send to Australia?" Alfred continued. "He sends the Peggottys, whose simple goodness is pretty close to stupidity, of course, and their fallen niece Little Em'ly—another tart to be saved by Australia. And he sends the hopeless Mr. Micawber and his family and turns Micawber into a colonial gent."

"This merely shows—" I began, but he cut me off again.

"So who does he send to Australia in his mind, Plorn? In the most important part of his mind? The criminals—the Artful Dodger to start, and that pageboy in *Copperfield*—and the reformed prostitutes and the stupid. And who does he send in his paternal imagination, long before he sent us, in fact? He sends his two sons. What does it tell you about what he thinks of those two sons?"

I thrashed about for something to say. Even though all had changed with the guvnor dead, it was clear that would not stop Alfred pursuing the same old arguments.

"Now you can answer me," he said.

I watched a line of eucalyptus trees along a billabong which were close enough to the road to harbor bushrangers.

I was stumped, until inspiration revived, and I asked, "What about the Staplehurst crash, then?"

"No," murmured Alfred. "It's too cruel."

"Too cruel? The guvnor was a hero at Staplehurst!"

"Maybe we can talk about Staplehurst another time. When there aren't bushrangers around."

But no bushrangers presented themselves, and we got to Cobar without incident. Alfred seemed dispirited at dinner but in a way that did not favor conversation.

~

In the evenings I read and reread *Charles Dickens' Proposal*, which confirmed and consoled my belief in the guvnor's essential virtue. Of course I already knew that in the late 1840s he and Miss Coutts had set up Urania Cottage for young homeless women found in the slums or coming from workhouses and prisons. Father had got advice on how to run the place from the governor of Tothill Fields Bridewell in Westminster, which housed women, and visited the crowded dormitories of Coldbath Fields Prison in Clerkenwell. I forget the name of the poet who wrote "As he went through Coldbath Fields he saw / a solitary cell; / And the Devil was pleased, for it gave him a hint / For improving his prisons in hell."

I could see the guvnor was fascinated by gaols and visited them to understand both how and how not to manage them. According to the Reverend Cooper he did not like the idea of the treadmill he'd seen at Coldbath. And I remembered on a rowing trip on the Medway one day he'd muttered to us boys something about the treadmill not teaching the rewards of labor but making the criminal resolve never to do honest work again.

His "An Appeal to Fallen Women" opened in a most humane way.

You will see, on beginning to read this letter, that it is not addressed to you by name. But I address it to a woman—a very young woman still—who was born to be happy and has lived miserably; who has no prospect before her but sorrow, or behind her but a wasted youth; who, if she has ever been a mother, has felt shame instead of pride in her own unhappy child.

A girl, that is, who deserved to live in a cottage and not a penitentiary. The guvnor must have been referring to Miss Coutts and her grand house in Piccadilly when he wrote that same appeal.

There is a lady in this town who from the windows of her house has seen such as you going past at night, and has felt her heart bleed at the sight. She is what is called a great lady, but she has looked after you with compassion as being of her own sex and nature, and the thought of such fallen women has troubled her in her bed.

He said that the house this lady had provided stood not in Piccadilly but on a pleasant country lane, and each girl could have her own little flower garden if she pleased. And after they had been there for a time and their conduct was good, they would be enabled "to go abroad, where in a distant country they may become faithful wives of honest men, and live and die in peace."

But the guvnor and Miss Coutts's net was broader than the fallen. The guvnor wrote in *Household Words* that he and Miss Coutts and other unspecified ladies of eminent generosity and sense recruited starving needlewomen of good character, as well as needlewomen who had robbed their furnished lodgings; they also sought violent girls committed to prison for disturbances in ill-conducted workhouses, poor girls from ragged schools, destitute girls who had applied to police officers for relief, young women of the same class taken from the prisons after undergoing punishment there as disorderly characters, or for shoplifting or for theft, young women held to bail for attempting suicide, and domestic servants who had been seduced.

Cooper wrote so clearly the arguments I could not marshal against Alfred to dent his sense of grievance. Despite his busy life, the guvnor had taken time to choose the furniture and select the materials for the young inmates' clothing. They should not wear uniforms, he said. They should have bright colors, like his waistcoats. He went to buy a piano for the place, said the Reverend Cooper, and the word got out, and virtuous people of the kind the guvnor never liked disapproved so much of a piano that my father spread a rumor that the young women would get one each, which Cooper said outraged the falsely pious even more.

As I read this history, celebrating the benign energy of my father, the assumption that he was still alive became irresistible, and I grasped at and wept more pathetically for that possibility than I had when Dr. Pearson told me he had died. My face was never dry through this rather exceptional spate of reading, and I acclaimed my brother Frankie's opinion that Father had been at that point of his life selfless and Christ-like, and I wanted to be able to tell him and applaud him on that, whatever his crimes in Alfred's eyes.

I read the entire pamphlet in two nights.

I had barely been to school myself when the guvnor took me out to London Fields' ragged school. The Right Reverend Dr. Cooper had been very taken with a description of that school in *Oliver Twist*, and there was something about learned men quoting my father that had the normal effect on me of abasement. I recognized the school as it was a landscape of my childhood and his campaigning, since he donated to the ragged schools. Places and days exalted and made eternal in his novels. Astounding that the guvnor could do that!

And then Dr. Cooper introduced me to the cases of some of the individual girls, and somehow, despite the scale of the Australian colonies, and of Momba for that matter, it all seemed curiously intimate to me. These tales showed the girls were not in colonial brothels but had an angelic and redeemed shine to them.

Case number forty-one, for example, was a pretty and quiet woman of nineteen years who was cast off after her mother's re-marriage, both mother and stepfather considering her an encumbrance. A clergyman found her sick on the streets and in a state "too deplorable to be even suggested to the reader's imagination." After a year and a half at the cottage, she was sent away, and found happiness in Australia. And so it went, with case number fifty, number fifty-eight, number fifty-one, number fifty-four, number fourteen, the latter "an extremely pretty girl of twenty" who was sentenced for disorderly behavior, a crime which the guvnor saw as mere protest at the cruelty of life.

Dr. Cooper quoted from a letter sent by another of the girls sent to New South Wales:

Honored Ladies, I have seen Jane and I showed my letter and she is going to write Home, she is living about 36 miles from where I live and her and her husband are very happy together—she has been down to our Town this week and it is the first we have seen of her since a week after they were married—my Husband is very kind to me and we live very happy and comfortable together we have a nice garden where we grow all that we want we have sown some peas and turnips, we have three such nice pigs and we kill one last week . . . My Husband has built a shed at the side of the house to do anything for hisself when he come home from work of a night. He tells me that we shall every nine years come Home.

I wished I had the names and places of these women so that I could ride round one day and tie my horse to their gate and drink tea with each of them and then we could both say, as colonials are required to say, how lucky they were to have been sent here. What a talking-to the woman of the letter would give to Alfred with his resentment and sniping at the high regard in which the guvnor was kept.

~

A conclusive letter arrived from Aunt Georgie soon after I got back to Momba. In it she wrote:

It was our grief when it happened that we could not instantly transmit the news to you by any means. That first night after his death, as he lay on the sofa the doctor had brought into the dining room for him, we were all conscious that you and Alfred would have been about your duties so far away with no suspicion of the light that had vanished from the world. There was a story here, copied from Australian papers, that you had the news broken to you by an outlaw they call a bushranger. I cannot imagine your grief and bewilderment, but according to newspaper reports you routed the desperado. How delighted would your father have been by that! It would have determined him to put it in a novel.

Your father died in familiar rooms, specifically in the dining room here. Your sisters were here before he expired, along with Mr. Beard for escort, and they were attentive and helpful all through the last long day. Your oldest brother Charley attended too. I know no one would have been of more service than you, Plorn, had you been here. He spoke of you with great affection the time before last he was here at Gad's. You can rest assured of his abiding love.

I wondered if Aunt Georgie had written the same thing to Alfred and put him in his place thereby.

I attach a copy of your father's will. . . . It was my belief and John Forster's that you should all have a copy, so that you would see you were equally provided for. You can look forward to considerable benefit from it on achieving your majority. If in the meantime you need an advance, Mr. Forster and I would be happy to make one of a relatively modest nature in terms of the scale of your inheritance, perhaps up to a hundred and fifty pounds according to need. However, I would make the point that you should not too closely examine the order in which the "Ts" and other parties are mentioned, or unfairly construe the emphasis that is put on this person and that. You will see that I have the great honor of being an executrix of the will, and I hope that you know how strenuously I will carry out that duty on your mother's behalf and on yours.

I had little appetite for reading a will and set it aside at first, but then suffered from a growing curiosity, not all of it of the highest order, to see how the guvnor had reconciled all his duties within this document.

I, Charles Dickens, of Gad's Hill Place, Higham in the county of Kent, hereby revoke all my former Wills and Codicils and declare this to be my Last Will and Testament.

And there, first off in the next line, before the call of blood, came, "I give the sum of £1000 free of legacy duty to Miss Ellen Lawless Ternan, late of Houghton Place, Ampthill Square, in the county of Middlesex."

Hence the warning about "Ts" in Aunt Georgie's letter. I did not like to see this blatant item in the will, both for my own sake and because I knew what its effect on Alfred and others would be. I knew, too, how it would be for my mother, reading it. "Was I on his mind at all?" she would have asked after seeing page one. I was pleased that Aunt Georgie had warned me not to put too much weight on the order in which things were addressed, or praise for parties, Aunt Georgie being justifiably esteemed above all others.

There were more legacies to servants, and then £1000 for my sister Mamie, together with a legacy she would receive up to the time of her marriage. And then, not Mother, but Mother's sister was mentioned:

> I give my dear sister-in-law Georgina Hogarth the sum of £8000. . . . I also give to the said Georgina Hogarth all my personal jewelry not hereinafter mentioned, and all the little familiar objects from my writing table and my room, and she will know what to do with those things. I also give to the said Georgina Hogarth all my private papers whatsoever and wheresoever, and I leave her my grateful blessing as the best and truest friend man ever had.

I felt unworthy in the resentment that now rose in me. Not to underestimate Aunt Georgie in the least, but I wanted to protest that there is a wife, and a mother. Finally Mrs. Catherine Dickens was mentioned, but only after Charley was left the guvnor's library, a silver salver presented at Birmingham and a silver cup presented at Edinburgh. Charles and my clever older brother Henry were to be given the sum of £8000 to invest and pay "the annual income thereof to my wife during her life, and after her decease the said sum and the investments thereof shall be in trust for my children. . . ."

John Forster was left the gold repeater watch presented at Coventry with its chains and seals and appendages, along with any manuscripts. For he and Forster had been friends so long, and Forster of the knotted brow was so often with us all during our childhoods.

He left Aunt Georgie with the decision concerning the sale of real estate. And the annual income from the sums realized would come to the children once "they shall have attained or shall attain the age of twenty-one."

Aunt Georgina and John Forster were to be the executors of the will.

And so I reached the end of the legal language with the sentence that began:

And lastly, as I have now set down the form of words which my legal advisers assure me are necessary to the plain objects of this my Will, I solemnly enjoin my dear children always to remember how much they owe to the said Georgina Hogarth, and never to be wanting in a grateful and affectionate attachment to her, for they know well that she has been, through all the stages of their growth and progress, their ever-useful, self-denying and devoted friend. And I desire here simply to record the fact that my wife, since our separation by consent, has been in receipt from an annual income of £600, while all the great charges over a numerous and expensive family have devolved upon myself.

I saw at once that one could consider the will would have been a more gracious document without this. Mother had, after all, borne ten children. Could that have been mentioned with a similar stress as he placed on the £600 pounds, indeed, as the justification for the £600.

He directed that he be buried in an inexpensive, unostentatious, and strictly private manner; and that no public announcement be made of the time or place of his burial, saying:

that at the upmost not more than three plain mourning coaches be employed; and that those who attend my funeral wear no scarf, cloak, black bow, long hat-band, or other such revolting absurdity. . . . I conjure my friends on no account to make me the subject of any monument, memorial, or testimonial whatever. I rest my claims to the remembrance of my country upon my published works, and to the remembrance of my friends upon their experience of me in addition thereto. I commit my soul to the mercy of God through our Lord and Savior Jesus Christ, and I exhort my dear children humbly to try to guide themselves by the teaching of the New Testament in its broad spirit, and to put no faith in any man's narrow construction of its letter here or there.

39

Alfred sent me a copy of a letter he'd written to Mr. Rusden, to whom I would be forever grateful for finding me my place at Momba. Alfred's letter was pitiful to read, because in some elements it was in contrast to his private thoughts, although it is possible that he believed utterly in what he sent me as a copy:

> *I do not think I probably realized the full extent of my loss till yesterday when my home letters came, and then all hope of some mistake or contradictions vanished. It is very hard to think that I shall never see him again, and that he who was so good, so gentle with us all, has passed away. There is but one unfortunate incident in our dear father's life, and that was his separation from our mother. As people will doubtless talk about this, may I ask you to state the facts properly for myself and Plorn, should you hear them be misrepresented. When the separation took place, it made no difference in our feelings towards them: we children always loved them equally, having free intercourse with both, as of old: while no word on the subject ever passed from the lips of either father or mother. Of the causes which led to this unfortunate event, we know no more than the rest of the world. Our dear mother has suffered so much, my eldest sister, Katie, in a letter said to me, "Poor dear she is better than I dared to hope she would be, and I'm sure that in a little*

time she will be more settled, and even happier than she has been for years, for she says what is true that she has already lived twelve years of widowhood, and now she feels that there is nobody nearer to him than she is." My heart is too full to write of any other subject than this today.

And I was sure that at that moment he was taken by tears, my poor brother.

❧

I was not long back in Momba and barely reacquainted with its pulse when, at table, Fred Bonney asked Willy, "Have you told Plorn of your plans, Mr. Suttor?"

Willy coughed a little but was frank. "I'm going back to run my place, Plorn, Goonawarra. Through the kindness of the Bonney brothers, I put together some money here and in Adelaide and I have resolved it is time to face the whole equation to take what comes. This year has been dry but not disastrously so. We wish for seasonal rains in the next year."

Fred was nodding. "We all wish you well. People who have been here years tell me that the kangaroo grass used to be so tall it met above the rider's head."

"That would be delightful," Willy Suttor said. "Very delightful."

"Would waist height be adequate?" asked Edward with a smile.

"Oh yes. Waist high would set us for life."

❧

By the time the whole riot of shearing came round, I'd not had time to confide in either of the Bonneys about my sighting of Maurice and his aunt. The frenzy of the shearing, sorting, washing, and pressing of wool consumed us. One day the shearers threatened to walk "off the board" because their boss was abusive and harassed them. In theory I liked the Australians' industrial sense of their own worth. They went back to "work the board" after Fred's intervention, and the sacked ringer went off to find a job on another station. Ringers were profuse with insults, and shearers were impervious to being called maggoty mongrels and being asked whether they were shearing the sheep or ****ing it? These insults were part of the casual music of shearing. But this ringer had insulted their women and the intelligence of their children and that was unacceptable.

The spring was busy with cricket, which I coordinated. Fred and Edward Bonney's interest was such that at least one of them rode out with us to play our various games. Fred came with us to Wilcannia—where our success against bank clerks and Connie's legal friend Malleson was recorded in the newly founded *Wilcannia Times*, whose correspondent wrote like a serious Home Counties cricket writer. "Mr. Dickens is not at all an agricultural player and his capacity to drive through the covers as well as his ability to late-cut the ball makes one wonder whether such a player, if at Home, might be fit for selection as a county player."

Fred said to me at dinner one night, "Edward and I have been wondering if you and your brother would like to spend Christmas with us this year? It would be a great honor for Edward and me to meet him at last."

"But you may have to ride down here yourself to keep that appointment," Fred told me. "We're thinking of moving some fifty thousand or more stock up north beyond Lake Peery."

"Yes," his brother said. "The big Wonkoo paddock up there has not been as heavy used lately as the rest. It has good stockfeed on it."

I said that as far as I could tell, it would make good sense.

"Wonkoo even has its own shearing shed," Edward further enlarged.

Fred pursed his lips and said, "Plorn, we think you might be sufficient in knowledge and skill to manage that northern end for us."

At this I felt raised by a tide of exaltation.

Knowledge and skill. I had acquired a new and unexpected definition.

"There's a homestead up there from the fifties. Three rooms and no doubt a few resident snakes. You should take firearms."

"And not chiefly for snakes either," said Edward.

I had an impulse to embrace Fred for making himself so pleasant to me. He considered I had applied myself. I had done all I could, and he and Edward had seen it.

"You'll have Cultay with you to settle in up there. And you'll have two stockriders to go with you, and there is of course the boundary rider up there. Whitelock. He doesn't use the house. Asks how anyone could need three rooms. But what do you say? You may miss some cricket, I'm sorry."

"I will do all I can, Mr. Bonney, to justify your and your brother's opinion of me."

"Very well," said Fred, apparently gratified, as his brother nodded his head.

"I could ride in there with the flock," I assured the brothers.

"But don't forget all cricket once you're settled in," said Fred. "It will take you only a day to ride into Momba for games. And don't forget Christmas here, either."

"And," said Edward, "if you run into that poor damned priest up there with the stand-alones, give the old chap a decent meal, won't you?"

Over the following days Fred issued me with further instructions. I was indeed to have an eye for the welfare of Father Charisse. If the blacks of Cooper's Creek presented, Cultay was to talk with them. If any white policemen led his native troopers to Wonkoo, I was to hand him a letter Fred was going to give me setting down his idea of what was permitted within the confines of Momba and its sundry pastures. He had told me the mounted police of Queensland

and South Australia recruited their black troopers from Victoria, south of the Murray. They were young darks who, being loyal to their own people, had no fellow feeling for the people they were set upon far from home.

"Armed with carbines," said Fred, "they have European thunder at their command! Divide and rule, as Philip of Macedon had it, and as humankind has practiced ever since. Set the piteous to kill the piteous. It is of course all tragic!"

When they asked me what stockmen did I particularly *not* want to accompany me, I said, as if it were a joke, "Preferably I would rather not Clough. He stood by and let me buy du Barry."

"The one Dr. Pearson took?"

"Yes. He gave us everything back except du Barry."

"It makes one wonder," said Fred, "if he is really cut out to be a bushranger."

The letter he gave me to hand to police commanders read:

Dear Sir,

Welcome to Momba Station, and I hope my submanager Mr. E. B. L. Dickens treats you with every courtesy and consideration, as he has been instructed. In return I seek to see the peace of Momba preserved and respected. If you should command a Queensland detachment pursuing wrongdoers across the border, may I remind you that you lack legal jurisdiction to take action against any person presently found within the limits of Momba. If your jurisdiction and command derives from South Australia, the same rule applies. If you command a New South Wales detachment, you have jurisdiction to pursue wrongdoers but not to commit violence on any individuals you encounter. Within those clear limits, you can expect every cooperation from Mr. Dickens.

Yours sincerely . . .

Drovers had brought in a huge flock of sheep from the southern paddocks, which were now massed in the home and neighboring paddocks, so that from the homestead veranda the earth could not be seen for the backs and heads of sheep. I was readying myself to join the rest of the drovers in herding the sheep up to Wonkoo when a postman arrived on horseback from Cobar with saddlebags full of mail from England, one letter from Mamie, and another from Katie.

After condoling with me for being so distantly absent from his deathbed and assuring me that they had informed my older brothers, Sydney and Frank, Katie told me dear close things about the guvnor. The Sunday before his decease, she said, she and Mamie had gone down to Gad's to see him and he had let her know he had ordered a voltaic band to treat his permanently painful foot. Katie—and many doctors—called it gout, but Father thought gout a disease of sybarites and princes, and always argued it was something else. Whatever it was, it was capable of near crippling him. And Katie was willing to admit she had wanted to talk to him about a plan she had to pad out her living as a painter by trying the stage—and of course the guvnor knew all the stage people—as her husband, Charlie Collins, was sick and—as the family had already somehow known—had never been much of a husband anyhow. He had taken to writing to plump out the little he made from painting in the manner of the Pre-Raphaelites, whom the guvnor had no time for. The guvnor published some of Collins's pieces in *All the Year Round*, but maybe that was more for Katie's sake.

Katie told me that after Mamie and Aunt Georgie went to bed, our father sat with her in the new conservatory beyond the dining room. When I'd left home the carpenters had been working on the conservatory, which the guvnor wanted to be the glory of Gad's Hill. When it was finished, though, he didn't have a lot of time to enjoy it. Anyhow, he and Katie talked for a long time still that evening and Katie told him she had received an offer to go on the stage.

The guvnor's advice, she said, was that she shouldn't. She was beautiful and might do well, he said, but she was sensitive too. "Although there are nice people on the stage," he told her, having after all named her (Catherine Elizabeth Macready Dickens) in honor of the great tragic actor William Macready, "there are some who would make your hair stand on end. You are clever enough to do something else." Then, Katie told me in her letter, he went on to inform her he wished he'd been a better father and a better man and started to speak of his health. He wondered would he finish his new book. "He spoke to me," wrote Katie, as she had no doubt to the other brothers, "as though his life was over and there was nothing left." She said his face had looked ravaged.

Mamie assured me she stayed with the guvnor's body all night to protect it. I wondered what she meant by "protect". Surely it would not be stolen. But it would have been like Mamie to think the night was full of body snatchers. She and Katie had been up the previous night too and must have been giddy with exhaustion. Mamie said she cut a lock of hair from our father's "beautiful dead head." The girls, as part of their vigil, saw to it that the guvnor's favorite flowers were cut to decorate the room.

But in whatever terms the sisters wrote about it, it all confirmed the death and established it as history. The ninth of June. Engraved now on the earth's air, on that of Britain, on that of all her colonies from the Arctic to the Antipodes. Unavoidable, ever ponderous in the calendar.

There were less ominous letters in the mail too. A letter from Hayward, the songstrel and manager of Toorale.

Dear Plorn,

Doleful news travels faster than good—and I am sorry that the news of your illustrious father's demise has penetrated the globe as far as

Toorale. I have the sad honor therefore to send you the warmest fraternal condolences. The world grieves for your father whereas for mine—as laudable a fellow as he is—barely a suburb. This must make your loss a little easier in itself—given that you are surrounded by so many condolers—but also much harder because you are reminded all the time that the loss has taken place and can never forget it.

I hesitate to mix issues of sacred and profane—or maybe more accurately sacred and sacred. But you should know that we missed your departure that night in Wilcannia when the Desailly girls and I had finished our singing. You should know, old chap, that no one was more disconsolate or worried at missing you than Connie Desailly. I thought you must know that—for it might help you combat, if I might say, a fatal misconception.

The offer to go sheep farming with you is still extant—I have my eye on Yanda on the Darling. But we shall meet at some cricket match or stock sale—and we can enlarge on the idea then. I hope by then that— though the death of your father will be an immutable day of grief for the whole British race—you will have recovered from the grief of loss—and rejoice in the richness of your memory.

Your friend,
Ernie Hayward

40

Fred and Edward Bonney accompanied us as we mustered the sheep to Wonkoo and Wonkoo South. We rounded up an additional ten thousand sheep from some of the nearer home pastures and met with flocks from other pastures at Peery Hills to herd them all onwards. There was something steady but acutely exciting about moving a vast flock in a vast country at almost languid speed. Our indefatigable dogs did the bulk of the work each day, pushing the sheep forward from their positions at the rear and flanks of the flock.

I brought along Momba Station's copy of *David Copperfield*, the title pressed upon me by Mrs. Wivenhoe. I'd decided I would prove my fitness to read it by succeeding at Wonkoo and prove my fitness to run Wonkoo by reading it.

The country was undulating as we went north, more intimate by the standards of the great openness around Momba homestead. Yellow and ocher rock on rises answered well to the saltbush scrubland. Emus ran away crooked-gaitedly but faster than a racehorse, inviting chase, but even the dogs were too engaged to think of running after them. We watered the flock on the broad shore of Lake Peery, which the older stockmen said was not as full as last year, opining that spring rain would be welcome.

∼

One day, on a ridge beyond Lake Peery, Cultay pointed to a place miles off where a party of Aboriginal people were traveling, as if above the ground, through air wavering with heat.

"Those men," he told me. "Those fellas in a hurry."

Without dismounting, I retrieved my telescope from my saddlebag and was able to discern, at the tail of the party, a ragged white cassock, which I surmised belonged to Father Charisse. There seemed to be no horse with the party as it disappeared in the wafery foliage around a far-off creek. I told Cultay that if he ever made contact with the group he was to invite the priest to come to dinner at Wonkoo homestead.

The homestead at Wonkoo was a low structure built of stone and designed, with its capacious roof and veranda, for coolness. The Bonneys bid me goodbye and a stockman named Bellows settled in with me then, to act as cook. The flocks watered themselves along Purnanga Creek, and with the help of Whitelock I drove some thousands of head into adjoining vast paddocks of Purnanga and Mourquong. We spent pleasant nights with the hutkeepers and boundary riders of these two paddocks, each of them a solitary man for whom previously the arrival of a supply wagon was an exceptional event. One had a particular interest in newspapers, and indeed all local news, and had spent time on an island in the Bass Strait, bludgeoning fur seals. Another frankly confessed to us that he'd been a machine breaker in Yorkshire, had been through the penal mills of Van Diemen's Land, and since only other people could judge a man, he avoided other people.

As I managed the flocks and dealt with the spring lambs in the Wonkoo yards, I was reading, actually reading, *David Copperfield*. The early pages were a test, but somehow in those homestead hours I was able to penetrate them, searching for the point of captivation which everyone had always assured me overtook them when they read my father's work. I was interested in the fact that David Copperfield had been born with a membrane of flesh called a "caul." This was seen by some as a sign that a baby would not drown, and that people would buy the cauls as a means of avoiding drowning.

I wasn't fully captivated, however, until I met David's aunt, Miss Betsey Trotwood. I still needed to negotiate the paragraphs, with their hedge of verbs and adjectives, spiky parts of speech, but I wanted now to know more. At last, when David was sitting with Miss Peggotty discussing crocodiles, the novel caught in me! And then when Mr. Murdstone arrived with David's mother, and clearly disapproved of David, I was hungry to find out how David's merit could emerge, as despicable Murdstone and his sister degraded him. I even daydreamed about the Peggotty family and the upturned fishing boat they lived in so cosily on the strand at Yarmouth. I was pleased that my father had an appetite for such a unique and playful habitation.

I was horrified to see David lost in the squalor of the company of Murdstone and Grinby. It was at Blackfriars, and we knew from intermittent references that the guvnor hated Blackfriars and its "crazy old houses."

David's progress and self-discipline led him to ultimate success, and marriage to Dora. But that union made me uneasy because of Dora's coyness, how she addressed so much of a conversation through her dog, and how she spoke all the time of her stupidity, using this artifice in all circumstances. I do not remember conversations between the guvnor and my mother partaking of this quality or mirroring those between David and Dora, yet I felt a little guilty as I saw on David's behalf the limits of such a relationship, which in the end was closed not by a separation but by Dora's death in childbirth.

Now I became engrossed in the professional debtor Mr. Micawber, for I knew the guvnor would consign the Micawbers to Australia, as he had the Peggottys, for whose class in any case Australia was the best of choices. Of course Mr. Peggotty prospered in the Antipodes, stirring my colonial pride, and he brought back to England news of Britain's fallen but colonially redeemed gentleman Mr. Micawber.

And Mr. Micawber wrote to David, saying, "You are not unknown here, you are not unappreciated. . . . Among the eyes elevated towards you from this point of the globe will ever be found, while it has light and life,

The

Eye

Appertaining to

Wilkins Micawber

Magistrate . . ."

At this point of the novel, I was in tears. David had by now married again, this time to the charming character named Agnes.

"The guvnor wrote this," I told myself and was breathless with amazement and awe. How could such a majestic mind as that give birth to a plain boy like me?

∽

One night when I rode up to the Wonkoo homestead after herding a flock along Purnanga Creek towards Whitelock's hut, I found Father Charisse on the veranda. He had let his beard grow long, and wore a kangaroo cloak around his shoulders, under which was his now thoroughly tattered cassock.

"Father," I said enthusiastically, with an eye out for Barrakoon's people nearby.

"Please, Mr. Dickens," he told me as if he understood my mind. "My people are a day's walk off. I am here by special dispensation of the remarkable Barrakoon."

I asked him to come in and told him he must join me for a meal.

He drank some sherry, which seemed to help him converse, and said of his new endeavors, "It is a strenuous life, Mr. Dickens, when the desert nomads decide to move quickly."

I said I was sure it was, and having had the informed Fred Bonney to guide me, I had never thought otherwise.

"It is what makes it worthwhile for me to attempt," he added. "I have little doubt I am where God wants me to be, bearing witness as I am intended to. If God is the God of deserts, then I am in the desert, with desert travelers."

I felt an urge to tell him to come back to his own people, but that was just bonhomie on my part. I was not equipped to argue the intentions of the Deity, and it seemed natural to argue that Father Charisse had misread the signs. Yet there was an authority both in his decision and to the way he looked at a person.

"Father," I said, settling for a humbler aim, "why don't you stay the night and have a good sleep? Cultay can take you out in the morning on horseback."

"That is very kind of you, Mr. Dickens. I know your intentions are good."

They were not as good as all that, though I did think that if he enjoyed a full night on a mattress, God's intentions might be clarified for him, to make them more normal, more predictable, and town-dwelling. For there was something shocking about his dedication.

"But," he said, "I do not have a night to squander away from my people."

"Do they accept you as theirs?" I asked. "A kinsman?"

"Yes. They think I am an idiot and help me at all stages of life. Their care for me is most touching and is far from the supposed emotions of barbarism. I doubt if any other society would have accepted me so quickly. Scottish Presbyterians, for example, would have thought me a child of the whore of Babylon. The native people have no such prejudices to overcome."

So he could not be argued with, and had not come to be argued with. His purpose emerged over a dinner of mutton and potato and split peas, all of which he devoured with honest appetite as if it were his nightly fare.

"I wanted to confide to you," he said as the meal went on, "something you can pass on to Mr. Bonney. I suffer from a certain unease about events when we were further north of here, I suspect in the colony of Queensland. Four of the younger men went off in a party on their own, and when they returned were talking to Barrakoon. I cannot gauge it, and no one will answer me truly. I do wonder whether they encountered white men, and whether there was a confrontation and bloodshed. We traveled south after that as briskly as we could, so my concerns were in small part confirmed. If they did engage in an incident of blood or plunder, or both, I do not want all the people paying for it. I would be grateful if Mr. Bonney could use his influence in this matter."

I assured him I would send a message to Mr. Bonney within days; that I had a letter addressed to any police commander who came to Wonkoo to say that Fred Bonney's eyes were upon him and that anyone from Queensland lacked jurisdiction in New South Wales. And if any such commander brought a party of troopers, he would be sure to call at Wonkoo for information and Mr. Bonney's letter would be handed to him.

Father Charisse was reassured, and after a brandy seemed set to drowse off in his chair, but then he thanked me and told me he would pray for me, as if I were in peril with the Supreme Tempter, as distinct from Mrs. Wivenhoe. After dinner, he told me he would get on his way and take some sleep later. The kangaroo-skin cloak would be very welcome, he said, for though it was spring the nights could still turn icy.

I saw him to the gate of the home pasture, but then he insisted I turn back to Wonkoo homestead. He continued forth, a penitential figure despite the dinner he'd had. He was a man who had abandoned all shelter for Christ's sake, and I could not avoid revering him. He was, in his way, a saint. The fact that he expected to achieve nothing measurable gave him more authority, since pious people were often strident about the results they would have. And even the guvnor had expected results from Urania Cottage, and achieved them. Charisse's achievement was the humble one and witnessed by no one but me: of going back to sleep on the same earth as Barrakoon.

～

Some four days later, two dozen Queensland troopers arrived in caps and blue coats and riding boots. The white commander of the troop, a very lean man of perhaps forty, introduced himself to me as Subinspector Belshire. He told me his native troopers were camped a little way from the homestead, making free of a well and the water from the Purnanga Creek. They sounded like a normal squad of young darks, hooting, teasing, musical when they spoke their native language. I presented Belshire with Bonney's letter and then felt bound to offer him the hospitality of Wonkoo, such as it was, though he assured me that to him it was a palace. It was his choosing, though, he admitted, to lead the rough life he did. He had gone home to Lincoln two years before but found it would never suit him again to live in Britain. "Queensland has well and truly cured me of that," he confided, although his confidences sometimes had the quality of policeman's edicts.

The sun set under long thin skeins of cloud, and I had got a good fire going on the hearth. He read the missive of Bonney's by lamplight, finished it without comment, and returned it to its envelope. Dinner was cooking in Bellows's kitchen outside at the time, and I was hoping our drink would be sociable and conclusive. I had a certain prejudice against Belshire to begin with, given that Fred Bonney considered men of his ilk licensed killers of the darks.

It was an evening when a high wind began moving, and spirals of red dust were kicked up, but by now I knew that atmospheric drama in the upper air did not necessarily foretell the arrival of a rain front. I served Belshire his rum and we sat at the table, face-to-face, avoiding the two easy chairs the room provided. I had poured a companionable rum for myself, but a small measure which I diluted with water from a jug. The inspector had taken off his belt and loosened the buttons of his jacket before he sat. He took a sip of his spirit, but not a hungry mouthful.

"Did you know that we caught Dr. Pearson?" he asked me. "Weren't he and his chaps the ones who held you up here?"

"That's right," I agreed, almost casually, as if Dr. Pearson and his associates had not brought me the fatal news.

"It was at Eulo. He took the entire town hostage and then boasted that he had a particular wild mare—a gray—amongst his horses, and that he would show how he could ride her in the main street. Well, she threw him so bad that his skull was damaged and his gang could not move him, yet had to move on themselves. And that was how the Queensland police got the doctor."

I would have laughed that du Barry had caused Pearson's downfall except that the main issue of Belshire's patrol was no laughing matter. I uttered a sincere hope that Pearson was not too badly injured.

"Well, now he will stand trial. He will not hang, but he will be long detained," he replied with considerable satisfaction, then said, "I've read your boss's letter. I have every intention of according with his wishes if that is at all possible."

"He is very insistent, Inspector, that you have no standing here," I said firmly.

"On the other hand, Mr. Dickens, I am interested in crimes

committed within my jurisdiction. There may be people on Momba who are suspected of the murder of two Welsh prospectors west of Toompine in Queensland. Besides, I see no other sworn enforcers of British law here, certainly not the New South Wales police. And the enforcement of law as it is recognized by our society, not some other fanciful one, is my vocation, my church, and my mandate."

"Within the colony of Queensland, however," I replied.

He took another sip of the rum.

"These niceties can't be maintained in country like this, Mr. Dickens," he replied. "The matter of jurisdiction is a civilized concept meant to regulate the behavior of servants of the law in places where they are thick on the ground. They are not thick on the ground here, or in southwest Queensland. Here the first principle of civilization, that the traveler should sleep safely, has not yet been established in the minds of the savages."

"Well," I said, "there is no need for the response to murder to be murder. I should remind you that if you are seeking to punish in this region crimes of the group led by Barrakoon, there is a priest with him, Father Charisse, from Belgium. He would inevitably be a witness to any actions you took, and thus you would be under the same scrutiny as if you were acting in a city street."

The inspector inhaled and opened his eyes wide to take account of this. "What work of your father's is your favorite, Mr. Dickens?" he asked me.

"Why, it's *David Copperfield*."

"*Bleak House* for me," he told me. "'An infernal country dance of costs and fees and nonsense and corruption as was never dreamed of in the wildest visions of a witches' Sabbath.' Such is his view of the law as practiced in cities. Besides, your good father seemed to think appropriate punishment a fine thing, whereas the letter of the law is a stumbling and silly thing. See his mockery of the prison system in *Copperfield*. So I have to say I am a little surprised to get here and find the son of the great man presenting me with that very letter of the law. Especially when two men were killed by their campfire."

"I regret their deaths," I replied. "The security of the night camp is a consideration all bush people place weight on. But I have no reason to believe the miscreants are anywhere on Momba."

The matter of the concern about the young men that Charisse had raised with me was, after all, nothing near proof.

"Mr. Bonney respects the Paakantji and is respected in turn by them. He wants nothing to blemish or destroy his connection with them. When the Cooper's Creek blacks come down here on their way to find ocher, Mr. Bonney allows them to spear whatever sheep they need. As a result, we barely lose a head. If we applied the letter of the law they would become criminals, and what benefit would there be to us in describing them as such? If you destroy the friendship between the Bonney brothers and the native people, it is certain they will not take it calmly and that it will be difficult to restore."

The inspector swallowed a large mouthful of rum now and its sweet acridity set his lips in a rictus. "So," he said, "I am to be concerned for a priest and the Bonney brothers."

"And for me," I felt I owed it to the Bonneys to say. "For me as well."

"Oh dear me," said the inspector with a short laugh. "I don't want to take on the Dickens family as well."

The next day there was a lot of inspection of police horses, the draining of a hoof abscess, and a great deal of walking back and forth of a suspect gelding. But then the troop saddled and set off in a southwest direction, where Belshire would encounter the western and lower reaches of the creeks that flowed from the Paroo, and thus less certain water.

41

A day passed at Wonkoo, and then another, and on the third day I was attending to the stock books at the homestead when Bellows came in and said there was a noise of firing from some miles south. I went out of the homestead and stood in the yard and could hear it clearly in the still morning. The human power to deny certain possibilities set in and I actually wondered if Belshire might have developed a head of resentment and was down there slaughtering Fred Bonney's sheep. I fetched my rifle and called Cultay and Bellows as all my other staff were collecting a flock from Purnanga. Cultay was so worried and fretful that I myself became unsettled. I saddled Coutts and gave Cultay a rifle, while Bellows wore pistols, and we rode off in the direction of the noise of firearms.

After no more than two hours' ride, we rose up the ridge and came down on Nippers Creek, where we found the firing had stopped. We continued on to an escarpment called Round Hill, where we heard a further scatter of fire, and a single shot resonating more sharply than the previous general fury of the fusillade.

We came upon the body of a young man on the north side of Olepoloko Creek, a watercourse that ran off from the Paroo. He had a broken spear by him and had been shot through the throat, the chest, and both legs. We dismounted and began to lead our horses through the tall grass, with Cultay intoning a death chant. There was another young man felled nearby, half-hidden by kangaroo grass, desecrated similarly by unnecessary wounds. A bloody club lay by him and it seemed one of his executioners had, after felling him, taken to him with his own weapon. I vomited immediately, without having time to excuse myself or move aside.

Bellows said, "Let me do the rest of the count, Mr. Dickens. You sit there."

But I gathered myself. I couldn't let that happen. I was the boss. The count must be mine.

We soon found two more young men, one of them with four bullet holes in him, and then another who resembled Yandi and was probably a cousin. This one had many bullet wounds in his chest, as if troopers had stood above him in a group, exhausting their ammunition. These younger men, it seemed, had gone forward to meet the attackers, so their people could cross the creek to hide. Further on, Cultay stood above two dead crones with mourning helmets of gypsum and seemed to take exact account of a frowning young woman with a dead baby beneath her body. One of the baby's legs was all but torn off by a carbine round. In the stream itself, we found seven women and older men, all dead. These we brought forth and laid on the bank. On the south side of the creek, a number of men and women and two boys about fourteen years old with hardwood clubs by them were stretched out full of bullet holes.

We heard a baby crying from further along the creek, and made our way there, finding two elderly women, kneeling in death, each with a little lump of gypsum in their hair. Here too was Father Charisse, lying on his back pillowed by a kangaroo-skin cloak, wearing a loincloth of rags with a number of bullet holes in the front of his body. Had he been wearing his cassock, I imagined he might have been spared. Behind him, a naked child of between one and two years was sitting up and howling. Taking the priest's kangaroo skin, I wrapped the child in it.

Twenty-four of Barrakoon's party were dead, though according to Bellows Barrakoon himself did not seem to be amongst them. I went to Cultay who was silent now, his face mute, and asked did he want to remain there. He said he would, with Bellows.

"Will we bury them?" I asked. "Would Barrakoon still be escaping?"

"Mr. Bonney ought to make a picture here," he replied.

"Yes," I assented. "Yes, he should."

I left Bellows there to mind the bodies and the live child and sent Cultay off to track down the shattered clan and to tell them the killers had gone, and that they would be welcome on Momba Station under the protection of Frederic Bonney. I then set out back to Wonkoo to collect my stockman and Whitelock, the hutkeeper, who were due at the homestead that afternoon. After a few miles I saw dust to the northeast and knew that Belshire's troop was on its way back to Queensland. I spurred Coutts crazily and chased the dust column for an hour and a half. When I overtook the group of twenty or so troopers they were riding in shirtsleeves, their elegant jackets stowed. Altogether they looked bored and dispirited. I rode to the front of the column and Belshire saw me coming—indeed he must have been aware for some time I was following.

"Mr. Dickens," he called, as if we were meeting by happy accident.

I began to speak but seemed able only to produce fragments of words.

"How?" I asked, "how . . . ?"

He called on his troopers to halt then pointed to a red gum which we rode towards.

"You murdered them," I accused him.

"I put paid to all that Barrakoon magic, I'll tell you that."

"You killed the priest."

"There was no priest."

"Yes, you mistook him for a dark."

This gave him thought for a while but not for long. "There was no priest in the group, Dickens. No one identified himself as a priest to me or my men. So you must be mistaken."

I told him I had seen the dead priest with my own eyes.

"Did you notice we got a number of young men and even young women?" he replied. "This will be fatal for the band. Within the year they'll be living on the stations and driving cattle. And Barrakoon will be dead of grief, as he well deserves. We could have pursued him but are at the end of our supplies. Best now to let him wither."

Like the boy I still was, I was tempted towards weeping in frustration, but instead I promised him, "Mr. Bonney and I will see you destroyed."

Belshire looked at me as if I were the deluded one and said, "Crimes against persons and livestock are not readily forgiven in the law of civilized countries. They are not available to be forgiven by you, for example, or by Mr. Bonney. Indeed, I would have thought the punishment of those who commit them was welcome to your boss. And I reiterate, there was no priest. We do not kill priests."

"You are an abominable man," I told him.

"If so, you will find that the Queensland government will not be interested in any complaint from you or Mr. Bonney. For I have brought quietus to those who have the intention to invade Queensland in the future and impose their treachery. Our carbines have spoken the majesty of law to the eternal rocks of Momba Station. I have been instructed to bring such majesty by my superiors, and my superiors will stand by me. Now, I'm getting on for the border, and you must report to Mr. Bonney. And get your stockman to bury the dead."

And with that he went back to his troopers, some of whom had been resting on the ground by their horses and commanded them up. In fairly short order they rode off, leaving me full of things to say but convinced of the uselessness of my utterances.

Back at Wonkoo, numbed and despairing, I sent Whitelock with a message for Fred Bonney telling him Belshire's Queensland troopers had massacred most of Barrakoon's party, including children and Father Charisse, and I thought he should come as quickly as possible to record the graves, and even the remains yet to be found, with his photographic device.

I then gathered my men and shovels. For Cultay had permitted the burying of the dead before Fred Bonney arrived with his camera. It took us the better part of a dreadful night and much of the next day to bury the slaughtered, and I sometimes felt an impulse to drop my shovel and lie like the dead amidst the grass. I maintained just enough intent to scratch the earth and dig, occasionally leaving it to men like Keogh to achieve a depth of earth appropriate to a grave.

After we'd finished, Cultay smoked the earth to re-sanctify it, and we camped overnight. Riding back to Wonkoo the next morning I grew feverish. I was bedridden the following day. Meanwhile, Cultay rode out to seek Barrakoon, and found him far off to the west. When he got back to Wonkoo he told us Barrakoon was wounded in the hand and very poorly in spirits.

Thankfully, Fred did come, raising me a little from my fever and flatness. One of the men accompanied him to the site of the massacre, where he took a photographic tour of the graves, opening three of them to make plates of the remains. He told me he intended to publish them to provide visibility to the slaughtered. At least, I felt, a recourse might be on its way.

By Christmas, no one had seen a trace of Barrakoon or his group, and they didn't appear at either Wonkoo or Momba.

The news of the massacre of Father Charisse and Barrakoon's Paakantji group was printed widely in the end. Fred sent his photographs to the coroner in Queensland and some were published. The Queensland Commissioner of Police acknowledged the Bonneys' letters and mine with the promise of a full government inquiry. Both Fred Bonney and I made statutory declarations through Malleson and they were sent off. My recall of the events was impaired by what I can only call a shock to the memory, into which imagination overflowed, and I felt my understanding threaten to slip, like an imprecise implement, as I wrote my account. And if I could not deliver such a tale, who would?

Belshire, the commissioner told us by further letter, had offered his sworn version, but for some reason we were not sent it.

It was soon clear though that if there was to be justice against Belshire, it would come very slowly. Yet on the other hand it took only a month before gossip began to undermine Charisse's martyrdom, calling him at best reckless, at worst fascinated by a Paakantji woman.

We would get used to waiting for a result for Belshire. And if the mounted police now became a little more circumspect, it would be little consolation to Barrakoon and his party.

When Fred went back to Momba, taking the live infant with him to pass on to the women of the Paakantji camp there, I was still oppressed as if by the taste of death—my father's and those of Barrakoon's people. I now harbored the thought that I had been fatuous trying to grow up into manhood in a measured way. Death made even application seem silly, a minor vanity. I was not consoled to think that Paakantji souls were in God's realm, and not consoled that my father's might be. All energy left my soul, all diligence my body.

A message was sent to Momba, and this time it was Edward Bonney who turned up three days later. He sat by my bed and asked me how I felt and what my ailment was. I tried to tell him. I felt flooded by death, by its persistence everywhere, by its capacity to swallow the known, striving world whole. It had swallowed Father Charisse and his ambition whole.

"It has so many servants," I told him. "And the commissioner of police in Brisbane—he doesn't want to know what his servants have done."

"You know, Plorn, I was never the sage my brother was," he said after a pause.

"You can't say that," I protested, but purely out of the politeness that was still left in me.

"No," he said, "to be a sage you need to believe men can be redeemed. Because of my proclivity, which I bear like a cross, I felt the crowd was always around me, ready to flay me. I don't speak to you lightly, Plorn. You are in agony. I have always been. I mean, I am a clergyman's son. I have never tried to be a sage because I know how fallen we are, and on what a ledge we live. My little brother . . . Well, it all came naturally to him. No strange appetites. He wonders why men are so given to deadly acts. To me the question is, why aren't we evil all the time? I think . . . forgive me, I'm not sure, dear boy . . . but I think you have seen so far out here that men tend to evil, even if they can be suddenly overtaken by acts of grace. Like my brother, you prefer to believe the reverse: men tend to good and are suddenly overtaken by acts of viciousness. You are always surprised by evil. You are in fact bedridden by it. On top of your dear pater's death."

"Is it worth rising up and walking about in a world where viciousness is everywhere?" I asked him.

"I don't know. I just wake and find myself living as yet and undertake the duty of life. And that's it. There's one thing my brother and I agree on. Even in this wilderness, Plorn, life is honey. Is it not honey for you?"

I could not stop myself weeping now. "It is not honey, it is gall," I replied. "My father is dead, and he never knew me."

"Ah," he said, as if he was approaching an understanding of me. "So it is your father more than the Paakantji."

"No. It is my father and the Paakantji," I protested. "They are the same thing."

"I see," said Edward. "I do understand, old fellow."

"Thank you, Mr. Bonney."

And again, I felt a revival of grateful life in me. Perhaps, I thought, more than if his brother had come with deft consolation.

Since the massacre I frequently sought out Cultay to see how he was faring. "How are you, Cultay?" I would stupidly ask.

"I'm grouse, Mr. Dickens," he would reply, "grouse" being the colonial word for excellent.

I couldn't tell whether he was despairing or had placed the murder of his kinsmen into a part of his soul where it could be viewed without bringing down the whole structure of his mind.

42

Before he left to return to Momba, Edward Bonney said, "Christmas is coming, and it needs to be celebrated by the living on behalf of the dead. So Fred and I have decided to make this Christmas memorable, to make it a gala. As well as you and Alfred, Fred has invited the Desaillys, and your friend Ernie Hayward from Toorale. What do you say, Plorn? Will you enjoy such celebrations?"

I decided I must go along at least to the extent of seeming well to honor their gesture amidst the darkness.

In the approach to Christmas, I fortified myself with my scattered achievements, reminded myself I had been entrusted by good men with the management of my own outstation. I was also now a man who had read a novel and could discourse on the qualities of characters. I demanded of myself that I feel almost equipped for meeting other people in society. Belshire was serious, and my sense of social inferiority to Hayward was nothing by comparison and need not be taken too earnestly. So I insisted to myself that I would not find anything threatening, as I had before, in the easy sociability of Ernie Hayward.

I rode south to Momba beside Cultay over a hot day and half a night. Back in my old room at Momba homestead, I forced myself to rise for breakfast and was delighted to find a very jovial Alfred had arrived from Corona, and was wearing a festive, checkered suit, and the kind of dazzling tie the guvnor would have approved of. For my sake he was in the highest good spirits, as if the guvnor had not died on us.

It seemed a mercy beyond utterance that the Desaillys were here, too, and their presence brought about a shift in my spirits. They proved that the normal was in many places splendid. Mrs. Desailly was very vocal and Mr. Desailly was smoking beside her, smiling at her high robust conversation with a mixture of pride and irony. I was comforted to reflect that I had lasted long enough in Mrs. Desailly's country for her to treat me as a familiar. It struck me, too, that the Bonney brothers had warned the company to avoid talking about the Belshire incident.

At the same time I'd somehow reached a judgment on sundry matters I'd never entertained until now. Belshire and his men's massacre of Barrakoon's people seemed to have induced more skepticism in me about many things. Had Father, for example, undertaken Urania Cottage in part from vanity, to impose on the lives of the girls the neatness he insisted we practice at Tavistock House and Gad's Hill? And even if this was so, it wasn't a crime, and I was prepared to argue that point with Alfred should the matter arise. But then I saw Alfred would probably be in agreement on it. Had Alfred simply wanted me to get over the childish illusion that our father, despite all, was impeccable? Belshire was a different man from the guvnor, though. Belshire was a man who had sought permission for savagery, a godlike and satanic warrant, and had got it from the Crown emblazoned on his helmet or from the hell of his own heart. I was sure that other policemen did not invoke the law as regularly as Belshire, and that was because they did not have that need to fortify themselves, sustain themselves from the wellsprings of authority as often as Belshire, to justify his going forth to cover territory with the blood and curses of the Aboriginal people.

With this newly settled moral confidence about the guvnor, I found myself talking afresh to the pretty-featured Connie Desailly on Christmas Eve. I noticed her face had become refined since we last met and seemed less florid and more womanly. I relished the fact that I could talk to her without too much artifice and teasing, which this Christmas I was not in such a mood for.

"So, you have plans for a partnership with Ernie Hayward?" she asked.

"I have agreed with Ernie to take up one of the stations between Wilcannia and Fort Bourke," I told her, proud that news of our enterprise had got around. "We'll be veritable grandees."

"I never doubted it," she said, "though Mr. Hayward is a loss to the music hall."

"But there is debt," I said by way of exaggerated humor, "and we'll suffer it like all the other great men of the Western Division."

Blanche did not intrude in any of this, for her suitor Mr. Brougham had arrived and all her attentions were for him.

Connie spoke as if her happiness was dependent upon her beginning in shorthand and pastoral bookkeeping at an Adelaide school, and the idea of such independence of skills suited my mood exactly that Christmas. Yet I wanted her company, and all at once I wanted more, and found as I talked to her that I was not a half spirit haunting the conservatory at Gad's or even that western creek of the murders. I was alive, and somehow the fragments of my body and soul had coalesced to be alive for her. I felt for her something of the sweet yearning of which the guvnor wrote in *David Copperfield*. Again I wondered why Maurice McArden had taken such an extreme exception to the guvnor's depiction of infatuation, for it seemed to me to have more in common spirit with *David Copperfield* than with William Blake's poems. This exchange of plans with

Connie was part of a serious project, the project of a life, where Mrs. Wivenhoe had been the project of one great, all-revealing night.

Hayward had to be inveigled to sing with Connie that night and agreed to do it if Mr. Brougham, who had a good voice, would accompany him and Connie to sing the carol. Thus we were graced with "Torches, Torches, Run with Torches," which had a strange effect on me, with its invocation of running all the way to Bethlehem, another town in another place and of heightened meaning . . . vast places, dry, too, on a small earth in a great darkness—or so it came to me as I heard it in my half-mad, half-healed condition. And Hayward and Connie were sublime and carried Mr. Brougham, who was not quite so.

At the end of the evening, I took a last drink, looking out at the immense night with Alfred on the veranda. "Well, Plorn, old fellow, this year has orphaned us, as regards the guvnor anyhow," he said. "But we can never be fatherless again."

I felt a brief sense here in this desert calmness of that gentle approving soul, Mama, and wondered how she had stayed silent all this time, while Alfred and I and others were vocal with our opinions.

On Christmas morning Frederic Bonney read some of the Christmas liturgy from the Book of Common Prayer. It was never much used in the Dickens house; it lay, largely forgotten, like a fire-hose in case of conflagration. The reading from the third epistle of John, like the carol the night before, rang in me this morning and I feared I might be turning religious, of which the guvnor would not have approved. "He that doeth good is of God: but he that doeth evil hath not seen God. Demetrius hath good report of all men, and of the truth itself: yea, and we also bear record; and ye know that our record is true." Was Belshire in some humid Brisbane church? I wondered. Did he hear this too? Did it strike home?

The record of the fatal deeds of Belshire! In that matter there was an epistle of Bonney, and an epistle of Dickens, humble documents, but with *our* truths and Belshire in their sights.

The Christmas feast began in the late afternoon and continued for hours. It was thoroughly delightful, and I went on feeling a tentative happiness in the company. I was aware certainly that I heard every plain and wise and humorous utterance, that they fell on us simultaneously, and that Connie Desailly and I exchanged gazes as if we saw common meaning. This was heady, I thought. This was the height of life. A week ago I had been disabled by recurring images of gunshot wounds, of the dead, bloody-chested priest on his back, of the child whose head was a daub of blood and bone and cerebral substance. I knew I would always be burdened by this image, but it would not burden me to the point of disappearance. It was Belshire, I saw now, who had the duty of disappearance.

I drank wine. Edward Bonney told a joke! It was not hilarious in itself, but for his efforts to narrate and his own amusement in it. It concerned a teacher in their father's grammar school who suffered from appallingly bad breath and would lean over boys, and when they averted their heads cried, "What is the matter with you, boy? You refuse to look at me!" And one hapless boy, blinking at the stench from the teacher's mouth, was reduced to saying, "It is the cologne water you wear, sir." To which the teacher with the withering breath said, "I don't wear a cologne, you fool!"

Then, suddenly, it was late at night, and I was tipsy from wine and from confirmatory glances from Connie. She and Hayward sang a few more songs—"Once in Royal David's City," I remember. It showed, said Edward Bonney, that we did not need Dr. Pearson and his gang to make us musical.

I felt I should see Alfred to bed again and helped him to his room. Yes, he had drunk very fully, but for some reason he was full of laughter, even after I managed to get him flat on the mattress and remove his shoes. It seemed the foreknowledge of his expected success in Hamilton made him jovial. I sat in his room awhile, breathing easily until he succumbed to sleep. I relished too the normal humanity of the night after the difficulty of past and lonelier nights.

I saw his copy of the collected poetry of his godfather, Lord Alfred, which was always by his side. Indeed, it was one of two pieces of Tennyson that traveled everywhere with my brother, the other being an engraved ring the poet had given Father long ago, I think at Alfred's christening, and Father had given Alfred.

It had been one of those daunting realities of who Alfred was, that his godfather was a beacon and a god. But given that I was a literary gent now, I picked it up, intending just to dip in briefly, as I had been told one could with poetry. Besides, I knew that Alfred Tennyson had written the great "In Memoriam" for his friend Henry Hallam and had always been impressed that Tennyson could have such a passion for a friend. Also, "In Memoriam" seemed a good tag for the year we'd had and for the horrors I'd witnessed. And on top of that, Connie had read from it before we left Wilcannia for the memorial service in Sydney.

It was obvious that Alfred had been consulting the same poem, for the page fell open and I read:

> I envy not the beast that takes
> His license in the field of time,
> Unfetter'd by the sense of crime,
> To whom a conscience never wakes.

Oh, my God! I thought again, as I mused about the reading from the Christmas ceremony. Belshire!

And then nearby, the great consolatory verse:

I hold it true, whate'er befall;
I feel it, when I sorrow most;
'Tis better to have loved and lost
Than never to have loved at all.

As I went to put the book back, a letter fell from the midst of the pages. Looking down, I saw it was in the guvnor's handwriting.

I picked it up. The letter was loose and I opened it quite idly. It had the letterhead of the Athenaeum Club, that cream block of male clubbiness that stood on Pall Mall. I had only ever seen it from the outside—as a fortress where eminent men went to mutter significant things and dine. The letter was addressed to Mr. Alfred Tennyson Dickens, and had been written on Friday, 20 May 1870. This was—what?—some twenty days before the guvnor's decease.

"My dear Alfred," it began.

I have just time to tell you under my own hand that I invited Mr. Bear to a dinner of such guests as he would naturally like to see, and that we took to him very much, and got along with him capitally.

I knew no Mr. Bear, but he must have been a colonial visiting London.

I am doubtful whether Plorn is taking to Australia. Can you find out his real mind? I notice that he always writes as if his present life were the be-all and the end-all of his emigration, and as if I had no idea of you two becoming proprietors, and aspiring to the first positions in the colony, without casting off the old connection.

From Mr. Bear I had the best accounts of you. I told him that they did not surprise me, for I had unbounded faith in you. For which take my love and blessing.

They will have told you all the news here, and that I am hard at work. This is not a letter so much as an assurance that I never think of you without hope and comfort.

> *Ever, my dear Alfred,*
> *Your affectionate father*

So, it was established then. My father had never known that I'd applied myself. I had failed to convince him before his death.

A hollow creature again, I folded and replaced the letter. All the humanity of the evening drained out of me. I left Alfred's bedroom and went straight to the veranda and—despairing of the homestead—out into the night. I knew how Dandy had felt now. Having come here to the extreme fringe of things, where could a person flee next?

It occurred to me to go to the camp of the darks. I had been there once already since I'd ridden to Momba with Cultay and delivered him to his wife. I had seen the child that survived the massacre.

So I sought the Paakantji camp again, as the only possible place of relief. I believed I barely had the breath to get there.

Given that Fred Bonney had not enforced Christmas upon the imaginations of the Paakantji in any evangelical manner, except as a day off work, the camp looked normal, unruffled by festivity. A number of men and women were soundly asleep in the open, due to the heat of the day just past. The child I had found after the killings was asleep next to one of the women. He would grow up without memory of the terror. On his mother's breast, as Bonney would have it, given the earth was their mother.

I felt grateful Cultay was there, sitting side-on to a small fire wearing a shirt and pants, with white paint across his nose, on both cheeks, and then up the bone of the nose to make a circle on his forehead. What was he doing in this priestly mode of his on what was for him a normal night, I wondered, unable to escape the suspicion he had waited up for me.

He said nothing, but turned a little towards me and the fire, and there was an implicit invitation for me to sit down beside him. I did not greet him, nor he me, I just went round the fire and sat with him for about three minutes, lacking the capacity to think of something to say that was worthy of him. All I could manage in the end was, "Cultay, I'm finished. I'm eighteen years old and finished."

He said nothing.

"I don't know what it's like in your world, Cultay, but in mine it's all useless," I added.

I was not doing well in my confession of despair, I knew, but there was something about him that implied permission to speak as he stared into the fire still.

All I could manage now was, "People make up their minds about you. And that's the limit you have to run into, forever. That's the limit of what you can be."

"You'll get better, Mr. Plorn," he told me. "That Belshire put a bad spirit on you."

It was in some senses obviously true.

"Mr. Plorn," he said again and handed me a lump of the same aromatic gum mixed with ash he had given me on the road to Corona the Christmas before. I had slept then. I had had a sense of being saved from something malign. I had dreamed too sharply and terrifyingly but had felt renewed at dawn.

"Take hold of it, Mr. Plorn," he urged me and put his hand on my head awhile, having never touched me before.

This time I took a reckless mouthful and began to chew the gum with its vegetable, ponderous flavor.

"You better lie down here," Cultay said.

I spread myself beside him, chewing away as if for salvation. I felt a strange sense of expansion within me, a leap of the muscles and inner organs as if they had all been mute till now but had developed an ambition to be something else. It seemed I went straight into a state of dream, without intervening surrender or drowsiness.

 ~

Thus I was now traveling down the moonlight-washed trunks of a rough aisle of ghost gums, and by one of them was the young man who'd resembled Yandi and whom the frightful Belshire had murdered. Streaks of white paint ran down the length of his body, from shoulders to ankles. He did not seem to resent what had befallen him but stood like an usher to accompany me. We went forward together as if to inquire into the night. It was a night as clear as the one I had left Cultay sitting in.

There was firelight ahead by the banks of a creek or billabong. I heard many voices rising and falling in casual conversation, including Wilkie's hearty voice. Mr. Thackeray was there amongst the trees with his pug face, unhealthy paunch, and decided frown. He was wearing a neat suit and an open collar as if he had been called from work, and he said, blinking, "Oh my God, doesn't he act it for every last tear? It's like Little Nell." He had made peace with Father on the Athenaeum steps, I knew, and they had shaken hands, but this sort of talk might make him an enemy again if he wasn't careful. Mind you, Mr. Thackeray had achieved the first level of inoffensiveness some years back by dying, like my companion. I heard then but could not yet see Daniel Maclise, the guvnor's Irish favorite. "Jesus, you were a beautiful young thing, Charles, when I drew you and Catherine," he said, pronouncing the name Charlless as he always jokingly had. He went on, "Billowy cheeks, lovely curls, misty skin, vaporous. Catherine looking as if she were made of mother's milk!" And then he added, "But translucent."

I could see nearly the whole company the guvnor had clearly gathered now. Everyone was there, it seemed—visiting the place for the first time and having a merry time. Wills, the real editor of *All the Year Round*, looked both sensitive and sensible in his great black fringe of sideburns, even though he'd been ill from the damage he'd done to himself in a riding accident. The Yandi-like man made no comment, but stood beside me, a patient attendant.

They were chatting, Father's friends, all along the banks of Momba Creek, and drinking punch from pannikins. I saw plump George Dolby, the theatrical manager. My godfather, Lord Lytton, long faced and a little sad, which seemed usual with him. "Here's Plorn," he called without any surprise, as if I were still in England and available to be encountered any old day. The barrel-chested and huge curly haired and double-chinned Mark Lemon was present, too, with his ox-like head. The guvnor considered Lemon had "gone across" to Mama, but there'd been a time when Father had considered him a good friend, and so here he was, all rancor forgotten, drinking punch with the others.

The Yandi-like dead man now took his station to one side of the company. Off in the trees, John Forster stood by frowning, wondering if he should impose order on the scene and the mourners. By him was old Clarkson Stanfield, who used to paint the guvnor's backdrops for his plays. A kindly old Papist who'd painted St. Michael's Mount in Cornwall—a work of utter genius, the guvnor had said. Better than those damned Pre-Raphaelites. Stanfield wasn't a great talker like the others, but he walked across and asked me what the light was like on Momba, and I told him distractedly it was very glaring. For I was more concerned still with Mark Lemon, whom I'd been told had died not long before the guvnor. I went up to him, and he surveyed me down the length of his ample cheeks.

"I thought Father was angry at you," I said.

"That's all changed," he told me with a wise smile. "That was a misunderstanding."

And as if in pleasure at the new arrangement, he drank all of his punch in one gulp. As he did so, I saw the guvnor. He was seated in a chair by the bank of the creek. His upper body was bound with rags and there was a blindfold over his eyes. The Yandi-like spirit took in his presence as well. It was as if I could feel the absorption, one in the other.

A little irritated about the way they'd treated my father, I told Lemon and Lord Lytton, "I want to speak to the guvnor." My god-father took me by the shoulders and looked me in the eye and said, "That bloody woman will be my death. My absolute death!"

I knew he was complaining about his Irish wife, Rosina, who wrote novels about what a bad husband and what a rake he had been!

"What if my mother was to write a novel about the guvnor?" I asked him.

"Oh, far too nice a woman for that, Catherine," said Lord Lytton. "Yes, a delightful girl. With too much pride to play that game, your mater."

Lord Lytton led me to my father, with the Paakantji spirit at my right. The guvnor was sitting on an ordinary kitchen chair. Under the bonds that held him to the chair he was in shirtsleeves, and there was a pannikin beside him on the ground, so when they were finished with the game they were engaged in, and untied him, he could drink. I wanted to save him from this silly game of blindfolds and rag ropes. When I arrived in front of him, I said, "I have applied myself, Father. I have a groove. You should tell Mr. Bear, whoever he is."

He seemed to me to be smiling at my voice. "Dear old Plornish, is that you? Come to the rescue. Take off this blindfold, eh? Undo it at the back."

I reached my hands over his shoulders and undid the knot at the back. The blindfold fell away as soon as I unknotted it. I wished so earnestly to see his face, but he had no eyes when the cloth fell away. There was a vacancy there that was deeper than a pit.

I asked him, "But what has happened to you?"

I felt a pity flowing from me for the father who had become a chasm, and a feverish ambition grew to save him. Yet there was casual talk all around me, talk of the Adelphi Theatre and magazines and the Academy, and of other men's wives. He stretched away from me, his was a mouth that opened in the earth, a great wound in the fabric. And still the others went on gossiping around him without any ill will, though their normality was an insult to him. For they could see, and he could not. The Yandi-like dead man was equally appalled and came up to watch me release my father from the chair. The Belshire victim led him fraternally out into the stream. I could see his thin shoulders and then I saw the flow of water and could not see him at all. The chair on the bank was empty.

Now it was obvious: my father, the guvnor of guvnors, wrote letters that were as piteous in their ignorance as was his present condition, his utter ignorance of the earth. He was not to be held to blame at all. He no longer knew of the sun, let alone of me. He was not to be believed anymore as a judge amongst the living. He had lost no power to charm but all his power to bind. Such a kind of father must be forgiven. The breathing and moving son was not to be assessed by one who perished too soon, bearing his old ignorance. This seemed so clear, so simple, that my despair appeared to me now to be at heart a peevish thing, not quite a trifle, but almost a conceit.

I woke at dawn in saffron light with Cultay sleeping on the far side of the dead campfire. The dust was mauve.

❧

That night the company was tired after the revels of the previous day, but when Connie and her sister presented themselves at the piano, I came forward and announced, "With your kindly permission I intend to ask the Misses Desailly to let me perform with them in a faulty tenor, much less in quality than Mr. Hayward's."

Everyone said it was a good and novel idea, and Mrs. Desailly said half-satirically, "What affront!"

I asked the ladies if they knew "Ae Fond Kiss." They did, and they had the music in Blanche's portfolio.

"On three," Connie whispered to me as Blanche played the introduction.

For the first time in my life, I was going to sing before other humans.

"*Ae fond kiss, and then we sever*," Connie and I began, like one voice.

At "sever" she smiled, and we gazed at each other amidst the long applause. Then we turned ourselves to the next lines, which were like a statute against the undue influence of death.

> *Ae fond kiss, and then we sever;*
> *Ae fareweel, and then forever!*
> *Deep in heart-wrung tears I'll pledge thee,*
> *Warring sighs and groans I'll wage thee . . .*

Yet I sang the doleful lines like an anthem of praise to some proposition just beyond the reach of my hands, which reconciled the living and the dead.

Acknowledgments

Apart from the works of the immortal Charles Dickens, I should acknowledge the major modern biographies relating to the author and his family. These include: Claire Tomalin, *Charles Dickens: A Life* (2011); Michael Slater, *Charles Dickens* (2009); Peter Ackroyd, *Dickens* (1991); Fred Kaplan, *Dickens: A Biography* (1988). John Forster's foundation work *The Life of Charles Dickens* (1872–4) is also essential reading.

Claire Tomalin wrote, as well, *The Invisible Woman: The Story of Nelly Ternan and Charles Dickens* (1991), and Robert Garnett did in this decade past produce *Charles Dickens in Love* (2012). Further dimensions were added to my story by Andrew Lycett's *Wilkie Collins: A Life of Sensation* (2013) and *The Letters of Charles Dickens to Wilkie Collins*, edited by Laurence Hutton (1892). Great light was shed on the career of Edward Bulwer-Lytton, Plorn's godfather, as it was on other notable Victorians including Thackeray and Dickens, by Clare Clark's charming (I assure you) book *The Great Stink* (2005).

For correspondence, of course the starting point is *The Letters of Charles Dickens (1836–1870)*, edited into three volumes in 1880 by Mary Dickens and Georgina Hogarth. In the matter of letters, I have done light editing of some I quote, and have in a few cases constructed letters from Plorn's siblings as a way of economically conveying the emotional luggage Plorn brought with him to Australia. The letter that causes Plorn such distress near the book's end is authentic, although also very lightly edited.

In the cases of Plorn's brothers and sisters, I was helped by Robert Gottlieb's *Great Expectations: The Sons and Daughters of Charles Dickens* (2012) and by Lucinda Hawksley's *Katey: The Life and Loves of Dickens's Artist Daughter* (2006). The same author's *Charles Dickens and His Circle* (2016) is also a most useful handbook. Sir Henry Fielding Dickens's *Memoirs of My Father* (1928) is of great interest since Henry was the Dickens who saw Plorn off to Australia and was close to him in age.

It is indisputable that Catherine Dickens has not drawn the eye the way her coruscating husband has, yet she is a fascinating woman in her own right and one who was, in the belief of some Dickensians, grievously wronged. Lillian Nayder's *The Other Dickens: A Life of Catherine Hogarth* (2012) passionately champions her.

As for Alfred and Plorn, the sources include *A Tale of Two Brothers: Charles Dickens's Sons in Australia* by Mary Lazarus (1973); Jeannette Hope and Robert Lindsay, *The People of the Paroo River: Frederic Bonney's Photographs* (2010); Bobbie Hardy, *Lament for the Barkindji: The Vanished Tribes of the Darling River Region* (1976); and Frederic Bonney's article, "On Some Customs of the Aborigines of the River Darling," *Journal of the Anthropological Institute of Great Britain and Ireland*, vol. 13, 1883, pp. 122–37.

Notice that Bobbie Hardy's book spells the tribal name of the people of the Paroo and Darling Rivers differently from the spelling I have chosen, as the way it is spelled in this text has become more common since Hardy's book was published.

Last of all, I must beg the tolerance of all Dickensians for creating what we do not know: the circumstances and means by which, in an Australia not yet connected to the United Kingdom by telegraph, the colonial Dickens boys became aware of rumors and then of the certainty of their dazzling father's death. I have also invented the Sydney memorial services. My hope is that these confections work well enough not to outrage anyone, and also to pay tribute, insofar as lesser writers can, to the incomparable inventiveness of Charles Dickens himself.